BOOK ONE - PART ONE

THE LUCIDIANS

INHERIT THE EXXON VALDEZ OIL SPILL

Alaska's Prince William Sound:

August 8ᵗʰ, 1988 - March 26ᵗʰ, 1989

BRIAN BUTLER

Book One
The Lucidians
Part One
Inherit the Exxon Valdez Oil Spill

ISBN-13: 978-0-9980955-0-9
ISBN-10: 0-9980955-0-8

DEDICATION

This book is dedicated to the people of the City of Cordova.
May they prosper, love, and enjoy the longevity of life that living in such a beautiful
and nutrient rich environment can provide. The fishermen of Prince William
Sound, the Gulf of Alaska, and the Copper River Flats have dealt with huge setbacks
yet continued to build, re-build, adapt, innovate and refine their efforts.
The trials of mega-quake and oil spill that Cordova has endured and recovered from
have forged this coastal city into a rare diamond, tempered with prudent
preparation for the worst and joyous creation of the best.

CONTENTS

WINTER 88 INTO 89

SUMMER 1988

PICTURE PERFECT

Jack stretched his legs and shifted his position constantly with the roll and pitch of the Emma Dawn. He piloted her from the top house wheel, standing, rather than sitting at the helm station. The sea was too rough to sit comfortably. It was a bright sunny day, but windy, with a wicked four-foot chop. Cheerful bright white foamy froths furled by the winds adorned the tops of each wave. All side windows of the top house were open just enough to block the light ocean mists that the Emma Dawn churned up as she bucked and lurched through the sea. Warm streams of ocean salt breezes laden with faint hemlock sap smells swept through the top-house.

The Emma Dawn's diesel engine was an efficient thrum, soothing, seductive, urging him to sleep. He refused, tuned his ears instead to the other layers of sound, creaks, rigging strain, the splash of waves off the bow. Jack felt the ocean through the wheel and her hull, the thrum and vibration as she lifted through a wave. He knew her tolerances, knew she was well within them, just a bit sloshy. He turned an occasional eye to the back deck each time a larger than average wave lifted and dropped her.

Hungry seagulls soared, dipped, and swooped, bright white against a blue sky, above the back deck of the Emma Dawn. She was loaded with salmon for the second time today. Bright silver fish all lined up symmetrically by the constant shift and slosh of her deck as she danced with the quartering sea.

From a slight distance, the blue and white hull of the Emma Dawn could be seen listing to port, bow higher in the air than designed, stern nearly under water, the occasional aberrant wave threatening to wash over the deck. Bow spray shot to either side in dramatic bright white plums, as she bucked and lurched.

A person with an unseasoned eye might catch alarm at the sight of the forty-two-foot Purse Seiner each time the stern was swept with an errant ocean wave. To Jack, it was reason to be wary. He had instructed his crew to lash the lead line to the side of the boat so the gear would not shift as they ran. Warry, but in a relaxed, peripheral way as a seasoned war veteran maintained focus during battle. He trained himself, and his crew, to keep many mental notes and scenario visualizations such as; that line could snap, it will fly at this angle, move to the left, keep feet glued to the deck, avoid getting caught in the deck winch... An unwary fisherman could be smashed, de-limbed, sliced, broken, or drowned during the normal course of any given day. A constant, yet peripheral, awareness was required for sanity, and happy survival. Constant relaxed awareness that allows the mind, at the same time, to enjoy the experience and think all manner of things. Once tuned to the environment, it becomes the norm, then the mind must contend with being confined to a boat with constant potential for harm, and, other people, crew.

For Jack, being stuck on a boat set his mind into a frenzy of imagination. As a child working with his father he had grown up referring to this as 'Boat World'. The mind was set free because the body was confined. Or, as he often wondered, he went a little insane while fishing each year.

He managed his crew from a light hearted yet deadly serious point of view. "*Don't die, catch fish, have fun, don't die*" His mantra, was engraved on a wooden plaque, and hung where it could be read every day by the crew - on the inner door of the head.

Jack stretched his legs better, held his arms up in a 'Y' shape, stretched and wiggled his spine. A shiver of pleasurable energy surged through him. Despite his tired limbs and sore hands, he felt incredibly good, vital. The knowledge that this was his second deck load of the day gave him and extra delight - that of a job well done, money to use for creative entrepreneurial projects. He finished his stretch and glanced at the back deck, eyes shifting over various safety points. Satisfied that the seine net had not shifted overly much in the wash, that the skiff was secure in tow behind them, it's tow line, lifted from the boom winch would not foul the net on the back deck, and purse lines were secure in the big plastic buckets, he sat in the large leather captain's chair and slid it forward, neatly into the heart of his helm. Jack then altered his course to shave by the shallow areas of Knight Islands rocky shoreline and take the Emma Dawn into calmer waters a bit sooner.

After a cursory scan for logs ahead, he picked up a coffee cup, a thermos, and poured himself a half cup of hot black 'stay awake' while shifting his weight and arms to keep the cup level and the pour true. Didn't spill a drop, this time. The carpeted deck of the top house was stained with brown spots, mostly coffee, from other not so true pours.

They were running north west, craggy Knight Island at starboard, into Snug Harbor from the Yellow Bluffs where he and four other boats had fished all day. It was late evening, the sun still high and warm to the west.

Knight Island, to Jack, was the most beautiful and bountiful place in the world. Tall craggy new mountains with sharp peaks showed visible fissures along the meadows where the 64' earthquake had lifted and dropped the island like a toy snake. The sudden cliffs, some ten feet tall, that lined the island showed a story, a testament of power, how the ground walked on had lifted, dropped, as force cause the entire island to ripple. Strong, healthy trees that had shared a root system with the fissures also told a story with time, righting themselves upward, some roots above some below, of recovery and adjustment, much like the community of Cordova, his home port.

His family had fished Knight Islands nooks and crannies, hiked the island for years. It was a good day when he was able to get off the boat and back pack up to a mountain lake.

Jack smiled as he noted silver water, just ahead, calmer seas, on the other side of a tide rip. He aimed a little more towards it; a tweak of the auto pilots manual steering knob. He felt the tide currents vibrations through the Emma Dawn's hull, as if it were piercing a veil, and then, the ocean smoothed out considerably. The mouth of Snug Harbor ahead, the sun was low in the west, casting an eleven-pm orange tint to everything. Another mile or so and he would be in the shadow cast by the forested hills and mountains above Discovery Point. Two other boats ran ahead of them toward the shelter of Snug Harbor which lay inside of Discovery Point. A few boats were still fishing at the Point, either not having loaded yet, or working on their second or third. His father's boat, the Alta Pearl, might be one of them, he wasn't sure. He had not used the radio to hail him all day, or vice versa, which usually meant they were both happy and on the fish. His Father and Uncle were both fond of Discovery Point while Jack enjoyed heading further away from the crowd that hovered and waited turns. He had learned a thing or two about plying the waters a bit further up, closer to where the salmon hit the beach. The disadvantage of running time back to Snug

Harbor not withstanding Jack had a good amount of luck this year in getting a tender or two to swing close and allow him to offload his catch. They were under way from Cordova to Snug Harbor, passing right by, why not?

The Emma Dawn entered the shaded area nearer Snug Harbor. A warm zephyr brought the heady scent of tree sap, wood, and earth, from the thick forests of Knight Island, through the open top-house windows. Jack smiled, inhaled deeply, savored the warmth and smells, forever logging it in his mind as the sweet smell of a successful day, in Prince William Sound, the most beautiful place on earth. To Jack it was and he would make good argument with anyone who would disagree. A surge of wellbeing and optimism flooded him - gratitude for being able to love what he did for a living and a deep appreciation for being able to do so in the most beautiful place in the world.

He rounded the turn to angle into Snug Harbor, keeping a shallow reef to starboard, and saw that the Lorem, his preferred fish tender, was at anchor. There were only two boats at each side of her, two offloading, two waiting. The two seiners waiting were about half loaded, sterns sunk to about half normal freeboard, a water level fisherman referred to as the 'money line' before everyone began to tank down and chill the fish with cold brine. Not all in the fleet had converted yet and these two were still dry holds, as were most smaller seiners.

Jack felt his heartbeat quicken as he hoped that Sarah would be working the deck. Her image flitted through his mind, pretty face, blue eyes, blond hair, cute chin with a slight divot. She was well rounded in all the right places and completely did it for him. He had not made any hard advances, just shared his humor and smile with her - was a bit nervous with taking the next steps. She had shown some obvious interest that he had dwelled on overly much, like an orphan savoring a sweet. There were times in his life when this was the death of any first moves. Jack brought the boat down to an idle as he entered Snug Harbor. It was rude to create a wake here, just as if they were in the harbor back home. The sudden reduction of engine noise was always a glorious thing. The crew would all wake up at the sudden change in tempo. Compared to the rhythmic roar of the engine while underway, the idle was near silent - like sweet music.

The little cove of Snug Harbor was flat calm - the mountains above in a caldera reflected in the water below, the boats as well. It was picture perfect. Jack turned to grab his camera then recalled he had let Wendy use it to take pictures of the deck awash with salmon and jubilant crew. He stuck his head over the hole down to the lower deck, saw Wendy ruffling her hair as she yawned and stretched.

"Wendy!" Jack barked. She jumped and glared at him. "Hand me my camera please, hurry quickly." Wendy glanced around, lips tight, spied the camera in the direction Jack was flailing his fingers at, wide spread, impatient. He did not want to miss the shot. It was rare to get such a calm reflection. Wendy moved slowly, as if to punish Jack for startling her. Picked the camera up and handed it up to Jack's hand. "Thank you." Jack said. "I still have coffee up here if you want some."

"I will make some fresh." Wendy said. "Shit turns to poison after the first twenty minutes Jack."

Jack was pleased that the light had gotten even better for a photo as the Emma Dawn slid slowly forward while waiting for Wendy to hand him the camera. He framed the picture, the Lorem, two seiners at each side, the steep mountain caldera that wrapped the mirror like water, the jagged shale shore line lined with huge hemlocks, boughs sagging with moss and lichen... He snapped the shot, framed and snapped another. The picture would be of the Lorem, with two purse seiners alongside, the mountain caldera surrounding Snug Harbor's water fall and beaches perfectly reflected like a mirror. Dazzling.

Wendy came up the stair ladder from below to stand beside Jack. She stretched, sighed, and stared out the widow as they slowly made way towards the tender.

"I would love a copy of that picture if you can remember to get me one. It's beautiful." Wendy said. She filled his coffee cup with what remained in the thermos, took a sip herself, fake gagged, and handed it to him. Jack took an appreciative sip, pulled a cigarette from his pocket and lit it. He exhaled out the open window; flipped a silver toggle switch to turn on a little fan to whisk the smoke away. Wendy ran her hand through her straight brown hair in hopes of smoothing its kinks. Didn't do much good. She wore blue jeans spattered with fish blood, brown deck shoes, and a long-sleeved shirt. She had forsaken her bra wearing at day three on the boat.

"I will share. Of course." He said. "It's beautiful, isn't it? A perfect end for a perfect day. I am proud of you and the crew. We worked like a well-tuned machine today, not one fuck up, no one got hurt."

Wendy nodded enthusiastically. "I love it." She said. Her voice was reverent. "Good money, good times

THE CREW

The two stand in a comfortable silence as the boat glides slowly across the water towards the caldera of Snug Harbor. Bart emerged from the cabin and began to piss off the back deck, his hair a mess, pointing every which way. When he finished, he made his way up to the top house from the deck.

"Aww, look at you two, all romantic and cozy like." He teased. He patted Wendy's shoulder and wedged himself between the two of them, a can of coke in his hand.

"Looks like they are about done offloading the boat alongside, about an hour wait after we tie off the back there." Jack said. He yawned. "I might catch a nap."

"Hey, that's the Lorem there, Jack. Maybe you and the voluptuous blond can make some more moon eyes at each other." Bart teased. A big grin played across his face, he waggled his eyebrows.

"Hey, woman here." Wendy said.

"Yah, sorry, keep forgetting." Bart said. He had tried to get with Wendy a couple of times when she first came aboard, but she played the married and faithful card. He gave her a grudging respect for that while Jack just knew better than to hit on her in the first place. If she wanted to do something she would have to initiate. Not him. Even if she did he wasn't sure if he would be inclined to aid her in cheating on her husband, Jack had met the man, liked him.

Wendy was thirty-two, married to what she called a Silicon Valley yuppie, first just as a kid for the stability, then, later, for real and for true. Jack respected her for that though he had warned her that, while on the boat, the men would want to joke and flirt. When he told her that she had shrugged, said she could be just a raunchy. In fact, she proved to be at ease with men and their advances, enjoying even, fending them off with humor and grace. She was hard bodied, not an ounce of fat on her, large breasts that had been slightly augmented, both of which, she was very proud of. Wendy was born and raised in Cordova, which explained her tolerance of raunchy humor - Cordovan's, especially on the heathen side of life, are exceedingly good with raunchy humor, crude language, and other forms of advanced communication skills.

Her mother was a slender graceful Eyak woman, and her father a big blue-eyed Swede who had come to Alaska to work in a partnership program with the Fish and Game. Jack was friends with her brother, Steve, and friendly with all the Castells. This was her third year with him and they had become great friends. Jack had asked her why she still came back, why, when she had a beautiful home in California, just an hour drive from Cupertino. He never forgot her answer.

"I come back because I would go insane if I stayed there. It is so nice, so wonderful, but people, bored I guess, make up weird shit to get fucked up about, drama, gossip, society stuff. I would friggin' love to make every bitch there work here, fishing for a living. Would make them better people. Like what you are doing for Mark and Ziggy this year, Vitali and Tuna, last year. Making spoiled rich kids become better men."

Knowing that the crew members would make passes and being ok with it was one of Wendy's more endearing qualities. She would, right from the beginning, announce that she knew they wanted to fuck her but they weren't gonna... Well at the beginning of the second year with him she did. The first year she sputtered her way around advances and Jack had to intervene with a few stern words on her behalf once or twice. This, ironically, had the effect of her feeling closer, more comfortable with Jack, something that bugged the rest of the crew. Perhaps that was why it was said that women were bad luck on a boat. Being twenty-five and the owner of his own boat put him in a particularly attractive position, one that he didn't mind taking advantage of and in fact, planned to do so with Sarah, this very night.

They rafted alongside the Brook, a forty-two-foot Ledford, to wait for the offloading to finish up. Once it did, they would cut loose from the Brook and her captain would slide her up into place while Jack jockeyed the Emma Dawn into the Brook's position.

Jack smelled butter and garlic wafting up to the top house as the other two crew members, Mark and Ziggy began to concoct something to eat. Jack shut the Emma Dawn down, enjoyed that moment of blessed silence, from his own boat at least, then and went down into the main cabin. He had placed sturdy hand rails in strategic areas that made descending the steep ladder stairs from the top house quicker and more fun.

Mark was on the radio, hailing Lana, his girlfriend, who was a crew member on another boat. He was a Harvard student from France, his father a nuclear physicist. Ziggy was the son of a wealthy corporate lawyer from New York, Michael Neufeld, a man who had been out on Jack's Dad's boat back when Jack fished with him. Michael fancied himself a bit of mentor, liked to drink whiskey, liked to laugh. He had also promised his services should they ever become a large corporation with lots of money.

All of them, except for Bart, liked to cook. Wendy, being a bit of a granola cruncher, disdained red meat and tried to get them to eat green stuff as much as possible, Ziggy, being Jewish, would have no pig, Mark was an admitted pig of all foods and often whipped up some astounding dishes which he always bitched would be better if there was bacon in it just to get under Ziggy's skin a bit.

Bart was a thick, well-muscled, local Cordovan, he fished the summers and as much as he could during the winters between hunting trips and fur trapping. He lived in Cordova year-round so, when dear and moose season opened, he was out to pack the freezer, save money on meat, eat better meat without additives. Bart was the oldest of them at 32, Jack's skiff man, one of the best in the business, and working on his fifth season. He was saving his money, working to get his own boat together, did all of his accounting with Jack's mother, Rebeca. He had only two seasons left with Jack, this being one of them, and then he would be getting his own rig the smart way. Leveraged to the hilt, and deep in debt, just like everyone else.

"I see your lover over there, weighing ze fish." Mark said. He spoke with a heavy French accent. He then spoke in the mic of the radio again. "Cape Hook, Cape Hook, Emma Dawn, you hear me?"

Jack glanced over at Sarah as she worked the deck of the Lorem. She had on rain pants, hair in a ponytail, big red rubber gloves, hoody over t-shirt. He seated himself at the galley table opposite Wendy.

"You must go to her. Tell her the way she makes you feel." Mark said.

Ziggy barked a harsh laugh. "You French, always about pushing 'ze' love, even while you try to get your own girl away from the clutches of that letch Captain on the Hook."

Mark shot him a look that could kill.

"Cape Hook back to Emma Dawn." Came a gruff voice over the radio.

"Ah, this is Mark, calling to Lana."

There was a bit of static as everyone waited the reply.

"She is busy." Came the answer.

"Tell her to hail me on the Emma Dawn when she is... Not busy!" Mark raised his pitch on the last two words, caused the crew, and Jack, to suppress laughter. He snapped the mic back into place.

"This cocksucker is keeping her from me! I know it! He knows she is a cool chic. I will keel him." His fists were clenched in anger, face red beneath a scruffy crew cut.

"Easy there, little feller." Bart said. "We like to share in Alaska. You don't want to be a poor sport about it now do you?"

"We share in France also, you asshole, but with friends, not stupid dickheads like that fat bastard." Mark waved his hands in the direction he imagined the Cape Hook and Lana would be.

"Hey, lady here?" Wendy spoke with humor, a roll of the eyes at the plight of being surrounded by crude boys.

"Yes, beautiful woman, you are here, so sorry..." Mark said. He huffed out some air, let his chest relax. "Lana is way to cool a girl to work with those bastards, she has told me things. You, Wendy, work with gentlemen, she works with pigs. There is a large difference."

Jack knew the captain and crew that ran the Cape Hook and Mark was seriously exaggerating things.

"There is nothing you can do right now so just relax. You are busy too." Jack said. "Like the Dali Lama said, 'Why worry? If you can do something about it, do it, if you cannot do anything about it, no amount of worrying is effective.'"

"Yeah, I know that one. But this is about a woman. One does not apply the Dali Lama's words to things regarding women. He is a virgin." Mark said.

Jack and the others laughed. "Really?" Jack asked. "If so you may have a damn point."

Mark was now grinning and nodding, his anger dissipating quickly, as it usually did.

"Right now, she is probably wearing the ugly rain gear like your girl Sarah." Mark waved his hand at Sarah. Jack's eyes followed. "But I heard the boat running in the back ground, they are not fishing. She could have talked to me." Mark sighed. "I sound like a school boy yes? It is just that she is my girl, not his, damn it. Frigging handsome captains of fishing boats have a huge advantage over magnate's kids, or, maybe not eh?" He winked at Wendy. She shook her head 'no'.

Ziggy rolled the big pot roast over and basted it with juices from the pan. The smell of it made everyone's mouths water, mixed with ocean air, food on a boat was just... Better. Mark left the radio and went to the galley to assist, or, rather, to make sure Ziggy didn't do anything he would disapprove of with the meal. He busied himself with carving slabs of roast and loading plates with potato chunks and peas and handing them out. The crew fell silent as they began to eat.

Jack looked out the window, into the boat next to him, two people moved about, the rest probably sleeping. He ate. The pot roast was excellent, potatoes good with butter and pepper, the peas smashed into them. Mark took his seat near the radios and turned on the stereo. Tom Petty's music began to work its magic turning the evening meal into a mutual sing along, "So let's get, to the point, lets roll, another joint, yeah, you don't know what it's like... you don't know what it's like... to be me..." And to this they began talking of the good day they had until the conversation fell to an easy silence. They were all tired and had another two hours to go before they could anchor up and sleep for four hours straight. For right now, Jack would have a nap. He had run the boat in while they all snoozed. They would wake him when they needed to.

FISHERMAN'S DREAMS

AUGUST 8 TH, MONDAY, 11:50 PM

The bunk on a boat becomes a fisherman's sanctuary. It is here his personal items belong. No one dare touch them. Sacred. Jack went back up into the top house and crawled, weary, into his bunk. He listened to the crew babble below, faint, the din of the tender as it's hydraulics squealed and fish-pump roared. Of everything there was to love about his boat, the delightful treat of non-active bliss and relaxation was the one thing that topped Jack's list of cool shit about fishing. Not just sleeping, but the dreams. Dreams on a boat took on a more vibrant surrealism than when on land. As soon as he closed his eyes and took a few deep breaths he entered the hypnogogic state. Images of sunlit mountains, azure blue ocean, the silver flash of fish in the gear, which had burned themselves into his retinas all day, came in clear and strong. He enjoyed the simple reverie, even smiled, as the images grew stronger. Jack focused his breath, into the center of his forehead and let the images become the dream. Wavering light cast up at him from the ocean below as calm waters reflected diamond bright on his floating body. He floated just over the ocean, the mountains of Knight Island and bright blue sky his scenery. He allowed his dream body to be pulled along, imagined that it was moving with the tides below, a diversion to solidify the dream just a bit more, then he commanded himself to travel. He flew fast, exhilaratingly fast, toward distant mountains where beyond lay Anchorage, the faster he went the more the images around him faded until he found himself flying along in utter darkness. Here Jack took deliberate breaths, focusing the breath through his forehead and affirmed that he would pass through the darkness, the abyss, and reenter a dream. He could feel atmosphere rushing around him in the pitch black and stretched his arms out, imagined himself a dragon. His form altered, took on the shape and feel of a dragon. A bright round sphere of light appeared in the far distance and he knew this would be a dream of Audrey's home, his current girlfriend as was his intentions on making himself travel. He flew confidently into the sphere and found himself at the door to the home that he shared with the woman.

Audrey was thirty-eight years old, blond hair, green eyes, and a quick wit. She was his college professor at one time and had seduced him with a trip to Alyeska to ski and stay in the hotel after taking an interest in him while teaching her psychology class. She shared a common interest with him in study of the occult and had many cool books by Allister Crowley, Abremalin the Mage, Enoch, Moses, Hebrew Kabala, a huge collection. Not just the common books but all of them, all books of the bible as well. She shared with him the ability to dream lucidly and they often experimented, unsuccessfully with entering a shared dream state. Tonight, was his own thing.

Now Jack hovered a few inches off the ground outside the door to Audrey's house, his intention fixed on entering and pulling Audrey out of her body for a little dance and a quick kiss. He noted that it was still bright and sunny in the dream even though in reality it should be the ever dusk of Alaska's summers. He turned his attention back to the door, reached for the door knob and found the threshold barred. He drew back, surprised, then realized that Audrey would have a strong threshold given all the occult knowledge she possessed. He focused on the door and there appeared a pentagram, crudely fashioned, but present. He focused on it and reached out. His fingers passed through the wood door and he curled them around the protective symbol and ripped it away along with the door. Tossed it over his shoulder. Audrey stood staring at him on the other side wearing a long pink night gown, arms folded across her breasts. She was smiling at him with a leer on her face that actually startled him. She crooked a finger at him to come in, turned and faded into the house. Jack had been expecting her to be in bed, and perhaps she was now that he rethought about it. He felt uneasy as he followed her into her house.

Audrey smiled at him as she turned her attention to a young man seated on her couch. She lifted her nightgown up and over her head and tossed it to the side before straddling him. Jack reached out and attempted to connect with the real Audrey, not this odd version of her that his mind had created. He felt the extreme warmth of her skin as his hand neared her back. He whispered her name, told her to come dream with him. She lurched away, as if burned, eyes angry as she stared at him.

"Stop it! Stop that Jack! You shouldn't be here!" She yelled. The force of her words took Jack by surprise. These kinds of dreams often ran a little weird. He looked at her, naked, breasts heaving as she breathed, legs closed around a thick blond patch of pubic hair, thighs tensing as if she were about to leap at him.

"Why are you attacking me?" Audrey snapped. Another Audrey came down the stairs into the living room, eyes squinting. "Jack? Is that you?" She asked.

The Emma Dawn's engine revved, the sound popped him awake with a start. Bart was maneuvering from the helm. Jack rolled out of his bunk and stretched, yawned as his eyes adjusted to the evening light.

"Thought I would let you sleep, not that you actually sleep while you sleep." Bart said. He was aware of Jack's lucid dreaming, as were all the crew, a few even picking it up and were thrilled with it. The ones who did he added to his list of known lucid dreamers. Built his private network.

Jack nodded. "Thank you for that Bart. And yeah, just had an intense one, like as if you took five hits of acid and huffed some ether and started seeing things. I have to write this one down."

As Jack spoke he felt his body thrumming with energy, especially at his forehead. He was taught by his yoga instructor to 'focus breath through the third eye' while meditating. He had applied this to the dream state as well, found it helped keep the dreams solid. Jack had also been taught by Sing-Kahlsa that the vibrations, the thrumming of energy he now felt, were from the spirit being snapped back into the body from the sort of dream he had just had. It was an odd physical sensation. Sort of a 'Vvvvvmmmm Vvvvvmmmm Vvvvvmmmmm' for about thirty seconds until it went away. The jury was still out on soul travel as far as Jack was concerned. He was more prone to believe that it was an abrupt shift from the Lucid Dream state back into the physical consciousness, and a tweak to the flight or fight response nestled in the base brain, that caused it. He was, however, certainly open to the possibility that his instructor was correct. The soul did travel and it did snap back into the body when needed, and this was what caused the weird thrumming of energy he often experienced. Or, it could be a surge of adrenalin combined with a hyper awareness brought on by the dream state that caused his body to thrum with a wave of energy. Wave energy, light, consciousness. The thought that perhaps it was the soul made him shiver, feel prickles of nervous energy wash over his skin, raised his hackles. Wonder just what the hell he was messing around with, experimenting and experiencing incredible things in an advanced alternate state of mind.

Jack took up a pen and a note pad and wrote down the time and date and title of the dream. He had an understanding with Audrey that she would do the same during the fishing season and then they would compare notes to see if there was any psychic connection of a shared dream time. Cool experiment. She had been his psych professor his first year of college and they had dated after the class was over basically because of their shared ability to lucid dream and that it was sort of taboo and cool to be doing the professor. Her field of study was paranormal psychology in which she held a PhD. Audrey, like Jack, held high regards for the mental and physical effects of Lucid Dreaming. To Jack, being able to dream while awake within the dream was something that God blessed him with more than anything else in his life. It made life mysterious, better, deeper.- At sixteen when he first started he had indulged in any whim he desired. He screwed every Hollywood starlet he could get his mind on, Cher being especially entertaining, used pyromantics to blow up and burn dream images, lightning summoned from the skies to scorch the dream earth, shattered the minds of dream images with his mind, used rage to drive a high-powered Dodge Charger through traffic as fast and recklessly as he could, ending in explosion against a wall and drifting off, staring back at the carnage feeling triumphant, engorged with power. But then things begin to change, he began to become aware of a residual effect of the dream, began to revere the opportunity to explore higher purpose. In dreams Jack sought out Jesus, drank the addictive draught from the holy grail, flew to the moon, past the moon, into the vast and cold expanse of the galaxy, entered dreams that he could not control, where things suddenly became frighteningly real, as if the images in the dreams were not of his imagination, but real, independent of him, and had always been there. He would levitate through ancient Greek cities, challenge his personal trickster, a shadow man who took form of a coyote-raven per the books, but, to Jack, was Arnold Schwartzenager, to duals that usually ended up with fleeing, hiding from the trickster. Jack continued his duals with the Trickster Arnold and eventually caught him and was about to cut his throat when Arnold told him he could not kill him because if he did he would kill a part of himself. Jack stayed his hand, released the Trickster, and it disappeared. He had awoke with a start from that dream, felt exuberant, vibrant, filled with power.

Jack then began unravelling the effects of his thoughts on the manifestations of the dream, compare them to his thoughts while awake. In this comparison, he found that there were many strong correlations between dream manifestation, and life manifestation. He concluded that life, was also a dream, just a thicker, slower moving one. In the dream items of desire manifested at will. Jack wrote down how it worked in the dream, found that it was the same formula for how it worked in life, just took longer.

The mental formula he kept working on, enhancing as he realized a new subtlety of mind over matter. He carried it with him, in his pocket, a little folded, stapled, paper pamphlet, so he could add notes when thoughts occurred and were clear.

When Jack put his formula to the test strange coincidences, synchronicities began to happen. He met the right people at the right time, found a book that explained and confirmed the experiences he was having by Dr. Carl Jung, which led him to take a paranormal psychology class where he met his professor, Audrey, and engaged her in long conversations about the paranormal. She was a manifestation, sent by God, and while he loved and enjoyed her, knew they were never going to marry, never going to be anything long term other than friends. He wanted children but she already had two beautiful little people and had her tubes tied at thirty-five.

Jack finished writing his notes in his log and put it away, focused back on the waking world, the slow-moving dream, meant to be savored, that was life.

NO PLACE I WOULD RATHER BE

Jack watched with approval as Bart skillfully maneuvered the Emma Dawn alongside the Lorem. Ziggy and Wendy tossed lines to the crew of the tender who caught them and began to pull the boat up snug against the air bladders deployed to keep the boats from grinding together.

He felt invigorated after having rested and dreamed. He stepped out of the top house, kicked off his deck shoes, and stepped into his boots, which were surrounded by his rain pants. Once his feet were in the boots all he had to do was pull up the rain pants and presto, he was work ready. He turned and saw, Ziggy, Bart, and Wendy in gear, waiting for the operator to lower the fish sucker into the open fish hold. Sarah was standing by the fish chute and smiled as she waved at him. Jack inhaled through his nose a large dose of mind clearing ocean air.

"You take her tonight. Somehow. You must make your interest known. Cordova is way too short on pretty ladies." He told himself.

Jack brachiated down the ladder forward, hands holding the rails behind him, feet finding purchase as he grabbed and swung from stay lines to land on the cap rail of the Emma Dawn, then hauled himself up and over the higher rail of the Lorem to land, with a tiny slip, upon the deck of the tender.

"Heh! He is on a mission!" Mark said. His accent made the crew chuckle. "Go get her, maybe we share, me and Lana huh?"

"Your disgusting." Wendy snapped.

"Oh please, pretty lady. Only a prude would not want two mouth and four hands pleasuring her at least once in this sweet and short life time. Tell me it is not so."

"It is not so… Maybe." Wendy replied with a giggle. She tossed a massive wad of pop weed at Mark who dodged and caught it, a smile on his face.

Jack hoped that Sarah did not hear them. He glanced her way, saw her standing, raingear glistening wet in the bright deck lights, strands of hair that escaped her pony tail wrapped around her face. She pulled these away, smiled and… Did she pink up a bit? Jack smiled back. Waved. The deck was loud with the whine of hydraulics and big vacuum system. To loud to talk. He just stood next to Sarah happily and watched as the crew worked the fish sucker tube back and forth in the fish-hold like a giant vacuum. The high-pitched whine of the vacuum engines changed volume as it began to suck fish and ice-cold salt water. His refrigeration system kept the salmon cold which was rewarded by an extra four cents per pound. The system was expensive but had quickly paid for itself. It was difficult, however, to keep the fish at the right temperature to guarantee the extra money and a good tender-man would be extra prickly about getting the reading with a thermometer to make certain he was getting the cold fish the cannery was paying for. Jack had rigged a thermometer to always read the right temperature, and had another actual thermometer hanging next to it. Black line pulled up the rigged one, white line pulled up the true. Ziggy was careful to check the actual with his back blocking the view. He looked up at Jack and gave him a thumb up. Today, they would not need the fake one, the brine was plenty cold. He watched the fish shoot up the translucent sucker tube and into the holding tank. Sarah opened the gate and the first of his sixty thousand or so pounds of salmon began to fill the weighing net.

Jack walked over to the chute, stood on the opposite side, and watched for the money fish, reds, kings, silvers, and dog salmon were separated into smaller totes for weighing, each being of a different, and higher value than the pinks.

"Looks like you had a great day." Sarah yelled over the whine of the engines.

"This is the second load. Fishing is good today everywhere I would imagine." Jack yelled back.

Sarah nodded, looked back to his fish, caught a big King and tossed it into a tote bin to the side of her. She looked a bit tired, cheeks still pink, maybe from Jack, maybe from being warm while working, sweating. He told himself it was the latter yet hoped it was the former.

The crane operator lifted the first full hopper of salmon and held it above the deck so the weight could be taken. Sarah waited for the digital read out to stop fluttering up and down and then called out the weight, giving Jack the high bounce of an extra ten pounds. She smiled as Jack nodded appreciatively. Every bit helped. Once the weight was taken a long lever was pulled that opened the aluminum hopper door to let the Pink Salmon pour into the fish hold of the Lorem. As this happened the sucker continued to scream and dump fish into a gated holding bin. Once the hopper was empty Sarah opened the gate to allow the flow of salmon to proceed down the slanted sorting table. Every bit of the machinery was fabricated from need, each tender with a little different system, but each with an eye to being the most efficient production line.

The work was quick, steady, and coordinated so that the flow of salmon rarely had to come to a stop. The salmon streamed by. Sarah quickly grabbed and sorted the money fish. This time of year the Silver's were running and were more prevalent than the others. Out of fifty thousand pounds of salmon, there would usually be about five or six thousand pounds of silvers, eight hundred pounds of reds, and so on. Jack stood next to Sarah, a little downstream, to see if he could catch any of the money fish she missed. It soon became apparent that she was not going to miss any and Jack relaxed a bit. He kept tally as the hopper was weighed, made furtive eye contact with Sarah at times, made her laugh with body language as odd little things happened during the delivery.

The hours passed and the end tally Jack held on his clip board was 51,878 for the pinks, 834 for the reds, 450 dogs, 2,340 silvers, and 230 pounds of kings. Jack smiled as he added them together, 55,732 pounds. He was pleased with his decision to run the boat with a full deck load. It had made his crew a little extra money.

Jack climbed the stairs to verify his tally against that of the Captain of the Lorem. Greg was a huge man, had to be close to four hundred pounds, sported curly brown hair and a usual smile on his pudgy face.

"You did good today! 57,160 this time!" He said.

Jack smiled and nodded enthusiastically. "Smooth fishing too." He said. He shoved his own tally sheet in his pocket now that it was useless and unzipped his water proof pouch to produce his purse seine permit card.

Greg took the plastic card from him, swiped it to get an imprint. He handed Jack the clipboard. Jack signed the bottom of the white copy, handed it back. Greg tore off the bottom pink copy and handed it to Jack. Jack smiled as he tucked it and the permit card carefully, reverently, back into the thick plastic. He would turn in all his pink slips at the end of the season, or as he needed to, and have the cannery cut him a check.

"Thanks Greg. I appreciate the good service. Haven't been on the radios or listening all day. Anything new?" Jack asked.

Greg inhaled and gave him a surprised look. "Well, nobody got killed or injured, that's the good news. Bad news is, the Fish and Game are closing us down for three days to allow for ample escapement of the wild salmon." Greg said. He winced as Jack's grin turned to a grimace.

"It's fucking closing?"

Greg nodded. "Yeah, announced it while you were off loading, shoulda heard the people talking, got a little nasty."

Jack clenched his jaw. "Fuck! I just got out of the red. The fish are here, streaming down the beaches, the Sound is full. I can't believe those fucking idiots are fucking closing it."

Greg shook his head then smiled. "We will be plugged after the next couple boats, so we gotta go to town and off load, be back early afternoon of the opener. You and your crew want to come along?" Greg asked.

Jack was still processing the new turn of events. He wanted to hit something but realized that would do no good. He relaxed his jaw and told himself to look for the angle... So what if they were closing it. It was a fact that the wild salmon were in, they were streaming down the beaches. The fish counters would call in favorable numbers and they would re-open. It would not be three days.

"Did you offer anyone else the opportunity for a ride into Cordova?" Jack asked.

Greg shook his head no. He glanced through the window of the wheel house down at the deck. Smiled. "Sarah wanted you to come." He said. "I am pretty sure she likes you. You been making the eyes at her all season long and haven't so much as flirted with her." He said

Jack felt his cheeks color a little and looked away, down at the deck where she was washing her raingear, getting ready to remove it.

"Yeah, I like her too. Just don't have the time to be messing around. Keep it professional and all... But we just got some time, didn't we?" Jack smiled. "Can you do me a favor?" He asked. Gregg nodded.

"Can you extend the courtesy of a ride to town to the captain of the Cape Hook, he is waiting to deliver."

Jack looked down at the Cape Hook as it maneuvered to hang off the stern of the Lorem. It was obvious that the Captain hoped to avoid a confrontation with Mark who was like a jealous Leprechaun protecting his gold where it came to Lana.

"And, could you spare Sarah if she would like to stay with me and my crew during our forced holiday?" Jack asked.

Greg nodded thoughtfully. "Sure, if she wants to stay she can, but she was looking forward to going to Cordova, party and what not."

To this Jack just shrugged. "I like it out here, maybe she will too."

Greg laughed. "All depends on how you ask her I guess. The shower is available; we will be taking on new water in town so enjoy a long hot one."

"You're a good man Greg." Jack said. He extended his hand and shook the man's huge paw.

Greg nodded in agreement. "Yeah, I like to offer my preferred customers high bounce every now and again." He said. "Saw you stuff your tally in your pocket there..." Greg winked.

Jack laughed as he left Captain Greg's wheel house. He moved swiftly, jumped over the cap rail, landed on the wet slippery deck of the Emma Dawn, caught his weight on a taunt stay line and scampered up the ladder to the top deck. Bart had maneuvered the boat around to the other side of the Lorem, so they could take on fuel, and to get out of the way of the boat waiting to deliver. The crew was still cleaning the deck and their gear.

"So, what was the final tally?" Bart asked. The crew always threw in twenty and tried to guess poundage of each days catch. Whoever came the closest won if they were within a thousand pounds, miss it by more than a thousand, and the pot grew. They had missed it for the last three deliveries.

Jack stood on the top deck, supporting his weight by leaning on the ladder railings and smiled at his crew. They looked up at him expectantly. He rather liked that.

"You guys did excellent today, great teamwork. I need to talk to you all in the cabin." Jack said.

"The tally Jack! What was it?" Bart demanded. The others nodded.

"Ok ok, greedy guts. It was..." He looked at the clip board through the plastic pouch at the pink slip. "Right at 57,160."

He watched for triumph but there was none. "Well who came the closest?" He asked.

Ziggy raised his hand. "I guessed 51.5, your boat is only supposed to hold forty-nine thousand pounds. The others are all lower than me."

"You missed it by more than five thousand. The pot grows!" Jack said. "Meet me inside really quick." He entered his top-house, placed his clipboard, which held the tally, and the precious 'Permit Holder' card he had paid to much for in a spring-loaded hatch he custom built to keep it safe, let it snap shut, flush with his bunk bed wall, then descended the inside ladder stairs to the lower cabin.

The crew filed in and took seats. Weary sighs and smiles.

"What a fucking day we had huh?" Jack said. "Over a hundred thousand pounds today. Imagine we can do it every day if the fish keep running, huh?" He said.

There were tired whoops, a high five. Jack smiled. His crew this year had come together from a rather rocky start.

"Showers are offered on the Lorem. I would normally draw straws with you all like usual but this time I gotta go first." Jack said. The gleam in his eye and his emphasis on the word 'gotta' told them he was up to something.

They all just nodded, Wendy produced four straws and they all drew quickly. Wendy would go next, then Ziggy, Mark, and Bart was last.

"Ha ha! You last Bart!" Mark said. Mark laughed. Bart wadded up the paper he had written his estimate of the tally on into a tight little ball and bounced it off Mark's forehead. Mark flinched, now silent, a surprised look on his face.

"I don't like to be fucking laughed at." Bart said.

Mark shut up immediately. The little wad of paper had been scrunched together so tightly in Bart's powerful grip it must have stung as it pinged off his forehead.

Jack tried to stifle his urge to laugh but could not hold it all in. A snicker escaped. Wendy began giggling, made a snorting noise.

"Good thing that nice judge in Cordova had me take those fuckin' anger management classes huh? Normally I would have just punched you in your laughing mouth." Bart grinned, raised his jaw, pleased with his new level of restraint.

Mark rubbed his forehead, a good-natured smile on his face. He had already had the shit kicked out of him in the Cordova bars for being an overly arrogant prick. Lessons learned. His own father had told Jack that he had hoped that would happen when he hired him to take his son as crew on the Emma Dawn.

Jack waited for them to enjoy a bit of mirth and when they calmed he drew their attention again.

"There is some bad news though, I need you all to hear me out for a second."

They calmed and looked at him.

"The Fish and Game are shutting us down for three days to allow for wild salmon escapement." Jack said. Everyone's faces slid into a scowl. He was proud of that. Of all the crew, he and Bart were the only ones who needed the money and yet those who did not need the money wanted to keep working as hard as they were just for the experience, and to earn back their father's investment, or come close. The two playboys were proud of their work.

"Hear me out though, I know it sucks but here is what I think is going to happen. They will only keep it shut for one day at the most, just until their counters see that the fish numbers are going up. I mean, the sound is full of fish." He made a motion with his hand cupped around his ear for them to listen. Under the din of the tender could be heard a steady 'sploosh!' 'sploosh!' 'sploosh' of salmon jumping. They heard it as well. Nodded.

Now Jack grinned big. "The Captain of the Lorem, Greg, is going to offer the captain of the Cape Hook the opportunity to make a grocery run into town. I am hoping he accepts because that means they will be stuck in town when the season opens sooner than expected."

Mark brightened and nodded. "You are devious Captain Jack." He laughed.

"Yes, well, you Mark, have got to use some of that French diplomacy, put away the hot head, and see if you can have Lana stay while they go to town. Me, I am going to ask Sarah to stay with us. I would suggest you find a way to politely ask Lana to volunteer to stay out on the boat. The rest of them go to Cordova and get stuck there - Greg plans on being back the day of the projected opener, early in the afternoon."

Mark nodded his head. "But where is the Cape Hook? Are they even going to come in here?" He asked.

To this Jack pointed towards the stern of the Lorem through the back door, his hand on the back of Mark's neck so he would look where he was pointing. It was not good timing for the whole diplomacy thing. Lana was just climbing off the bow to the back deck of the Lorem and received a little pat on the ass from the Captain of the Cape Hook as he helped her safely to the deck. To this she made a little 'o' with her lips and wiggled her butt at him, a smile on her pretty face.

Mark made a funny little gasp noise in the back of his throat as if her were trying to inhale and talk French at the same time.

"That... That cocksucker" Mark yelled. He began to bounce up and down on the balls of his feet. "I will gut him like a feeeesh!" He made to pull away from Jack but Jack squeezed his neck a bit harder and held him back.

"Easy Mark, I don't want to have to fly you to town on a med-vac. She didn't seem to mind it, they probably are just comfortable with each other, fooling around, you know?"

"Yes, Yes I know, I don't want them fooling around! He touched her ass with his filthy hand..."

"Can it for fucks sake." Jack snapped. "It was through three layers of clothes. You tell me about how the french are all cool about sex then get all jealous over this girl, offer to share her with me, then get mad she is being friendly with others?"

"My offer to share her with you was in jest Jack, because I know you are too uptight for such things." Mark said. He shrugged. Jack felt the tension go out of him.

"You are right though. She is a cool woman. I just... I think in my blood is the instinct to protect her because she is so cool. They might take advantage, that is different, like rape. No one rapes my woman."

Jack let go. Mark did not move towards Lana or Captain Ray of the Cape Hook. Instead he fidgeted as if still considering bolting out the door for a confrontation with the Captain. For being a Harvard educated man, Mark was lacking in what Bart had called, 'street smarts.'

Lana then walked straight down the side of the boat towards the Emma Dawn and stopped at the rail looking down at them as they stepped out on the deck.

"Hi you two." She said sweetly. She began to throw a leg over the rail and Mark leapt to help her.

Jack sighed with a bit of relief. He darted up the ladder to his wheel house and grabbed some fresh clothes, stuffed them into his groom bag and made his way to the Lorem. He saw that Sarah had ended her shift, another fellow was doing her regular job and he crossed the deck to the big oval shaped metal door of the Lorem's cabin. Jack passed through the gear locker and into the hallway that led to the galley. To the right of the hall was another hall that led back to the shower area and stowage.

He found Sarah sitting at the galley table munching an apple and reading a book. She looked up at him over the book, blue eyes bright, and smiled. "Hi Jack." She said.

Jack smiled back at her although it felt like a coil of eels battled about his stomach region.

"Hi." He said. He paused, feeling the battle of his mind. These were the moments in life that reminded him of lucid dreaming. He knew he was about to do something to cause the dream to change, but for some reason irrational fear would take hold of his mind, even though he was fully aware he was dreaming. While dreaming there was a split second of a split second to reign in the minds fears, or fear would cause to manifest monsters instead of the nice thing of original intention. This, was one of those moments.

Jack inhaled and stepped forward, towards Sarah, his hand held out to her. He focused on projecting a 'devil may care attitude' confident, and broadened his smile a bit.

"I am going to take a shower and I would love it if you would join me." He said. "Our little secret?"

Sarah stared at him, mouth slightly open, eyes wide, beseeching. The book dropped to the table. Her eyebrows raised and lips puckered in what might be anger. Jack grinned bigger, tilted his head and raised his eyebrows.

Sarah's would be anger showed a flicker of a smile.

"You are such a shit. We haven't been on a date, have not even had so much as a conversation more than polite yells on the deck, and you want me to just jump in the shower with you?"

Jack could now tell she was faking her incredulity. His confidence grew.

"We have had many a good conversation, most non-verbal, but to where we are comfortable with each other. You have to admit there is a thick sexual tension between us after an entire summer of stolen glances and cavorting about to make each other laugh." Jack said.

Sarah slipped and nodded. A tiny nod, then shook her head, 'no'.

"It's all that nice stuff that is keeping me from bouncing this coffee cup off your stupid head right now."

Jack gave her his best 'please I really want you' face. "All that nice stuff was our 'dates' and I liked it but let's move forward. Do you want me? Right now?" Jack asked.

Sarah looked up at him, her face softened, a grin grew, her lips parted, tongue caressing her plump bottom lip in such a way that Jack could feel the lust emanate from her. She sighed and blew a stray strand of blond hair away from her face.

"Yes. Now." She said.

Jack closed the distance between them as she stood. His hand slid behind her neck, tangled in her hair, as he took her hand in his. They kissed lightly, Jack's lips just brushing over hers. Sarah moved her head forward, her tongue urgent against Jack's.

They hurried to the shower, stripped and stepped into the hot water. Sarah was not the least bit modest or shy once she accepted his offer, she took pleasure in Jack's admiration, as he explored every inch of her full round-ness. Jack likened her to a Rubin painting, voluptuous, sensual, beautiful. Most men loved a skinny body, the model look. Jack preferred a rounder, fuller body. Sarah was a delight to his senses, her hips round, abdomen sporting a soft pad, not fat, just more, like an Arabian belly dancer.

Sarah was no wall flower when it came time to consummate the full sum-mer of flirting. She sighed, wiggled, shifted positions, stroked, teased, demanded, urged, and gasped as Jack danced with her under the hot water. He would like to believe that he had ravaged her in the shower but the truth was, they lit into each other with equal hunger, gentle, rough, and above all, with heart pounding passion.

When they were finished, they toweled each other off and opened the door to the shower. Wendy stood in the hallway, waiting her turn, a cool smile on her face, eyes moving up and down both of their bodies.

"I hear you two have gotten to know each other a bit better." She said. "Congratulations."

Sarah giggled as her cheeks turned pink. Jack just gave a little sheepish shrug. They stepped past Wendy into the area where they had left their clothes to get dressed, not bothering with modesty. Wendy gave a little 'tsk, tsk'

"Just going to let it all hang out huh?" She shrugged and stripped off her own shirt and pants. "Guess there isn't much sense in being overly modest, we share the same boat and all." She said. She turned her back to them, removed her bra, stripped off her panties, and stepped into the shower with a cute wiggle of her muscular ass.

"Which brings me to my next question lovely Sarah." Jack said. Sarah looked at him and smiled as he pulled her closer, still naked, nipples just grazing his belly. He gave her a quick kiss. "Would you like to stay aboard the Emma Dawn while Greg runs into Cordova. He said it would be ok."

Sarah laughed as she looked up at Jack. "He gave his permission, did he? I should hope so." She slid her hands around Jack's waist, fingers sliding over his butt. "I love it out here." She said and stood on her tiptoes to kiss him on his lips and cheek. She put her mouth close to his ear as his hands stroked her back. "And right now, there is nowhere else I would rather be, than with you, on your boat."

PRINCE WILLIAM SOUND MAGIC

Jack and Sarah agreed to meet up after she had finished her next shift. They grinned at each other on the deck of the Lorem. Jack made his way back to the top house of the Lorem and Sarah, re-clad in rain gear, made her way to relieve her deck mate.

A quick check in with Greg and Jack learned, to his glee, that Captain Raymond of the Cape Hook had eagerly agreed to travel aboard the Lorem into Cordova and that Lana would be left behind after she had asked him very... persuasively. Greg was still a little steamed up as he chuckled and shook his head in the telling of it.

The Emma Dawn was tied alongside the Lorem, her decks fresh and clean, cabin lights on, engine purring as she waited below. Jack gazed fondly at her from the top deck of the Lorem.

A fresh shower, wet and a bit awkward sex, a calm pastel ever dawn and the promise of a sunny day off, with a beautiful woman, made him giddy with pleasure. He sneaked aboard the Emma Dawn like he used to sneak back onto his father's boat after a longer than approved beach party. With practiced stealth he entered her top-house and closed the hatch to the lower deck. This was to ensure privacy as much as it was courteous to the people below. With both side windows open and his fan on to blow the smoke out Jack poured a cup of coffee, lit a cigarette, and opened his log book to note the day, the tides, add to what he had already jotted down, while he waited for Sarah to finish her shift.

There were no other boats to offload, so remaining at the Lorem's side was approved by Captain Greg with the contingency, of course, that they depart with haste should a late straggler enter Snug Harbor. The wheel of the Emma Dawn was dead center of the top-house, a captain's chair and navigation center occupied the corner of the bridge, starboard side of the standing helm. Jack had designed this area himself after purchasing the boat. He changed all the electronics with the help of Tunashima-san, a Japanese electrical engineer who loved computers and tinkering. Jack had him aboard during the 1987 season.

Now he could sit in the navigation center, pull out a slide away desk, and make his notes in comfort. He envisioned adding an onboard computer, with satellite uplink so he would be able to keep in touch with his business efforts and family while fishing. He had discussed this with Tunashima-san who believed that one-day computers would be integrated with everything. He also cautioned that this was not necessarily a good thing. Jack didn't see though, how it could be bad, and shared his vision of how he wanted to integrate furniture with computers. From that conversation they began immediately to design his helm with expanded computer usage in mind.

He pulled the desk into place and organized his books, pen, coffee, ashtray, lighter. He opened his fishing and maintenance log, noted the date, the amount of salmon caught, place, weather, tide stage, and mechanical performance of the boat. He had checked the oil in the morning, added a quart to the engine. He then put the boat logs away and opened another log. This one was full of designs and drawings of ideas. There were pages and pages of ideas, some that he had fabricated, others that were simply to elaborate, well beyond his skills and means. The slide-out desk he was currently using was on page one, as was the lay out of the navigation electronics, the radar monitor on a swivel so he could use it while at the wheel, or in the navigation seat, the placement of the auto pilot, the loran, radios were all carefully thought out so he could make the best use of each station. Tonight, he had an idea for a different way to release the aluminum bins the tenders used to weigh the 'money fish' so that the tension could be lessened on the deckhand releasing it. He had watched Sarah pull and jerk with both hands on the lever to open the hatch each time she opened it to empty the bin into the fish hold. He drew the original release mechanism, had closely inspected it earlier, then added leverage, then added a small gear box with a remote-controlled release. Then got rid of the crane operator and made the crane remote control as well - no batteries to charge though, hard wired right into the 110 inverters, the remotes plugged in with water proof rubber insulation to protect the user from shock. He then designed a protected pod where the remote user could stand or sit to get out of the weather and be protected from flying parts and pieces should something break and zip across the deck.

It was two thirty in the morning when Jack saw Captain Ray, and two deck hands, step off the cap rails of the Cape Hook and onto the deck of the Lorem. A bit of glee lit Jack's smile. They had taken the offer to go to town, had bought the ruse. Jack chuckled as he made his way down to the deck and into the cabin. It was dark save one light over the galley table where Ziggy slept sitting up, slumped against the wall, face pressed against the window, drooling. Wendy was asleep in her bunk, Mark in his below hers.

"Whats it?" Ziggy said. He wiped his mouth. Looked about as if there was a disaster about to happen.

"We need to cast off pretty quick. What happened with Mark and Lana?"

Ziggy snorted. He didn't do anything stupid this time. Was, owe you zay? Diplomatic. Like you suggested."

Jack nodded. "Good. And he is asleep instead of obsessing over Lana."

Ziggy nodded. "They had a conversation. It went well, until the groping started. Then it got a bit awkward but I didn't leave, stayed right here and watched. She's purdy. She snuck back aboard her boat when they were done."

Ziggy was the youngest of the crew, an awkward nineteen-year-old, well-educated and spoiled by his father's wealth. He had been the toughest nut to crack into the teamwork and comradery. First half of the season he had been a bit sulky at having been told, by his father, that he would crew aboard the Emma Dawn with Jack, but now, was pulling his weight, enjoying the experience. Ziggy had come aboard with an air of superiority, as if his father had somehow purchased his spot aboard the boat and that entitled him to make requests. He got off on the wrong foot with Bart right away, asked him to fetch a bag, assumed he was help for the experience. Bart had laughed, pulled out a long Buck blade.

"You every skinned a moose kid?" He asked. He did not wait for an answer, Ziggy was frozen, eyes locked on Bart's knife. "You are crew on this boat. Wendy is your deck boss. I am skiffy and first mate. You have no idea the world you just entered and what it has in store for you. You listen to what we tell you and we will help you survive without injury. Now, fetch your own fucking clothes you wet behind the ears over privileged little shit."

After his initial, 'culture shock' Ziggy went into survivor mode, took notes, made the best of his situation. He was studying to be a lawyer, like his father, and from what Jack could tell, would make a great one some day.

"Bart is still showering I assume, once he gets aboard, and Sarah, we will go anchor up and get some sleep. We have earned it." Jack said. "Might as well let the bunk rats sleep all the way through." He clapped Ziggy on the shoulder.

"Wendy did mention that you two were going at it in the shower." Ziggy said. He grinned.

"We didn't just go at it Ziggy, we humped, sucked, fucked, and twizzled. Don't ask me what twizzling is. I think Sarah made it up."

Ziggy shook his head. "Mark was happy you finally mounted ze woman." He said. He enjoyed mocking Mark's French accent. Mark, in turn, did a funny rendition of Ziggy's New York Jewish accent as well as what he called Jack's lack of accent at all.

Jack went back up top and fired up the Emma Dawn. The big Cat diesel engine roared to life then settled to a low rumble. The morning skies were clear, the mountains cupping Snug Harbor black silhouettes against faint blue light of Alaska's ever dawn. Prior to midnight, ever dusk, after midnight, ever dawn. He saw Sarah walk out on the deck and went down to meet her. She tossed him a stout canvas bag and smiled as she climbed nimbly over the rail and onto his boat.

"Hi Jack." She said.

"Welcome aboard Miss Sarah." Jack said. He took her hand and pulled her to him, her body warm, soft against his.

"Have you seen Bart?"

"I am right here." Bart said. He stepped down, to the cap rail, spun and stepped forward on the fish hold, feet sliding in a controlled manner as he passed them.

"Cast off then?" He said. He was fresh from a long shower.

"Yes, anchor and sleep." Jack said.

"Not sure how much sleeping you're gonna get Mister." Sarah said. She smiled coyly and batted her eyes at him.

Bart disappeared around the bow as Ziggy came out and moved to the stern. Jack sprinted up the stairs and watched as the lines were released and tossed aboard the Lorem. Bart moved down the cap rail, one hand on the railing mounted in the side of the cabin, raise his leg and put his foot against the Lorem's metal hull. He gave one good shove and the bow of the Emma Dawn moved away from the Lorem's side. Jack put her in forward and turned the wheel so his forward motion would swing his stern clear.

Sarah looked around at the top house as Jack stood at the wheel and gave Bart the signal to drop anchor. He had chosen a place well away from the Cape Hook so as not to tempt Mark to yell for Lana in the morning. He wasn't even sure if Mark knew she had managed to stay behind so she could spend a little time with him.

Once Bart gave a thumb up to indicate the anchor had taken hold Jack shut the engines down. Everything went silent. Blissful. The plunking sound of jumping salmon grew loud, the sounds of the Lorem pulling her anchor louder. Jack sighed. He felt Sarah's hand slide under his shirt and up his belly.

"I am very happy that you finally hit on me." Sarah said. "I was beginning to double triple analyze your every eye brow twitch and glance my way."

Jack nodded, his eyes drinking in her lovely face, half open flannel shirt, swell of cleavage showing in the gap. "I was beginning to do the same thing, over analyze. I guess we have that in common." Jack said.

Sarah nodded and gazed around a bit, her eyes coming back to Jack's after a lingering travel up his body.

"You have a very cool wheel house. Comfy and cozy. Your navigation area here is nicer than the Lorem's. Of course, Greg is a bit lazy and prone to being a slob." Sarah said. She sighed and smiled at Jack a happy smile, eyes sensuously fixed on his cock. Jack moved his hands to his button up jeans and began to slowly, unbutton them. Sarah took the hint, and opened the front of her pants, hooked her thumbs in them and slowly worked them down. She tugged at his jeans buttons until they popped opened. Her warm hand snaked inside his open fly and palmed him, pinned his cock along his leg and gently rolled it back and forth. "Again Jack, dry this time, so you can feel the wet." She winked and removed her shirt. Jack's eyes drank in her naked body as she moved to the lower bunk and slid into it sideways, her legs spread, feat on the floor. The bunk was about a foot and a half off the floor so this made her thighs spread wide and her pink show a bit. Jack knelt between her legs and smiled.

"See, nonverbal communication is just as good as a good conversation and..." He put his mouth on her and stopped talking. She laughed then trembled with pleasure as he continued to communicate nonverbally.

Jack awoke at five am. He had two hours of sleep. Sarah's head lay on his shoulder, smooth leg over his. She was on the inside in case he had to roll out quickly. He raised the covers and looked at her, sighed and shifted a bit. It was lighter out, he knew if he was on the open water the sun would be bright and full, but here, in the confines of Snug Harbor, the mountain shadows prevailed.

He was wanting to drift off and sleep, maybe until nine. Seven hours of good sleep. And dreams. Wonderful boat dreams, in boat world.

"You better get up and look at this." Robert said.

Jack groaned and looked at his dad. He was standing in the wheel house looking down, out of the window.

"What is it?" Jack looked out of the window. He looked down, into the water. Rocks had raised up out of the water all around the boat.

"Did you look at the chart before you anchored here last night?" Dad asked. "Tides going out, we are friggin' surrounded by rocks."

"Huh? Yeah, Snug Harbor doesn't have rocks like this... Glacier Bay maybe. Like that one time we ran right though them and by the grace of god did not hit one..." Jack's eyes were not believing what he was seeing. Huge black rocks loomed, dripping, wet, laden with kelp all around them like the teeth of a bear trap.

Jack lurched as there came a sickening grinding thunk noise against the hull of the boat.

"Get down there!" Robert yelled. He pressed the start button, the engine cranked, fired. "Get down there, tell me what side the rock is on! I can force us off it a way while still on anchor. Then you pull anchor!"

Jack didn't think, just turned and leapt from the top house to the deck, his feet passing through the fish hatch cover to land in a large pile of slippery, silver bright fish. He floundered about, had to get back up and tell dad were that fucking rock was!

Jack's eyes popped open. He inhaled sharply as he realized he had been dreaming then breathed easy, his heart still pounding. He chuckled. "Shoulda known that was a dream. All the signs were there." Sarah smiled but was asleep, her breasts against his side, head resting on his shoulder, her hand resting upon his morning wood.

Jack carefully slipped out of the bunk and stood. He stretched and yawned, naked, hard on sticking straight out and saw that the Alta Pearl was tied up to them, wheel house just a little above his, his mother looking at him, her eyes round, mouth in the beginning of an 'oh my god' statement.

"Oh... Sheeiitt." Jack said. He fished about and found his pants, pulled them on.

"What's the matter?" Sarah said. She tossed the covers off and was about to get up.

"No, no, just stay there." Jack said. He was too late. Sarah stood and stretched, all her naked glory, right in front of his mother and father.

"Um... My dad tied up to us while we slept." Jack said.

Sarah made a screech noise and ducked back into the privacy of the bunk bed.

"Why didn't you tell me?" She demanded.

"I was wondering why my mom was on the Alta Pearl... She doesn't fish with us anymore..." Jack said.

He picked up a book, looked at the writing, read, "The rocks were real and they put a shroom bash in the rear hole sphincter staash sh shh! It's not that... It could happen in shrunken water..."Jack smiled, inhaled, and blasted through the roof of the Emma Dawn, up high, staring down at his boat as it, and the Alta Pearl, shrunk beneath him. He was amused that the rocks from the first dream were still there, surrounding the two boats, only in this dream they were still submerged, only visible from his vantage point through clear blue sea. "Gotcha this time." He said. "And now, to indulge in a bit of dream flight..."

Jack turned his eyes to the surrounding mountains against blue sky. He saw what looked like smoke coming from one and flew to investigate. A moment of vertigo made him wobble bit as he realized how high he was off the ground. Jack inhaled sharply and affirmed to himself that he was safe, an adept dream flyer, there was no fear of falling. But there was, a little. He felt confidence fill him again and swooped down towards what caused the smoke alongside the mountain.

Jack settled next to an ornate rock fire place on a cobblestoned ledge overlooking the blue, white capped ocean a hundred feet below. The stone that enclosed the fire pit rose up from the cobblestone to form a half sphere, seamlessly built into it. Warmth emanated from the round stones. A woman in a light blue dress sat next to the fire holding a large crystal goblet of red wine. She smiled, said nothing. Behind her was a wood door set in the side of the mountain, windows wrought of stone showed that a home was there, meshing perfectly with the mountain side. Jack looked down the cobblestone path. It wound along the mountainside to an arched bridge that spanned a deep ravine to a ridge across from him. Small sail boats breezed along, white sails against a blue ocean below. A rock spire just a way off juts out of the water and curved over into her mountain forming a natural rock bridge. He could see that there were people along the side of it, presumably standing on cobblestone paths such as the one he was on.

There was a warmth of energy and beauty that Jack could feel as a palpable thing in this place. It was very peaceful. He turned to the woman drinking the wine. "What is this place?" He asked.

She nodded. "Good question Jack. Much better." She was suddenly right next to him, eyes large, penetrating. She thrust a bag of coins into his hands and winked out. Jack looked at the coins. They were lumpy, old, a figure eight on one side, a roman like persons head on the other as he held them in his hands. "Denarii's for the times of the Black Horseman." Her voice said.

The dream faded and Jack awoke. He was buzzing pleasantly in his mind, his body felt like a large blanket full of static energy was moving close to him, then away, then close again.

Jack carefully removed himself from Sarah's side and glanced out the windows before he stood to stretch. The coast was clear. He put on his sweat pants and deck shoes, pulled on a sweater, and made his way to the work deck. As he pissed over the side he wavered a bit, adrenalin kicked in and he caught his balance. His piss stream landed on the side of the boat as it wavered with his sudden lurch. He was certainly awake this time. Heart thudding a bit faster Jack pulled up his sweats and returned to the warmth of the top house. It was the ninth of August and already there was a fall smell and feel of change in the air. Fall would come with September this year.

Once back topside he noted the boats anchored up all around him, hoped no one had seen him pissing off the side. His father's boat, the Alta Pearl, was anchored with his Uncle Conner's boat, the Alabaster Lady, tied off to the side. He glanced at his watch. It was six ten am. Sarah snored cutely in the bunk. Bart seemed to echo her with a trumpet of human flesh that emanated from the back of his throat clear through the hull of the boat to the top-house.

Jack sat in his chair and opened his dream log. Wrote down the Titles, Denarii's for the times of the Black Horseman, Bad Anchorage, Eyes All Around, then the dreams. As he wrote another dream memory returned, then another. He mused upon them for a few minutes, let the symbols steep within his mind. He felt stronger. He had been given a compliment, and a bag of coins. Denarii's. He did not know what Denarii's were, though that maybe he had read a book about them and then his subconscious kicked that out during the dream. He just knew that they were powerful, mystical.

Jack put away his pen and paper and made his way silently down to the galley and put on a pot of coffee. Everyone still slept. It was very peaceful. He practiced his art of silence, coffee yoga, while he poured the water, ticked the lid down over the water tube for the perk to soak through its many holes and turned the stove up a notch. He then stepped out, to the back deck, into the cool early morning air of Sung Harbor. He watched salmon jump, a school of them disturbed by a seal from beneath thrashed the water and darted off in all directions. A bald eagle warble shrieked as it circled the stream at the head of the harbor. A brown bear looked up at it, went back to fishing. Jack stared at the bear for a while as it ambled up the fish laden creek bed, occasionally dipping a paw in to pluck out a dark humped spawner.

Jack silently said the lord's prayer in his mind as he had grown accustomed to doing when things were very good. Being grateful for his life, his good fortune, was something he believed kept him in tune with opportunity, helped turn opportunity into synchronicity, synchronicity into the making of a thing, or situation, desirable. Lucid dreaming had done that to him, made him reverent of God, aware of God in a way he had never experienced. It was impossible to him that he could have come up with the visions such as the Denarii's dream, fully immersive and experiential, on his best day of being creative. The scene came from somewhere else. Something way larger and more talented than him. The same thing had created Snug Harbor and all it's critters.

Jack stealthily climbed the ladder, entered his top house. He glanced at Sarah as she slept and shivered with delight. The same thing had created her, for him, a companion. She was so very sweet and proving to be smart, a necessary attribute in Jack's mind for any relationship longer than a week. He had picked up on her intelligence while working on the deck from the non-verbal communications.

Jack crept back down into the cabin to fill his thermos with fresh hot coffee. Mark was up, already glassing the Cape Hook. He put the binoculars down and sighed.

"She is not up yet. Supposed to come over here once she wakes up." Mark said. He gave Jack a clap on the shoulder. "It is good you finally spoke your heart to the blond. I was beginning to think it would be up to me woo her."

Mark said. He spoke in low tones, courteous of the crew, Bart to be specific. Mark had a good deal of respect for Bart's wrath.

Jack smiled and nodded, pointed upstairs, made sleeping hands. Mark nodded.

"Umm... We heard you two down here. Next time, start up the generator, cover noise huh?" He sniggered into his hand. Glanced at the bunk area. Bart still snored.

"The Cape Hook was last to deliver last night. I doubt your Lana is going to be awake before nine. And, starting the generator is out of the question. Waste of fuel and machinery just to cover up some grunts and groans."

"You are right..." Mark looked at his own bunk. "I will lay down and lucid dream about her." He said. He nodded to himself and went back to creep into his bunk as quiet as possible.

Jack hopped he would have the lucid dream he spoke of. Mark had found the idea fascinating, was into the I-Ching system of Chinese divination and all sorts of things esoteric. Jack had seen him reading a thick book on the subject and asked him about it. That question led to an in-depth conversation regarding lucid dreams, tarot cards, and Carl Jung who, ironically, had written the foreword to the I-Ching book Mark had brought aboard.

Although Mark said he would learn to lucid dream, he had not yet been able to do so though he liked to claim he had. Jack could tell the difference. There was a distinct change in an individual as they attempted to express their utter astonishment at having been successful with the first lucid dream. Jack still recalled his first one, that feeling of having stepped into another reality, of being able to perceive on a new level, the creations of the mind right down to the vascular lines of a leaf, the concentric rings raindrops make on the surface of a mud puddle...

Jack filled his coffee cup and stepped back out into the cool air of the back deck. He leaned against the ladder to the top house, took five minutes to simply enjoy the morning, the sight of the sun slowly trickling into Snug Harbor as a steady band of gold that made more vivid each thing it illuminated. He reverently sipped, savored, drank in the moment. Hot, fresh, black coffee. Beans ground fresh every three days or so to bring out the rich aroma and savory flavor that brought back many pleasant memories. Over and over Jack used coffee to anchor the most pleasant times of his life, the most productive, the most revelatory. Coffee was his anchor and trigger for the better side of him, the creative, productive, and appreciative.

In the morning Jack practiced Coffee Yoga while being silent, a thing he picked up so he would not awaken his mother, who was way too chatty in the mornings for his still mind.

Coffee Yoga involved everything that was Kundalini Yoga combined with the creation of a pot of perfect coffee, and the subsequent enjoyment of the savory first cup.

Jack formed a plan for the day in his mind. He would show Lana and Sarah the most beautiful country in the world. First, though, boat maintenance. Jack set about the engine room, quietly lifted the floor hatch, descending to the power source of his boat and business. He had organized his maintenance schedule to perform a daily checklist of tasks that always served to make him feel good about his boat being in the best possible operable conditions. He put in a good hour and a half as he ticked off his checklist. Belts, hoses, fuel filters, oil, electrical connections, ground wires firm, hydraulic tanks topped off – they always needed a little every three days of hard use, six days of regular use – sea cocks and strainers flowing the right way, rather than into the bilge, which could sink a boat rather suddenly – the white painted bilge and engine room inspected for metal shavings, unusual spatters of oil, water marks, sea spray from the water pump... Jack performed his maintenance inspection every day knowing that being intimate with every functioning system that sustained his boat, livelihood and survivability would clue him into even the most subtle of hint that something was going wrong with one of the systems. The habit had served him well.

"You take care of It. It will take care of you." His father said. Jack held his father's voice and wisdom in his mind with a fondness, a wisdom imparted from master to student, parent to child.

By nine they pulled anchor, picked up Lana, and began to idle along slowly out of Snug Harbor. The sun was bright, warm, sky and ocean blue, the smell of breakfast being prepared wafting up the now open hatch into the wheel house.

"Mmmmm! Smells good down there!" Jack yelled. His arm was around Sarah as he eased the engine up to running speed. The Emma Dawn left the remaining shadows of Snug Harbor and was lit a rich morning gold with sunlight. Bart stood with his back to them, rigging a thick fishing pole with a halibut hook on the top bunk of the wheelhouse.

"Gonna use a circle hook at first, then switch to a jig." Bart said. He loved fishing, any species, even more than Jack, and that was a lot.

"I am going to our favorite spot... We might catch anything or nothing but there have been times I have hauled up big halibut and ling cod there." Jack said.

"Put a twenty on the biggest?" Bart asked.

"Yeah but you have to guess the weight within ten pounds to win it." Jack said.

"Fuck you." Bart replied. There was no ire in his voice. It was just deadpan. He had only won the pot twice the entire season. Even after worrying an entire page of full of calculations.

"And fuck you, get your own pole ready."

"Fine, you surly shit. Just take the wheel." Jack said.

"Food?" Came a voice from below. Lana handed Sarah tin foil covered plates through the hatch. Then she emerged with Mark right behind her. Lana stroked Jack's back. "You are a much handsomer Captain than that pig on the Cape Hook." She said. She giggled. "If I were fishing with you Mark would not have to worry about me getting groped because I would be doing the groping to be sure." Her hand slid down and squeezed his ass. Sarah shook her head but had a small smile on her face. Mark, surprisingly, did not get all bent out of shape. Jack looked at him and he just smiled.

"See Jack? I am not the insane jealous person you thought. Lana has told me of the crude and unwanted advances her Captain is making on her, like a constant yapping desperate dog."

Lana nodded. "Yes, but I can handle him ok, he is just a big kid really. Lack's what do you call it... Charm?" Lana nodded. "Yes, charm." Lana now turned her attention to Sarah. "I hope you are not offended by my playing?" Lana asked.

Sarah smiled. "Depends I guess... But no, I think you are interesting."

"Good, we will be friends then." Lana said. She hugged Sarah to her and kissed her cheek. Sarah blushed. Lana smiled and cupped her cheek. "You are very pretty, very, sexy." Lana said. She stood a couple inches taller than Sarah, had a bit longer but very pretty face, an air of experience and sexuality about her that was alluring.

"Thanks, so are you." Sarah said.

Lana pulled Mark to her side and stepped forward to the side of the wheel to look out at the ocean. Both fell silent. Which was rare.

Bart dropped anchor just outside of Discovery Point after Jack had circled the area to get depth readings and drift. They were on a reef of about fifty feet depth that was tall and craggy, surrounded by deeper water. It was an area they were very careful not to get snagged up on with their nets while purse seining the outside of Discovery Point.

All reefs were areas that Jack regarded as sacred. Need food? Tired of eating salmon? One drift along this magical spire provided a gourmet fair of rock fish, halibut, or ling cod. He imagined the Ling were the guardians of the castle of rocks below them, though he knew they ate everything they could get their mouths around, including their own. Ling protected their young fiercely when they were the most vulnerable while they hung around the birth nest. Once the young were considered adults though, then they could be eaten. Jack found them fascinating as a species but each that he studied had traits, idiosyncrasies that were equally as interesting. Salmon. They always returned to their place of birth to give birth. Why and how? That was still not clear. Some said the bio chemistry of the place of birth could be smelled. Some said it was a form of genetic memory, like a programmed species, they were designed to function that way...

"We are right above a hundred-foot-tall rock spire." Jack said. He breathed in the fresh salt air.

"We gonna catch some butt!" Bart said.

"And some dragons. There are dragons down there too." Jack said. He winked at Bart. "Protecting their castle. Occasionally they bite the bait, sometimes they latch onto the fish you have caught as you bring it up."

They let the lines down and Jack showed Sarah how to jig. He had opted to go with a half of salmon head for bait. Bart had attached a salmon tail.

"You tap the weight on the rocks down there then lift up about two feet, sweep this way then down again. If you feel something tug, you give a tug back and start reeling, you will know, then, if you have something." Jack said. "It will tug back, hard. Get the dip net ready, I have a feeling there is going to be a big one on my hook soon." Jack said.

"You can't catch fish, you kill to many with the net, bad fish karma." Bart said. He laughed. "Me, I just follow orders you give, so no bad karma there."

Jack handed the pole to Sarah. "Just up and down and when you feel a tug, you set the hook." He said. "Way more sporting than using the circle hook Bart has on."

Bart whooped and began to reel. "See? It's on buddy... This one's a little feller though."

"Little ones are better eating anyway." Jack said. He grabbed the gaff hook as Bart reeled his fish up, there was a slight bend to the pole and then, suddenly, something hit hard. Bart made a loud grunt and the pole bent down harshly,

"Oh fuck I think one of those dragons just swallowed my whole damn fish!" Bart yelled. He reeled, then paused as the fish took drag, made his real squeal. "Ohh yeah!" His grin was huge. Mark, Lana and Ziggy stared at the water, Sarah had forgotten all about her bait as she watched Bart.

Bart cranked the fish in, playing it just right, letting it take drag when it wanted until it grew tired.

"We have color!" Bart yelled. "It's a dragon!"

All eyes went to the water.

"Oh my god!" Lana gasped. "It is... A dragon!"

Jack laughed. "Anyone got a camera? It's hooked good Bart. Just keep him on so we can get some pictures while it's under water.

Sarah yelped with surprise, her pole jerked from her hands, landed on the cap rail. She dove for it and caught it by the handle just as it was about to go over. All eyes turned to her as she regained control of the pole and began reeling.

"Ha ha! There you go Sarah, bring it in!" Jack said. Her pole wiggled as she reeled then bent steeply as like Bart's had. Line played back out of the reel as it took drag.

"Help me with this one quick." Bart said.

Jack bounced back over to him, his gaff hook still in hand. He looked at Ziggy. "You get some good pictures?" Ziggy waggled his camera and nodded.

"Fuck the pictures man, get my damn fish aboard." Bart snapped.

Jack looked at the Ling Cod. Its huge mouth was open, a gapping tooth lined maw. It had swallowed the fish and hook. It's side fins were spread wide close to it's head which really did give it a dragon like appearance. He marveled at the creature as Bart played it back and forth just under the water to keep the line tight, the hook set. Jack poised to set the gaff hook in its head.

"A little closer... keep it flat..." Jack struck, the gaff crunched through it's skull. The big Ling Cod jerked Jack's arms back and forth as it thrashed. Jack laughed, almost lost his footing, smashed his hip against the cap rail as he fought to bring the fish up the side of the boat. It flopped on the deck and began to sweep its tail back and forth. Bart bashed it in the head with a fish bat, jabbed his knife into its gills and sliced its jugular vein. Lana was standing well out of the way, an amazed expression on her face.

"Ok its aboard! Now Mine!" Sarah screeched. Her fish, a nice halibut, thrashed as she pulled it's head out of the water.

Jack quickly hooked the fish and lifted it aboard. It was only about thirty pounds but it was thirty pounds of energy bouncing up and down on the deck as it thrashed, flopping so chaotically it knocked over a deck bucket, slapped both Jack and Sarah with it's tail and sent the gaff hook skittering across the deck as Jack whacked at it with the fish bat. He caught it with a solid blow to the top of the head and it went stiff, quivered. He cut the halibut's jugular with a quick stab through the gill plate. Thick red blood spread around it's jiggering head until it went limp.

Within thirty minutes they caught another ling, two halibut, two yellow eye, and a tiger stripe. Jack took great delight in seeing them whooping with excitement each time they caught a fish - how Lana was a bit squeamish about killing them with the bat, but when she brought hers aboard, beat it's head in rather enthusiastically. The water was as clear in the sunlight and the fish they caught visible down to about twenty feet.

"I think we have enough meat, keep going and we will be filleting all day." Jack said. He put his arms around Sarah from behind and hugged her.

"It is amazing here. Magical." Sarah whispered. Jack kissed her neck lightly. The sunshine on her face, the winsome gaze in her eyes as the sea breeze lifted strands of blond hair that has escaped her pony tail, locked in Jack's mind.

"Bountiful and beautiful." Jack said. "That is exactly what Prince William Sound is." He smiled.

Jack headed the boat towards the Bay of Isles in the mouth of which they had dropped some shrimp pots. As they headed away from Discovery point porpoises began to sprint along with them. Ziggy, Lana, and Mark all moved to the bow of the boat, cameras in hand. Mud Ducks, aka Cormorants, black with long necks, lifted off in groups of fifty and a hundred, skimmed the water away from the boat. Tern's flew in their odd dipping and swooping manner as they fished herring and salmon fry just below the surface. Seagulls, bright white against blue water splashed and fed in a frenzy on the same, all in a huge clusters to the starboard and port.

The Emma Dawn glided along at an easy eight knots over the flat, blue, mirror like surface of the ocean. Jack and Sarah stood next to each other at the wheel station looking down over the bow as they watched the porpoises dart back and forth under the water, coming up to breath quick then back down. Jack's eyes widened as he saw what he thought was a giant porpoise coming upwards at a sheer angle from the depths. His hand automatically pulled the throttle back to reduce the speed of the boat. He saw the Orca's mouth open as it rose fast from the depths, take one of the frolicking porpoises, broke surface of the water in a splash of sea and blood and dive downward on the other side of the bow leaving a thick swirl of crimson.

"Wow!" Jack yelled as it happened. Sarah's mouth was open but nothing came out right away. "Oh my god... What was that? I mean... Was that a Killer Whale?"

Jack nodded. He went to the side window.

Lana had shrieked in surprise, the others were pointing and hopping up and down. Mark's face was red with rage.

"Did anyone get a picture?" Jack yelled.

Ziggy frowned and looked at his camera, shrugged. "I might have. I tried." He yelled back.

Bart was laughing. "It... It happens... Ahahhaha all the time... "He was trying to explain to Lana.

Mark put his hands on his hips and broke into a string of French obscenities. Lana started laughing and shaking her head.

"Zat cocksucker whale ate it. He ate ze porpoise. I will kill it. It's a monster! A monster!"He yelled.

"Happens all the time!" Jack yelled. "Just very rare to see it, third time for me but never, ever, like that." He was excited, thrilled. "That was friggin' awesome!" He ran the boat back up to speed and hugged Sarah to his side, her eyes still amazed, as were his.

Jack ran the Emma Dawn lazily along back towards the Yellow Bluffs after emptying the shrimp pots. A decent amount of shrimp awaited supper time to accompany fresh Ling and Halibut. If Mark was inclined to perform, the guy could provide a cream sauce that would impress even the most seasoned pallet.

As the boat chugged along Bart entertained the crew with a lesson in filleting and properly storing the variety of fish they had caught. Soon the smell of pan fried rock fish filled the cabin as Bart continued the lesson on how to consume, with great pleasure, the various flavors of the fish. Mark was paying rapt attention as Bart spoke and kept interrupting with questions that were flattering to Bart so kept him talking about things. Mark was a chef at heart, though his educational direction was still up in the air. Part of the reason his fathers cast him into the crew position aboard Jack's boat, to open his eyes as to what he wanted to do. Mark had laughed. "I want to do nothing... Is zat so wrong?"

Jack handed Sarah a pair of binoculars and had her glass the ocean for a pair of orange buoy's. She quickly found them and pointed so Jack could see.

He leaned in over her shoulder, smelled the scent of her hair, her body, a faint perfume mingled with hormones, and looked down her line if sight as he aimed the boat towards his remaining shrimp pots. They had been soaking for three days.

Yellow Bluffs was where they had loaded the boat twice. A wall of shale bluffs covered in yellow lichen ran to an 'M' shaped bite of heavy forest, then resumed being yellow bluffs on the other side of the valley of forest. It was as if the cliffs guarded the shallow entrance. The scenic little bite was exposed to the weather and not great for anchoring overnights. On a calm day though, it was just fine.

Jack piloted the Emma Dawn into the narrow gap between the fifty-foot-tall bluffs and entered the little cove. He idled close to the shore until the depth finder showed a hundred feet then gave the order to drop anchor. Once Bart had the anchor well set Jack killed the engine and smiled as he enjoyed no longer hearing the noise. From his windows he heard a bald eagle shriek overhead, seagulls chuckle. The warm summer breeze filled Jack's nostrils with scents of sun warmed tree bark oozing sap.

They put out the lawn chairs and basked in the sun, breathed in the heavenly scent of ocean tinged forests in the warm breeze as the boat swung slowly on anchor. Sea otters lollygagged along in groups of threes and fours, hundreds of birds, feeding at the ocean's surface, flashed in the distance. Salmon, ten and twenty at a time, leapt from the water, their bright silver bodies flashing in the sun before splashing down. Jack could identify what type of salmon made what type of splash noise - pink, pink, pink, red, pink,

pink, silver, silver, pink, dog, dog, dog, dog, dog, walking dog - sort of like music in the back of his mind.

Off to the starboard side, the side facing the ocean, came a loud whooshing noise as a pair of Humpback Whales began competing with the sea gulls for food, porpoises made bright splashes as they darted about making the whales puke up what they fed on by ramming them in their gullets.

Jack used a napkin to wipe a trail of grease from the fried fish away from the corner of his mouth as he watched the distant feeding.

"Man..." Bart said. "We could load up three times today."

"We should listen to the radio a bit, see if there is word of a bit earlier opener." Jack said. "Three days suddenly seems extreme." He grinned big. Bart nodded. "You are a devious bastard." He said. Jack grinned bigger.

Sarah giggled as Lana shrugged off her top.

"Oh common, don't be a prude Sarah. Your breasts are beautiful, and just like handsome Bart there, his shirt is off, his titts are magnificent yes?" Bart made his pecs bounce and grinned, his eyes casually swept Lana's breasts. "Oh, wow... Forget the whales." He said.

Sarah shook her head no as they laughed. "Look back at the whales Bart, back and the whales." Wendy said. She had a mischievous grin on her face as she stripped her shirt off and sat next to Lana and Mark.

Jack smiled at Sarah. "It's ok, let those puppies show. Kind of a tradition out here." He said.

Sarah sighed and lifted off her shirt with a little tilt of her head and wrinkle of her nose. She blended well.

There came a whooshing noise and Jack could see that the humbacks were heading towards them.

"The Humpbacks are moving towards us." He looked down in the clear water, could almost make out the bottom from where he was. Between the surface and the depths winked thousands of bright silver specks of salmon fry. Ziggy was torn. Six beautiful breasts, or a pair of humpbacks. He aimed his camera at the whales but continued to sneak semi-casual glances at the lady's breasts.

Jack could tell that Sarah was rather uncomfortable, at first, but she lost herself as she watched the whales lazily swim toward them. The two hump-backs were getting rather close. Jack looked at Bart who had already taken a couple of steps back from the edge of the boat. Wendy moved forward, camera ready, Lana close to the cap rail, Sarah next to her. Jack grinned as he moved across the deck, down the side of the boat to where the cabin was between them and the approaching Humpbacks. Bart was right beside him laughing under his breath. Jack positioned himself, with his own camera, so that he could get a good shot of the girls in all their glory as the whales came within twenty feet. The humpbacks were adult, about fifty feet in length. Their grey backs neared the surface of the water, broke surface just twenty feet from the side of the boat and exhaled a double plume of whale snot high into the air. Jack snapped shot after shot, caught the delightful expression on the ladies faces, as the whales surfaced, caught the spray of snot jetting out of the whales blow holes.

"Wow! Cool!" Lana yelled. He snapped a photo as the whale plume settled over them, a thick stinky mucous, basically whale snot that smells like cow breath, and the shocked expressions on their faces as they were coated in the thick, stinky mucous.

"Ewww! What the hell?" Sarah shook her head, flinging slippery clear slime everywhere. Lana just stood looking down as snot rained over her, dripped from her perky breasts. Wendy darted to the side after the initial snot rain landed on her. Ziggy and Mark were drenched but Mark was laughing so hard that it made Ziggy smile. The girls danced about, repulsed. Jack snapped picture after picture of the groups expressions. Whale snot on sun bathing beauties. Great title for a picture.

Bart was laughing and slapping his knee then fending off Wendy and Lana as they grabbed him and began to rub up against him to smear him good with their coating of snot. Mark jumped into the fray.

"We are slimed by ze whale, makes for good lubrication no?"

"No, no, it's full of bacteria, we have to wash immediately!" Bart said. He began to laugh even harder as they froze at the thoughts of that and stepped back, staring down at their drenched pants, running their hands through their hair to squeeze the now grey, viscous fluid out.

Jack fired up the generator and they turned on the deck hose and began spraying and washing down the entire deck, and themselves, until everyone was drenched and smelling of joy soap. Sarah donned her t-shirt during the fray, though, sans bra in a wet t-shirt, she looked even more alluring. Jack smiled into her eyes as he worked the deck brush.

A day of golden sun, grilled salmon, shrimp and halibut as the main sustaining proteins, an exploratory hike through the historic gold prospecting camps, and the Fish and Game announce the opener for six AM, the next morning, just as Jack had foreseen.

Jack grined at the news and looked at Lana. "You are welcome to stay aboard with us until your Captain is able to catch a flight out." He said.

Lana laughed and gave Mark a squeeze but then sobered a bit. "My 'Captain' is very..." She searched for the English word, "Cunning." She said. "He will be back in time and I had best be on that boat in the morning or he will be pissed."

The entire crew were in the galley of the Emma Dawn, which was most of the cabin space save the four bunks and head to the bow. Mark tuned the radio to the talk channel and they listened for Lana's Captain to hail the Cape Hook for a bit, then lost interest in the radio chatter and turned it back down again. Jack sighed and hugged Sarah to him.

"It was a most excellent day eh?" They all nodded, Sarah gave him a look that he read as wistful, perhaps sad, yet she was smiling. "Hey, what's that all about?" He asked.

Her smile broadened and she shook her head. "I am just kinda sad it's over and you go back to fishing and I go back to tendering." She said.

"Yeah? Well, it aint over yet, it's only six in the evening, and the sun doesn't go down until eleven or so."

Ziggy, in the bunks reading, grunted. "I for one am looking forward to getting back to work, make a little money." He said. He had been in a bit of a funk about being made to watch the boat while they had all gone on a hike to explore one of the old mining cabins on Knight Island and believed that Bart had screwed Wendy during the excursion. Something that for some reason he felt was his entitlement should she decide to be unfaithful to her husband.

While on the hike they had found all sorts of core samples stored in the cabin, which was actually was a conventional, for the 1918's style, large, two story house, nestled behind trees from the shore line inside Yellow Bluffs cove. The core samples, hundreds of them, were stored in racks in long rectangular cardboard boxes. He could tell they had been labeled at one time because there were old yellow tags of tape with tiny bits of paper triangles still stuck in them. In his imagination he could see the people tearing the labels that identified the core samples off, in a last-minute ditching of the area due to the only available ride out about to leave. In fact, there was evidence of a very hasty exodus from the site, dishes still in the cupboards, on tables, dirty in the wash basin, bedding layered in dust, curtains half drawn.

He had wondered, aloud with the others, as to why people in a hurry to leave would rip off all the tags from the core sample boxes. Must have been trying to hide their findings, or to attract an investor so they could come back. No one had ever come back.

Jack loved gold. He always brought a gold pan with him during his hikes around the Sound. He had found a little, here and there, and noted the places on his own secret map. You never know when a stash of gold might come in handy. Two such gold producing streams in Prince William Sound were marked by drips of coffee on his nautical charts, hidden in plain sight. Right now, however, salmon were his gold.

The grill was fired back up, halibut chunks, shrimp, and some yellow eye rock fish layered in onions, bell peppers, mushrooms, sour cream, mayo, and mozzarella cheese, sizzled and steamed in tin foil, as Bart eyed the tasty concoction carefully, to avoid the sin of over cooking such tender meats. The music was on, lounge chairs circled, the sun made a golden descent into ever dusk as Jack and his crew ate, told tales. They paused now and then to breath in the gifts of sap laden warm summer air and enjoy a seal snorting near the boat, or a whale sounding, tail black against the evening's golden ocean.When they pulled back into Snug Harbor it was still ever dawn, just past midnight. They caught about five hours of sleep before the opener.

CALLING IT QUITS

The jellyfish sodden bunt dropped down from the power block high above. Jack let the snap line connected to the heavy bunt web, the money bag, the place where everything cinches up on a purse seine and needs to support the weight of thousands of fish, slide through his hand as his other hand controlled the hydraulics for the big power block high above.

As usual, gravity and the law of tonnage won. Jack let the line slide the rest of the way. The gear dropped the last ten feet, splattered jelly fish and salmon gury, as it did every time. Mark cussed. As he did, every time. His deck hands then began the adept ritual of spreading out the net, exposing the rigging, prepare for the next double pin set.

Jack watched them with a strong sense of pride. Bart motored the seine skiff around to the stern, hot dogging it atop a wave into a tight spin and drop down the other side, his eyes wide as he hard-reversed to break his forward momentum. Jack winced as the boat dipped in the trough of one wave, while the skiff crested higher than the heavy bow bumpers and impacted with a loud whump, sent out a spray of fiberglass. Ziggy dove to the side. Mark yelled and shielded Wendy, most chivalrous, yet the bump was well over before he had gotten there. They were undeniably all awake now. Ziggy lunged and grabbed the skiffs hook up line, held tight and flipped the heavy ring close to the bear trap. Wendy snatched the hook up ring, slipped the cock of the bear trap into it, folded it back along the trap, and latched it down. Jack flipped on the hydraulics to the deck winch, wrapped the heavy line that was connected to the bear trap and sucked the line tight, the shiny aluminum disk of metal connecting the two lines vibrating in the middle, the bow of the skiff now snug against it's protective air bladders a bit squished.

Bart hauled the double pin end of his lead through the bow rollers and Mark took one side, Wendy the other. Then he leaped over the bow of the skiff to the back deck as a favorable lift from a wave aided him.

"Fuck Jack! Sorry! Shit! Could have killed someone. I will repair the bow. Fiberglass it and paint." Bart said. His eyes were still wild, adrenalin still surging.

Jack smiled a thin smile and nodded. He regarded his crew on the back deck, their raingear plastered to their bodies as the wind shoved rain against them, hoods up, faces wet, dripping, sleeves raining water. They looked good. Salty. Jack's smile broadened. He took a snapshot with his mind. This would be their last day.

"I think we have had about enough of this don't you? I am for calling it quits." Jack said. He watched the expressions on their faces. It was consensus time.

"I vote we quit. Do we quit or continue?" Jack said. His voice was raised, to be heard against the wind and rain.

The boat lifted slowly atop a swell as the crew considered. They had been fishing all day outside Latouche Island. The swell from the gulf was slow, like a gentle roller coaster, the chop on the top at a manageable three feet. It had rained now for the last eleven days. Unbelievable, copious, drenching and ever present rain. Grey mists and fog every morning, the odd sight of a flat calm ocean, which would be brilliant blue in the sunlight, hissing and bubbling as rain like the teeth of a comb churned the entire surface. Mesmerizing rain. Top house wiper, middle window, directly in front of the helm, had failed on day four. Jack found parts and pieces stashed from another incident with the wipers, cobbled together a gear, replaced it. Two days of cussing and a lot of Joy soap and paper towels to at least defog. When he flipped the switch for his wiper and it sang a little huuuuuuuaahhhhhh across his top house window, the crew had cheered and passed around cigarettes. This had become a tradition, throughout the seasons, one that Wendy and Bart taught the fucking new guys.

Another swell rose behind them as the boat rocked in the chop and rain blatted down pockmarking the rising grey waters, raised bubbles like blisters, popping wetly, an instant on the eyes, to be replaced by four more - constant, mesmerizing.

They had just made their fourteenth set of a little over two hundred pink salmon, a little over eight thousand pounds. Jack had made his nut in early August. These days were profit, and gravy, but they were getting scary. Winter was looming, it's scent heavy in the air, it's crisp air causing heavy winds to erupt out of bay's and passes.

Wendy's hair, the strands that had escaped her bun, were soaked and plastered to the outside of her hood. She was the first to raise her hand. "We quit." She said

Bart shook his head. "Not yet."

Ziggy had been complaining that he needed to get back to New York for the last few days. His hand shot up. "Quit." He said.

Mark nodded eagerly, hand raised. "We quit. Yes, warm socks, this day to me, is more precious zan zee pussy. I want pussy back and no need for sock on the sands of the Rhine."

Jack looked at Bart. The rest of the crew glared at Bart. Bart felt the pressure. Jack looked at the shattered bow of the seine skiff. The damage was superficial, but left unattended to, would saturate with salt water, swell the wood beneath the fiberglass, cause all kinds of havoc. He raised an eyebrow. Bart shrugged.

"We are still making better money in this miserable rain, than we could at any job. At forty-five friggin' cents a pound we are making..."

"Exactly an average of 600 per day after food and fuel." Ziggy said. "But I have calculated a growing percentage of poundage decrease each day. Staying at this point is stupid. Risky. No longer enjoyable."

Jack nodded. "Ziggy is talking the math of the business Bart. We are taking a beating out here for less and the less is increasing nearly incrementally. One mistake, like the bow of the jitney there, and I am set back all the days we worked."

Bart began to laugh. "Alright, alright, fuck you guys, I vote we quite." He raised his hand. Looked a bit sheepish. "Just was being a hard ass... You know. And I guess it would be nice to spend my money without a cast on."

Wendy whooped and clapped her hands a loud pop. "I could kiss you right now if you weren't such an asshole." She said. Then she kissed him anyway and turned and planted an especially lingering kiss on Ziggy. "Wouldn't want you to feel left out." She said. Ziggy's face flamed red, which was funny looking against all the grey water and mists, like a bright red tomatoes enfolded in the green lettuce of his rain hood.

"No one should be left out huh?" Mark said. He spread his arms in anticipation.

Wendy harrumphed. "You are too far away over on those leads." She said. Wendy had tossed the corks all summer, Ziggy web, and Mark on lead line and rings, he had a talent for it, in addition to a constant string of curses in French and English at the jellyfish and falling rings which he had learned to be agile enough to dodge.

"I would swim an ocean to feel your tongue on mine." Mark said.

"Fuck you Mark." Wendy said... "If I were not married I would have fucked all of you guys actually." She broke out in a peal of laughter as the others gave her stunned expressions.

"Rig for travel!" Jack bellowed. He headed up the ladder to the bridge, paused at the door to the house, and turned, to regard his cavorting and proficient crew as they began to enthusiastically rig for travel. He felt a poignant moment as he realized he would not be seeing this for another year all at the same time he grinned. It was over. He would not have to act and think, and wear the mask of Captain, which was a drain on his natural spirit, for a long time. Take off the mask, put it on the shelf, become himself again, work towards self-actualization and esoteric studies amongst others seeking truth. Follow the inspiration and dictates of being a Lucidian. Being Captain was about over. The relief palpable, a regret poignant.

Once at his Captain's chair he pointed the Emma Dawn toward the end of LaTouche, barely visible as the fading daylight and grey rains shrouded it. They would travel around it, and straight into Crab Bay where he knew the Lorem rested at anchor, awaiting deliveries. Sarah would smile at him, act casual as she finished her shift and headed in for a much-needed screw in the private confines of her state room in the belly of the Lorem, where the iron bulkheads muffled moans.

Jack steadied the boat into the face of the chop, way off course, but safer, as he watched his crew drop the skiff back a good fifty feet and raise the tow line well over the corks using the center boom winch. He then climbed the mast to the crow's nest, raingear plastering to his legs and flapping on the other side until he entered the confines of his fiber-glass and aluminum crow's-nest at the highest peak of his boat's mast. Away from all, he could see the crew easily, the lay of the waves, and the exhilarating tilt and sway of the boat. Jack realized his decision to climb up and run the Emma Dawn in from the crow's nest was bat shit crazy, but he had not been up in the crow's nest for a good week. No need when fishing was slow. It smelled musty, the fiberglass and aluminum mingling with salt and rain. He smiled as he saw his thermos and pack of smokes where he had left them on the wheel housing.

Jack slid the door shut behind him and flipped two stainless steel toggle switches to turn on the PA system and navigation lights.. He had custom built his crow's-nest to be comfortable for two, lots of built ins, and entirely enclosed from wind and rain. He equipped it with a sonar, compass, complete steering and power controls, a cassette player - the speakers below overridden by his choice of music, something fondly tolerated by the crew, at times. He had a CB to hail the crew via the P.A. System. The electronics were entirely encased, insulated against moisture. The crow's-nest was heated by a small electric heater which came on whenever the generator was on or could be manually switched on without the generator. The forward windshield had a functional wiper, which he turned on immediately upon closing the door. It moaned and sighed back and forth, clearing the rain.

Jack took control of the Emma Dawn from the crow's nest, gave the wheel a spin to check her turns, straightened her back into the chop and glance down at his crew, made a line and rigging check. The crew cavorted as they washed down the deck, secured the seine skiff for travel on swell and choppy sea. They had the skiff dropped back about fifty feet behind the boat, tethered to the boat by line which was tied off on the deck winch, hooked and lifted by the boom winch so it created a shock absorber in the middle as well as held the line high above the purse seine so it would not sweep the big net overboard. Jack smiled as they were bopped about, laughing, full of energy now when just twenty minutes ago they had all looked dogged tired. It was the right decision to quit.

Jack turned his eyes forward, smiled as the rain and wind beat against his crow's nest window. He took a quick mental tally of what had been accomplished this season, what new ideas he had come up with, innovations, mods for the boat, and felt a surge of elation. He picked up the mike to the loud speaker.

"Boys and girls, this ends the season of 1988, you have all done well and I, Captain Jack, your delightfully brilliant skipper, am very much richer than before we met. This of course means that you have all earned an excellent income for just three months and one and a half week. I will run us into Crab Bay, get your asses inside after securing the deck and get some sleep. I will put my head alarm on in case I nod out. Relax." Jack chuckled ominously over the speakers. "No problems." They knew he had no head alarm, it was one of his ideas though, fishing was great for brainstorming and sudden inspiration. He had already filed it under "great idea, no time for it."

Jack watched the rising and falling hills of waves before him for logs, deadheads that could shoot up out of the water and smash through the hull of the Emma Dawn. There had been a day, long ago, when they had been in water like this, surrounded by such logs. Each time a swell and wave lifted and dropped a new log, shaggy with kelp, barnacles and green algae would shoot up out of the waves. They were amazed at the sight as they slowly, carefully picked their way around the perimeter of them. A logger had, long ago, lost a boat load overboard and, over time they became water logged, heavier and less boyant at one end causing it to sink down ward until it still floated, vertically, just the end of the log showing like a stump in the ocean, hence the name deadheads. Jack shivered as the memory returned to him. Had his Dad not turned the boat they would have run right into the rising and falling algae laden logs. Like green sea serpents they dripped sea water as the waves moved faster around them. It was filed away in one of his strangest memories of things in Prince William Sound.

There were a few logs, easily avoided and easily spotted from his vantage point as he ran the Emma Dawn towards the end of Latouche. He spotted the Alta Pearl, Dad still plugging away and hailed him on the cb.

"Alta Pearl, Emma Dawn."

"What's going on kid?" His dad came back.

"We are hanging it up old man. Been a good season, time to quit."

"Not for us, I am going to make these guys work until the fifteenth if they just keep it open. Take it easy, maybe get a couple deer on the islands."

"Enjoy dad. You make dawdling about enjoying the Sound for a bit an excellent idea. Why run away just because the season is over. This is paradise is it not?"

"Yes." Robert McKnight came back. "Out."

Jack smiled as he put the mike back in its hanger. The old man was tough. Abrupt. Jack knew he would be more than ready to quite in just a few days.

The crew would begin to grumble. Best to do as he did. End on a high note, on a shitty weather day.

The wind was gusting, ripples lashed into foam left the tops of the curling white caps. Jack felt the lurch of the boat as it hit the waves, the bow spray arching out then whipped back by the wind. The forecast was for a rising wind in the evening but not this bad, had to be forty knots in gusts. Jack eyed the end of Latouche Island, shrouded in mists, the evening light beginning to fade already. He had about five miles to go he guessed. He cut the wheel a bit as a large comber topped a swell, braced his legs like he was flying a surf board, held on to the wheel. He cussed and reached to throttle down as the bow of the Emma Dawn spread the next wave, her hull shuddering, sheets of bow spray covering the top house as the wind took it. The crows-nest lurched atop the mast, forced Jack into the wheel as he strained to counter the motion. He hit his ribs, not hard enough to break, but enough to knock the wind out of him. Jack cussed and throttled back a bit more as the Emma Dawn began to rise again.

Five miles to go until he could shelter in the lee of wind, use Knight Island to get to calmer waters. He lurched and steadied, realized he was more trapped up top than not. Would not want to try and climb down into the top house in this weather.

He grinned and picked up the mike.

"Dad... You better head in. I am bucking into it at about five knots, trapped in my crows-nest."

There was static on the CB for a few seconds. "Har! Dumb kid. We are heading in. Stay up there fer Christ's sake."

"I can see your lights..." Jack said. "You see mine?"

Static and wind...

"Emma Dawn... Hailing Alta Pearl..."

The rigging shrieked, the Emma Dawn plowed her bow under a steep wave, sprays of plume jetting left and right from her bow. Jack felt his first twinge of gut clenching fear.

"Alta Pearl!" He said. He glanced behind him, saw his dad's boat lights, a white plume off the bow, the lights lurching upward, much as he was. Jack backed down the throttle yet again, angled his line more towards the path he imagined his dad to be running.

"Yes?" Came Robert McKnight's most patient attempt at calm. Jack smiled.

"I am angling a bit in front of you. Gonna be a fun ride." Jack said.

Static and wind. The bow smashed into a wave, the mast, atop which he was perched, creaked and strained against the stay cables. Jack watched the ocean, cut to the right, then left, focused on bringing the Emma Dawn's bow into the best angle for the next wave.

"Dance baby. You are a tiny dancer. In the waves." Jack muttered. Sweat made his clothes damp, trickled into his eyes. He felt like he was riding a bull and piloting a boat at the same time. He again reduced the speed a tiny bit, glanced back, saw the dip and rise of the Alta Pearl.

Jack still had the presence of mind, or perhaps the ingrained intuition, to check the back deck. He cussed as he saw that the purse line had spilled from the heavy rubber baskets that held them. He flipped the switch to the deck loudspeaker.

"The purse baskets have dumped. Secure them. Secure anything you think might need securing. And bring me up a cup of coffee." He said. "Kidding about coffee. Fix my deck!"

Jack steered, then hazarded a glance down to the deck. About a hundred and thirty yards of purse line lay loosely coiled and slid back and forth on the deck. If one end slipped out a scupper the entire purse line would be sucked over and possibly foul the screw and rudder. Then they would be fucked in this weather. Ziggy appeared on the deck, his rain coat whipping as he hurried to stuff all the line into the baskets.

"Make sure there isn't any already going overboard." Jack yelled through the loudspeaker.

Bart appeared and lent a hand even though this was clearly Ziggy's fuck up. Ziggy was just in his socks and long johns under his rain jacket. He and Bart cussed and worked hard to get the lines stuffed into the baskets than lashed them down so they would not slide.

"I bet you remember next time." Jack said through the P.A.

The crew had prodded at Ziggy for the first half of the season to turn him into a good deckhand, a functioning part of a well-oiled machine that fit Jack's standards. His end of the season crew was fast, efficient, and held a genuine affection for one another. Good training and a good contract - the rest was a gift Jack had with getting people to do the right things at the right times by stressing that process makes winners over and over until the crew repeated it as a catch phrase. A positive and motivated crew was as good as gold aboard a commercial fishing vessel.

Ziggy shot Jack a look that could have seared a steak, but then nodded and grinned as he clung to a line for balance against the rising and falling waves. Jack smiled back. Character, the boy had developed a bit of character, his father would be proud, and it was his father's idea that Jack mentor the sons of the wealthy to make them better people.

For the past two years Jack had experimented with running adds in exotic places such as France, Russia, Japan, New York, California, Chicago, and Denver, for deckhands. He did so at the advice of Michael Neufeld, Ziggy's father, and a McKnight family friend. Michael Neufeld, during a rather intense conversation, aboard the Alta Pearl back when Jack was sixteen and still working with his dad as skiff-man, had convinced Jack that it was not only smart, but would, in a small way, make the world a better place. Michael had, all along, been thinking of the effect commercial fishing would have on his own son and if he thought it would be a great experience for his kid, others would as well. Things worked out. Synchronicity, plans within plans, hard to read because of subtlety and the slow moving life dream.

The add Jack placed read:

"Do you have a son or daughter, eighteen to twenty-five, who you are concerned about? Do you believe they might benefit from an experience that will cause them to grow up, develop good character, learn to be part of a well-oiled commercial fishing machine, compete and win against 250 other boats and crews in the exciting and beautiful waters of Prince William Sound? I can provide that exact experience for them by putting them to work aboard my boat, with my experienced hands, who will train them to become a commercial fisherman in Alaska.

His or her pay will be eight percent of boat proceeds, standard green hand pay. The experience will cure boredom, complacency, over partying, laziness, and disrespect - or they will be fired. Some do get fired.

$20,000 up front. No refunds. Let's talk. This will be the best education you can provide for the money.

My name is Jack McKnight and I am a second generation commercial fisherman residing in Alaska, fishing out of Cordova...

Jack did not actually believe he would get any takers. What he got was interesting - new friends like Mark and Ziggy whose fathers were wise enough to see the value in what Jack offered.

Ziggy's father, Michael Neufeld, was a wealthy, high powered lawyer based in New York City, and had met Robert McKnight one evening at the Reluctant Fisherman, and asked to accompany the family aboard the Alta Pearl. The Mark's dad was the CEO of Areva, a nuclear energy research and operations company that had been nationalized by the French Government. Each of the fathers had spoken with him at length over the phone, had flown to Alaska to meet him, and shared with him their eagerness for their son's success, except for Michael Neufeld who had been the one to give Jack the idea - he simply sent Ziggy with a check in hand, an expensive set of leather suitcases, and a petulant expression on his face.

Another steep wave crashed over the bow of the Emma Dawn. Jack cursed. It would not be good to get a powerful man's son killed - a remote possibility that Jack had been advised to prepare for with a well written waver by Michael. The irony of this did not escape Jack.

He shook his head.

"We won't need to use the fucking waiver, not this day, not any day." He said through clenched teeth.

The time passed slowly. Muscles in Jack's back began to ache as he stood the wheel. Sweat dripped into his eyes. Each time the boat rose and into the next wave, Jack counter balanced and braced. It was like riding a bull in slow motion for hours.

Jack glanced back at his father to see the Alta Pearl slowly gaining on him every now and again, a sort of reassuring sight, those running lights bobbing up and down against a darkening grey daylight. His legs were spread, tight but relaxed, shock absorbers against the pitch and lurch of the Emma Dawn, body sideways to the wheel one hand on it, one hand gripping the lip of where the covered top of the crow's nest had been bolted to the regular crow's nest.

The storm from the gulf made the sky an angry black band behind them and chased the remaining day light away a bit but Jack knew that he would reach the point well before the pitch black. He had left the area they were fishing along the back side of LaTouche three hours earlier than normal. Jack calculated that he was at half his normal speed. The run time as the storm rose behind him, pushed him, nudged, at the Emma Dawn's vulnerable quarter pushed him a little more off course, would add hours to his dumb decision to run from the Crow's Nest.

Time slowed, his body ached, but he kept his eyes on the point where he knew the waves and howling wind would diminish by about half, and thought of Sarah, her smile, her charming laugh and hungry eyes. She was the prize and he just needed to get the boat in one piece around that damn point ahead. A black wall of wind lifted the green ocean and turned it to foam. The howl of roar of the wind was tuned as it went through the Emma Dawn's rigging into a high pitched lonely wail. The boat had just been overtaken by a wind squall from her stern, as it was lifted by a wave. As the wind and wave hit Jack felt the Emma Dawn speed up and so straightened her into the next wave to feel the bow plow deeply into the green water. He was pitched forward toward the wheel but managed to grab it with both hands, saw the bow take on water. For a moment Jack felt like he was falling. In that moment, he jerked back the throttle to slow the boat. The Emma Dawn shuddered. Her rigging screeched, and she righted upwards as the wave swept by. Jack felt a wash of relief as his position in the crow's nest became less of a pendulum. He shook his head and whooped. The squall had passed, he could see it's black line racing down the Montague Straights. He glanced over his shoulder as he realized there might be another squall right behind that one. When he looked forward again he wasn't sure he had not seen one.

He hailed the Alta Pearl, static. Glanced behind him, saw her lights much nearer. Scanned again for a squall. There was a black line alright but it wasn't advancing on him like a wall of wind, just hanging, a forbidding storm front.

A chill went up Jack's spine. He was sure he had just narrowly avoided a cap sizing. The weather forecast had not been bad, this was a local peculiarity that happened between Montague and the end of Latouche once and a while. Jack realized he was in one of those many prayer appropriate moments that he had found himself in from time to time while growing up as a commercial fisherman. And pray he did, made deals, promises, and solemn vows during his conversation, well, his begging, with God until he reached the point, rounded it into slightly calmer waters. Here Jack relaxed, brought the Emma Dawn back up to full speed. He thanked God and reaffirmed that he would be extra good as he toggled the mike for the P.A. speakers.

"Can someone run the boat while I climb down from this fucking crowsnest? Please?" Jack asked through the speakers below.

"Come on down. We have a fresh thermos of coffee and some grub for you that the Frenchman whipped up." Came Bart's reply over the CB. Jack keyed the mike to the CB twice and made his way carefully down the ladder.

Back in the warm and certainly more stable confines of the top house Jack found Bart standing at the wheel, a thermos of coffee and a grilled cheese and ham sandwich with two large slices of pickle on a plate next to it. Double bonus.

"Nice ride up there? Dumb ass." Bart said. Jack laughed.

"I feel like a bead in a baby rattle. Got pounded like a whore's cervix on Navy pay day." Jack said. Now Bart laughed, shook his head.

Jack poured a thick wide mug full of coffee and topped off Bart's own cup.

"That reminds me of a conversation I had with my Dad once. "Jack said. "He told me it did not matter if a woman was a whore, or a respectable lady they all deserved to be treated the same. And I, being just fourteen at the time then asked him why he wanted me to treat them all as whores. Of course, that is not what he meant, but he got a good laugh out of it. He meant I should treat them the same but left open exactly how to 'treat' women. Never has told me... I just assume he meant well... Treat them all like Mother Theresa."

Bart snorted and laughed, spit his coffee out to add to the carpet stains.

Jack took a bite out of the grilled cheese, glanced at the navigation array, radar, compass, noted that Bart had already set the Iron Mike. They were still about an hour out of Chenega Bay where the Lorem waited, where both Ladies waited.

"Jesus... I thought we were going over when that squall hit." Jack said.

Bart shrugged. "I must have slept through that."

"Fuck you Bart."

Jack rested his hand on the dash of the Emma Dawn and thought how lucky he was to have such a beautiful lady, such a faithful and dependable sweetheart. Her heart beat at eighteen hundred rpm, her bow rose and dipped steep to port as she took the quartering sea, not her best ride. Jack was thankful it had not been on the side on the way in.

They rounded next point into Crab Bay. It was dark now, raining sideways with the wind. The boat lights ahead showed that the Lorem was at anchor, one seiner to her starboard. Jack nodded and smiled.

"No wait. My reward for running the boat so well." Jack said.

Bart nodded. "Can I please have a shower before you and Sarah get in there?"

Jack laughed. "No." He said. With utter finality.

Bart nodded. "You suck."

"It's good to be Captain." Jack said. He bobbed to the left to avoid a playful punch from Bart.

"Chicken." Bart said.

"Yeah. Your last 'playful' poke at me cracked a frigging rib." Jack said.

Bart relinquished the wheel and went down to ready for securing the boat to the tender. Jack took a seat in his captain's chair and felt his body immediately relax. He inhaled deeply, exhaled. He hated putting his boat through a rough sea. Always seemed to stir things up, tweaked engine belts, hoses, stirred up sediment in the fuel tanks all kinds of odd effects of vibration, frame twisting ever so slightly. A good hull flexed a bit which then transferred through the entire boat tweaking things, testing tolerances. Jack said a silent thanks to God and made himself relax a bit more, his muscles ticked as they cooled. He brought the Emma Dawn to an idle and switched off the auto-pilot. A little ping of excitement washed through him as he thought about Sarah, about the end of the season. Since the last closure they had gotten together whenever the Lorem was servicing Jack's delivery area. Increasingly he was craving her and she professed her lust for him with eager hands and words of adoration. He was in love plain and simple. Mark was loves harshest critic. Even while he was losing his mind over Lana's whereabouts he would take time to spout off about love being an illusion, a trick of chemistry in the brain that could be reproduced using food and vitamins. When Ziggy heard that he immediately began grilling Mark as to what foods and what vitamins and the two began to devise a way to produce such and effect, bottle it, and sell it to people. Love, in a bottle.

Jack's feelings of pleasure grew in intensity as he recalled that conversation. Nineteen eighty-eight had been an excellent season, crew wise, money wise... He had made his nut by July 13th and the rest of the season had been profit. The Emma Dawn was still the banks but her worth was far more than what he owed.

He could, if he chose, pay her off entirely this year or put the money into a capital construction fund towards a new boat, one option he had meditated on quite a bit. A beautiful craft capable of multiple uses, seining being its primary function, tendering during the Copper River Flats gillnet season, longlining for halibut and black cod, crab. Fisheries he had done and wished not to do any longer after a few storms.

Jack had designed a boat capable of favoring his personal balance, his comfort zone of boat versus ocean. He knew a great boats potential, had watched other captains, owners in Cordova, talked with them, studied their business success, and believed he could carve a slice of the pie for himself as well. Having the right boat was part of that. Jack believed his skills were exceeding the capacity of the Emma Dawn, as was his father, Robert, and Uncle, Conner. The McKnight's, needed and upgrade.

Cordova was a meld of powerful families. The McKnight's were a small and only a second-generation family. There were tenth generation families, as well as the people who had always been in Cordova, thousands of years, the Eyak, along with the Chugach, the Tlingit, Aleut, and Tsimshian. Not all of these great 'Houses' as Jack liked to think of them, wished the McKnight's well.His eyes focused on the Lorem, still ten minutes off, as he idled the Emma Dawn between other seiners at anchor. The lights were very dim in the wheel house so Jack could make out the silhouettes of the other boats, their anchor lights and a few cabin lights glowing warm inside against the black of night, wind and rain.

He thought of Sarah. They had talked much of the future, well he did, she smiled and nodded, eyes merry and thoughtful as he spoke of many things. The new boat, of the new generation that was moving into the sound, how things were developing, innovations of gear and the inventiveness of fabricating things that worked better and better. The fleet in Prince William Sound was getting better, faster, far more efficient at catching salmon. The hatcheries had been built, the herring fishery developed, all by hard work and through the vision of people like William Bligh, Happy Joe, and Gyles Knowles. This year alone heralded the arrival of six new limit seiners to some of the more prominent visionaries of this new generation, sons of the aforementioned men. Limit seiners with three engines, fifteen knot cruising speeds, dual arms mounted with powerful cable winches, automated power blocks that slide up and down the boom to aid in stacking gear as well as lifting heavier bags of salmon over the rails and into the boat. And this year was an even year, next year the fishing would be twice as good, the odd years always were.

Sarah had listened and nodded, asked questions. Jack wondered if she saw herself aboard the boat he had described to her. He imagined the two of them married, raising children, teaching them the ways of Prince William Sound, of commercial fishing, and so much more. He always pictured himself in Hawaii or other sun-drenched paradise, being a college professor during the winter months and living in Cordova, fishing the waters of the Sound during the summer months. Would Sarah want to share such a life with him? He knew she loved it, the good and the not so good, everything, about being out on the water.

Jack blinked as he realized the seriousness of his thoughts regarding Sarah. It dawned on him that his feelings were very real. He was indeed, in love with miss Sarah Lohtelli. He grinned as he neared the Lorem. She was not on deck. That meant she would be in the cabin, sleeping, or reading in the galley.

His mind flickered through several different scenarios. Would he be able to take care of her? His plans were grand, a new boat, investing, taking a risk here and there on other more entrepreneurial interests...

Jack grinned and nodded with a giddy pleasure, so much potential, so many cool things to do. Always cool things to do at the end of the season, winterizing and storing the boat, settling pay with the crew, celebrating the end of good season... Which meant there would be drinking, boasting, tale telling of harrowing, bizarre, and funny events on the Sound, something that Jack loved about the end of the season. Of course, he would be able to take care of her. Just the two of them for a while, in his place in Anchorage, then, as they worked and expanded his little empire, a couple of kids and...Jack recalled Audrey, and took a reality check. She was sweet and wonderful and so so smart. He knew now that he was going to have to talk with her and ease out of the relationship, knew there would be some damn tears on both sides. Would have to say goodbye to the boys as well...

The Emma Dawn idled towards the Lorem at an angle, bow first. Jack put her in neutral, cranked the wheel hard to starboard, shifted into reverse, brought up the rpms, just enough to kick the stern over towards the Lorem, then shifted back into neutral. Forward momentum defeated, the stern now drifted closer towards the bladder dangling alongside the Lorem. Lines were tossed, and the Emma Dawn snugged tight in position for delivering their fish.

Jack stepped down from the top house to the back deck, flipped the hydraulics on, and loosened a boom winch line with a snap on the end of it. He removed the snap from its harness and handed it to Bart then fed him more line out of the winch so Bart could attach it to the fish sucker and aid in lifting and moving it as needed.

Ziggy stepped out on deck with a clip board in hand as Wendy and Bart heaved the hatches off to open the fish hold for the sucker to be lowered into.

"What is your guess on poundage?" Ziggy asked. His curly black hair was shifting in the wind as the rain pressed it closer to his skull, his dark eyes playful. This was the favorite part of the day for Ziggy. A bit of gambling. Jack considered.

They had made fourteen sets, each one yielding about three hundred salmon, at three and a half pounds each, about the same as the day previous only they had made seventeen sets that day.

"Make my guess at one thousand, nine hundred eighty pounds lighter than yesterday." Jack said.

"Damn…" Ziggy said. "That puts you like two pounds from my guess." He smiled. "We might have to split the pot."

"Put away the clip board and get to work you scheming Jew bastard." Bart said. "And tell that lazy Frenchman to get the fuck off the radio and get out here to work…"

Mark stepped on deck. "Lazy? You take a nap in the skiff all day and you call me lazy?"

Bart shrugged. "I have a skill." He said. "And one earned after doing your job for years."

"Yeah? You can't pull seniority and experience on me. That is not fair simply because you were born into a elite trade."

Jack cocked his head at that. He was surprised Mark considered what they did 'elite'. Mark came from a cake life in France, flitting about the country side, partying in towns, villages, and cities he loved, enjoying the wealth of his father. Now, at the end of the season he was beginning to show that he had an appreciation of hard work, of a hard work ethic, and a love for the scenery and wildlife.

Jack held a clip board and his plastic permit card in his hand and made his way across deck to climb up over the cap rail of the Lorem to her decks. He felt a bit guiltily that he wasn't sticking around to help the crew and engage in witty and crude banter. He thought about telling them that they had the deck, but decided they knew by now, he was off to get laid. He settled his guilt with some erotic images of Sarah, of the times he had been with her, of times he wanted to be with her. Did she want him on a long-term basis? This question, now at the end of the season, weighed heavy on his mind. One part of Jack laughed at the thought. Of course, a young lady would be charmed and in love with him. He was a stud. But another, more doubtful side crept in right alongside that thought. What if she just considered him a short-term fling? A momentary distraction in her Alaskan adventure that so many people from the lower forty-eight romanticize to the point of finding out for themselves, most with their expectations far exceeded, some simply realizing that being stripped down by raw nature, the sheer weight of a beautiful, but unforgiving environment, was not for them.

Jack relished the memories of the days they had shared together on the boat, picnicking, laughing, hiking, fucking in the woods, and how she was so eager to please and be pleased. They had shared much during the Fish and Game closures, and he had seen and talked with her just about every day when they off loaded their salmon. So much so in fact that Bart said it seemed that they had their own personal North Pacific Tender.

Jack crossed the wet slippery deck of the Lorem and entered the cabin. The crew seemed busy, none of them hailed him, just a quick nod as he passed them. Larry, the twin to Captain Gregg, gave him a small smile and a nod, where he usually had a smart assed remark or wit to share. He quickly cast about for Sarah, not in the galley, not in her bunk, he went up the steep stairs to the top house. There he found Gregg sitting in his captain's chair, a small uncasy smile on his face. The man was dressed in sweat pants, his huge body stuffed into the big leather chair.

"Hullo Jack." Gregg said.

Jack picked up an unease in the man.

"Hi Gregg. Is Sarah hiding somewhere?"

Gregg plucked a thermos up and offered Jack a mug which he accepted. Gregg poured steaming coffee into the mug.

"It's McKnight coffee." Gregg said.Which meant it was heavily laced with whisky.

Jack smiled and took a reverent sip.

"And I am only sharing it with you because I have to tell you about Sarah..." Gregg muttered.

Jack felt a pang, a cold wash, he knew, the crew avoiding eye contact, Larry with the odd smile, sympathetic now, Jack got it. She was gone. He looked out the window at the dark, a few lights from Chenega, sideways rain streaks in the bright deck lights shinning down from high above on the mast. The scenery now seemed a bit dimmer, forboding, the freshening wind wislte through the slightly open window nearest Greg, the one that vented the man's constant cigar smoke.

Jack took a long drink from the strong coffee, gazed at the warm glow of window lights from the homes of Chenega Village. The lights reminded Jack of playing in the snow outside his mother's kitchen window on a cold, dark, starlit night and feeling reassured by her presence when he could see her inside the warm light. He took another sip of coffee. Processing what he knew Gregg was about to tell him.

Sarah had to go today, she took a flight out early this morning, is heading back to Oregon." Greg said. "She left you this." He held out an envelope, sealed, a letter inside.

"Did she say why?"

Gregg gave Jack an apologetic smile. "Naw man, she said she wrote it all down for you and that I should just let you read the letter. I guess she thought I would just fuck it up."

Jack took it and nodded. "Sucks." He said. It was all he would allow himself to say. He felt that cold pang in his stomach as Gregg confirmed what he had deduced. It was not pleasant.

He sat the coffee down, pried open the envelope and pulled out a single page letter. Began to read it, silent.

To my handsome captain dreamer, of Prince William Sound,

I am so very sorry that I had to leave so suddenly... Sorry about a great many things, but none of them about my love for you, Jack.

I did not tell you much that I should have. You swept me off my feet and I will always cherish the memories of the times we had...

"Fucking new it..." Jack muttered. "Just a distraction during her great Alaska adventure."

Gregg shrugged. "She was pretty damn distracted all right. Cried like for two days..." He sighed as if impatient, took a swig of his own spiked coffee.

Jack read on.

"The things I didn't tell you is that I am engaged. That's the big one. I never wanted to be unfaithful to him, but you made me realize that he sucks. Before I met you, I believed I could tolerate him, maybe even learn to love him again, but after being with you I realized how much of a dick he is.

I don't know how much you know about arranged weddings and wills. My dad expressed a desire, for me to marry into wealth. Corbin's wealth is a tad bit greater than mine. He and I were high school sweet hearts, meaning we partied a lot. After high school - more revelations here - I became addicted very badly to cocaine, the entire lifestyle. The Lorem I bought two years ago and have been living on her and working her to stay away from it. The Lorem is my rehab. Captain Gregg works for me..."

Jack looked at Gregg. "You are employed by Sarah? She owns this boat?" Jack asked.

Gregg nodded, a puzzled look on his face. "Sure, thought you knew that... She is worth millions. I really thought that is why you were working her over."

"Work her?" Jack snorted. "No way... I am amazed by this..."

"Well, I gotta hand it to you then... You made her love you and didn't even know that she is worth like twenty-six million dollars." Gregg said. He chuckled. "That's got to pull some weight with her. I mean you liking her and not even knowing she was rich. You just liked her cause she was her. She aint used to that shit...If I were you I would chase her, catch her and make her marry me. Bam! Insta-rich!" Gregg smiled jovially. Jack felt the man's words genuine even though he knew he was just trying to cheer him up a bit. He smiled back, grateful.

Jack read the rest of the letter, reading between the lines one way, and then another, dumped, was the basic message.

At the bottom of the letter was her address and phone number. She asked that he call her once he got to town. Told him to call just after six pm as she would be able to talk then uninterrupted. Jack thought on that. It meant she would be waiting, each day, for a call just after 6pm, from him. He smiled... Then frowned. A wave of depression sweep over him, like a cold wash inside the stomach and a hot wet blanket across his face. He sighed and gave a small shake of his head. Told himself to get a grip, there were lots of other good things in his life... Namely Audrey... He had been cheating on her as well. But he had told Sarah of her. She had deceived him in many ways. That hurt. He ran his mind through a litany of erotic images of Sarah, then of her face, smiling, so sweet, her laugh rich, lusty and all the while she knew she was holding secret her fiancé and her wealth.

"There seems to be a little hope. She left her number, asked me to call her." Jack muttered. He took a larger swig of his whisky coffee.

"Today is the last tally for me my friend." Jack said. His voice was strong. Captain Jack's voice. He felt it best to put the hat back on, put the matter of Sarah on the shelf... Until he could use a phone.

"Shit. Really? That leaves just four more boats out here to take fish from then. The pace is so slow that I am going crazy." Gregg shrugged. "I get paid daily to be here, so I guess its kina cool though." He said.

Jack smiled. "I doubt you mind to much getting paid to read and putter about the boat."

Gregg snorted. "Hey now... Well not so much. But I and bro are a lot more active than you think I would say. At the end of the season we run this bitch down to Mexico, Sarah has a cool villa there by the way, and we have hogs there, ride up into California where we join brother Hells Angels and then go from there."

Jack laughed. "No shit? You and Larry are Hells Angels?"

Gregg nodded. "Yeah but it's not all violence and shit - like you think, Larry and I are accountants. We work for them kinda, help out with avoiding troubles with all kinds of paper work."

Jack laughed surprised. "I am amazed just how little I fucking know about the people I associate with."

Gregg nodded. "Yeah, you usually just business, then became Miss Sarah's business. Larry and I don't like Corbin Jennings fucking Cole very much. We been Sarah's hands for a few years and have had some ugly shit with him and her, fighting, cops getting called, that kind of shit. So um... We hope you get her."

"Glad you two are on my side... So, are you going to share McKnight Coffee with the Hells Angels?"

Gregg shook his head. "Naw, there we just call it coffee." He said.

Jack took another drink, felt the whisky burn a bit, warm his moods.

"I am not going down without a fight." Jack said. He recalled a line he had read in a book - the source of all misery is unrealistic expectations and being unable to reconcile the reality to the expectation in any given situation. Something along those lines.

He took stock of himself and his situation and managed to shrug it off, close the matter for now to a certain degree. Things were damn good in his life even if there was the occasional blind spot.

SHOTS AND STRATEGERY; WRAPPING UP THE 88' SEINE SEASON

"So, she just left it like that huh? And you feel challenged to go and see if you can rescue her from a bad marriage, marry her yourself, and be rich? Good plan." Robert McKnight said. He was not using his megaphone voice. Jack was grateful for that. His Uncle Conner on the other hand, was boisterous enough for the two of them.

"You got some interesting girl troubles. Another shot!" He barked at the bartender. He held up three fingers. The bartender, a well-rounded dirty blond with big pretty brown eyes, poured three shots and smiled. Jack held his gaze friendly to hers, was not feeling flirtatious.

"To beautiful women." Conner said. Loud. They downed the shots to that. Conner winked at Cara with the pretty brown eyes. "Another please beautiful woman." He said. He held up three calloused fingers again. Cara blushed. Poured.

"Yeah, and I have Audrey to think of. She is smart, sexy, great, a real woman..."

Conner raised his shot. "To two beautiful women!" He said. They chuckled and downed their whisky. Conner wiped a dribble of whiskey from his beard. "Forgot about her when I heard about the millions of Sarah."

Cara cocked her head. She was listening. Jack made that eye contact with her he had been avoiding. Smiled, managed to look guilty as she made an odd face that at once said, I disapprove, yet am intrigued.

They were sitting together at the Anchor Bar, drinking beer, doing shots, smoking. Jack only smoked on occasion. Bars and the end of a great fishing season was one such occasion.

The Emma Dawn was prepped and winterized for her long, cold, rest on braces at the city marina. The crew was paid as of ten in the morning. Everyone had plans to leave within days - save Mark who would wait for Lana's Captain Shithead to end his fishing season.

Ziggy had shaken Jack's hand and then broke down and gave him a huge hug, thanked him for a summer he would never forget, lessons he would always remember. He told Jack that he should come to New York, that he and his father would love to show him around. Jack took a rain check. He had immediate plans to attend college for the winter at the University of Alaska, Anchorage. He also had Sarah to contend with. If there was anything there he had to know, had to try and convince her to marry him.

"You are young yet Jack, got college to finish, something you keep putting off to pursue other shit. Hell, you are twenty-five, you should have graduated at twenty-two with a four-year degree." Robert McKnight said. "Talk of marriage, kids... Yeah it's pretty cool to make a family and you are getting old actually. I was much younger when I got together with your mom."

Conner nodded. "Times change. It's older that they marry now."

Jack sipped his beer, puffed his smoke. "It's actually kinda odd. I had no idea that I felt so strongly about her until I imagined our kids playing on the boat... Then it kinda hit me. I love this girl. Then she was gone and those thoughts blew apart in the winds, and rain..."

"Twenty-six million dollars..." Conner said. He whistled. Indicated for Cara to give them three more shots. "Marry her and you graduate from college quick. You are only going to have a good paying job during the winters, that much money removes the entire issue."

Jack shook his head. "I wish she didn't have the money. I make enough to take care of us. All it does is complicate things... But she was smart to not tell me, at least now we both know my feelings are genuine."

"Sure son, you make enough, but can you offer her a villa in Mexico in the Sea of Cortez?" Robert asked. He wasn't being helpful. "I mean; you have Audrey. She appreciates you, your efforts. And the family loves her."

Jack nodded then shook his head, eyes focused on Cara's large round ass as she bent over, then his beer, cold in his hand.

"Audrey and I are not serious, we both know she is too old for me, already has children. We are just living together, having fun. I mean I love her, she is a wonderful woman, make someone a great wife. Just not me. I gotta' see if Sarah will want me instead of the guy she says she thinks sucks... Which is odd. She thinks he sucks but leaves me to marry him... I don't get it."

"She wants you to chase her." Cara said.

Jack looked up from his beer to see Cara leaning towards him, breasts resting on her arms, cleavage showing, there is a certain sexual spark between them. Jack looked her in the eyes.

"And then there is you, bending over, very nice, distracting from my thoughts of love and being faithful and stuff... And then enlightening me. She wants to be chased..." Jack purposely gazed at Cara's breasts. "What time do you get off?" He asked.

Cara laughed merrily and moved back, her breasts falling with a nice jiggle, fat nipples now showing.

"She wants to be chased McKnight. As I do, by a man who wants to make me his forever."

"Yes, but is he here now? All I am asking is for is some fun between consenting adults. So... What time do you get off?" Jack said. He could care less what her response was. And that made all the difference.

Cara pinked up a bit but smiled a little. She walked closer to Jack and spoke with words intended for only him to hear.

"Three. And yes, I like to have 'fun.'" She added. "As I have heard you do from several of my friends."

Conner laughed and Robert groaned.

"My son is a slut. And we have made him that way by example." Robert said. Conner nodded.

Both Robert and Conner McKnight were large, powerfully built men with full beards. Loud, boisterous, yet also very perceptive and reverent at appropriate times. Jack often fondly thought of them as a bit like full sized dwarves.

"Conner, you got married when?"

"At twenty-two I met and fell in love with my Alabaster Whore." Conner said. "Dumbest smart thing I ever did. Got three cool kids and a nice, nice family estate." Conner said. He eyed Robert critically. Conner still held a bit of a grudge that Robert had sold the mile five homestead and moved his family to Anchorage.

"Like you said, times change, but I am twenty-five, have had a lot of 'fun' sex... He winked at Cara. "...and am thinking about really, really, getting serious with my 'Alabaster Whore' who is also a multi-millionaire. Life is so sweet sometimes." Jack grinned. He downed the rest of his beer and stood. "Gotta go dad, Uncle Conner." He hugged them both, felt a bit woozy.

"So soon?" They asked.

"Yeah, I have some stuff I need to do on the boat, hauling her out early with high tide tomorrow." Jack said.

Robert nodded. He knew Jack's sudden need to be alone with his thoughts.

"Don't wear that big brain out kid. You need it when you are my age." Robert said.

"Yeah dad, I think it needs constant exercise and then at your age there comes a wisdom to add to it. I don't have that yet."

"Take my wisdom now kid. Forget the girls. Come longlining, let the ocean clear your mind a bit and add to your bank account."

Jack frowned and glared at his dad, as he often did when the man was frustratingly right. He shook his head and smiled.

"You are right. But college will pay off in the long run don't you think?"

Robert shrugged. "Learning is good, earning is better if you ask me."

Jack laughed. "Fucking make it hard don't you dad? I agree. So, it's the women and the 'it's finished here now' feeling I have, I guess. Hell, that's why I am going to the boat." Jack said. Robert nodded.

Jack made his last eye contact with Cara then made his exit from the dim confines of the Anchor Bar. Before he made it outside Conner barked at him. "Don't you think of disappearing before you stop by and say good bye to your Aunt and Cousins Jack."

"Wouldn't dream of it." Jack said.

Once outside he inhaled the air deeply, salt, ocean, spruce wood smoke, from warming fires, and birch smoke from the salmon smokers, a craft that, at the end of the season, was heralded as the tasty results of hard work, as well as some world class salmon curring. That was the bouquet that hit his sense of smell. The light was grey, the sun setting, the rain a fine mist from low smoky looking clouds. It was moose season, deer season, duck season. Jack loved this time of year. Everyone pitched in and helped harvest meat and berries for the winter, cool nights, crisp air scented with wood smoke, dogs barking, kids playing, people chain sawing meat for the table and wood for the stoves. He had not participated for a few years now because of college overlapping. He missed it. There was always the December deer hunt though... He sobered a bit as he made his way down to the Emma Dawn, shedding the effects of too much whiskey in to short of a time to the fresh cool air.

The galley was warm, smelled of cinnamon and herbs. A pot of water and cinnamon sticks with various green minty smelling leaves was warm on the diesel stove. Jack stared at it for a minute. Andrea Staffan had given it to him. A very thoughtful gift. She and her husband owned the Bystic Mitch that was usually docked directly across from the Emma Dawn. It was gone now, already dry docked. Ron had to cut his season off a little early to get back to his co-ed scuba diving job in California where he owned a certification school. Andy had to get back to her mobile home park that she owned and managed during the winter months. Jack had also cut his season off a bit early because of college. He had a Bachelor's of Psychology with a Minor in Business then decided he would get a Bachelor of Business, then got frustrated with the system that made him start over again with bullshit classes that had nothing to do with business until a professor pointed out, over a beer, namely Audrey, that it was wise of the college to make people take classes they didn't need because of the money it generated and the college was, in much need, of revenue, at all times.

He sighed and opened the heavy round hatch to the boats diesel stove to peak at the red sooty flames that danced as he turned the knob to increase the flow of diesel, in effect, turn the heat up a notch. Patiently he waited and watched the flames writhing like flickering soot demons until they grew stronger, hotter. He made sure that they stopped growing to satisfy his paranoia regarding the entire stove malfunctioning and catching the boat on fire and then lowered the heavy iron lid to seal the hole up again.

The pot-pouri that Andrea had given him did not completely mask the comfortable smells of saltwater and wood, faint diesel and bilge but it's scent increased as the stove grew hot. Jack opened the windows a notch now that the heat was turned up. Fresh damp air began to stream through the cabin in an acceptable ratio to the dry heat of the stove. Jack then began to methodically make a pot of coffee and arrange his objects of power on the galley table. Pen, calculator, paper, ashtray, smokes, phone, various journals.

When the coffee was ready he poured himself a fresh black cup, sat at the galley table, lit a cigarette, and selected from the journals one entitled, 'Musings'.

Jack took a sip of coffee and listened to the ticking of the stove, the drops of water pattering the deck from the constant mist collecting on the rigging, growing heavy and falling, the creak of lines securing the Emma Dawn tightened in the breeze. It was warm, pleasant in the cabin, the little pot of cinnamon sticks Andy had given him mingled with boat smells and his cigarette smoke. Jack watched the smoke leave through the port window and felt himself relax.

 He began to muse. He had turned down halibut season in favor of college. He wanted now, a business degree. Ironic that he would turn down the potential money of a seventy-two-hour halibut opener in the gulf because he had to be present to enroll and begin classes in business in Anchorage. Seemed like bad business.

Jack doodled a quick caricature of Bart and drew a line from him...

Bart, who normally would go with Jack as crew, had quickly jumped at the opportunity to crew for Robert. In fact his father was already overseeing the conversion from purse seiner to long liner on the Alta Pearl for the three day halibut opener. Price was good at nearly four dollars a pound. Last opener his father had caught over fifteen thousand pounds even with missing a day due to rough waters kicking sediment up into his fuel lines from the tanks.

Jack flipped open the 'Musings' note book. He began to doodle as he thought, write down titles to thoughts, sub titles. He would have Bart run his boat, take it long lining rather than just hang it up. He could have him use his permit, lease it. That would be good. Jack smiled as he made notes, picked up the phone, called Bart, made him the offer, told him he would smooth things over with Robert and help find someone to take his place. Wendy would be perfect if she could be convinced to stay for another week. One more adventure before returning to her cake life in California. Cousin John would be with Conner,

Bart was nearly there with his down payment for a boat. He had been saving for three years, was driven, would make an excellent Captain. Jack was pleased with himself. Bart would treat the Emma Dawn well and would be able to experience firsthand being the decision maker in all things.

Hopefully he would load the boat with Halibut, that would make a nice paycheck for all. It was a much better business decision. It then occurred to Jack that he would be losing Bart, his one experienced, dedicated crew hand, the best one he knew. There were many others but they were loyal to their captains or were family to their captains, which implied loyalty. Given the success of hiring spoiled rich kids and charging twenty thousand each to their concerned fathers Jack new he would be doing the same next year. It would be more difficult getting them up to speed without Bart's gruff mannerism regarding safety and doing a job right as a team. Bart and Wendy were both outstanding deck boss'.

Jack did some quick calculations. He suspected that Bart would do better than him by about five thousand pounds. This meant that he would earn 25,000 dollars. They had agreed to a fifty-fifty split after crew, food and fuel. That was a far better offer than the crew share of 10 percent his father offered.

The phone on the boat kept calling to him. He stared at it, thoughts of Sarah and Audrey flooding his mind. He wanted to call Sarah. Per her letter she would be getting married October 5th. It was now September 14th. He had little time.

Jack reached toward the phone, hesitated once more, then began to dial Audrey's number. She answered on the third ring.

"Hello Beautiful." Jack said.

"Jack! I was just thinking about you and hoped you would call." Audrey said.

"I just wanted to let you know I will be home in five days, September 19th."

"What time? I can pick you up at the airport."

"I am driving, taking the ferry."

"Oh shit! That's right... Duh! I am sorry. Been a bit spacey and preoccupied today." Audrey said. She gave out a sigh. "The boys have been getting their first week back to school issues off their chests."

Jack smiled upon hearing of the boys his hands wandering to the items on the galley table, his writings, journals. He picked up a LePen ink pen with a fine tip, slender and with a good weight to it. He pulled a sketch pad to him as Audrey went on about the boys, half hearing her, half wondering why he didn't care anymore. The boys, Sam and Ashton, eleven and thirteen respectively, had come to accept him, listen to him. It would be them more so than Audrey that would be his sadness in leaving. He knew Audrey would understand, she was a wise and resilient woman. In fact, he believed he could keep in touch and have her be part of his life, forever, because she was wonderful. A quick clean, well-spoken and respectful break. Let her go, find the real thing for her. That would be the best thing.

Jack frowned at what he had doodled on his sketch pad, a hanged man dangling from a dark tree...

"Ok Audrey, I got to hit the sack, long day tomorrow, have to get the boat ready for longlining." Jack said.

"I can't wait to fuck you when you get back... Got a little surprise for you." Audrey said. Her voice sultry, in the mood to talk dirty.

"I have something hard to give you too." Jack said. He winced, yes, it was going to be hard, to let her go, she was amazing in bed, a great mom, excellent professor, liked to hike and ski, had traveled to stay with him on the boat once and wowed the crew with her charm and personality, especially Wendy who had highly advised Jack to marry the woman.

"Mmm it's been a good while." Audrey said.

Jack smiled. As promiscuous as Audrey had been before they got together he was certain that it had not been all that long at all. He hadn't... Guilt pangs.

"Yeah? When I get home, I am going to take care of your needs as best I can sweetness. I have a lot of pent up nasty thoughts and things I have imagined doing with you." Jack said. He went on, enjoying the effect his words had on her.

When he hung up the phone he had to readjust his pants a bit from the nasty things she had said to him, her voice very much was made for dirty talking. He smiled, sighed, re- circled his objects of power and focus around him: purple plastic ashtray built on top of a rubberized no skid bean bag special for the boat, yet another spiral journal, a steaming hot cup of coffee, his LePen, black Bic lighter... As he began his routine the guilt pangs of having just lied to her about his arrival time in Anchorage niggled at his mind a bit. It was a justifiable ruse, he told himself.

Jack began to write, to create, to place on paper his ideas, dreams, goals, to keep his mind off of Sarah, Audrey, the boys, and focus instead on his end of season ritual, that of prognosticating his goals and aspirations for the winter transition.

"September 14th 1988

Goals for 1988-89

Areas of focus for this year.

1. College. Attain psychology and business degree.

Take a full load of interesting classes.

2. Design and build cool computer desk, fabrication shop, helm designs...

- What the hell do I want to do? Have a Bachelor's of Psychology, next step bachelors of business? or Master's degree? then PhD. Job as a professor in Hawaii requires only Master's degree, get that, and start applying for the job. Two more years.

Conflict:Bills are paid. 78,000 in the bank and potentially 25,000 more from halibut. Looking at four more years of college, another fifty k for education... with a pigeon hole opportunity for return. IE I gotta use the degree in the fields available.

- Have need to fly down to Sarah in Oregon. Fuck college. Get girl, get money.

Jack slapped the pen down on the galley table, took a drag off his cigarette, a sip of coffee. That was it, the deal, clear his head by dealing with Sarah. If she spurned him for Corbin so be it. He would accept it. That was the only thing he could think of to do, to rid himself of the 'what ifs', he would put himself in her face and charm the fuck out of her. Then he could focus on college.

Jack glanced at the phone again. He had not called her since he got back to town and now knew that he had intuitively avoided calling her for this reason. It would be pointless. He had to see her, face to face, and have a conversation that could change both of their lives, vastly, for the better, or the worse, but it was what the heart wanted now. So be it.

He stared at his paper, his thoughts rapid, exited at the prospects. He would step up his departure time. Get into Anchorage tomorrow. Check in with the ferry terminal in the am, see how soon he could get out. This would put him in Anchorage tomorrow, the 16th, way early, he would have more time to speak with Audrey. He had told her that he would be home the 19th...

Jack relaxed his shoulders, focused on easing the gut roils caused by worrisome thoughts. and gazed out the rain spotted windows of the Emma Dawn at the harbor, lush green mountains shrouded in mists warped by the rivulets of rainwater and tiny round beads of water.

This was his last day in the harbor, on the boat. He went over in his mind all that he would do tomorrow, some he could do this evening. This evening he would go through the boat, inspect and note fixes and repairs needed as he undid the winterization he had already completed before his decision to allow someone else run his lady, his Emma Dawn... He would then begin to gather his belongings, clothing, gear, personal items, from the boat. Packing was a ritual, a departure from one thing of significance as it ends, and an arrival to another thing of significance as it begins.

Jack looked at this page of serious statements. He hadn't gotten far. Ended right at 'fuck college'. He cocked his head as it dawned on him that he loved learning, and that he was always, truly, in college. He put the pen to paper and wrote.

"Fuck college? I love college, college earth. Tuition free. Pick something up and learn how to use it well for the rest of your life."

But with no paper to prove you have learned, and just demonstrable experience, people still will not hire you. Companies want that degree! The Master's Degree is the key that will unlock many doors to being able to teach during the winter time.

College. After Sarah..."

Jack smiled, sipped his coffee. He liked the concept of college earth, just sitting in the galley there were examples all around him of skill sets he had to know to operate and keep functioning, his boat. The thought inspired him. He began to write them down.

"...1. Carpentry - sort of hazy on the 'it has to be level' thing - but proficient at.

2. Fiberglass - a job you call in well to because you feel too good to do the work. - It allows form to shape from thought and is a great creative tool. May open a fiberglass design shop one day...

3. Net mending. An enjoyable meditation in the sun, something to hurry the fuck up on in the wind and rain to close a hole to catch the fish.

4. Mechanical -When I put it back together it works, or not, an ongoing challenge, hire a pro.

5. Commercial fisherman - above average, comfortable where I am, will get better, smarter, more intuitive, like the great ones.

6. Captain - love running my boat, training the crew, leading, is intuitive, natural, and enjoyable.

7. Book keeper - Mom has taught me well in keeping books, but I keep many more kinds of books..."

Jack smiled and glanced at his various journals. They were fabricated of folded typing paper stapled together to form books, each with a title, a variation of the Lucidian symbol he had designed to represent the person able to awaken in dreams, and a symbol representing Alta Pearl Fisheries he had designed, three sea lions encircled by a ring with a ridge of Hemlock trees at the top. Doodles, nothing brand specific other than "Alta Pearl Fisheries Inc." written along the circle band.

8. Procurement agent - I need to find better and better channels of good gear cheap.

9. Fabricator - give me a torch and I will make it myself. Might do this in combination with fiberglass, design cool stuff.

10. Bachelors of Science in Psychology - interesting field, have no interest in hopeless mental cases, more like the worried wealthy. Them I might like. Need Masters. Teach co-ed scuba diving. Or something.

11. Lucid dreamer - the gift from God. No idea why I am so strong at it, why I have a vast appreciation of human potential, or why I feel so compelled to do something about it, show it to others, teach, learn, become more even though I feel like I already have it all. I have a great urge to show people the magic of lucidity. Show them the magic! Put others in touch directly with the super consciousness, synchronicity, manifesting life dreams and desires. As I feel it happening, learning it's subtle web, how it all inter-relates with living an advanced life style on a day to day basis. It is nothing short of walking with God, knowing that there is a great realm of unknown and untapped potential just waiting to help make life better, more magical, a sort of enlightenment. I don't see how this would fail to help others, should I do it full time someday.

12. Public Speaker - have had many occasions to talk to groups, filled in for Audrey as a guest teacher while she was out of town. Enjoy orating to the crew..."

Jack stood, stretched, poured himself another cup of coffee. The wind freshened through the windows, brought him back to the here and now. Things to do...

He spent the next three hours mapping out his grand plan for the year, something he did every year at the end of the fishing season. He structured his costs, his taxes, his strategies for money management. He contemplated where he had been successful, where he had failed and what he could do better. He wrote down lofty goals, dreams of grandeur, while imagining their attainment, what it would feel like to enjoy doing and creating. At the center of his aspirations lay commercial fishing and building businesses to generate additional cash flow. His education was needed for the stability of income during the down time of fishing, the winters.

He detailed out yet again the new boat, saw the financing coming together, the contractor showing him the deck, the fish hold, the hull and cabin design. It would be a versatile boat capable of taking out guests. Bear and deer hunters paid good money to be taken out on hunts, live aboard a boat in Alaska, in Prince William Sound, a place of rare beauty. There would be two extra state rooms for them, a captain's state room in the top house, 67' length, 58' keel length, a sleek thing of beauty and power. Dual turbo diesel engines would power her up to 15 knots with a 10 knot cruising speed.

When he was finished he glanced at the time, it was now 11:15 in the evening. Jack pushed away from the galley table and leapt to his tasks.

The engine crawl space was well lit by three light bulbs, the thick plywood that covered the bilge channel showed a slight ding upon its white paint. Jack liked to keep a clean engine area, painted white to alert him of new spatters. He had also installed tattle tale strips of plastic his friend Tunashima-san had presented him with after observing his maintenance habits. The strips turned red from green if water was sprayed upon them - a great tool for checking the water pump. Jack lowered himself down into the engine room from the cabin hatch. He nimbly crawled through, turned fuel and water valves back on, emptied the coolants he had added for winter, checked belts, hoses, sea strainer, fuel filters. He turned the fresh water back on for Bart to use while long-lining halibut. Once done he rechecked everything quickly, hopped up out of the engine room, lowered the heavy wood floor plate back over the hatch, and covered it with a thick layer of neoprene matting and carpet.

Jack turned the diesel stove down a couple of notches, inched the windows closed a bit, not all the way, and began to pack his things. He had other gear in storage at Uncle Conner's he needed to get. It was late but they were most likely still awake even though school had started. If they were not, he would at least have fulfilled his obligation to tell them goodbye.

He stuffed his duffel bag, dirty on the bottom, clean on the top, dirty rumpled, clean rolled into tubes, something Jack believed removed wrinkles. It certainly made clean clothes easy to identify from dirty.

Packing was a ritual, the closing and moving away from a thing well done towards a new enterprise, challenge, something to be done well.

Transitioning from the captain persona to the student, only this time it was to the romantic and possible husband persona... Kids. Jack heard laughter in his mind. He was an only child but his family was large, always together, and he loved the chaos of children, laughter, good times, they were his memories, his life. He wanted to add to the din a bit.

Jack left his personal items he had gathered for packing on the boat until he could bring down a few boxes, slung his duffle bag over his shoulder, and made his way to the Anchor bar to speak with his father.

THE NEED FOR NEW SLAVES

He found his father and uncle very much in their cups, Cara all bright to see him. His conversation with Robert went well. He spoke in son to dad speak, something he had learned also worked for business associates and very well for negotiating, though the cadence of speech changed a bit. In a clear voice, using formal language, he told his dad of his plan and asked his blessing. Robert laughed and clapped him on the shoulder when he told him he stole Bart back. He was pleased his son had decided to sublease the boat, earn some money, said it was a smart thing to do. A beer, some advice on women from Uncle Conner, who was dragging Cara into the conversation, and Jack was on his way.

Jack drove from the Anchor Bar out to his Uncle Conner's estate. He had an apartment there where he mostly stored his gear, held office if he needed to, crashed when Uncle Conner made him drink too much, smoke to much weed. Jack had a deep fondness for his uncles, aunts, cousins but it was Conner who he held the greatest history with. They had been in business together for short periods of time, most foul, most adventurous.

It was dark, his headlights on as he weaved to avoid the deep potholes of Whitshed Road. Uncle Conner's estate was a large piece of property, and entire point of land that jutted out into Orca Inlet. From the house could be seen Hawkins Island and Cordova nestled amongst the hemlocks in the foot hills of Mt Eyak one way, and the other way - the end of Hawkins Island where it misted together with Hinchenbrook. Conner had purchased the land the year before Robert had sold the Mile 5 estate which had been the main gathering place.

Jack took a right off Whiteshed Road and onto Whisky Ridge Road - Conner had not named it, though he loudly claimed he did - and made his way down the narrow dirt dyke over a stretch of wetlands that the neighbors called the McKnight mote, then to the Hemlock lined driveway of the McKnight compound. He parked by the huge garage doors, near the stairs up to the apartments above the garage. From there he could see across the parking lot into the main house. The lights were on in the kitchen, and the girl's bedroom. Cousin John's truck near the decks of the main house. It was midnight plus some.

Jack pulled a little bag of dog food from his pocket as he walked and scattered nuggets all about the deck and railing as he crept along in the dark. He smiled. The ravens would appreciate his dog food gift. He glanced into the windows to see who was awake, caught sight of the twins, Marci and Cindi, in their panties, no tops, laying on their beds, reading, each with their Walk Man headphones on, listening to music. He looked away quickly, continued walking towards the porch door, upon realizing what he was seeing.

Jack reflected on Audrey's beauty, full, vivacious, sexy - yet sagging with age, in contrast to the near perfection of youth. Youth, however was replaced by an undeniable sexiness, in Audrey's case. He shrugged, someday his body would do the same.

"Jack! You peeping-tom pervert!" Cindi shrieked. She had a smile on her face as she clutched a shirt to her chest and leaned out the bedroom window.

Jack jumped. "How the hell did you see me. I mean I was just looking to see if you two were awake, not actually trying to be a peeper... Though you ought to consider some curtains or something. Other people might think those tiny things on your chests are cute or something."

"Fuck you Jack! They are cute and you know it." Marci said. Cindi giggled.

Jack entered the foyer and removed his shoes. Aunt Felice would brain him if he did not. He liked the policy. Enforced the same on the boat and in his home.

Marci and Cindi met him as he entered the kitchen and gave him hugs, each sighing as he squeezed them to him. Little John smiled at him from his bowl of cereal. Little John was huge because he ate cereal at twelve something in the morning.

"What are you doing here this late?" Cindi asked.

"Yeah, are you leaving?" Marci asked.

"I am. Tomorrow. I wanted to say goodbye, pick up some things from the apartment."

The twins, now covered in long t-shirts, their feet adorned in bright blue fuzzy slippers, pouted.

"It's too soon Jack, we have not done the Big Dinner."

"I am very sorry I am going to miss the Big Dinner." John said.He looked genuinely sad as the twins shot him harsh looks.

"I know, it sucks, I hate to miss it, but I have to get to Oregon, somehow get Sarah back, or at least know I gave it my best shot and put her out of my mind." Jack said. He opened the refrigerator door, pulled out a Mickey's big mouth. Frowned at it. Wondered how long Uncle Conner was going to insist you might as well drink shit beer if it's alcohol content was high.

"I knew that girl was going to make you do dumb stuff." John said.

Jack laughed. "You are correct, Sir! As you well know."

John nodded. "Yeah, I am eating cereal at one in the morning. Becca was a bit of a bitch tonight." He took a huge bite of Cheerios.

"It's romantic Jack." Cindi gushed.

"Yes, you are tossing away your family, so you can get back into some bitch's panties again." Marci said. She pouted most cute, batted her eyes at Jack.

"Yes, it's romantic, and yes, it sucks that I will miss the Big Dinner... Really sucks. But I want to have kids like you two and if I get started now, you will be the cool second cousins who can teach my kids all the wonderful things you know. When they are your age you two will only be thirty." Jack smiled.

The twins smiled, yet with reluctance, petulant. "You just want some child slaves to crew on your boat." Marci said. Cindi nodded.

Jack sighed. The twins crewed aboard the Alabaster Lady, Uncle Conner's boat. John had fished with Conner until he was fourteen, then bought into gillnetting at the same time many his school friends did. Jack had held out for a purse seiner, did not like the waters and conditions of the flats much after David, John's older brother had been killed in the breakers at just nineteen.

"Yes. I want fresh slaves." Jack said. His voice low, evil. He chuckled a sinister chuckle. The twins nodded.

"We knew it." They said.

Jack finished his beer and hugged his cousin's good bye, they were sad to see him go, as was he them, the three of them were his Lucidian protégé's, had learned to lucid dream very quickly. They were correct about him. He had to see if he could get back between Sarah's thighs and, if so, see if she would start a family with him. Marriage. Happy children.

AN ADEPT ESOTERIC: A BIT ABOUT LUCIDIAN'S

1988, SEPTEMBER 15TH, THURSDAY, 1:11 AM

Jack sat once more at his galley table, arranged his objects of power around him, purple ashtray, black lighter, LePen, cold cup of lemon water, and his notebooks. He eyed them. Thoughts rapidly played as he read the title of each notebook. One he was very fond of was his address book. Inside was people's names and addresses and interesting notes on every person he knew or did business with. In the back of this book were pages left blank and here he listed people specific to their level of lucid dream ability or interest in lucid dreams as a source to make a better life, for self and others. Those he was certain were lucid dreamers were compiled in the last few pages of the book. The number was currently at ten, Audrey, Cindy, Marcy, John, Mark Remua who had also introduced Jack to the I-Ching and Tsun Tsu's Art of War, Michael Nuefeld, father of Ziggy, wealthy corporate lawyer residing in New York City, Vitali Mikhailov, son of a wealthy Russian ex-mafia guy, and Tunashima Wakaba, son of a wealthy textile merchant based out of Sapporo City. He was delighted to add Mark's name. The Frenchman had told him, his first night trying, that he had succeeded in having a lucid dream, Jack knew though, that he had not. Towards the last days of the fishing season Mark came to Jack, eyes wide, a big grin on his face, told him that he had his first real lucid dream, that the others he just thought were lucid, but this one was big, huge, incredibly vivid. Jack knew then, Mark had indeed actually had his first fully Lucid Dream aboard the Emma Dawn.

Jack had started lucid dreaming at sixteen and had indulged himself in flights of fancy, screwed every starlet or sexy dream image he could, crashed a hundred cars, flown boats through purple clouds, shot lightning out of his hand, altered the weather, engaged in any experience he could imagine, until these activities became old. Then he used lucid dreams to study the nature of his consciousness, to see how deep he could go into the dream, into the subconscious. He found that he could get to a place where he could no longer control the dream or all the characters in it. Jack would awaken from these dreams in a panic, a cold sweat - experiencing an intelligence that seemed to be entirely independent, with a will of its own, within a supposed dream, was, at first, Terryfying. This gave credence to the Yogi version of soul travel, the Christian beliefs in a hierarchy of intelligences. Jack filed these thoughts under 'possibly true.' One thing that Jack filed under 'absolutely true' was that he was in direct experience, part of a thing much larger than himself while Lucid and this larger thing might very well be God.

Another thing that he found to be absolute truth was that lucid dreams were a great place to try ideas, inventions, and often mined the dream for inspirational designs, some of which he had brought into form and been quite pleased with. This, he had decided, was the mark of a Lucidian. To bring from the dream to form a thing of value. To manifest reality from thought. To make magic. Jack had begun to think of the Lucid Dream as both being in direct contact with God, and gaining inspirational ideas was a side effect. God was generous with the amusements.

His Kundalini Yoga instructor, Nirvare, taught him of god energy, prana. That which sustains the body, and brain, oxygen, also sustains the mind, spirit, and soul. A breath was a powerful thing. Sanskrit for 'live breath' prana was God Energy. People breath all day long without realizing they are breathing God Energy. Practiced and trained breath was the foundation of Kundalini Yoga.

To cloud the mind by limiting breath was like denying God. Jack puffed his cigarette. He chuckled. Cigarettes limited breath, clogged the bodies process of oxygen, and muted the bodies vibration. Jack had started smoking for this very reason.

At the age of twenty, after two years of Kundalini Yoga, Jack was experiencing an extremely high level of phenomenon during his Lucid Dream experiences in combination with his waking life. His Psychology Professor, Audrey, had asked a young man from the class to stand against the wall and then instructed her students to attempt to view his aura. Jack was familiar with the concept of an auric field surrounding the human body from reading about the occult, Yoga, Buddhism, Aleister Crowley, Madam Blavatsky and the like. He thought the exercise laughable but wanted to please Audrey who he had become infatuated with during the semester. Even though he thought it unlikely, he gave it an honest try. Jack focused his breath into control and through his forehead like in dreams, as taught by his Kundalini instructor. He held the belief that it could be real, what others said they could see, what T Lobsang Rampa said he could see, perhaps he could too.

When the vision came, there was a corresponding slightly euphoric, physical sensation in his forehead. Jack was so startled that he exclaimed when he saw a bright oval of smeared colors, mostly yellow, streaked with greens and pinks, a bit of black and crimson. He didn't just 'think' he saw it, he frigging saw it. He had actually blurted out 'I frigging see it! Not just maybe but bright and frigging obvious! Wow." The class had laughed at this. Audrey asked Jack what he saw and he described the colors and the size. As he spoke he glanced at her and found he could see hers as well and it was a soft egg of lavender and pink lust, shot with fiery tendrils of crimson. He smiled and told her hers said she wanted to go to bed with him, to which she blushed deeply and laughed. Told him to stay after class for a discussion on appropriate behavior.

Jack often joked that seeing his first aura was then rewarded with fantastic sex which is what made him such an adept esoteric, as Audrey fondly called him while in bed. "Mmm, come here my adept esoteric..." only when she said it, it was very hot and sexy.

It had also been Audrey who told him that smoking tobacco would shut down his chakra's when he needed to shut them down and not experience some of the odd stuff as he developed stronger senses for the spiritual world; reason he had decided to take Paranormal Psychology in the first place.

Jack exhaled his smoke. Took a sip of coffee. Audrey was in his book of Lucidians, secreted away in the back of his address book.

He had retrieved his things from the apartments above Uncle Conner's garage and returned to the boat to stay one last night. He brought with him a dolly, left it on the dock where he would find it in the morning, stack it with boxes full of his stuff, and say goodbye to the Emma Dawn for another winter. Let Bart fish her, keep her warm, plug her holds with black cod and halibut.

Jack turned the diesel stove up another notch, opened the window on the lee side of the blowing rain about three more inches, removed his clothes and climbed into the starboard side bunk he claimed once in harbor to keep a bit warmer than the top house, which was fine during summer but a bitch to heat during fall and winter.

He settled in, thick sleeping bag tucked around him, switched on the overhead light and got out his book, Roger Zelazny's, Chronicles of Amber, Lords of Chaos. He let his mind enter the book world, visualize the characters until his eyes no longer could focus and images of Sarah started popping into his mind. Jack reminded himself that he would be entering a dream in just two minutes as he let the book fall in the little carpeted shelf made for holding such things in a delightfully small bunk area to dream in. Just two minutes. Do not loose awareness, remain vigilant of your mind as your body moves into sleep phase.

The ocean was bright blue, white sand and palm trees adorned the beaches, fig, date and olive trees grew in lush green clusters around tall marble buildings. The sun was warm on his skin as Jack drifted towards a harbor filled with sail boats of all sizes and function.

"This is a pleasant, Greek scene, where the hell did it come from?" Jack wondered. He saw from the harbor, as he allowed himself to drift languidly along, an enormous pillared building sitting on top of a forested green hill and recognized it as how he had pictured the Castle of Amber only jumbled with Greek imaginings. He moved without effort, without thought, letting the dream take him where it might while focusing his mind on pleasant thoughts. The tingling he felt when he floated out of the harbor and over homes peopled by beautiful women sent a sexual urge through him and he thought he might land and introduce himself.

He lit on the green grass in the sunshine, looked across the lawn at several ladies all dressed in thin white linens that the sun made see through, leaving the most enticing silhouettes. They were all beautiful and lithe. Jack approached the first female he made eye contact with.

"My name is Jack." He said. As he spoke he projected psychic will at the woman, his intentions sexual. This normally worked on dream images so Jack moved forward, confidently, hungrily, his hand reaching for the dream beauty. And he stopped short, his breath caught in his chest, heart thumped with a sudden surge.

The woman pulled away from him, her eyes enraged at first then shifted, scrutinized him as if he were a curious bug. Jack felt himself fixed in place by her power, her large, violet eyes, hair silky long, auburn, the reds caught and held the sun's radiance.

"You are undisciplined and arrogant." She said. Her eye's held Jack's. He could not tear himself away from her gaze.

"To get the prize you must change that." She said. She held her hand out, slender fingers wrapped around the neck of a translucent gossamer bag. Jack was now able to remove his eyes from hers. He now fixated his gaze on the bag. The shimmering bag. There were coins inside. Eight powerful coins, each a powerful lesson, each a stepping stone to the other. He felt the coins, knew their history, and shivered with dread and elation. He wanted them, badly, wanted the prize the woman spoke of, his eyes studying each of the coins, learning, feeling the different meanings of them, understanding their unique symbols. Jack reached out to take the bag from the woman, eyes still locked on hers, his dream body experiencing a swelling, euphoric sensation where his forehead would be. She pulled it away.

"Arrogant!" The woman's voice was now in his head, her lips did not move.

Jack awoke with a start. The same euphoric sensation in his forehead. His dream sensation had created a corresponding physical sensation. His pineal gland was strengthening, opening, being exercised.

Jack rose, opened his dream journal and jotted down the dream.

"Amber: Violet Eyes, and Arrogance."

He sketched the coins that he had seen, attempted to get the symbols on them correct. One of them he recognized as similar to the symbol of uranium, others like circuit board patterns. These coins were much more refined in make than the coins in the Denary dream.

The wind had kicked up a bit harder now, rain drumming on the deck of the boat in irregular patterns, the boat rocking gently, lines creaking as it strained against them. Gentle, natural music.

Jack relaxed to the soothing sounds and sensations of the boat, the soft bed, warm sleeping bag. He focused on the slight euphoric sensation that lingered just behind and in the middle of his eyebrows. The Third Eye, the pineal gland, the odd pressure that he felt during dreams. He imagined it was a sort of psychic awakening, a dormant ability that he was exercising, thought it might come in handy one day if for no other reason than to enhance his focus in the dream time.

Undisciplined? Arrogant? He relaxed further, mind alert, until he suspected his body was asleep, his mind tricking him into thinking that it was still awake with a layer of dream that simulated being awake. He raised his arm, and pushed against the side of the carpeted bunk wall. His hand passed through the carpet and into the hull, confirmed his suspicions. Jack took a breath and sat up, separating from his physical body, which felt like pulling two static socks apart, or at least was how he dreamed it felt.

He entered the galley of the Emma Dawn. Everything was slightly warped; the wind could be heard but he could not see out the windows. The stove was in the right place, the coffee pot still on. Jack knew he had taken the pot off the stove in waking life. He smiled.

Jack focused on the coffee pot, raised it with telekinesis up off the stove, floated it over the sink and dumped the remaining coffee out. He used his mind to hold the pot in place, turn on the water faucet, and fill the pot with water. As he performed this task he breathed steady, energy sustaining lungful's of oxygen - prana as he had been taught - to hold the image of the dream, to experience using telekinesis in a controlled and refined manner. He knew, as he did this, that his physical body was also breathing deeply, could feel the attachment to the physical body through his breathing, could feel the thrumming of energy just behind his forehead.

He woke himself and jotted down the experience, turned out the light and surrendered to the dream time again, this time, not bothering to remain vigilant. That was good discipline... Wasn't it? He thought as he drifted. He wondered vaguely if that thought was his, or the redheaded dream woman's. And why there were some lucid dreams that he could not exert his will over, or was it that he truly could in all of them but a part of him believed in higher beings and so created them to fit his belief? Or was he experiencing a form of Archetype on a Jungian level, the woman being his anima, or the trickster or something? And what was up with the coins again, the first ones were lumpy, ancient, these last ones, were like advanced mini computers with lines that glowed that reminded him of motherboards.

Jack mused over these things while listening to the wind and rain upon the windows and drifted off into new and strange dreams, with the resolve that he would simply enjoy them. He awoke a half an hour later with a start. He had tried to remain aloof. But the dreams morphed as if his own mind was challenging him with the shear bizarre nature of finding it so very hard to resist sampling drugs offered by a demon giraffe while partying in a thickly wooded rain forest, happy little wood nymphs laughing and pretending to hide behind trees, their round bums sticking out, as they buried happy, giggling faces in the emerald green moss so he could take them from behind. He heard the demon giraffe laugh as he caught himself up one of the little nymphs as she cried out in dismay and beat at his chest with her little hands.

He snorted in disgust, placed his mouth over the top of her head, bit the top of her skull off with a surgeon precision then held her by the waist and used his long purple tongue to stab at her exposed brain. Jack stared in horror as her little legs twitched then danced as the demon sucked her brains of her skull as if he were drinking a divine elixir, which it turned out he was. The next wood nymph he caught by the hair as she ran screaming, did the same to her and offered it over. Jack stared at the poor little wood nymph's brain as it pulsed pink and frothy with an energy he began to covet. He drank, and awoke in a cold sweat, chest heaving, heart pounding.

CAPTAIN BART

SEPTEMBER 15TH, THURSDAY 7:00 AM

J ack began his day at seven in the morning. Six and a half hours of sleep seemed a luxury. He rolled out of his warm sleeping bag into the damp chill of the boat. Cold Cordova autumn rain had won over the low level of heat he had left the diesel stove on. He turned the knob to crank up the drip rate of fuel and watched as the soot demons began to dance through the top hatch of the stove as he held it up with a lever handle so he could see. He was cautions with this stove, held a wary respect for it. Satisfied that the increased drip of fuel was burning well, and hot enough to boil coffee, he replaced the heavy iron disk and stowed the handle in a shelf mounted above the stove right in it's place next to the salt and pepper, garlic and his mother's own, smoked birch syrup salts. He stretched his hands, feet, legs, back, while making coffee. After taking yoga his first three years of college Jack developed the mindset that 'everything is yoga'. Morning sadhana, became, morning coffee yoga. A blend of western and eastern philosophy.

With a bowl of oat meal, a fresh lemon squeezed into a glass of water and chia seeds, and a hot cup of black coffee, Jack began to prognosticate his day. He picked up the phone and dialed Bart, let the phone ring twice, hung up. He waited a minuet, dialed Bart's phone number again. Bart answered on the first ring.

"Morning Jack." He said. His voice was horse.

"Morning. You are hung over like an overindulgent doofus."

"Ha, yeah I am also naked and crusted with Cara frosting." Bart said. He chuckled. "Thanks for warming her up for me, said she was mad at you so jumped my bones and told me to tell you how good she was."

"Yeah? How good was she?"

"A gentleman never kisses and talks." Bart said. He managed to sound truly offended.

"Whatever my friend. I have two female hearts to contend with, not wanting a third even if she swears she just casual, they still put their hearts into the deal, no matter how brazen."

"Did you call to babble your weird wisdoms at me or for some other reason?" Bart asked.

"I am leaving today..."

"I know, you said so yesterday."

"I want you to keep the boat working as much as possible. Black cod, halibut if there is a second opener, see if you can get moved up the list for tendering the flats next spring. See if you can get into herring, talk to me about your findings, I will partner financially with you, and... I hope you have enough to get in because I have good news my friend..." Jack paused. He heard Bart take a drag of his cigarette, eyed his own, rejected them. Cigarettes were not morning sadhana, unless there was some serious brainstorming going on. He continued. "I heard rumor that there is a Delta for sale, the owner..."

"Dale Jacobson!" Bart exclaimed. "Spoke with his crewman yesterday, told me to go talk to him today. Shit. I gotta get moving on that!"

"And please, you know my maintenance obsessions, take care of my Emma Dawn." Jack said.

"Man, I will treat her like you do, I get it, prevention, cool." Bart said. He then laughed lightly. "Yeah, thanks Jack, I am about twenty grand short of getting my own rig you know? Doing this over the winter might just get me over the hump."

"Don't rush. You are the best crewmember in Cordova. I want you on my boat next year. But, you know, if you do get your own boat at least remember greasy eggs and bacon." Jack said.

Bart laughed, coughed. "I will, you got that and back from me too."

Greasy eggs and bacon was code for being on the fish between Jack, Robert and Conner McKnight.

"Can't vouch for the old man or Unca Conner but you got me baby." Jack said.

"Yeah, speaking of which, your dad going to be ok with me jumping ship?"

"I spoke with him. He is fine. Wendy will take your place." Jack said.

"It's a very interesting thing... Love. Isn't it?" Bart asked.

Jack hesitated, taken back by his friend's question. The tone of Bart's voice was sincere, gave Jack the impression that he was gazing at Miss Cara as he spoke.

"Like a drug I guess." Jack said. "I want me some more Sarah."

"I would too, especially now that you know she is rich." Bart said.

"Not true actually. I am rich by most standards. If she was poor, she would have dumped this guy for me already. The money is a complication."

"Yeah, whatever you say Jack, you are a fool in love. Good luck. I will make us some money while you bop around the country chasing pussy. That's fair." Bart said.

"May you find yourself doing the same in a couple years." Jack said.

"Um... don't curse me like that. It just isn't the right thing to do to a friend."

Jack laughed and hung up the phone. Thought for a moment about what Bart meant. Shrugged as he realized that it might well be a curse. A fine and pleasant one if it all worked out in the end. If it didn't... At least he had taken action to make it a thing, like in a dream. Like a dream, slower, subtler, were life's thoughts to things. But only if combined with action and stratergcry.

SHITTIER IN WHITTIER

SEPTEMBER 15TH, THURSDAY, 6:30 PM

Jack stood on the solarium of the Bartlett as it pulled into the dock at Whittier. The town was shrouded, as usual, in heavy gray mists, rain constant, straight down, drenching. Jack was impervious to its mood-altering drabness. Inside, he was sunny. He often wondered about the people who lived in Whittier. Most of the one hundred and sixty three residents lived in a fifteen-story condominium complex that had four hundred condominiums comfortable ensconced within the facility, a post office, a general store, a threater, city business offices, laundry facilities on every floor. It had once served as a military barracks when Whittier was a strategic fuel depot during World War II. The other large building that dominated the tiny deep water port was condemned. A huge hulk overlooking the town, it was once the largest building in Alaska and had served as a military commissary, recreation, and officers' quarters. In it's youth the building sported a pool, bowling alley, cafeteria, ball room and an Officers Club.It now stood abandoned, boarded up, a foreboding husk of its once useful days. Jack wasn't sure why but believed that the 1964 earthquake had destroyed the building. He had memories of exploring that great grey ruin.

When he was younger one of his friends, Brian Henderson, had fallen into the empty pool while running headlong into the dark to avoid being shot by a paint ball. When they trained a light on him they found that he had landed between huge chunks of rebar laden concrete. The fact that sheer luck had kept his buddy from being impaled on rusty rebar spikes was very sobering but Brian had not, yet, been shot with a paintball. Jack, after determining that Brian was ok, shot him in the thigh with a nice red splat of paintball paint. Brian held that against him for quite a while.

The train pulled out of Whittier at eight p.m. sharp. Jack's Ford F-350 chained to one of the vehicle cars which was just a flat car, no rails. Jack relaxed in the driver's seat as the train slowly made it's way toward the Whittier Tunnel. It would be about a twenty-minute ride through the two and a half mile tunnel and on to Portage where the train would stop, the vehicles off load. From there the train would continue into Anchorage hauling fuel, timber, materials to keep a city running. Whittier was a very well-kept secret logistically speaking. It was a wonder of engineering that was forced into existence by World War II. Had there never been a war, the need to hew a tunnel through the mountain to get to the deep-water port would not have happened near as quickly as it did. The military punched the hole through in record time and with little red tape or legal bullshit. It was needed. It happened.

Jack's truck rocked gently on its suspension as the train began to make way toward the towering cliffs of a mountain that wrapped around the head of Passage Canal and outward into Prince William Sound. The canals waters were grey, the air thick with rain mists that dimmed the beauty of the Kitty Wake rookery and huge waterfalls on the far side. He gazed around at the scenery, amused that his truck was strapped down to a flatbed train car and about to enter a tunnel and pass through a mountain.

He flipped on the dome light in his truck when the train entered the tunnel and passed the time with a note book and a pen. He doodled designs he had dreamed about for a desk, literally. In the dream he had waved his hand over the desk and it turned on. One part of the desk itself was a computer monitor, its surface sleek, pockets and clever drawers everywhere. When he awoke from that dream, he had begun making designs to create that very desk. The desk had become a hobby, something he doodled and designed on over and over for two years now, while vowing to build it for himself one day, to bring it from the dream, into reality.

Once on the other side of the tunnel Jack noticed that it was not raining, was, in fact partly cloudy with sunny patches. He smiled and rolled his windows down to get some fresh air into the cab.

"It seems that shittier in Whittier is true today." Jack mused. He had spent some nice sunny days there though, during the seine closures when they were fishing close by Esther or Perry island. A shower at the harbormasters building and a hot meal at the Anchor was always a pleasure during the season.

Sarah was on his mind as the train slowed into Portage to let off the vehicles.

THE WISDOM OF REBECCA MCKNIGHT

SEPTEMBER 15TH, THURSDAY, 8:51 PM

Jack drove fast along the Seward Highway to keep up with the flow of traffic. The evening was growing dim fast but Turnagain Arm did not fail to inspire awe right up until the last of the sunlight failed. Headlights on, the back bumper of a Chevy Astro Van in front of him, Jack drove, music on, head bobbing, towards his first stop. Home and mom. Rebecca would be crushed if he drove through Anchorage and did not stop to say 'hello'. That and she wanted his financial information for accounting and tax purposes, something that she badgered him about constantly, albeit briefly, every time he spoke to her over the phone. Just a quick badgering, "Remember to keep your receipts, taped, to paper, paper in a three-ring binder, thank you honey."

Jack backed his truck up to the garage door, in ready position for stashing his Cordova Gear, neatly, in his designated space, next to where his father stashed his stuff. He grabbed his leather satchel with his tax papers in it as he slid out of the truck. The badgering worked. It reinforced Rebecca's belief that badgering was good.

Rebecca was in the kitchen window, peering out between giant Iris flowers that grew from twin stone boxes to either side of the outside kitchen window. She smiled and waved, her face bright, auburn hair framing it. She met him at the door with a big hug.

"Your father told me you would be in but he wasn't sure when. I made you some meatloaf and some mashed potatoes and gravy with peas about four hours ago. You can heat it up in the microwave."

He felt his stomach rumble with hunger at the thought of his mom's meatloaf, he hugged her a little tighter.

"Thank you." Jack said. He gazed at his mom, hands on her shoulders. His smile broadened as he registered the love for him he saw in his mom's face.

Jack removed the satchel slung around his shoulder. Held it up for her consideration then opened it and took out the accounting journals and receipts in three ring binders, placed them in a neat stack, on the kitchen counter.

"My accounting for taxes." He said. Rebecca nodded, her smile approving.

"Tell me about her Jack." His mom said. She smiled at the folders and nodded again. He felt pleased that he had pleased her. Always did.

Jack gave his mom another hug. "She is just like you." He said.

Rebecca beamed a smile but cocked her head. "Thank you, Jack. You know what I mean though. How did you meet and all that? Are you really dashing off to try and stop her from marrying someone else?"

Jack laughed. He told his mother the story of his summer as he waited for the micro wave to heat up his meatloaf dinner that Rebecca had thoughtfully plated and Saran Wrapped for him. He devoured the meat and tatters, peas, and butter with black and cayenne pepper as he told his mother all about how they met and answered all her other questions.

"I can't wait to meet her Jack." Rebecca said. She spoke with utter confidence in her son. Always had - other than sharing with him her business perspective which was always ultra conservative. "Safe bets pay!" Rebecca always said. She frowned much on his entrepreneurial ventures. Being an accountant, she had seen many failures.

Jack pressed on with his multitudes of side ventures anyway. He believed that each thing he did was a success, even if he lost his money, which, so far, other than fishing, which his mom called a 'safer bet', had been the case. He was still recovering from his most recent failure, that of the Alaska Float Center, but already had plans for a new venture, a Fabrication Shop that designed advanced ergonomic furniture as a side to handling orders from people needing interesting things built. Engineering and design had always been a fascination. While fishing and watching the mechanics of how things worked, the work flow aboard the boat, he came up with some good tweaks to his own gear, why not share those tweaks with others who might find them valuable.

Rebecca sat back in her chair and sighed, eyed Jack's folders.

"I will get to your tax estimate tonight, not doing much anyway."Her hair was big, sticking out everywhere in its brown red glory. She wore no bra under her t-shirt. Jack was used to seeing her nipples jutting forth when she was excited or happy. He teased her that they were like mood rings, they were soft and gone when she was down, feeling pensive, and hard and pokey when she was happy and excited, which was a bit over half the time.

Jack had admired his mother's form all his life and she was not entirely modest. All of Jack's friends were very polite to his mother but eventually they all teased him about her being so damn sexy. Rebecca knew it, always put the willing thralls to work doing this task or that while flashing them just a bit of flesh here and there. They would work tirelessly for her.

"I will call you tomorrow before I get on the plane." Jack said. "Promise. Unless... Audrey kills me when I tell her I am in love with another woman."

Rebecca raised an eyebrow. "Umm... You shouldn't worry about that. Audrey and I talk... A lot. We have gone out for girl's night a few times." Rebecca rolled her eyes.

"What? I mean, yeah I knew you two have talked, didn't know you two have been social together. That is very interesting..."

"Silly boy. I do her taxes and we both sit on the Republican Woman's Committee. She is nearer my age than she is yours and she is damn funny. I really like her. In fact, I am going to take her out after you do your thing... Maybe tomorrow, Friday night at the Midnight Rose, should be fun." Rebecca said. She laughed at the amazed expression on Jack's face.

Jack just shrugged. "Audrey is good and I kinda feel stupid for what I am about to do, all for a girl who might just say, 'Hell no!' and send me back to Alaska with my tail between my legs..." Jack said.

"Sweetheart, you are in love with a woman who can bear your children and is wealthy. Not stupid. Natural. Wanting children is natural, healthy. It is also honorable, required of you, and I was eighteen when I had you, your dad a charming rogue less so than now but nevertheless." Rebecca sighed and smiled. "He was irresistible." She shivered.

"You talk with her about all this and please, do not, Jack, burn a bridge with her... "Rebecca cupped Jack's face with her hand and looked into his eyes to emphasize her words. "You know she loves you. She will always love and think about you." She removed her hand and her face turned a tad bit concerned. "I will maybe just get her pizza and some ice cream and go visit with her tomorrow night come to think on it."

NOT WANTING TO WASTE AN OPPORTUNITY

SEPTEMBER 16TH, FRIDAY, 12:36 AM

Jack's guts hurt as he drove out to Peter's Creek, his buddy Jessy's house his destination. He was worried about Audrey not taking it well, yet kept reassuring himself that his mom was right. Audrey would be gracious about it, had probably run the scenario through her mind, knew Jack wanted children, new crew, to further the McKnight line.

Jessy had agreed to store Jack's truck out in Peters Creek. He did not want to leave it at the airport. Nor did he want to drive it to, park it, and sleep at, Audrey's to alert her he was in the house once she returned from wherever she was. After he had his conversation with her there was no longer going to be a space in the garage at her place.

He had called before he left his parents' house and there was no answer. It was a Thursday night out that turned into a Friday morning out? When he reached Jessy's house his buddy gave him a ride in his Camaro to surveil the scene. Audrey's van was not in the drive way.

Jesse also had offered a ride to the airport, dinner, and a keg party. The keg party had been planned already but was a happy coincidence. A rowdy Peter's Creek party with some very cool people, artists, heavy equipment operators, dudes who still lived with their mom's, and all the unmarried females from his famous senior year and two grades down, sometimes four grades down... Young and tender newbies to the throng. Most everyone had good jobs save a few lovable slouches who were still sponging off their parents while working at partying. Wasters who lacked motivation and loved marihuana. They still held potential and contributed to the joy of a good party as much as any of them.

This was his Chugach crowd. His father had moved him to Anchorage, enrolled him in Service High School, to further his education, and opportunities, as well as strategically place his family in a cheaper cost of living environment than Cordova. Jack had a good Cordova friend going to school at Chugiak High and had developed friendships outside the Service High crowd who were a bit to 'city' for him. The kids in Peter's Creek knew what hard work was, knew the value of a good blue tarp, were far more resourceful.

Jesse owned an auto body repair shop, always had cool hot rod projects going on. He lived in a home that was once a fourplex but now turned into a giant family one plex were he shared the place with his six sisters and five brothers. His father was Chinese, his mother Latina. Jesse Yhay, pronounced 'Way' was his full name.

Music rolled heavy across the lawn as they approached the open garage. Jess was animated and gregarious, introduced his new girl, Ronda, all high and smiley. His buddy Bush had been doing pushups, asked if Jack wanted to feel his pecs and firm chest as he pumped and sweated in front of the girls. Some who knew him rolled their eyes, two new ones riveted on Bush's form.

"Perfect timing, end of the summer party, and you show up." Jesse said. "We have a shit ton of barbecue, two kegs, a bunch of 'everything'." Jesse said. Ronda gurgled and nodded. Jack smiled and shook his head sadly at her. She frowned.

At one am Jesse drove Jack to the home he shared with Audrey near Mirror Lake. He had insisted they take the cherry 1970 Oldsmobile 442 to make the run. Jack's palms were wet and heart pumping hard as his mildly intoxicated friend shot up the on ramp from Peters Creek to the Glen Highway at well over a hundred miles per hour to pull off the highway at Mirror Lake while feathering the brakes to keep from losing control of the car.

Her van was still not in the yard. Jack let himself in with his key and snuck up to the bedroom. As he passed the boy's room he saw they were not home, staying the night with friends he assumed. A tiny wave of relief flooded through him, they would be gone in the morning.

Jack eased open the door to the bedroom, found the bed rumpled, swept off the covers and inspected the sheets. They were stained with... Stuff. Audrey was fond of satiny dark red sheets. They were indeed sexy, but also showed even the slightest smear of bodily fluids. She always toiled extra time to get the spots removed as much as possible, but stains remained. These stains were obvious, and many. Jack felt his stomach flutter and tighten as he understood that she was indeed getting laid with someone else. He had suspected, and she had been very subtle in her mistakes of events during some of their conversations during the long summer of his absence. He looked closer, could make out an actual imprint of a sliding smear as she skootched off the bed. Very recent.

Jessy gave him a ride back to the party where Jack reveled with his friends to take his mind off things. He found an unoccupied corner of a room and crashed at three in the morning.

Jack awoke at seven in the morning. He jolted upwards, ready to move, shook off the haze of sleep quickly. He had indulged more than normal in alcohol but kept it very reasonable, knew he needed clear thought for the day. Jack stepped over a cute, chubby blond who was curled around a guy he didn't recognize, and made his way to the shower.

After a quick, cold shower he felt far more refreshed. He drove his truck, mind considering that the odds were high that he was about to catch Audrey in an undeniable situation. It wasn't so much that he minded her getting laid, not after his summer events, it was the kids that had to listen or meet the guy in the morning over a bowl of cheerios. Awkward for a kid. She did have them staying the night with friends though, that was certainly thoughtful, would need to hide her doings from them as well as him.

Audrey's van was in the yard, a nice Buick Skylark parked next to it. He immediately knew the guy, had casually mentioned to him that if anyone was to nail Audrey in his absence, it should be him.

Mark was a bartender at the McKinley View Lounge, where Audrey liked to work night shifts as a server to pick up extra cash. Mark's black 78' Buick Skylark was a beautiful muscle car, a fitting car to the man himself, fit, and handsome. Jack could understand her attraction, yet was puzzled by his sense of being betrayed even though he was on a mission to separate himself from her because he had fallen in love with another woman himself.

It was with a sense of mixed consternation that Jack let himself into the house. It was early, seven thirty am, and he knew Audrey would be asleep but about to awaken soon.

Jack recalled the dream he had as he silently walked through the living room. Audrey had gotten a new couch and loveseat, lamps. Nice. The living room was nothing like he had left it, like he had recreated it in his dream. Two plates and two wine glasses on the coffee table. He entered the master bedroom and found Audrey laying on her side, naked rear end facing him, covers tossed off in her sleep. Mark was on his back snoring, Audrey's arm around his chest.

Jack kicked the bed.

"Hi Honey. I am home." He said when her eyes flickered open.

Mark sat bolt upright. The shocked look on his face was comical. Jack smiled a small smile intended to put Mark at ease. Audrey on the other hand was tragic. She immediately began crying and hid her face in her hands.

"It's ok lover." Jack said softly. "I am going to the kitchen, make some coffee, let's all talk nice down there."

Audrey looked at him, eyes brimming with tears.

"O... Ok Jack... I am so sorry Jack... "

"Me too but I am no better... I am sorry I woke you suddenly, just thought it might be funny one day. Mark certainly looked stupid." Jack gave a bit broader smile.

Audrey sighed. Her guilt and shame turned to exasperation. "Go make coffee Jack McKnight!" She said.

Jack made coffee.

Audrey and Mark came down and the three of them sat at the table. Jack shared his own secret with Audrey who nodded.

"Honestly Jack, I knew... I picked up something subtle, don't recall what, but when we talked I could feel it."

Jack nodded. He had made strong coffee, added a shot of whisky to it, McKnight coffee. This warmed him a bit, soothed out the night's overindulgences. The party had been fun, ended about two in the am, then just couples pairing off, which he abstained from. He sighed, let his nerves sooth out.

"I am very, very fond of this woman Mark. And..."

"Can it Jack. You are going to marry another woman and dumping me... Which, you realize, she is fucking her fiancé right?" Audrey said. She was amiable, but getting her digs in nonetheless... Jack winced.

"Yeah... I suppose. So?" He said.

"So, no reason for you to be all prude. I want to do that thing we talked about... You know, two guys at once." Audrey said. She immediately shrugged and blushed. "Why waste this opportunity?"

Jack stared at Audrey in disbelief but a smile ticked the corners of his frown up.

"My mother was so right about you." He said. "Said you would handle it just fine."

Audrey laughed, rich, warm, and sexy. Her laugh always made him breathe a little harder.

"I love your mom. I suppose she knows all about this thing you have for the girl already?"

Jack nodded. "We talk." He said.

Audrey stood and let her robe open, her breasts jiggled a bit as she lowered it slowly to the floor. She extended her hands to both men. Jack took a hand, Mark the other, Audrey sighed and pulled them upstairs. Jack and Mark spent the next hour competing to see who could make her moan, shiver, and tremble with pleasure the most. Jack let Mark win... Or believed he did.

FALL 1988

GETTING TO SARAH

Jack arrived in Port Townsend in a rented Ford Taurus, four door, black, power windows, door locks, tilt steering, cruise control, comfortable seat, decent stereo with a cassette player and AM-FM radio. During the drive from the airport towards Sarah's house Jack played with the radio, heard new rock songs he had not yet heard, while being out of touch fishing. He also caught up on the news.

Doom and gloom, droning about the ozone layer, greenhouse gas effects, and some hopeful stuff as well, the Soviets were downsizing, the Iran Iraq war had ended, the PLO acknowledged Israel's right to exist, it looked like George Bush would be the next president... Jack nodded. Good. Reagan had been awesome. The economy was doing well, things were looking up nationally and internationally. Except for the ozone layer. Aerosol cans were creating a hole in the ozone layer. The environment was getting more and more messed up - carbon dioxide was collecting in a layer around the world and creating a greenhouse effect which had caused the severe droughts in the farming states of the U.S.Jack snapped the news off as it began to get repetitive.The Ford Taurus was user friendly and ate up the road between him and Sarah. He smiled as a Stones song came on. "Satisfaction". He thought of the worlds issues for a bit, shrugged. Not his realm, he was a tiny life in the bigness of it all. The world he saw was beautiful. There were no changes in Prince William Sound, it was fresh, abundant, teaming with life. The pollution in California did not effect it yet the talking heads on the

TV would have him believe there was a crisis within the environment. Not his, though he did wonder, as he had stared out the windows of a jet during a flight down to California and saw the never-ending lines of headlights and taillights to the horizon how long such a sight could be sustained? He had asked himself questions. Can this sustain itself? How the hell do we sustain that kind of fuel use daily? The number of cars on the roads and the amount of roads for the cars was mind boggling. It was no wonder city people believed that humans were ruining the environment.

Sarah's letter was folded and tucked into his back pocket. He had switched clothing styles from Alaskan to just a little less Alaskan which was a new pair of Levi 501s, leather deck shoes, new black t-shirt, and a knee length Norwegian overcoat for mild weather - which was bunched up in the back seat. It was damn hot, seventy degrees with high humidity. Jack disliked the heat. Always visited places of the world during their winter to keep his trips as cool as possible which was convenient because he was busy all summer fishing.

Jack stilled his mind as he pulled onto Cedar View Heights. The mailboxes on the road were as large as outhouses. This was one of Port Townsends high rent districts, as his father would put it. Jack thought it a bit intimidating. These people already were where he wanted to go... His own wealth and fame dreams were just the wealth part. No fame.

His mind drifted to his lifestyle with Audrey and the boys in the little three-bedroom home. It was very nice. A shop outside for tinkering, large fire place. Homey. The boys had accepted his leaving well enought. Jack promised them that they would both one day be crew members on his boat. He had been a part of their lives for about a year and a half and in that time, had grown closer than he thought he would.

Jack drove Cedar View Heights at a brisk pace, hoping to catch Sarah walking. Laughable. He still had not called her to let her know he was in town. It still didn't feel right using the phone. He wanted to see her and speak to her while he looked into her eyes. That and he was curious about where she lived, how she went about her daily life, what this guy she was to marry looked like.

He found the drive to her house on top of a rise that overlooked the rest of Cedar Heights. 3410 was a large estate, not gated but surrounded by a black iron fence with square brick columns interspersed every fifty feet. The entrance was arched black iron with an elk symbol at the top of it. His father belonged to the Elks. Interesting. Jack passed the home by as he marveled at the size of it, the grounds around it. Opposite the road and home was a down slope, lightly treed, what appeared in the dark, to be a golf course could be seen through the trees, a lines greens lights aimed down over the grass to light its perimeter. Jack slowed and made a U-Turn further up the road, passed by Sarah's house again, looked into the brightly lit windows for a hint of her. He could discern nothing. A car approached, headlights bright. Jack suddenly felt like a criminal casing a home and wondered what the hell he was doing, sighed and shook his head after the car passed. He was exhausted from his flight, didn't sleep well the night before with all the partying going on at Jesse's house, all his thoughts, worries, about Audrey and the boys. Jack wondered if he was a fool for having left her in such a hurry. Didn't even get all his things out of the house. Sure, she had been cheating on him, but he believed her when she said she loved him. Love, no honor. She fucked the bartender. The surprise invite to indulge her fantasy was very awkward, yet he had enjoyed her, admired her temerity at assessing the situation and deciding to make the most of it. Opportunistic slut. Jack smiled as he stepped on the gas, now in a hurry to leave the beautiful neighborhood. He thought of Wendy, how she lived in a similar environment after being raised in Alaska. Her Cake Life, as she called it, drove her nuts. She hated it, yet looked forward to getting back to it, and her husband.

He toured down town Port Ashton and found it rather stodgy, very little night life. It was Friday night for shit's sake. He found a bar, pulled in, parked, entered, had three McKnight's, smoked. He paid with cash.There were only about twelve other people drinking, talking, mostly couples, some together a long time, some exhibiting body language that would indicate they were in the early dating stage. Four men were playing billiards, balls clacking over soft rock juke box music.

Jack caught the attention of the bartender.

"Where do you recommend a guy might go to meet some real upscale girls on a Friday night in Port Townsend?"

The bartender smiled prettily at him and batted her eyes. "Right here of course. Well... Usually anyway. There must be an event going on in town." She said. "Can I get you another?"

Jack nodded. He gazed around again. From his seat at the bar he had a view in the mirror of the door behind him, could see everyone who came and went. It was Friday night, soon to be Saturday morning. He had selected a bar in the nicest area closest to Sarah's neighborhood in hopes that they might run into each other. He had made reservations at the Palace Hotel in downtown. His key in his pocket was calling him as he finished his fourth McKnight, the whiskey was making him a bit sleepy wired. Tired wired. A common issue with Jack when he felt like he had not accomplished much. He chuckled at that thought. This day was long enough, in fact it was over, past midnight. Jack paid and tipped the bartender.

"Shank you for the wonderful dinksh." Jack said. He smiled at the bartender. She smiled back.

"You are most welcome kind sir!" She said. Her fake British accent made Jack laugh. She scooped his tip up and nodded. "And thank you for the tip and the eye candy." She said.

Jack flushed a bit. But he took a good three second look at the gal. It dawned on him that he was a horny rascal. He told himself he could rein it in, did so, and left the bar.

He drove the Ford Taurus gingerly, it's lighter than truck steering suddenly very prone to oversteering, to the Palace Hotel. Parking was a bit risky but he managed and felt relieved, his tensions eased with deeper more relaxed breaths. He locked the car and opened the trunk with the push of a button. Cool feature. Jack pulled his suitcase out of the trunk, closed it and strolled towards the Palace Hotel. The place that had been a bordello in the early nineteen hundreds and was newly renovated. Recommended to him by the rental car agent.

Once in his room Jack found it very well put together. Tall ceilings, crown moldings, modern heating rather than what once was radiator heat, though they made the new system look like an old radiator system, a desk, lamp, ashtray, coffee pot... Jack was wired tired, which meant he wanted to lay down and sleep but knew if he did he would just think about all he was doing over and over, weird scenarios that became tedious. He had learned it was much better to do something productive, fix something, draw something, design something, write something, while working out the issues. Or not. Then sleep. Dream. Seek a solution. Fast incubation.

Jack sat and granted himself a glass of water and one beer from the stocked hotel refrigerator. He picked up a pen and used the pad of paper to jot down a design he had for the desk - sort of a swirly wrap around desk that incorporated a personal computer - as he thought of Sarah.

"She is fucking her fiancé..." Audrey's words and her tone went through his mind over and over. "Intimate with him. Or perhaps, since her brief time with me, she has grown colder to him?"

That thought made him smile. It could be true... He doodled a heart into the design of the desk... His mind then flitting to a scene of Sarah on a nice bed, her legs spread, another man between them, then him making that man disappear, and himself moving over her and she smiled with approval for him to penetrate her. He focused hard on the image of being between her legs, feeling her, smelling her, hearing her breath quicken, her moans and cries as she came on his cock...

"Damn, I gotta get me some Sarah soon." Jack said. He adjusted his pants, then just took them off, lay down, and thought hard about Sarah for a good ten minutes, Audrey slipped in at the end.

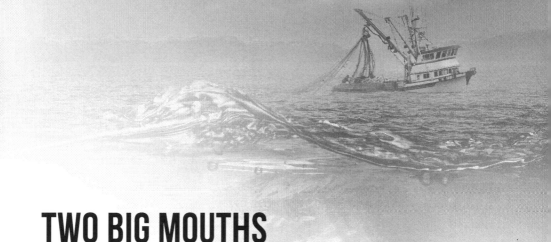

TWO BIG MOUTHS

Jack awoke at eight am. He was a bit hung over. The urge to piss stumbled him into the bathroom. He admired his rumpled hair in the mirror, his piss erection pushed his shorts out, the fat head winked at him, his belly button a butthole it was straining to get into. He turned on the Victorian style shower tub. The sound of running water made the urge to piss stronger. He stripped off his underwear and stood under the chilly water - urinated a long time into the drain.

When he moved back to the coffee pot, a surge of energy pulsed through him, excitement, joy, he was in love, horny, and in the best shape of his life. Felt good, very good. Energy coursed through him, a vibrant, eager, life force that he savored in a very conscious and grateful way.

Jack performed his morning sadhana - coffee yoga. "Wake up the body, wake up the mind." He chanted. He lifted his arms and stretched as he inhaled. He was still naked, damp from the shower. "And the coffee wakes the body and mind." He said and chuckled. He sped through the process and jumped into the shower again. The water he kept tepid then gradually warmer as he lathered. "I will buy a ring and get in front of her and propose to her myself. She can accept or deny. Then I will get my fucking life on with, back to school. Late enrollment or just skip an entire semester and get back to it in January. Late already."

He thumbed through the Port Townsend yellow pages and found a jeweler, jotted down the address, and performed his first action of the day towards winning his love, purchased her a diamond engagement ring. Something shiny for the ritual, like a mallard and his pretty feathers.

Once back at the hotel he put the diamond ring on the dark brown wood table, turned the lamp on to make it sparkle. The phone next to it. A pang of doubt gnawed at his guts. He forced it away.

"This is like a dream." He thought. "I am going to do what I am going to do and expect and believe that it is going to happen for the best possible outcome, she will marry me, and let it go... And believe, believe, expect and believe."

The phone was white, pushbutton instead of rotary. He reached out, hesitated.

"Drink two beers to calm your nerves, then do your oration." His public speaking Professor's voice rang out in his head.

10:30 AM

"You are hitting it a bit early huh?" The cashier said.

Jack nodded as he peeled a fifty from a roll of cash and paid for his 'early' beverages.

"Just to ease my nerves so I can make some important phone calls." Jack said.

As Jack exited the liquor store he inhaled deeply and smiled at his beautiful surroundings. Victorian downtown Port Townsend reminded him of a bigger Cordova. He wanted to explore it, visit the harbor, take some time to enjoy being here, in this unlikely place, that he had in no way foreseen while beginning his fishing season, nor, even, after he had met Sarah. The ocean air was fresh in his nostrils, sifted out from the other smells of car exhaust, dust, fragrant flowers which hung bright and colorful along the Victorian era street. Jack smiled, felt very good, but then turned towards the car and found his way blocked.

The man held a knife in a hand that bore scabs on the knuckles. Tall, lanky, blondish hair, unkempt beard.

"Gimme your cash!" He hissed. His blue eyes darted about nervously. Jack smiled, shrugged, reached into his pocket, pulled out the money, tossed it on the sidewalk between Lanky's feet. The man looked down. Jack kicked him in the nuts. Hard. The results were not as Jack expected. Lanky's eyes widened, furious, muscles bunched. The knife was a Buck, he recognized the curve of the silver blade as it flashed toward him. Jack had a two-part attack in mind for Lanky and had already begun to swing his plastic bag with the beer in it, hard, in an overhead arch as he also pulled his belly backwards to avoid the thrust of the knife. Two Mickie's Big Mouths crashed into Lanky's head. The man's long dirty hair flew up as the plastic bag broke open. Jack flinched his belly away from the knife jab but felt the blade poke him in the belly. The step back had been a great idea. A cold wash of panic flooded through him. He watched, in slow motion, as the two green, keg shaped beers fell to the sidewalk, burst with loud pop noises while Lanky collapsed in a heap upon the sidewalk. He stared at the man, saw his eyes rolling, his legs jerking. "You... Fuck... Kill you..." Lanky gurgled. Then he was out.

Jack put his hand to his coat, the blade had gone through it, through a little paper note pad he kept in an inside pocket, and into his belly. He did not feel a tremendous amount of pain. He heart clicked fast as he opened his coat and pulled up his shirt. Blood flowed. Jack wiped it away with the fabric of his shirt and saw the the slice was about a quarter inch wide. Not deep. Not into the guts. He told himself. He wadded up his shirt and pressed it against the wound with the palm of his hand.

"Are you ok dude? I called 911." The cashier said. Jack looked at him and was never happier to see anyone in his life.

"Thanks." He said. Sirens could be heard, a good sound. The cashier began to pick up Jack's money.

"Don't touch anything just yet. This is a crime scene." Jack said. "If that guy dies I need you as a witness and I want the cops to see exactly what happened. Jack kept his feet planted where he stood, things replaying in his mind. The knife was still in Lanky's hand; the man was not moving. The squad car came to a screeching halt just outside the row of parallel parked cars, another one on the way, siren wailing in the distance.

"Yeah, I saw everything man..." The cashier said. He was breathing heavy, excited.

"What's your name?" Jack asked.

"Jimmy. Jimmy Jones." The guy said. He shook his head, eyes wide with disbelief.

"Shit like this happen around here often?"

"No way, well not until recently. I think this guy has fucked a few people up lately. But there is new stuff, drugs, pcp and meth and all sorts of shit." Jimmy babbled.

"Step away from the man and keep your hands where I can see them." The officer barked. He had his gun out. Jack looked him in the eyes and raised his hands, made his belly begin to ooze blood again. The cop looked down at Lanky, holstered his gun.

"Leonard." He said. "Go ahead and press that wound son. I see his knife. That your money?"

"Yes." Jack said. "He wanted it."

The officer was in his forties, brown hair, stern face, but he smiled and nodded. "I can see what happened here."

"Yeah, that guys a real creep, been hanging around, probably the guy that knifed that hooker, that might even be the knife!" Jimmy said.

"I doubt that." The cop said. "He was with me the night she was killed, drinking beer, while I tried to talk him into going to rehab. Leonard here, is my half-brother from a different mother."

Jack clenched his jaws. The officer used his radio to let the approaching cop car know everything was ok. The approaching sirens went quiet. Scenes of corrupt cops and wrongful arrests began to play in Jack's mind.

The officer removed the knife from Leonard's hand, bagged it, felt for a pulse, nodded.

"He might live. You clobbered him pretty good huh?" The officer said.

Leonard groaned, tried to sit up.

"Stay down Leonard or I will knock your dumb ass out myself." The officer said.

Leonard groaned, clutched his crotch in his hands, and puked.

"I... Got nothing left." He muttered. "Fights gone. Balls hurt."

Jimmy snickered. "Yeah, took a mean kick to the sack and just kept coming. If I got kicked that hard I would have been done."

"PCP." The officer said.

Images of small town justice left Jack's mind as he rationalized that he had a witness, Jimmy, and that the officer seemed very rational.

"Your wound is pretty light. Bleeding has almost stopped already. But, if you want I can take you to the hospital on the way to taking him to the station."

Jack pulled his shirt away from the puncture. It was sticky already, just oozing. He sighed.

"I will be ok, just need a band aid."

"I could see the tip of the knife was all that went in when I bagged it. You are very lucky. But stupid. He would have taken the money and run away. Instead you could have been killed. That was dumb."

"Yeah... I would a..." Leonard whined.

"Shut up."

The officer held his hand out to Jack. "Jesse Addington." He said.

Jack introduced himself, shook the man's hand.

Officer Addington took statements from the cashier, from Jack.

"Why are you here in Port Townsend?"

An ambulance pulled up and the EMT's loaded Leonard onto a stretcher and took him away. They gave Jack some iodine and a bandage after inspecting the wound as Officer Addington questioned him.

Jack told him everything he wanted to know until the man put his note pad away and sighed.

"Not every day you have to file an arrest report on a brother. Half-brother though he is, we have been together since we were very young... But!" And here Officer Addington brightened a bit. "Him going to jail right now is the best thing I think. Straighten him up. I guess I owe you a thank you. And good luck with the woman..."

Jack smiled and nodded. "Yeah, and now I have a little extra story to spice up the romance."

Officer Addington chuckled. "Who did you say this girl was?" He asked. It was a cop question. Jack had not said who she was at all.

"Sarah Lohtelli. You know her?" Jack asked.

Officer Addington nodded. "Oh yeah." He affirmed. "I know her, her family, her fiancé." His face had an odd, amused tone to it. "Her Daddy died from a heart attack about two years ago. Left her and her mother a hell of a lot of money, millions. How do you know her?"

Jack felt a moment of hesitation to tell the whole story without knowing Officer Addington's personal affiliations. Several different versions flitted through his mind until he just decided, once and for all, that Officer Jesse Addington was a good man. He then told him how they had met, fallen in love, and showed him the letter that Sarah had written.

"I believe she wants me to fight for her or she wouldn't have given me her address." Jack said.

"Fight?" Jesse cocked his head.

"Figuratively." Jack said. "I am a lover, not a fighter."

"Yeah, you loved my brother into the hospital." Officer Addington waved his hand in the direction of the ambulance.

Jack shrugged.

"You are here on a romantic adventure. I get it. But like I said, she is worth millions, you could be an alcoholic weirdo who she doesn't want anywhere around for all I know." Officer Addington indicated the broken beer bottles. He looked at Jimmy. "You better clean this mess up." He said. Jimmy nodded and bustled off.

"However, I feel you are an ok person. Stupid. But ok. How well do you really know this girl?"

The question surprised Jack. His mind flashed back to all the conversations he had with her. They had talked of many things, love, hypnosis, lucid dreaming, fishing, creativity. In fact, the bulk of their conversations had been her eagerly asking him questions; mining his brain for what he knew. He had enjoyed that very much, found it flattering, but there were times when he had attempted to engage Sarah about Sarah and found a wall there. She would shift the conversation back to him, or move towards dreamy romantic sensuality.

"Not that well I suppose. She was a bit elusive when I asked about her life but just seemed fascinated with my life. She hid the fact that she had money from me." Jack shrugged. "I might do the same thing if I wanted to know someone liked me for me, and not my money."

Officer Addington nodded. "Or perhaps she avoided it because she did not want you chasing her around the country trying to get her to marry you?"

"Her letter sort of dispels that. I mean. I made it through the damn trial period of liking her just for her. You know?" Jack said. He was feeling grateful for Jesse's line of questioning now.

"I bought her a ring. I will propose to her. If she says yes, then I will be very happy. If she says no, I will only be less happy and will leave her to her chosen life willingly. Go back to mine. Which is pretty fucking cool if I do say so myself. But, if she says yes, I am going to make her a happy woman."

Officer Addington nodded. Extended his hand again. Jack shook it.

"Shit kid, she is marrying Corbin Cole, one would think she is happy already. His family now owns the largest construction company not just in Port Townsend, but most other counties in this area as well. But who knows? Maybe she will say yes." There was a twinkle in his eyes as he spoke. Jack read it as approval.

"So, if she says no, you go away, let her be, that's good. But, be aware, if she says yes, Mr. Cole may raise a little hell, and he has lots of friends here."

Jack squinted his eyes at that as he shook the man's hand. "I can defend myself." Jack said.

"Exactly what I am worried about." Officer Addington said. His eyes were sincere, thoughtful. "When I was your age I would have popped Leonard in the head too." He said. "So, use your head, be wiser at your age than both of us would be?"

Jack smiled. Nodded.

He watched the patrol car glide down the road, felt the roll of bills that he had risked his life for in his pocket. Jesse was right. He had been foolhardy and took entirely too much risk for twelve-hundred dollars.

"Here you go." Jimmy said.

Jack jumped, turned to see Jimmy holding a fresh bag, a six pack of Mickie's Big Mouths in it.

"On us." He said. "That guy was hanging around all week, creepy looking."

Jack accepted the beer.

"Thanks Jimmy. Gimme beer and you have a friend for life." Jack said.

Jimmy laughed. "Good luck with Sarah. I heard you. Um... Her guy, Corbin? People either work for him, hate him, or don't know him. I personally hate him. Worked for him at one time. He... Is a cocksucker."

Jack nodded. "I am beginning to read between the lines on that one."

"Between the lines? Nothing like that with me. I don't like him. And, he is dangerous, so watch your shit."

Jack nodded again. "Got that too." He said.

AN INNOCENT RUSE

As Jack entered his room back at the Palace the reason he had gone and gotten the beer came back to him. The phone loomed huge on the desk. He ripped the cap off a Big Mouth and gulped down half of it - realized he was being compulsive, and lit a cigarette. He sat and felt the letter in his pocket, pulled it out, along with Officer Addington's card. He looked at the letter, then at the card... He laughed as an idea popped into his head. It was brilliant. He dialed the number on the card, asked to be put in touch with Officer Addington and left his number with dispatch. He was still booking his half-brother.

Jack began to thumb through the yellow pages again. He scanned the various businesses in Port Townsend, made notes of phone numbers and addresses of interesting marine shops, restaurants, bars, harbor stores. He plotted out the most likely places he would meet cool people. Lucidian's to add to his list. This became a list of two book shops and then the phone rang.

Jack snapped the phone up before the second ring.

"Jack McKnight."

"This is Officer Addington, what can I do for you?" The man's voice sounded quizzical, curious.

"I need a tiny favor and it is in the interest of protecting the peace." Jack said. He had finished his first beer, half way through the second.

There was an ominous silence of the other end.

"Could you let me ride in your cruiser, take me over to Sarah's house and get her to come to your car. Like say you need to talk with her, ask her a few questions, have her volunteer to stand in a line up, something? I will then propose to her in the back of your car. If she says no you can be assured that I will let it go at that. If she says yes you can just let us out somewhere, back at my hotel or something...."

Laughter. Jack stopped and listened to the man laugh, then finish with a sigh.

"No way. But as far as testimony against my half-brother, I want him put away for at least a couple of years. Aggravated assault with a deadly weapon. You can sign a statement, if it goes to court you will be called as principle witness. Gonna need a picture of your belly scratch."

Jack spun a few rebuttals. "I gotta get back to college. In Alaska. Does the state pay for airfare?"

Officer Addington chuckled. "Are you trying to bribe me?" He asked.

"Um, no just pointing out how difficult it will be to return to Washington." Jack said.

"Please, I just need to see her, ask her face to face to marry me. I just can't do it over the phone, you should see the ring I got her, it's pretty, she will love it."

There came a sigh.

"You know, I want my brother to do time, best thing for his wretched soul right now. I remember when we were kids, he was funny, quick, great sense of humor. How about I work something out for you on this and you testify if need be to guarantee he gets sentenced?"

Jack was a bit surprised.

"You want him to go to jail?"

"Yes. He deserves to. It will also be good for him to get clean. And, I have a solution to your problem all worked out but it needs to happen tonight, around five when I get off. I will get you at the Palace."

When Jack hung up the phone he was elated. He picked up his list of places to visit, things to do, and set off to enjoy a bit of Port Townsend, the library being his first stop. Find out a little about the Cole family. Is good to know your enemies. He then went to the municipal building to check the status of construction contracts, location of projects, who won what bids. There he discovered that Port Townsend Construction Services, owned by the Cole family, held most of the large contracts, also learned from a chatty young lady that Wendal's Construction Co., owned by Sarah's daddy, had been purchased by the Cole Family for a 'shit ton' of money.

THE FISHERMAN HAS BALLS

Jack met Officer Addington in the mezzanine of the Palace Hotel after the lobby attendant called to let him know a Police Officer wanted to talk with him. As Jack approached he could see that the lobby guy was looking a bit nervous and that Jesse was playing it up. He smiled, a merry light in his eyes as he nodded at Officer Addington.

"Am I a suspect again?" Jack asked.

Jesse nodded. "Yes. Come with me and get in the back of the car or I will cuff you, and drag your ass."

"I suppose I will just go willingly this time." Jack said. He began to walk towards the exit.

"Not that way." Officer Addington barked. "Follow me."

Jack turned and followed Addington past the lobby clerks desk, raised his eyebrows and shrugged as he passed the nervous looking man.

"Don't you worry; I will be back to stay the next four days here. He don't have nothin' that will stick." Jack said.

The clerk nodded once, stopped, frowned.

Jack took the back seat at Jesse's directions. The squad car's blue vinyl seats smelled of lemon Lysol, the interior warm.

"Kinda comfy back here." Jack said.

Officer Addington chuckled. "You have no idea what has been on that seat. We try and keep it sterile back there but you are sitting on a mile of shit, puke, blood, and an ocean of tears."

"Wow." Jack said. He stared at the seat with a different perspective, more reverent. "People actually shit themselves back here?" He took another quick whiff of air, now imagined an undertone to the Lysol of human filth.

"Yup, and don't you and that girl get carried away if she says yes. I don't want to spray n wipe again tonight."

"You clean your own car?"

"Yeah, we have a motor pool and all but they do a quick shitty job. We redo what they say they have done."

Jack nodded. He held an entirely different view of the police in later years, after having acquired things he had received through hard work there was a time or two where the Cordova Police Department had helped him keep those things, and retrieve some after having apprehended the thief that stole them. When he was younger he had made a great attempt to be invisible to them and had been collared, after several years of illegal shenanigans, by Officer Dunston, who, instead of flat out arresting and booking him, talked to him, scared him, told him to live up to his true potential, and let him go on the promise that he would clean up his act.

"So you mentioned you met Sarah while fishing in Alaska? You are a commercial fisherman?" Officer Addington asked.

"Yes sir, since I was ten years old, bought into purse seining when I was eighteen."

"That's hard work, no wonder you knocked my halfwit brother out."

"Ah, that was shit luck and a couple of Mickie's Big mouths." Jack said. "In fact, I about shit myself when that whole thing was over, started shaking all over, breathing hard, then, literally, had to dive for the head. Had the squirts bad. Like my fear and adrenalin turned whatever was in my stomach to hot, acidy, burning, liquid."

Officer Addington laughed. "Some people puke, some people shit. After shock, we call it. When the body cools down from adrenalin. Personally, I prefer puking. Not always around a toilet."

They fell silent as Jesse turned onto Cedar View Heights.

"My favorite neighborhood in Port Townsend." Officer Addington said. His voice was sincere, reverent.

"You would like to live here?" Jack asked.

Jessed nodded. "I would love to raise my kids here. Let my wife enjoy a wonderful life of wealth. I mean, we aren't doing too bad but just not as well as these folks. There are so many interesting stories of smart living and thinking that got them here. I am good friends several people who live here, high school friends and new friends."

Jack nodded. "It is beautiful, manicured... Well kept. Alaska is nothing like this, but is to me, more beautiful. A mobile home, by a lake, surrounded by pristine mountains that glow green in the light of the aurora borealis is far more valuable to me that all of this..."

Officer Addington laughed. "Why is it that every Alaskan I meet just gushes about the beauty of the place. Must really be something to see."

"It is." Jack said. "But we have this kind of stuff too, manicured places. In Anchorage. Wealthy people in Alaska are just different, non-ostentatious for the most part. Most anyway. Millionaires in Alaska wear Levi's and flannel shirts."

"I know. My brother, the guy you knocked out, has fished out of Dutch Harbor, King Crab, for the past few years. Which is why I am impressed that he didn't run you through with that knife."

Jack nodded. The thought sobering. He had come close, very close, to being gutted this morning. Most mortals would have collapsed immediately from that kick to the balls, all it did to Leonard was give him pause, made his knife thrust slow.

"So... How are we going to do this with Sarah?"

"I am going to ask her about an incident and tell her that I need to talk to her in private. Politely, I am not going to push it if she says no."

"Sarah is pretty smart about things. What if she says no?"

"I will tie it in with an actual incident. Her and her pretty boy were involved in a bar fight that resulted in considerable damages and cost to the establishment."

"I take it that you don't like Corbin very much. What can you tell me about him?"

Officer Addington swung the car up the driveway towards Sarah's house. Jack could see that there was a silver BMW in the drive, an 8 series. The thought occurred to him that Sarah may have many things like this.

"Is that her car?" Jack asked.

"No. It is Corbin's."

"Great."

"And no, I don't care for him much. He is a rotten fucker. Is on his second DUI now, in court, using a lawyer to impugn the law. You know, he is not the wealthy one, his daddy is, Corbin knows full well that once he marries Sarah she will open her trust fund. Twenty-six million dollars is a lot of money. Makes people do things. I don't want things done. Got it?"

Jack nodded. "The thought has occurred to me."

Officer eyed him in the mirror, suspicious like.

"Another thing Jack, she has been in love with Corbin since they were kids. High school sweethearts."

Jack's hand squeezed around the little felt box that he carried in his pocket. He hoped that she would not laugh at it, that it would represent the truth of his feelings. The more he learned about Sarah, the more he began to feel doubt. He had rehearsed in his mind what he would say to her, and to her mother. Had even written it down, then rehearsed it again. Discovering that Sarah was, or had been, in love with Corbin wasn't helping much.

The U-shaped driveway with the silver BMW in it was raised slightly near the stately looking stairs to the pillared porch and huge front doors. The drive was lit in layers of warm yellow lights against the evening twilight. As the squad car came to a stop Jack forced away all doubts, told himself this was like when he was dreaming, that he was acting to alter the dream and must focus all his energy on the positive outcome that he desired to manifest. This sudden pang of awareness, much like awakening to the dream, made him smile. His spirits elevated. He turned that emotion up a notch with a deep, reassuring breath, and focused on Sarah saying 'yes' and throwing her arms around him.

Jack hid himself in the shadows of the back seat as Officer Addington knocked on the front door. He could see from his position and watched as the door opened. He caught his first glimpse of Corbin Jennings Cole then. Tall, sandy blond hair, wearing a pair of black pants and a loose fitting tropical print button up shirt. Jack could make out a bit of shaking of the head, the body language hard to read from the distance to the door, but it appeared Corbin was not pleased. He opened the door wider and stepped to the side. Sarah emerged. Jack's breath quickened.

Officer Addington made a motion to Corbin and he remained in the doorway, stared suspiciously, as Sarah walked towards the car. She looked different, great. Jack had never seen her with makeup on or in feminine clothing. Her long blond hair was now curled in soft waves down her shoulders and she wore a thin yellow dress that clung to her body perfectly as she walked towards the cruiser. He loved the way her body jiggled so slightly, so sexy beneath the fabric of her dress. Jack's pulse ramped up as she drew near, a perplexed look on her face as Officer Addington opened the back door for her, used his body to hide Jack as much as possible from Corbin's observation.

Corbin yelled something that Jack could not hear but he did catch the end of Sarah's statement back to him. "… Is no big deal!" She got into the back seat of the police cruiser. Jack looked directly into Sarah's surprised eyes as the door shut.

"It's me, Jack." He said quickly. "Please don't get out of the car, I really need to talk with you."

Sarah's mouth opened, her eyes wide with surprise. A brief flicker of anger and outrage crossed her face but was replaced with a delighted smile. She gave a short laugh.

"Well what do you know. The fisherman has balls." She

"I thought you figured that out already." Jack said. He smiled into her eyes.

Officer Addington eased the car down the driveway, blinker on to turn left onto Cedar Heights.

"Keep your head down and don't appear to be talking to anyone damn it."

Jack had sat up straight to greet Sarah, but he did so under the cover of shadow, hoped it would be enough. He now slouched down out of sight again. Sarah, eyes locked with his, slid down as well.

"Not both of you. Jesus Christ. Try not to look suspicious." Jesse barked.

Sarah broke her gaze and sat up straight. She giggled and ran her hands over her face, swept her hair back.

"Oh, I figured it out." She said. "Just didn't think you would not call me and then show up, a week later, in the back of a cop car."

Officer Addington gunned the engine and powered down Cedar Heights a bit over the speed limit. Jack lifted upwards and took Sarah's hand. She let him pull her to him for a hug and exhaled a big sigh, her body molded to his, soft, hand warm on the inside of his thigh. She parted from him and looked down, hair falling forward to hide her face.

"I am sorry Jack... Sorry I didn't tell you. We were not supposed to fall in love..."

Jack turned to face Sarah, knee touching hers. Sarah continued to look down, he could see her chin trembling through her golden curls.

"Please look at me." Jack said. His voice was soft, yet serious. He waited until Sarah lifted her head, her blue eyes brimmed with tears.

"It is my hope that I will be able to make your life wonderful though I know that things are a bit complicated right now. I know that what started out as just a fun sex thing turned into something more than either of us expected."

Sarah gave a small laugh. "Yeah, you started talking and I listened." Sarah said. "You were supposed to be a fun fling, a romantic interlude, not someone who falls in love with me, not the me who is rich, but the simple deckhand me. I own the Lorem by the way, just hired Greg to run it for me because I don't know the first thing about running a boat."

Jack nodded. "Yes, I fell in love with you, Sarah, not your money. The money and the fiancé just complicate things because I think that if you didn't have either of them, you would not hesitate to say yes when I ask you to marry me."

Sarah gave a sad smile. "Yes, I would not hesitate." She said.

Jack pulled the velvety little box out of his pocket and opened it, held it out to her.

"Will you, Sarah, marry me?" Jack asked.

Sarah stared at him, sucked in a big breath, her blue eyes big, moist with fresh tears, shifting back and forth, from his eyes to the ring, back up to meet his gaze, lips curling upward, happy, eyes lighting up.

"I... I am... I mean, I will but... I already have one of those." She said and held up her hand.

"Take off his, and put on mine. It is that simple." Jack said. His voice was soft, his smile sincere. He had heard her say she would, she will! It was happening, the dream was manifesting.

Sarah smiled and shook her head, giving in. She reached for the ring and pulled it out of the box. It was far smaller, less expensive, than the one Corbin had bought for her but she yanked that one from her finger as if it was suddenly toxic and slipped Jack's on. Her face broke into a bright smile and she began to breath a bit heavy. She threw her arms around Jack and her lips press hot against his as she giggled. "This feels so good!" She kissed him again, a wet, tongue slithering, lingering kiss.

"Oh fuck... I can't believe this Jack. But it feels so good, so much a relief!" She reclined in the seat beside him, hand on his leg which he slipped over the top of hers. "When I got back to Port Townsend and got together with Corbin I was sick to my stomach but told myself this was my life, that you were not real and when you didn't call I thought that you thought I was just a plaything, and probably just went back to your girlfriend."

She pulled his hand, secretly, to her crotch. It was warm, soft. Jack took the hint and stroked her a bit with his fingers.

"Fuck Jack, I masturbated four times in one day thinking about you!" She whispered. Her voice carried undertones of urgent need and humor, a hungry, sincere voice. Her hand gripped Jack's inner thigh tightly in quick playful little jerks.

"Ah! Ow! I get the point." Jack said. He pulled her hand away as she laughed. She slid it back up his thigh again as soon as he released it, this time much higher, much gentler. Jack pulled her head towards him and they kissed again, his fingers now mindfully above her dress, touching her side.

"After being with you Corbin's mannerisms became tedious, boring, the lies about where he had been when I knew he had been off fucking around, that is how he is but in front of my Mother, a complete angel, a fake. I could see it all because of you, because I could still hear your voice talking real shit to me, not bullshit, your plans, your thoughts, your weird excitement about ideas, about my ideas." Sarah said. She took a breath and shook her head. "By the way, before you think I am an innocent little thing I need to tell you all my dirt. Ok?" Sarah said. Her eyes were serious, Jack nodded.

"I have been to rehab twice. That is why Corbin and I got along so well. We both like drugs, Cocaine to be exact. That's what this summer was all about, sort of my third rehab. I bought the Lorem, worked on her, saw beautiful things and fell in love with an amazing fisherman. Long hard work was far better than actual rehab. I cleared my mind, my heart. The problem is, it worked. I now seriously hate Corbin, can't stand the sight of him and have been pushing him to quit drugs."

As Sarah spoke Jack's memories of his own drug use came pounding back. Times with his Uncle Conner... Narrow escapes of the law. He wanted no more to do with it, although, it had made him a far better money manager.

Sarah sighed. She leaned over and traced the outer edges of Jack's ear with her tongue.

"Is there somewhere we can go? I want you to make love to me, nice and slow." She whispered. Her voice a warm breeze filled with sexy little words that were as much sighs as they were coherent language. Her hand was gently stroking his cock, which was already full, now growing fuller. Jack clasped her hand, held it gently away from his crotch.

"Any more stroking and I won't be able to get out of the car without embarrassing myself." Jack whispered.

Sarah pouted. Jack gave her a quick kiss.

"We are about five minutes away from the hotel. From what I can hear, she has agreed to marry you. Congratulations." Officer Addington said.

The reality came to sharp focus, like a slap to the top of the head, in Jack's mind. This was the prettiest fish he had ever caught as well as most poundage in one day. Nothing would be the same. Everything better... Maybe. Money complicated things at the same time it enhanced them.

"Wow, yes. Thank you." He looked at Sarah. She was beautiful, her smile to him thoughtful, she held up her hand and wiggled her ring. "You are mine now Jack McKnight." She said. Her laughter at his suddenly wide eyes made him smile and shrug. "Wow. That is true. This is huge." Whap!

Jack felt a surge of elation, disbelief, nagging doubts, hope and joy smack him again. Slapped by Fate, smacked by Destiny, a tangible dread shook his guts. His adrenal system pinged upwards, hands became wet, clammy. Jack shrugged the confusing jumble of feelings off. This was his moment. He had opened the door in the dream to find exactly what he wanted to on the other side rather than the fearful manifestation. Yet the thunk was there... Heavy and heady, made Jack's mind swim a bit, made waves of nerves, ice cold prickles, sweep up his spine and to the top of his scalp. These moments were to be savored in life. Jack breathed easy and let joy rein over the rest of the emotions. Warmth spread, his heart won, his prick the hearts grand ally, grumbly guts eased as the prick and heart aligned. Jack chortled with glee.

Sarah pulled his head to her and rained little warm kisses on his cheeks, her tongue eventually slipped into his mouth to flutter rapidly against his own. She pulled away, eyes bright, smile mischievous, her hand sliding up his belly, fingers finding the bandage under his shirt, giving it a tweak. Jack smoothly caught her hand and kissed it to avoid her alarm. The sting was intense though, made him wince despite his efforts.

"What hotel are you in?" She asked. Her giggle warmed Jack's heart, set him on fire. He pressed his thumb and two fingers together tightly and anchored the sexy, joyous feelings coursing through him firmly in his memory. Such wonderful emotions might come in handy latter. Jack did this with each elated moment in his life. It helped during the darker times, clear his mind, focus, with a press of the fingers to the thumb.

"I want to congratulate you two. Sarah, Jack is, from what I can tell so far, a standup guy. He knocked my bother out this morning..."

Sarah laughed. "No way? He cold cocked LeoNard?"

Jack caught the way Jesse winced at the way Sarah pronounced his brother's name.

"Yeah, and I take it you know him?"

Sarah sighed. "Used to, kinda, he partied in a different circle but we overlapped. Another thing I find repulsive about my old life."

Jesse nodded. "I commend you for cleaning up Sarah. I have seen many a kid handed wealth go bad. I knew your father, and he was very aware of this, it's why he said you could not get your money until after you married."

Sarah nodded. "Had I gotten it all when I was using I would probably be dead, or just brain dead." She said.

The squad car came to a stop in front of the Palace in Victorian downtown Port Townsend. Jack's excitement jumped two notches, three. He smiled broadly and shook Jesse Addington's hand.

"Thank you. I will never forget what you did for me today." Jack said.

"Doubt I am going to forget it either." Jesse said. He smiled and gave a little nod as they stepped out onto the sidewalk.

Jack took Sarah straight to his room his heart beating fast, her hand warm in his as they strolled past the hotels front desk to the elevators. The man behind the counter looked nervous, dropped a key as Jack made eye contact with him and winked.

"Told you he had nothing on me." Jack said.

OTTER TAI-CHI

Jack awoke to find Sarah sitting in a chair staring at him. Her hair was rumpled, legs pulled up in the chair and spread, yellow satin panties wet in the middle, bare breasts peaking from between her legs. Sarah radiated an easy sexuality even as she held, for a moment, a frown of contemplation on her face which slowly diminished a bit as Jack stood, naked, his cock semi-erect, muscles and lithe strength making her mouth water a bit. Jack was completely aware of the effect his body had on her, on most women who liked him and was awkward with it at the same time, self-conscious, something that Audrey had told him made him even sexier, which made him even more uncomfortable about it. With Sarah, he felt much more confident, sexy, and able to relax into it.

"I can see your mind working." Jack said. "I kinda had a reality check myself."

"Oh, um..." Her eyes traveled over his body, lingered on the bandage covering his knife wound, back to his eyes. She looked sexy. "Does your dick ever go down all the way?" She asked.

Jack looked down, shrugged, and loosened his belly muscles to let it stretch down ward, then jumped it up and down like a snake.

"Oh, my God!" Sarah said. She giggled into her hand. "You never did that before."

Jack smiled. "Kinda hard in a boat shower or bunk..." He eased closer to her as he spoke, made it bounce rhythmically. "Didn't think of it when we were frolicking in the woods." He said. "More like trying to not get our asses eaten by mosquitoes."

Sarah giggled as he proudly bounced closer and closer to her. "Kinda like a one-eyed porpoise, isn't it? Just-a swimming right towards you?"

Jack reached out to her and she let him pull her up out of the chair, her soft curvy body melting into his. He brushed his hands through her hair and enjoyed the slide of his cock along her belly.

"What's on your mind?" Jack asked.

"It's just you right now." Sarah said. Her hands slipped behind him, cupped his ass, pulled him tighter to her.

Jack felt a surge of lust love flow through him. He wondered if it was real love. Was this the feeling? It was wonderful, giddy even, to be with her. That, and she had millions. He frowned over her shoulder. The money was shading his motivation, or making him feel guilty, perhaps a bit unworthy, uncertain.

His fingers explored the surface of Sarah's skin down the small of her back, diving under the waistband of her panties. He growled like a horny sea otter. Sarah gasped, body tightened. Jack knew she was strong, he had worked next to her all summer. Her hands squeezed into his hips and her eyes blazed, accepted his playful challenge. Jack's cock strained harder as he watched her belly muscles tighten, breasts swing as she twisted to thwart his attempt to put her on the bed. Jack smiled into the blaze in Sarah's eyes.

"The object is to pin the other... Then do what thy will." Jack said. Sarah nodded, showed teeth.

They twirled and twisted, danced in a strong, yet gentle, blend of sexual judo. Jack grunted as he pushed the wrong way, on purpose, and let Sarah's strength topple him on the bed.

"Aha!" She yelled. Jack laughed as she swung a leg over his head and lowered her plump pussy, adorned in yellow satin panties. "Lick it loser boy!"

Jack finished inside Sarah, staring into her eyes as he ejaculated, her hips bucking upwards in spasms and jerks, her mouth working open and shut. A long wailing keen shook the window panes, her eyes wide, unbelieving, mouth in a fixed 'o' shape. Jack was pretty sure she wasn't faking.

"Wow... That was... Gooooood." Sarah said. She shivered and twitched, her thighs trembling, a light sheen of sweat coated her body. Jack was sweating a lot.

He stood swiftly from the bed, sloppy wet cock dripping here and there. "You like that? I learned it a long time ago from a beautiful native girl who called it Otter Tai chi. Get it, you Otter Tai chi, oughta touchee?" Jack said. He moved to the coffee pot, his hands automatically building a pot of coffee.

"So, you want to tell me what you looked so concerned about before I dick-stracted you?"

Sarah giggled, then sighed and fell silent.

Jack pushed the brew button, breathed in the first few motivational vapors of coffee.

Sarah sat up against the padded head board of the hotel bed.

"I was planning, thinking, considering, worrying." She said.

Jack brought her a cup of coffee, black, she took it and sipped thankfully. He sat naked beside her.

"I am good at that kind of thing, planning, thinking, strategizing, but not very good at the worrying part. I have Buddhist training that aids in eliminating the worry." Jack said. He grinned as he recalled Mark Remua brushing off the wisdom of the Dali Lama because he was a virgin. "So let's go over our plans and strategize together. You don't have to work through it alone." Jack said. He slid one hand over her thigh, sipped coffee with the other.

"My mother is going to shit bricks." Sarah said.

Jack laughed. "I had Officer Addington slip a letter into your mother's mail-box explaining myself. Does she check the mail in the morning?"

Sarah began to giggle. At first it came as a slight titter, then a full-on gale of laughter. She hugged Jack lovingly.

"Silly boy, my mom is not going to be convinced with a letter, but it was sweet of you to do that."

"I write a pretty good letter… But I don't know your momma like you do."

Jack set down his coffee and slid down the bed, hovering over her, his lips grazing her belly then thighs as he moved, catlike between her legs. Sarah realized he was trying to go down on her and closed her legs. It didn't take much pressure at all and she relented, legs fell wide apart. Jack's tongue and lips traveled up her inner thigh.

"At your own risk." Sarah whispered.

"Good thing I am a risk taker." Jack replied.

His tongue and lips came to her mons, then down, the tip of his tongue tracing her contours, then back up where he paused, drew in a breath and gently blew warmth over her clitoris. Sarah moaned and arched her back. Jack provided more contact, more friction, his tongue feeling her with buttery soft strokes. He focused on her breath, the tightening of her belly, the grasp of her hands as her ass lifted, thighs twitched. His hands slid into the flesh of her cute round belly and pulled it upwards, made her spread and protrude a bit more for his tongue to flick, his mouth to suck.

Jack enjoyed the control he exerted over Sarah's pleasures. It was intoxicating, powerful. As she neared climax he backed off a little, allowed her to cool down, then brought her back up. Three times and then over the top.

Sarah let out a long wavering moan, her belly clenched tight, hands clenched to fists in his hair.

Jack relished the way her fat padded belly shook and twitched as the muscles beneath rippled, the way the super fine, golden hairs along her belly caught the rays of morning light through the window. She was so pleasantly rounded and full, beautiful...

"You do that too well... Was the best orgasm I have ever had." Sarah said. She was still breathing heavy. Jack grinned and wiped his chin with his hand, smeared his hand across his belly and down to his cock.

"You can thank Audrey for that, she was a stern instructor." Jack said.

Sarah made a pouty face. "You always talk about women before me. The sexy Otter chick, the stern professor. What am I? You know, I have slept with just Corbin since I was seventeen. Before him was two boys, one when I was very young and eager to try. Had to show him what to do. And then when I was fifteen.

"You are Mrs. McKnight, the incredibly sexy and smart woman, who, even though she is a head shorter than me, flipped me onto the bed and had her way with me. That's who you are."

"Mmm... You forgot rich, perky tits, fat round ass and strong legged ..." Sarah wobbled her breasts with a subtle gesture. "...Blond who kicked your ass." She said.

Jack laughed and nodded his head. He moved in for a kiss. It was a hot kiss, though her tongue was ice cold against his. He smiled into her eyes. "You came good huh?"

"For the fourth time this morning - Jack of all Fuck Techniques." Sarah said. She smiled brightly and cocked her head. "And certainly, master of one..."

She opened her legs and wiggled her tongue at him. Sarah giggled as Jack bit the side of her neck playfully.

He then whirled off the bed and strode to the coffee station, opened the refrigerator, and pulled out a plate covered in saran wrap. A cluster of grapes, Jarlsberg Cheese, and some marinated sirloin thinly slice, piled the plate.

"I thought we may feel a bit hungry after we woke so I put together this little plate for us to share."

Sarah laughed and clapped her hands. "I am a lucky girl." She said. "He is the greatest pussy eater and feeds me as well."

Jack sat naked, Indian style in front of her, pulled a grape from the vine, and offered it to her.

Sarah took the grape between her lips and giggled at her own attempt to look ultra-sexy for Jack, like in a bad movie - leaning forward to optimize the fullness of her breasts, litheness of her torso.

The phone rang. Jack felt jarred out of a pink dream. He turned and stared at it, memories, and logical clicks as to who the caller might be and the direct course of conversation he would need to take. He picked it up in the middle of the second ring.

"Hello." Jack said.

"To whom am I speaking?" Came a man's voice, angry, tight.

"This is Jack, who is this?"

"You are the fellow who has Mrs. Lohtelli all upset, you kidnapped Sarah! We want her back at the house immediately and your charges will be lowered to harassment."

Jack couldn't help himself. He burst out laughing.

"This must be Corbin. You must know that she came willingly."

"She was lied to and brought to the station by Officer Addington."

"She came willingly. Over and over I must add."

There was a silence of speech. Jack could hear Corbin's anger through his breath. He indicated to the phone and mouthed a silent, 'Wow, he is pissed!' To Sarah. Her eyes were wide, her hands covering her mouth.

"I have called the police. They should be there within seconds." Corbin hissed. The phone clicked abruptly.

"What did he say?" Sarah asked. She looked a bit panicky.

"That the cops are about to be here." Jack said. He went to his Levi 501s crumpled on the floor and pulled them on then to the door and opened it with a quick tug.

Jack smiled at the bewildered officer's face whose knocking fist was just about to knock upon the door which made him do a little awkward punch move.

"Come in please." Jack said. He stood in just his jeans, no shirt, no shoes, hands out to show he had no weapon. "You have been given false information by a spoiled rich kid who has lost his girlfriend." Jack said. He took a step back as the other police officer lunged at him, not enough to evade but enough to lessen the force of impact. Jack fell backwards in a controlled manner, non-resisting.

"I am not resisting!" Jack yelled. His voice was a clear, loud tone. The same he would use to talk over the engine on his boat. The boat-voice. They rolled him to his belly, and Jack held his hands behind him so they could click the cuffs on. Despite his obvious submission they put the cuffs on painfully tight. They always did. The tussle also removed the band aid that was covering the knife wound and he began to seep blood as it stung fiercely.

"You are arresting my fiancé. Let him go immediately or I will have my mother sue and ruin your lives."

The two officers used his arms and wrists to lift Jack to his feet. Pain flared through his wrists and arms as they twisted.

"Think about your actions. They are about to ruin your lives." Sarah's voice was a firm, clear, authoritative tone. She stood gracefully from the bed, the sheet slid from her body, Sarah was naked and beautiful before them. "You can see that I am here of my own free will. The room smells of good sex. There is food where we were sharing a meal on the bed when you knocked."

Jack took simultaneous delight and dread at the tone of Sarah's voice. She had once again assured him that she intended on marrying him and at the same time affirmed his mounting fear of her mother's power over her decisions.

The officers holding him apparently felt the same way, at least with regard to her mother.

"Your mother is who called us." One of them said.

"She called because Corbin most likely found out about Jack and I and lied to her." Sarah replied. She pulled a shirt on and the two policemen made efforts to give her the respect of privacy. Jack felt relieved. This was turning reasonable quick.

"Are you certain you are in no danger or harm from this man Miss?" The Knocker Officer asked.

"I am in pleasure with this man's company. Not yours at the moment." Sarah snapped.

"There is a card in my pocket. Officer Addington's. He witnessed my proposal to Sarah, he can verify if you call him." Jack said.

Officer Knocker seemed to relax the faster than the others. "Front or back?" He asked.

"Back wallet." Jack said.

Officer Knocker fished it out along with his wallet.

"I think we have made a mistake, that little fucker is manipulating us. Let them cuffs off him." The officer said.

It felt good to feel the cuffs come away, at first, then the blood rushed painfully back in to fill his hands. Jack winced and rubbed at them, moved his fingers about, not wanting to look like a wimp.

"Sorry for the misunderstanding and um... Congratulations on your recent engagement mam."

The officers left.

Jack sighed. "That could have gone bad if they were idiots." He said.

Sarah laughed, long and loud, near hysterical, until the phone rang. They both fell silent and shook their heads. Sarah answered this time.

"This is Sarah." She said. "Hello mother. Everything is fine."

...

"Corbin is an idiot. I don't love him."

...

"No Mother. It is not too late. It is just in time. I changed. Can't explain. I don't love him!"

...

"I can't believe you would do that to me. Maybe we need to talk later."

Sarah hung up the phone. She inhaled and forced a smile. Her eyes met Jack's. He felt a zing of excitement at the same time full relief flooded through him at having the officers leave. Compared to them, mom didn't seem like such an issue.

"We will elope. Go to Vegas." Sarah said. "Have you ever driven a BMW M6?"

Jack shook his head 'no'.

Sarah smiled sweetly. "You are in for a treat." She said. "Once we are married mother must deal with the fact that I am not marrying Corbin. Now, she thinks she has a chance of having her darling, rich, son in law. He is smart Jack, scary smart, has her all played into his plans. That and I am sure we need to leave before his thugs get here."

"Thugs?" Jack asked.

"Yes, large dumb guys, usually violent?"

"Oh, thugs." Jack nodded. He shrugged. "I am good with vacating fast."

They stopped and got a good cup of coffee, and a couple of flakey cinnamon cookies, at a small cafe that overlooked a harbor in the sun, sipping and plotting their next moves. They were a good fifteen miles away from the hotel, in a tourist area, lots of people about. Sarah was confident that Corbin would have his friends out looking for her but doubted that they cover much ground very quickly.

"We should let your mother get used to the idea of me and then be involved in the wedding as well. Corbin can charm her, surely, I can as well."

Sarah shook her head a firm 'no'.

"Corbin is very wealthy, well, will be if he pleases his daddy. I think perhaps my mommy and his daddy are in tango some nights, even though Corbin's daddy is married to a nice younger girl. A pauper like you would upset her very much."

Jack frowned. "A pauper? I make good money, own my business in good standing, not a pauper. Besides, who talks like that? Who the hell says pauper anymore?"

Sarah reached across the table and tweaked Jack's nipple, not meanly, but seriously enough to get his attention.

"My Mother talks like that, she is a condescending, judgmental, rich bitch - something else I found myself less tolerant of when I got back from Alaska."

Jack shook his head. "I just can't believe that under all the crusty drama shit she has no heart for her daughter, or secretly would want you to be happy with someone who isn't addicted to drugs, who has done well for himself in life without the benefit of being born into money."

Sarah sighed. "Guess you must learn for yourself. We will end up eloping anyway." She said.

"It will at least be an honest gesture that she will have to turn down, then reflect on for the rest of her life. Or, she might just decide to go with it after we meet. She can only resent herself in the future for having rejected witnessing the wonderful marriage of Miss Sarah Lohtelli to Squire Jack McKnight."

Sarah laughed. "Oh, my sweet Jack. She does not reflect, she only projects. You shall see when we try. Just promise me one thing?" Sarah squeezed Jack's hand.

"What?"

"That you will still elope with me after we talk to my mother."

"Deal."

When they reached the driveway to Sarah's mothers home Jack felt his heart rate elevate as he focused on the outcome he wanted - no less than Sarah's mother's acceptance and respect. He would use his most polite formal speech as he did when addressing his father.

"Shit, there she is, in the doorway." Sarah said.

"I feel like we are fifteen or sixteen the way you are acting with regards to her." Jack said.

Sarah shrugged. Giggled. "That how she makes me feel." She said. "It does get old."

Jack parked the Ford Taurus nearest the steps to the porch and they approached Mrs. Lohtelli. Sarah's mother stood just out of the doorway, wore her black hair in a bun, her face beautiful but in a way much different than Sarah's. Stronger chin, exquisite cheek bones, full red lips, emerald green eyes which gazed intently from behind black rimmed glasses, her arms folded in front of her. Jack admired her figure and smiled as he looked at her forehead rather than her eyes, which he had already read, appraising him, finding him lacking in her judgement. Despite that he found her stunningly beautiful. And then the beautiful woman opened her mouth and Jack knew she was foul and black inside, under that beauty.

"Well Sarah, you have totally screwed this one up, haven't you. Poor Corbin is distraught, spent the night here waiting for you. Screwed up again, like always. And you!"

Jack met her fierce gaze and kept his face as blank and unreadable as he could.

"How dare you abscond with my daughter like that! Like a thief. That's what you are. A heart thief. You stole her heart. I am going to have that looser cop's badge for helping you. He is an accomplice now."

Jack fought to retain his composure. Officer Addington was not a looser. Sarah did not always screw things up. This woman talked in self delusional lies. She was poisonous.

Sarah stopped walking towards the door, placed her hand on Jack's thigh to indicate that he should stop as well. Jack stopped, breathed a heavy exhale. It would take a bit more than the regular charm magic to work. She needed to calm down a bit before he could address her respectfully. The game was on, her swords were out, his mission wasn't going to be easy.

"You may not simply impose yourself on my daughter. I do not want you as a son in law. You tell me you want to marry her and then not wait for my approval, just propose to her, after literally kidnapping her from the safety of my own home!" She folded her arms in front of her and glared harsh eyes at Jack. "Just who the hell do you think you are?"

"I would love an opportunity to introduce myself to you." Jack said. His voice was formal, an even cadence.

"I read your letter, I know who you are. Your actions already show that you are not trust worthy." She spat.

"Please Mom, you are so angry. Let's go inside, calm down, have some wine, and talk about this. Jack is wonderful to me, and I am so in love with him. He makes my heart full and happy just seeing him smile." Sarah said.

Jack felt a pang of love sweep through him at her words but her tone was fawning, a little girl seeking her mother's affections after she knew she had done something wrong. He could imagine Sarah spending a lifetime cow-toeing to her mother's anger and fears.

"We don't need to talk. I read his letter. Anybody can write pretty words. Your actions have already showed that you are not trustworthy. That makes you a thief and a liar in my eyes." Karin Lohtelli said. Her voice had calmed a bit, was now cold, collected.

"I am not going to let Sarah make the biggest mistake of her life by marrying some ignorant fisherman. What if your business fails? What if you can't take care of my daughter?"

"Mother you know full well that he doesn't need to take care of me. I will have my money; we can use it well to capitalize in any business or market we want to."

"Oh? Oh? You think you are getting your trust fund, do you? Not if you marry him!" Her long, perfectly manicured finger pointed at Jack's face. Ruby red, nice... Jack thought. He licked his lips, noticed Karin's breasts as they wobbled beneath the black satin kimono looking garment she wore.

"Hah! I will not sign off on it. It goes against your father's will, it does not honor his wishes for you. This boy here has you dazed so you can't see he just wants your money. You really think he is 'the one'?" Karin let out a harsh laugh.

"He loved me before he knew I had the money. I never told him. He thought I was just a deck hand on the Lorem, not the owner." Sarah said. Jack was proud of her tone this time, a bit more firm, assertive.

"You can keep the money." Jack said. Karin blinked and stared at him, mouth about to speak but silent. Jack decided this would be his only opportunity to speak.

"I can understand your point and concern for your daughter. A business woman such as yourself recognizes potential threats to her own empire, her authority. My business is seventy percent equity and generates a net income well over a hundred thousand a year. You can appreciate that I would, if given the opportunity to co-manage Sarah's money, consider it carefully and invest it intelligently."

Karin stared, but listened. Jack could see his words and tone jarred her a bit.

"I own a very good business, have excellent credit, and my money is well invested in assets. The fishing business will not be my only business. I will diversify, create my own empire, with or without the opportunity that Sarah's money represents."

"Your net worth is very little." Karin spat. "You are a joke, a commercial fisherman, with one boat, and one fishery. And when that fishery fails, so will you. What will you do then?"

Jack held her gaze, kept his face neutral. He was used to such conversations with his father, not full of spite and vehemence, but argumentative, confrontational. Point counter point, business cadence. Jack had learned to use this voice to address his elders, people of respect, to make propositions, to be heard, and carefully considered.

"I would like to respectfully point out that my net worth started when I was eighteen. Your husband did not get his first business phone until he was 29 years of age." Jack said.

"He was twenty-eight. And how can you possibly know that?" Karin snapped. "You have done your research, haven't you?" Karin nodded, a thin smile upon her face. "There is your proof Sarah. He is a gold digger! Already researching into our family's history and connections. I will keep the money, and it will be safe. Corbin loves you and is devastated by your treacherous whoring around with this dangerous young man." Karin said. She glared at Jack only this time, behind the utter contempt was a flicker of something else. Something that Jack read as interest. He had gained a small win. And she had used the word 'dangerous', something he felt as more of a compliment than a slight.

Karin Lohtelli stepped through the door and slammed it behind her with a muffled whump.

"I told you." Sarah said. She looked down, eyes brimmed with tears, chin trembling. Jack held her as she cried, her body heaving against his. He felt bewildered as to why this had such an effect on her. To him it was a minor argument, a disagreement that would, in time, wear away with the result being her mother's blessings, begrudging at first, then evolving into better feelings. Then again, maybe never. Some people were simply unwavering in their convictions right, or wrong, they believed they were right.

"This will get better. We just continue to wear at her until she understands, or at least gives up, which is a sort of acceptance I guess." Jack said. Sarah sniffled. He felt her wipe her eyes on his jacket.

"I wanted at least one really nice wedding..." Sarah whispered. "But never to Corbin. I would rather go to Vegas and have you as my forever after than wake up the next morning with Corbin after the most beautiful wedding in the world." Sarah said. She then laughed softly. "On the other hand, the arrangements and flowers and wedding shit was really choking the life out of me."

Jack nodded as Sarah spoke. He had never fantasized about a formal wedding. Rather, he had fantasized how to skirt the cost of one yet still marry a wonderful woman, a companion, a genetic match for the intelligence of his children.

"You go back to the hotel. I will gather some things and meet you there." Sarah said. "She can't control me anymore. It is time she learned that." She gave a little laugh. "Fought me hard on the idea of purchasing the Lorem as my own personal re-hab. Her fears were right. My eyes are open. Bitch."

Jack looked after Sarah as she turned and walked away from him, towards the side of the house where the garage was. He watched her fast-angry gate, admired how her ass wiggled beneath the thin yellow dress, smiled, and jumped into his rental car.

He hesitated for a few seconds before putting it into drive. He glanced over to where he had seen Sarah go around the corner. Through a large window he saw a garage door open, then heard a car engine start, rev loudly, tires squeal. White smoke filled the window, and a jet black M6 shot out of the garage, turned into a fishtail, streaked down the drive out onto Cedar Heights road. "Wow." Jack said. His hand felt the clunky gearing of the Ford Taurus as he put it in drive. He began to chuckle, then braked hard as Corbin, curly blond hair, well-trimmed, jumped in front of the car and came stalking towards him.

"Get out of the car you punk!" Corbin yelled. Jack sized him up, believed he could take him should it come to that. Not today, he had promised Officer Addington he would be cool. He popped the Taurus in reverse, mashed the gas, gained speed in reverse and cranked the wheel hard over, sending the front end of the car into a controlled 180 whip. He had the car in drive again before it stopped sliding and stomped the gas pedal to the floor. The result was not as dramatic as the M6 but it sufficed to increase the distance between the car and Corbin - who was now running along behind the car, instead of blocking its way. The wheels squealed as they spun on the loose gravel on top the asphalted drive. In the rearview mirror Jack saw Corbin pick up a potted plant and hurl it at the car. The effort was comical, the pot too large, it's distance way short. Jack laughed as he caromed into a hard left onto Cedar Heights Drive.

GRAND DADDY SUPERCONSCIOUS

Jack and Sarah stopped at a hotel on the way to Vegas in Twin Falls Idaho along route 93. The ride in the M6 had been fast, with Jack testing the sport coupes limits every chance he got. Sarah talked with him about everything and anything, laughing, carefree for the most part. She shared with him the implications of her not getting her money. Told him she didn't care. Jack cared. He wanted her to get her money and could tell that she was stuffing a great deal of conflict within her mind as well. Just as he would be in the same situation. Being treated as she was by her mother was most likely the most hurtful thing. The woman was hateful, spiteful. He wondered if Karin would kill Sarah over twenty-six million dollars. People do weird shit when it comes to money.

Jack threw his extremely well packed duffle bag on the hotel room bed, king sized for a little extra room to romp.

"We should call your mother, tell her where we are." Jack said.

"You think she gives a rat's ass? She just got what she has been wanting all along - the trust fund." Sarah said. The anger in her voice burned along Jack's mind, made his shoulders tighten a bit. He breathed, did some subtle shoulder rolls, relaxed them up a bit.

"I would think she loves you, not the money. You are her life, an only child. I find it hard to believe that she values money over you." Jack said. He watched

Sarah as she fidgeted with her purse, a turquoise leather designer bag with a clever gold snap to hold it closed. She was still in her clingy yellow dress and looked sexy even though, after driving late into the night, the dress was wrinkled and her hair was a bit flatter from the curls she had worked into her long blond hair.

She made a disgusted grunt. "I doubt it." But there was a softening of her tone, like maybe she believed, or wanted to believe, what Jack was saying.

"Call her now or in the morning?" Jack asked.

Sarah shrugged, unbuttoned the top two buttons of her dress, began to wiggle out of it.

"In the morning. Let's shower, like we showered on the Lorem."

Jack grinned and shoved his pants down. "But then we were awkward, eager but restrained, not knowing each other's likes or buttons. I would rather..."

"Stand there blathering?" Sarah said. She whisked off her panties and flung them at his chest. He caught the little flimsy and inhaled her scent.

"Mmmmm... My favorite. Pee-cum with road grime."

"Eww! Shower!" Sarah said.

Once in the water her giggles turned to sighs as Jack wolf licked the side of her neck down to her shoulder where he growled and bit her gently.

"Oh!" Sarah yelped. Jack smiled, hands slid over her back, warm soap slippery fingers caressing her tense muscles, feeling them carefully. - "Always feel with your fingers, measure your effect..." Audrey had taught him. Jack smiled, felt joy flood through him. He put Audrey's teachings to good work as the shower steamed the mirrors.

The king-sized bed served them well until two in the morning when they eventually drifted off to sleep in each other's arms. Initially anyway. Jack soon felt his mind stealing free of normal awareness, flickers of bright road and mountain images formed strong as he watched.

Jack carefully disentangled himself from the soft warm body of his soon to be wife. He lay on his back, head comfortable on a pillow, breathed deeply and allowed his mind to slip back into the place where images formed and sometimes made him jump because he believed he was taking a step downward like making an unexpected step at the bottom of a flight of stairs because he believed he had already stepped down the last stair or anticipating an extra step at the top. He held no agenda this dream time and sought to simply observe with a passive awareness and see what Grand Daddy Super-Consciousness presented him with.

Jack made a small laugh... Or believed he did. Grand Daddy Super Consciousness. The thought struck him as funny and he began to feel an overwhelming sense of hilarity burble through his being. He began to laugh. There was no form to this state, it was the blackness he had learned to be comfortable with. This time it was different, no weird rushing sensation, no vertigo, no awe, or fear, but instead, humor. Jack felt it as a bodily sensation, warm, amusing, incredibly funny and entirely joyous and pleasurable. The sensation welled through him. Jack giggled in uncontrolled spasms, his laughter echoed back from the blackness in which he floated. Then there was a bit of movement, as if he righted his dream body to orient within a scene. The blackness faded and, warm deep sunlight, bloomed, over a grassy field that Jack's feet landed upon perfectly. The scene solidified. He stood next to a tree on a little hill which overlooked fertile farm lands and green stands of cottonwood, the gold light infused the scene and his mind at the same time. The humor grew around him only now the sound of his chuckles was joined by a much deeper, richer voice. Jack's breath was taken away as huge laughter emitted from within him, all around him, awesome booming laughter that rolled through him, back and forth as if he was in a narrow canyon. Jack felt huge, expanded, as if he was the canyon, the plains through which the laugh thunder rolled. He immersed himself in the extreme pleasure of humor, and knew something more, realized something that drew out a sense of awe and then, even more sweet, pure, bubbly, laughter, joyous, playful, and care free, the humor of God.

Jack knew he was laughing with God, believed it with all his being. This was God's humor. He giggled joyously and watched the sunlight grow deeper gold in hue, warmer.

"God's humor is joy and love mingled to form delight. This is God's sense of humor, and he, it, prana, Grand Daddy Super-Consciousness is a joyous, lighthearted, overwhelmingly pleased, loving joyous and good-natured sense of humor. Pure... Mirth." As Jack spoke these words he felt joined with another being that spoke through him. He awoke as he uttered the word 'mirth'.

Sarah sat, looking at him, bewildered eyes darting back and forth. Jack realized that she must be a bit freaked out but felt the humor still, and her face was quite funny. He tried to focus on her as he continued to giggle uncontorlably.

"I... Had a funny dream." He said. His words were choked with giggles, uncontrollable and bursting from him. Jack shrugged and giggled louder, his sides slightly sore, his stomach tight from laughing, his cheeks wet with tears. Sarah grew a silly smile on her face, a look of love and amusement lit her eyes, and began laughing herself.

"What were you saying, something about God as you woke?" She asked. Jack beamed at her and for a moment all that love and delighted joy poured out of him and into her. He saw her feel it, eyes widening, breath catching. A little gasp escaped her lips, eyes amazed.

He hugged her to him, kissed her lips. Sarah pulled back and stared at him, her breathing fast. Jack was covered in a light sheen of sweat, was amazed at how much his stomach muscles hurt from laughing so hard.

"I... Um..." Jack began. He felt the need to explain himself. "The words were..." He struggled to recall the words that welled through him at the end of the dream.

"You are weirding me out. Now you tell me right now what you just did to me!" Sarah said. Jack had seen her feel it, she was still smiling, half laughing. Her eyes were wide, not frightened, but intensely curious, voice breathless. "Tell me what you did." She implored.

Jack took a deep breath to compose his thoughts. This would be difficult to explain. He had spoken, briefly, about lucid dreaming with Sarah while playing with her during the summer.

"I had a Lucid Dream of sorts and God and I were laughing, or I somehow tuned into the joy and laughter of God... I think that is more like it – I tuned into the ever-present flow of God's Mirth and like, swam in it, or was surrounded by it, very intense."

"That is some weird shit Jack. You are saying you swam in God's frigging sense of humor?"

"Yes. Or at least dreamed it." Jack said. He breathed easier now, more concerned with calming Sarah down than the dream.

"How? How did you do that? With the kiss? I felt it go into me."

Jack shook his head. "I have no idea. Weird huh? Like I transferred a bit of what I was feeling to you, like a static shock or something."

Sarah nodded, eyes wide, lips now in an amused smile. "Tell me about the dream?"

"I was beginning to enter the dream state without losing awareness. I knew it was happening. There is often a vast darkness and I rush through it towards a dream. It can be scary at first but you realize that it happens when you are usually not aware, every night, and that helps to get through it while you are aware and doing it."

"Why do you enter the darkness? Why not just start dreaming?"

"I don't know but sometimes you do seem to just start dreaming but it is only after you lose awareness a bit then re-awaken, so I believe that during that loss of awareness you always pass through the black void, span the abyss and then re-awaken once you begin to dream. Depends on how tired the body is, like at first you are supposed to go through the deep rest level, the blackness, and you are not supposed to be aware of it at all."

Sarah was nodding, blue eyes intent as she listened. Her breasts distracting. Jack glanced at them smiled. Sarah giggled.

"Later for that." She said. "The flying through the black part is not what I am talking about. I mean, tell me how you did that thing you just did to me, made me feel what you were feeling, like you pushed a funny thought into my head. Which is fucking weird Jack. Tell me how you did that." Sarah demanded.

"Oh, that, well… Have no idea. It just happened." Jack said.

The look on consternation on Sarah's face made Jack laugh, and wince a bit as he felt his muscles tighten in his belly.

"I am aware in the darkness quite often. In fact, at times like this, exciting times, when I am doing things by the seat of my pants, following my heart, like to come rescue you from the clutches of an evil prince dude, my dreams become even more intense."

Sarah beamed and nodded.

"It is like when I live my life like it also is a dream, I also have far more intense lucid dreams."

Sarah beamed and smiled. "Maybe you can teach me how to do it sometime." She said.

Jack nodded. "I intend to, you would love it, it is very eye opening but it can be scary, fear tends to mess things up, make you wake up. Without some rational sense of how to grasp it, how to believe it is ok, safe, then evolve that into pleasant even. This time, as I was passing through the darkness, and when I say passing through I mean it is often like hurtling through space but with just a light breeze, which can be a bit disconcerting."

Sarah began to giggle. Jack joined her easily then shrugged.

"I know, weird shit, but you asked." He said.

"It is fascinating Jack."

"It makes my life wonderful I believe. Joyous." Jack said. "Anyway, what happened to you I can't explain really well. It was sort of a tangible transfer of energy where my laughter, my pleasure inside me, moved to you, affected you."

Sarah nodded. "It was like I was worried you were having a freak out, and overdose or something. You were laughing and I could see tears rolling down your cheeks and then when you started talking in that weird voice and woke up you startled me at first, then I saw you smiling and felt how happy and funny you were, or are, or understood that you were. Something like that. Then I just became very happy, like when I am in a warm bath, content, with a glass of wine, music, and candles." She said. "It, you, made me feel very good, like I had taken a drug." Sarah giggled. "A warm bath with wine, music and candles drug."

She sat Indian style in front of Jack now. His eyes traveled from hers to her nude curves and back, tongue flicking.

"You can have me any way you want." Sarah said. Her tone was breathy, eyes hooded ever so slightly. "After you tell me how you did that and if you can do it again. I want more of that."

Jack nodded, lifted to his knees, stretched, and slid into the Indian position. He smiled as Sarah's eyes locked on his belly.

"Anyway..." They both smiled lust at each other. "This time, as I was passing through the darkness I was sort of blasé about it, aloof, not tense at all and then I had this thought that I just wanted to relax and observe what Grand Daddy Super-consciousness had to show me. And that is what set me off. I thought a funny thought in the darkness, in the void, and began to laugh, and the darkness began to laugh with me. It was like I was laughing with God or was experiencing the mirth of God."

Sarah was staring at him and nodding slightly. Then she shook her head, as if to clear it of deep thoughts.

"You are very odd Jack, weird but I love it. You were laughing so hard in your sleep. I just watched for a while until I thought maybe you were having a laugh seizure or something. Then, what was really, really weird Jack, was that you began to talk, and your words vibrated like, um... you were inside me..." Sarah lifted her hips, eyes on Jack's as he feasted his upon her body. "Like a gentle orgasm or something sort of flooded through me as I heard them but I can't remember what you said."

Jack nodded. His cock throbbed. Sarah ran her fingers over her pussy, dipped inside a bit, spread wetness upwards.

"It was cool. Are you like, ah, psychic or something?"

Jack shrugged. "We all are to some degree, something we have inside our minds that we don't develop much and mostly remain ignorant of, but it's there, waiting to be developed, exercised."

"All I know Jack, is that when I go to church, I feel nothing like what you just made me feel. Now fuck me, because, I am very awake."

Jack felt it to. Like his batteries were fully charged, his cock rampant, heart pounding with excitement. He crawled over Sarah as she reclined beneath him, legs spread, hips raised for a pillow to be stuffed under her. Jack penetrated her, felt her warmth, her twitches around him as he moved in delightfully slow motions, savoring each sensation.

Showered, shaved, breakfasted, coffee, sunglasses, and gear, all in order, Jack fired up the M6 and hit the road. It was six twenty-two in the morning. Sarah grinned as Jack made the tires squeal at the takeoff, eyes bright, hands cupped in her lap, seat belt tight between her breasts. Jack could still hear the mirth of God in his mind as the finely tuned six cylinder ate up the road in bursts of entertaining speed, and exhilarating corners... Then they grew silent for a long while, each thinking their own thoughts, comfortable in the big leather seats of the BMW.

Jack decided he rather liked the car, would like to have one. It was nowhere near as fast as his Lincoln but way more fun to drive. For one, it was new. There was also a feel to the lay out of the car, everything was in arms reach, well thought out. He wanted to copy this design into an office desk someday. Not a new thought - he had left designs of the idea in his desk at Audrey's place... He let his mind wander to Audrey.

She had a sexy laugh, throaty, like a middle-aged actress who was wringing life out for all it was worth. Jack smiled as he recalled how she blushed red, her arousal obvious, her chest and neck bloomed rose petal pink whenever she turned on. He then realized that he loved Audrey, not in a possessive way, but just her, as a person. A mixture of guilt saturated with realization and giddy reality set in. He looked objectively at his situation as he often found himself doing while experiencing happy emotion. Like a drug, happy emotion caused him to pull back, analyze the situation, remain wary. The rule was, enjoy the day, the happy, but look to your blind spots, see from outside the situation then re-immerse in the happy emotion. Worked with angry emotion as well. He had learned it from lucid dreaming and called it 'The give over, and the take back." The rule in the dream, realize you are lucid, awake while dreaming, but 'give over' to the dream to fully experience it and, if things got out of hand, do a 'take back' and reassume control of the dream, or, rather, control of the self within the dream, control actions, thoughts, and mindfulness, which would then have an effect, usually pleasant, sometimes mind boggling, on the content of the dream.

Jack felt a wash of pleasure as he recalled first realizing that the lucid dream technique was echoed in life, that now, he was doing exactly as he had learned to do in dreams. He made a conscious decision to release control and glanced over at Sarah.

She held her head high, a peaceful look on her face as she gazed out the window at the dawn tinged scenery. She was pretty, curvy, young, and fertile. He smiled happily. '*Oh yeah... Rich too.*'

The M6 thrummed down the road, ate up the miles between them and Las Vegas, with heart pounding enthusiasm, at one hundred and fifty miles an hour on the straight stretches.

A WRINKLE IN THE OINTMENT
HOLDING THE FLY

1988, SEPTEMBER 19ᵀᴴ, MONDAY, 10:30 PM

Las Vegas was an amazing thing to Jack but he felt very out of place, eager to leave, and hot, hotter than he had ever felt in his life. This time back home there would be Geese honking over a chilly lake, Cranes rah rahing as they headed south... So, this is where the stupid birds wanted to go. Jack laughed softly. Sarah gave him a sideways glance, shook her head.

"I am a lucky girl to be with a man who is so easily amused." She said.

He followed her gaze to a trio of women, bronze skin in tiny bikinis.

"I wasn't... No, I was thinking about..."

"Tits and tan?" Sarah quipped.

One of the ladies winked and held out a little pamphlet to Jack. He looked at it.

Sarah took it with aplomb. "Thank you." She said. Her cheeks were a little pink. Jack looked at the colorful booklet, saw that it was a menu of sorts, for adult entertainments.

They kept walking. The air was sweltering hot. It was nearly dark, but might as well have been, the lights of the place drowned the sun, and added to the

169

heat in the air. It was like dual directional hot. No escape. Jack matched his pace to Sarah's but wanted to hurry faster, get out of the sun, get into air conditioning.

"Where those... Hookers?" Jack asked. Sweat rolled down his forehead, wet his shirt, still flannel, against his skin. He noticed people in loose fitting clothes like pantaloons, shorts and sandals, and envied them.

"Yes, and it's just a little further." Sarah said. Her voice was excited, she was sort of pulling him along by the hand, which she would not let go of, even though he had tried to do a polite release - her hand was hot in his, another layer of heat, one he had no control over either.

"Is there... A way... We can never come here again?" Jack panted.

Sarah laughed merrily. "I like the heat Jack." She said.

Jack looked at her like she was crazy and pictured many miserable vacations with her to hot places.

They entered the Bellagio and the rest of the evening was spent in the cool smoky areas of the great Las Vegas indoors. Jack found himself enjoying the clamor and glitz as the third whiskey set in. He had no need of money. Sarah paid for everything, insisted he play the dollar slots with her. She whooped and giggled each time she got a win. She sat on the stool next to Jack, fondling his cock through his pants whenever he started winning.

"Mm... I love a winner." She purred.

When he started losing she would flash him her new sheer panties up her new pumpkin colored skirt. "Look what you are gonna get when you start winning, or get if you lose, just to help you feel better."

They gambled, lost, went up to the room and practiced their Otter Tai-Chi, then ate, shopped for more clothing, caught a show, drank the entire time, then made their way back up to the room. Sarah was pulling him along an excited bounce to her steps. Jack was out of sorts, feeling a bit like a country bumpkin, but having the time of his life. Then Sarah produced a gram of coke.

When she dumped it out on the glass coffee table Jack just stared at it. Memories flooded back of all the friends he had watch destroy themselves with the stuff, how much he had sold to the man who sold to them, the scenes of covert pickups, near misses with the police, women easily manipulated by their lust for more. The thoughts were seductive, the memories guilt inducing, yet the experience had tempered him in a positive way.

"Uh, no thanks, you go ahead." Jack said. "I used to be a dealer. Have used enough, watched it ruin people."

"Square." Sarah said. "I am feeling down, and want some to perk me up. A bit of this might help get my mind off my mother... even help with the courage to call her." Sarah looked up at Jack, over the pile of coke on the glass coffee table, a wry smile on her face. "It isn't going to kill you. I promise." She said.

Jack realized that she was referring to the expression on his face as he stared at the little white mountain atop the smoked glass coffee table. He blinked and forced a smile, felt oddly uncomfortable. His mind rejected the idea that Sarah still liked her coke. It was repulsive to him.

"The last time I did coke my heart stopped. I quit immediately after a painful half second of panic. Now, whenever I see the stuff it sends a cold hatred through me." Jack said.

Sarah's eyes met his and were merry, understanding, and a bit defiant.

"You did too much dummy." She said. She took some from the pile on a nail file, a neat little sparkly cone of yellow white and inhaled it with her left nostril. She served her right nostril the next little cone atop the smooth side of her nail file.

Jack shrugged. "I did. And was taught a fast lesson. One I did not ignore." Jack said. "But now that you have done a couple toots lets go back to the subject of your mother."

Sarah held her fingers to her nose and sniffed a second time, pulling the drug further into her sinuses as she simultaneously nodded her head in agreement with Jack.

"I want you to feel comfortable talking to me about anything Sarah. I have seen lots of couples that are tense and rigid around each other, and can tell they have a lot of unspoken issues, each with the other. I want you and I to be relaxed with each other, open, sharing..." Jack said. He layered his speech with purpose knowing its hypnotic effect, knowing the effects of cocaine. He wanted to tap her confidence, to open up, to call her mom and remain rational, focused on the outcome.

"I know that we have moved very quick, that you may feel that you just gave up a lot to marry me. I don't want that to ruin our happiness though. Can you be happy? Married to me, a 'poor' commercial fisherman?"

Jack stood in front of Sarah looking down her blouse at her breasts. She had removed her bra upon entering the room, leaving just a thin layer covering.

She lay back on the couch and ran her hands up her inner thighs, pulled her skirt up over her sheer pumpkin colored panties. Cute.

"We have moved quick Jack... My mother is such a cold bitch - you have no idea... But the answer is yes - yes, I can be happy living with a 'poor' commercial fisherman. But I could also be happy living with a very rich commercial fisherman once I can get my money. My mother has complete control over whether I get my money because of my own stupidity and having to go to rehab."

Jack nodded. He eyed the cocaine again, a meaningful glance.

"Are you going to talk to her or am I going to?" Jack asked. He pulled a scrap of paper from his pocket and picked up the sleek push button Bellagio phone from the side table and moved it onto the coffee table, next to the coke cone.

Sarah sighed heavily and reach again for her nail file with dragonfly embossing and what looked like another dragonfly sealed within the amber colored handle. Jack figured it probably was amber, and very costly. She used it, a dainty scoop to each nostril.

"I have given this some thought." Jack said. "I have some lawyer friends in New York who might be able to help us. It will cost a bit, but they are good, very good."

Sarah sniffed a wet slurp of coke snot into the back of her throat then giggled, embarrassed at how un-lady like it was, all the while her eyes big on Jack's.

"You know lawyers in New York?" Her face was a bit hopeful yet her tone skeptical. The sound of someone ready to be convinced.

Jack nodded. "Ziggy's dad is Michael Nuefeld, he is worth nearly a billion, a corporate lawyer. But he may know the right angles on the trust fund thing. He invited me to visit and stay with him in New York at the end of the season. Said he wanted to introduce me to his friends, and that his friends were people who made things happen, Donald Trump types, and the Trump himself even. I could call him and see if he is ok with us taking him up on his offer."

"You have not yet ceased to amaze me. But I have never heard of him." Sarah said. Brighter but still a bit skeptical.

"Doesn't matter, he is good, very good, at what he does. And, he is a friend, might not charge as much." Jack said.

Sarah smiled big, hugged Jack to her, and let out a big sigh of relief.

"So that was it? You were stressing out about losing a few million dollars?" Jack teased.

"You damn skipy. I mean you are wonderful and all, but just think how good things could be if I actually had my money." Sarah said.

"Let's call your mother, talk, tell her that Corbin is a drug addict, that you are no longer using drugs and he is, and that you want to get away from that circle, that downward spiral. She certainly doesn't want to be pushing you to marry a drug addict, right? That would make for a horrible person, let alone a mother."

Sarah laughed. "My mother enjoys a few evenings out on the town herself. She drinks way too much expensive wine and has nice and legal prescriptions for dandy little mother's helpers. Plus, she likes the cocaine as well. She and Corbin do drugs together on occasion. She believes he is just in a phase..." Sarah laughed a bitter laugh. "A phase that has lasted since we were high school sweethearts." Sarah shook her head. "No, my Mother is a shallow, selfish, controlling cunt. Cunt is the right word. It fits my Mother. My Mother is a cunt." Sarah said. Her tone was angry, scary with its finality.

Jack paused in his thoughts. Took in what Sarah was saying. He leaned closer to her and slid his arm around her waist, hugged her to him. She tensed away from him, body rigid.

"Please... Not now. I am not in the mood for lovey dovey shit." Sarah snapped.

Jack pulled away, a bit of anger flaring through him.

"You say she is a cunt, she raised you. I am not going to argue with that. Take a deep friggin breath and hear me out. I will call her, allow her to prove herself a cunt, but at least give her the option to accept me and be happy for you."

Sarah shook her head. Her smirk of disapproval not exactly honey-mooner-ish.

"You will see how hopeless it is. She thinks she has won. Go ahead, call the bitch." Sarah spat.

Jack raised his hands. "Easy sugar - God you're even prettier when you are mad. Fierce and sexy!" Jack spoke 'fierce and sexy' with a British accent, his impersonation of Sean Connery that nobody knew was Sean Connery.

"This is just a chess game. I wish we could record our conversation but that would be inadmissible as evidence in any case. So, I call her, and she is a cunt, then I call Michael, I am sure he will be able to help. For the price of about thirty thousand we will be able to sick him on her bullshit."

Sarah shook her head but now her face was filled with a genuine smile. She was beginning to build confidence.

"You remember Ziggy right? Real name Zebadiah?" Jack asked.

Sarah nodded.

"His dad contracted with me to take him out fishing, make a man out of him, teach him accountability and a number of other side effect lessons a person can learn while commercial fishing - sort of like you did with buying and working on the Lorem. It was, in fact, Michael Neufeld's idea that I contract with him, and others. I met him through a friend of my Uncle Conner's, Calvin Strom, a great guy, invented and marketed those neoprene rainbow sandals everyone in Hawaii is wearing, made a fortune."

Sarah nodded rapidly to match the quick flow of words from Jack's mouth, the small smile on her face no longer as doubtful.

"Calvin and I hit it off, became friends, in fact I have a standing offer to stay at his home in Hawaii. I would love to introduce you to him. He introduced me to Michael Nuefeld about four years ago because he knew through my uncle Conner that I was into what Conner calls, 'weird dream shit'. Michael is still Calvin's lawyer to this day and at the time we met he was on a what he called, a spirit quest. Like when a Christian goes to Israel, kinda like that. Michael and I hit it off and created a secret society called the Lucidian's. We came up with the idea talking and drinking. I took it all seriously, he kind of humors me along I think.

"You are into some weird shit... And this guy was into it too? A lawyer?"

"Yup, lawyers got souls too you know." Jack said.

They shared a laugh.

"A 'secret' society huh?"

"Yes, well, not really super-secret. It's ok to talk about it because anyone can join. It's more like a mailing list of people who know how to Lucid Dream and believe that it enhances the way they live their life. Once a year a query letter is sent to each member in the address book asking if new members have been met. It seems to grow in spurts. One year just ten, the next year was about 15, the next 27."

"That's close to exponential Jack." Sarah said.

"Yes... I am sorry I am losing my point. My point is he is very smart, and very cool. He will help us out, plus, show us an excellent honeymoon in New York City, a place I actually dread to visit."

"I went there when I was a little girl with my dad." Sarah said.

Jack saw her eyes mist, then brim with tears. She smiled as they ran down her cheeks.

"You loved your dad very much."

"It's been three years Jack, I miss him, and he loved me very much. My mom seemed ok back then too actually but she changed when we bought the big house. It was like she had arrived, she got what she wanted, that house, dad didn't want it. Only did it to make her happy. Call her now Jack, you will see, happy isn't her thing."

Jack nodded and picked up the phone, dialed the number.

"And... Jack... I love you. I think you are wonderful and am happy, elated, that you love me enough to marry me knowing there is this drama."

The phone was snatched up half way through the first ring as if the call had been anticipated.

"Lohtelli residence."

Her voice was smooth, controlled, sexy.

"This is Jack Mrs. Lohtelli. Can I please talk with you?"

Jack used his best formal tone, as he would be addressing his father regarding a very serious matter.

"Talk with me? Or to me? You don't seem the type for 'with' after you selfishly ruined Sarah's life with Corbin and then stole her from me."

Jack felt his cheeks flare. He glanced at Sarah who nodded.

"She is on her third by now, she usually gets into verbal tongue lashings about this time." She said softly.

"What you say is true Mrs. Lohtelli, I ruined her relationship with Corbin but only because she did not love him, he is a drug addict and not a very nice person."

"And he has a small dick!" Sarah yelled at the phone.

Jack cupped the receiver and shot her a stern smile and furrowed eyebrows. She licked her lips, her eyes on his cock.

Mrs. Lohtellilaughed softly."I heard her Jack, and I agree, I was looking at your cock when you came over. I saw how you were looking at me too Jack. You are quite the stud, aren't you? Marrying my daughter, the lucky little bitch gets a much handsomer man than Corbin, and with a bigger cock. But without the money honey, you are just a nice fuck, and she is simply too naive to see through your intentions to get her money."

Jack was careful not to breath or respond for a second though Sarah was creeping towards him, trying to distract him, or to lighten things up, let him know all was ok no matter how his conversation went. She pulled his pants open...

"I think you are a very beautiful woman Mrs. Lohtelli and yes, to someone like you I would be a good fuck that you could discard when you are done. I have been guilty of doing that and having it done to me and in all honesty, it is shallow and has no love in it. Love makes a good fuck a mythic fuck Mrs. Lohtelli."

Now Sarah's mouth was open in disbelief rather than about to suck. Her fingernails dug into his cock, a tiny bit, but enough to make him flinch and inhale sharply. Jack removed her hand and took a good step back, his eyes playful, his feet momentarily tangling in the jeans around his ankles.

"You can be a great lover, be the ideal romantic, but you are not the better deal where it comes to Corbin. Sure, he has his flaws, drugs are one, but that can work to her advantage. He dies early. She has all his money left to her. Just one example, there are others... You will never be able to provide her with the wealth that he can."

Sarah moved towards him again, fast, got on her knees.

"She can say what she wants, use sex, be seductive, she is good at that." Sarah said. "I will be gentle. Promise." She looked up at him, big blue eyes submissive, apologetic. Jack held himself up for her lips.

"... So, you see, there is little hope she will get her money once she marries you." And here came the pause Jack was waiting for. He had touched on things that made the woman prickle a bit, loose her seductive thing, which had been working, a tiny bit, her image played in his mind - something that concerned him a little.

"I sure wish we could get along Mrs. Lohtelli. I desire your respect and alliance now that I am your son in law. Sarah and I got married here in Las Vegas and are wanting to come back visit you, to get to know and maybe even, like each other. If not then we can at least be civil." Jack managed to finish talking, without a waiver, as Sarah slipped her mouth around his erection.

"So, you are in Las Vegas..." There came a thoughtful pause and a light chuckle. "Staying at the Bellagio no doubt, Sarah's favorite. You know Jack..." Another pause. Jack could hear ice clinking in her drink as she sipped. "You two might be staying in the same room that Corbin and his buddies shared a very high young Miss Sarah. Oh, I know he mistreats her, makes her do things, dominates her, she is so easy Jack, such a slut. You have no idea what you are in for. She will never be faithful to you, especially with men like you."

Jack found the slanderous bullshit coming out of her mouth very clever. Even though his mind rejected it he found himself wondering, just a bit, if what she was saying might be true. Found his mind clicking through all the possibilities. There were many. He watched and felt Sarah sucking, with much saliva, hungrily on him, bubble butt moving back and forth in time with her mouth.

"Nevertheless Mrs. Lohtelli, she has chosen me, out of all those handsome men she has let take her, to legally marry." Jack lurched backwards again as Sarah raised her head up off him, eyes blazing anger. The phone cord came tight and jerked the phone out of his hand. He held the receiver firmly to his ear, squatted and caught the phone, careful not to push the hang up button.

"She is lying." Sarah whispered. "Just pretend you believe her or it will get worse when she thinks you are offended."

Jack nodded.

"I have to ask you, mam, to not speak poorly of Sarah even though you may tell the truth, it is unseemly to desire to cast your own daughter so delight-fully into such a dark and low light. Although, I have had my fun in such ways as well. I do not care, mam, what her past is and would hope she forgive me my own past actions. I just know her present which, now, is very happy, loving, and..." Jack smiled down at the top of Sarah's busy head. "Gentle." He said.

"Jack, I saw you look at me, I know lust when I see it. I want you to listen to me. I am being very real to you. You speak of getting to know and like each other but it is not about that. I am sure I could like you just fine, like you a lot even. This isn't about love, it is about wealth, the uniting of two families, as her own father expressed a desire for her to do. She can marry Corbin, have you on the side for all I care, me too, have you on the side, a little mommy daughter action. You will love it, and with the right amount of coke and whiskey, Sarah will love it too. Let her go and I will pay you a hundred thousand dollars. Tell her I want to meet you and give you a chance, you are clever, then I will pay you in secret and you disappear with the money. We do it that way so you have the money before you break up with her. I know you wouldn't trust me, give you credit for being smart. Do you understand what I am proposing?"

Jack found himself considering, for a moment, gave himself a huge moral kick in the ass.

"I understand that you can do better. You were right, I was looking at you as well, but not with lust, I was seeking approval, and appraising you as a person. I felt that you were a good person, that you were just overly protective and in need of control. It is, in fact your control that made me call. And I still seek your approval, like a million-fold more that the little thing it is now." He said.

Mrs. Lohtelli giggled. "Oh, good, I knew you were clever. This can be so much fun, and once you two get here you and I can sneak about and you can be that good fuck. I like handsome clever boys Jack and am a bit of a slut myself. But not a million sweet Jack, five hundred thousand and a sweet piece of ass."

Jack was enjoying the dual. He began to ejaculate in Sarah's mouth while willing himself to quit visualizing Mrs. Lohtelli as she moaned into her pillow.

"I... I think that would be good. Yes. Yes, we will celebrate a little here, just getting married and all, and then we can all sit down and maybe have a bit to drink to loosen things up, work out our differences. You have made me very happy and pleased Mrs. Lohtelli, restored my faith in people's ability to be reasonable and kind to one another." Jack said.

"If she is done going down on you, could you put her on the phone Jack?" Mrs. Lohtelli asked.

Jack paled a bit, let out a sigh he had been repressing."Certainly, nice talking to you. Goodbye."

Jack held the phone out towards Sarah as she wiped her chin, swallow a last bit, licked her lips, ran her tongue over her teeth daintily. He wondered how Karen Lohtelli had known, surmised that she just knew her daughter well, that she had been right, she was a slut, and predictable. Or was it that she heard a slurp noise?

Sarah looked at him, eyes asking him not to do this. He smiled and held the phone out towards her.

"It's ok." He winked and put his finger alongside his nose. "She wants to talk to you, we were able to work things out."

Sarah smiled and made mean eyes at Jack. She took the phone.

"Hi." She said.

She listened, her face altering to a relieved and happy smile then back to suspicious, but she began to nod her head.

"Um, ok. Sounds good, we will see mom. Good bye."

She hung up the phone a look of disbelief on her face, her eyes appraising Jack up a little level of awe.

"I can't believe you did that. She was still a bitch, but said she had to at least try and like you, then chewed my ass out for marrying in a sleazy little Las Vegas chapel." Sarah smiled and cocked her head, curious. "Why did you tell her we got married already?"

Jack smiled. "Just wanted her to think it was too late, that it was already legal. Take away a bit of her win as well as gauge her reaction." As he spoke his sadness was heavy for Sarah, his face long, drawn.

"So, we will play in Vegas for a while then we go back and um... Meet my mom all over again. Just like that." Sarah's smile faded as she caught the look on Jack's face, the slow shake of his head.

He saw a wash of hurt sting her that caused a flare of anger to momentarily take him.

"No Sarah, you were right. Your mother is evil. She believes she has a deal with me to sell you off for five hundred thousand dollars." Jack said. He left out the part about her offering her body as part of the bargain.

Sarah flushed red with anger. "I told you she was a bitch..." She cast about for something to throw then changed her mind. She looked at Jack, a forced pleasant smile on her face. "And thank you for telling me. That means you wouldn't betray me for half a million dollars. That... Means a lot to me."

"So, we are off to New York." Jack said firmly.

"Yeah. We better get married first though." Sarah said.

"Chapel is open twenty-four seven." Jack said. He caught the look in her eyes, her body language. "Don't worry Sarah. We can have a real family type wedding with my family."

Sarah beamed and hugged him. "Yes, your family. I hope they like me."

"They will love you Sarah." Jack said. He slid his hands down to cup her butt and pulled her crotch into his cock by the cheeks of her ass. "And I want to love you right now." He whispered in her ear.

"Mmm... "Sarah hummed. Jack jerked open her dress, stripped it down and off her hips. He playfully shoved her on the bed. Sarah bounced nicely, legs splayed, ankles tangled in her panties. Jack stripped off his pants eyes, on her clean-shaven creases and folds as they popped open for his view while Sarah kicked her panties free. He wondered if Karin Lohtelli might be a little right about Sarah being a slut.

JACK'S WAY

Jack's eyes popped open at exactly five thirty a.m. He smiled as he stared at the ceiling, dreams strong in his memory, interesting. There had been a large two mast sailing vessel, on wheels, a Road-Boat, it was called. Larger and wider than a semi-truck and trailer yet still able to get down existing road structures nimble because four wheels in the front and back both turned to help maneuver the vehicle. There were others as well. Teams of them. They fought to capture other Road-Boats like pirates, driving fast, boarding other vehicles using paint ball guns. Unlike a harmless paint balls though, when the rounds hit they flared in tiny explosions the size of a bowling ball. Jack had fired one of the weapons as they passed alongside another Road-Boat, watched as the blooms of fire made sizzling, smoking wood splinters fly, left fist sized black scorch marks along the side of the rival vehicle. The return fire was shielded by some mechanism in his vehicle, but Frank, an old school chum, was yelling that the shields wouldn't hold long - and that theirs were down - that the dumb fucks had probably not invested in any at hub gear up. The game was being played in the streets of Cordova, was a friendly rivalry, with teams comprised of captains of purse seiners and gillnetters, the crew of the boat he was on was comprised of old and dear friends, those they fought against, of school mate's classes up and down from them. An elaborate game, complicated, inspiring. By playing it they were constantly training for actual warfare. Jack hummed to himself as he penned details of the dream into his journal. There was a magic in the dream, an organization, history, like he had done all of this before and was a very skilled strategist with many wins accounted for. And then he recalled the blimps. Huge blimps hovered over Cordova as they played the game. For coin the blimps would share a birds eye view of where the enemy RoadBoats were located. But they were not just for the game, they belonged to the City of Cordova and were used to haul cargo in and out of the town. Huge domes located out the road near Sheridan Glacier were used to grow and export fruits and vegetable, there was a huge economy based around these blimps, and, he knew, just as he knew how to fire the paint ball guns, that the energy needed to maintain cost effectiveness was coming from a power source located at the tops of mountains, that constantly charged banks of advanced batteries. It was as if Nicola Tesla's offer to power things from a distance was metered into a form of payment for energy that was much more abundant, taken, right out of the air and magnetic field of the earth.

Jack poured his thoughts into the dream, expanded it, simplified it, imagined it as a strategy board game, start as crew, assemble a team based on reputation and coin accumulation. He added the central gear up hub Frank had mentioned, then changed it to command central, where everyone was monitored, and teams were bet on, much like organized sports, bookies occupying space within the command center to take bets on teams to win, and a myrid other fun gambling combinations. The gamblers could watch 'live' from around the world via local cable tv and call in bets as they wished. They could even 'sponsor' a candidate or purchase a 'resurrection.'

Jack smiled more at the realization that he was back to his normal habit, which was what he liked to call extra-normal, of awakening very early and beginning his day of living the dream. He stared at the neatly written dream, doodled images he had quickly flipped out of the pen and onto paper. Smiled. The title of the dream changed to 'Wicked Game.' A little surge of fright flooded him as the words shifted but then he realized, he was still dreaming, and awoke immediately, heart pumping, breath heavy.

He slipped silently and stealthily from Sarah's side and stretched as he gazed at her, breathed in huge lungful of oxygen, prana, the energy of god. Jack moved silently over to the coffee pot, exaggerating his own grace in a comical way and, upon spying his reflection in the mirror, gave it a devious and joyous smile. "*Fade from Dune.*" Jack laughed. He moved with great stealth over to the coffee pot.

"*Always remember your coffee yoga Jack.*" He whispered. His hands deftly created what he imagined to be the best cup of morning coffee yet. Coffee yoga, mindfulness, physicality, Jack's way. That thought triggered a memory. One of Mean Green Mountain Man Gene eating bear meat, at a camp fire in Cordova's Hippie Cove. The man's tree pitch stained cheeks and hands blended with the dark as he tore strips of fresh cooked bear steak with his fingers and popped the meat between the huge black beard that guarded his mouth hole. His black eyes bore into Jack's with an intensity as he spoke.

"I have my way, and it brings peace and power. You will find your way. Jack's way. You will, I see it, I see many things while sitting on stumps in the forest. Especially after mushroom tea." The fire light reflected orange flames in Gene's eyes as he gave a big grin, showing a row of jagged teeth; prominent canines.

It turned out Mean Green Mountain Man Gene was right. Jack was sixteen at the time Gene spoke to him. Gene had a Harvard education, yet shunned society to live in the forests surrounding Cordova. He hunted deer with knife and stealth, bear with pit and spear, spirited in and out of town, lived in several different dwellings, some old abandoned cabins, some structures he built himself using knowledge of stone and mortar from clay, tree and limb. For fun he built pyramids up on top of the mountains and along popular hiking trails arranged in a pentagram. He called these Portals when he taught his Way to often bewildered college students and travelers who migrated to Cordova to work the canneries.

Back to his norm. Jack's Way. He inhaled the steam wisps coming off the coffee as he carried the cup to the desk where he had laid out his objects of power. A LePen, an ashtray, smokes, two spiral note books, and completing the circle, the cup of coffee. He sat on the comfortable leather chair at the hotel room desk, and began to prognosticate his day.

He opened his dream log and wrote down the title. "Wicked Game" then detailed what he recalled plus dream number two about recording the dream and elaborating on it. Chills streamed through him as he found that there was a complete game in the dream, easily stitched together with a little waking imagination. Entirely satisfied, he closed his Dream Log and began to give thoughts to the boat he wanted to have built, the desk he would build that would incorporate some of the interior elements of the BMW, and as he did this he reveled in the thought that he would have the money to create such things. He drew a depiction of Sarah's mother and circled it. Under it he wrote. 'Confirmed Demonic.' A shiver went through him. How could a mother be so cold? He thought of his own mom, Rebecca McKnight, so full of love for him, for his dad, for the entire family.

Jack went to his duffle bag and found his small leather address book. He sat again at the desk and incorporated the phone and address book into his circle of power. He opened the book and thumbed his way to the back pages where he kept his list of Lucidian's and found Michael Neufeld's entry. He dialed. It was early on a Tuesday in Las Vegas, an hour later in New York.

The phone rang and was answered by a polite, soft, feminine voice.

"Michael Neufeld please. You may tell him it is Jack McKnight." Jack said. He used his formal business tone, one he hoped would be confident enough to bypass Michael's gatekeeper. She put him through. Jack's mouth went a little dry. He took a sip of coffee, relaxed.

Jack hung up the phone gently. He was giddy with excitement. Michael had warmly invited them to stay at his place, had expressed confidence that he could help secure Sara's trust fund. His enthusiasm and grace set Jack at ease and he was soon able to joke and share laughter with the man.

He had been anxious about talking with Michael on this particular call whereas he had never been anxious while talking with him in the past. Jack studied why, came to several tentative conclusions, the most prominent being that he had tremendous respect for the man, didn't want to come across as weak and needy, by asking to visit and for help with dramatic issues.

Jack's next call was to arrange a flight from Vegas to John F Kennedy Airport in New York. He then called Michael back but had to leave a message with his secretary who very sweetly informed him that Mr. Neufeld would have a car and driver waiting for them when they arrived.

ANOTHER GIVE OVER

S arah squeezed Jack's hand as the airliner was about to touch down. "I hate this part." She whispered.

The planes tires screeched, there was a thump and a roar as the captain used the jets to brake.

"Me too." Jack replied. "But now all is well because we are on the ground, rapidly slowing." Jack held his body back against the rapid deceleration of the aircraft. He liked to be the driver, the captain, and disliked flying when he could not see the pilot. In float planes you sat next to, or just behind them, and knew if they were drunk or not, or detoxing, in which case it was wise to feed them a little whisky to balance things out. In this huge mobile home with wings, the pilots were locked up, way up front from their seats in coach. There was no way to tell if they were drunk or in need of a drink or not.

"It is even worse in coach, butthole." Sarah said. Her words were intended for Jack's ears only. She had not been pleased that he had booked the cheap seats, never had to squeeze in with the people before. While this amused Jack, he did kind of wish he could be up in first class.

Despite the cramped space they had both managed to fall asleep during the flight with Jack enjoying fleeting dreams and making little reality checks to muse upon his visions. It had been a whirlwind day as Sarah sniffed the rest of her cocaine on the way to the wedding chapel. Jack had asked that she not get anymore after they got married. Asked her to give it up for him. She had agreed after some back and forth and a bit of emotional smoothing of things out.

They got married at a place called the Little White Wedding Chapel that was quite cool - had wedding rings for sale and everything. The guy who married them was a little hung over. There was laughter and a lighthearted feeling to the event though the priest admonished them to please understand that they had just entered a sacred and legal union.

The air outside the airport was stale, hot, and cloyingly humid. Jack took several deep breaths, noted the scent of jet exhaust mingled with moist vegetation. He held Sarah's hand, his duffel bag over his shoulder and Sarah's bag in his other hand and cast about for the car that was to pick them up.

Just as Michael had promised a black Cadillac with a chauffeur was waiting for them in the arrival area of JFK International. The man held a sign board that read Mr. And Mrs. Jack McKnight. Sarah saw him first and tugged on Jack's arm.

"Common Mr. Jack McKnight." Sarah said. Her mood and tone was now happy, energetic. He found himself wondering if she had used a bit more coke as he dealt with the humidity and lack of fresh air.

"Do not deny new love anything for it will soon fade and be replaced with the reality of who we have really chosen to be with." Michael had told him upon hearing of his wedding to Sarah.

Jack knew, had his awakening moment to the reality of Sarah, and just accepted it. She was flawed, he was flawed, they were now married flawed people and they would have flawed children. Perfect. Audrey had taught him that as well. As he recalled the sexy college professor he realized that he loved her, in a way larger than marriage. He also realized that he wanted a woman like Audrey and that Sarah was really nothing like her. At all. Deep thoughts were not Sarah's thing. Audrey would have grilled him for knowledge, challenged his logic and reasoning with regards to the Mirth of God dream. Sarah was certainly not stupid though; her intelligence was just tuned into different things. Things that money could afford, investments, business. Purchasing the Lorem and working on her for a wage was, to Jack, brilliant. Jack's mind was open to Sarah, objectively, yet he was enjoying the subjective now. Playing a bit at the 'give over' for as in dreams, so in life.

Sarah bounced into the back of the black Cadillac and made a happy exclamation.

"Look Jack! Flowers!" She said. She held a brilliant red bundle of roses in front of her face. "I love flowers. Remember that and we will live happily ever after." She said.

Jack smiled at the stoic face of the tall olive-skinned man, wearing a black turban, a black beard, who held the door for them. His memory formed quickly of conversations with Ziggy about the big Sikh who was head of Michael's security.

"Thank you, Hamaul." He said.

The man blinked, quickly hid his surprise, and gave a short nod.

"You are welcome, sir." Hamaul said.

Jack entered the car and Sarah glued herself to him, lips kissing the side of his neck. There was a privacy window between them and the driver. This was not a normal Cadillac, more of a mini limo - the plush leather seats reclined and provided foot rests much like a living room recliner.

"These seats are way more comfortable than your BMWs." Jack said. Sarah slid down between his legs, knees on the carpeted car floor. Her hands tugged at his belt, fingers nimbly undoing his fly.

"You ever wanted to get a blow job in the back of a mini-limo while driving though New York City, now is your chance." Sarah said. Her warm fingers stoked him through his underwear. Jack glanced in panic at the dark privacy glass as it began to come down with a whirr. Sarah flipped around to seat herself like a proper young lady as Jack fixed the front of his pants.

"Welcome to New York City." Hamaul said. "You will find, in addition to the roses, that Mr. Neufeld also thought to provide champagne in the mini fridge, and cigars in the humidor. Please enjoy them as this drive will be approximately two hours and ten minutes until we arrive at Mr. Neufeld's residence."

"Excellent! Thank you, Hamaul." Jack said.

Hamaul smiled and nodded. "That you know my name means that Mr. Neufeld holds you in high confidence as I am head of his security as well as his driver." Hamaul said. "May I ask your relationship with Mr. Neufeld?"

"We met through a mutual friend, Calvin Strom, in Alaska. His son recently just finished an interesting season with me doing commercial fishing."

"I see! You are the Alaskan Jack. He has spoken of you often." Hamaul said. He then made an interesting gesture that took both hands off the wheel.

He made a quick triangle of his thumb and forefingers and held them to his forehead.

"You are a fellow Lucidian." Hamaul said.

Jack nodded. "Yes. Though I have never seen that hand sign."

Hamaul nodded. "I am a practicing Sikh, a warrior saint."

"I have had some experience with Sikhs." Jack said. "My kundalini yoga instructor was a genuine turban uniform wearing Sikh." Jack said.

"We have much in common. I cannot see through the glass when it is up, just so you know." Hamaul winked and slid the glass partition back into privacy mode. Sarah did not, however, resume the position but busied herself with popping the cork.

She handed Jack a fine crystal glass of champagne and raised hers.

"Here is to the first of many adventures we shall have. Did I tell you I own a house in Aspen? You like to ski Jack? Colorado is beautiful in the winter."

Jack clinked his glass to Sarah's and drank down the champagne. It made him thirsty for more and he held out his glass for Sarah to pour, then took the bottle and poured for her.

"I do love to ski. And I am very curious about the house in Aspen... Are there any more houses and cool stuff I don't know about that you have?"

Sarah nodded, a gleam in her eye. "I started investing when I turned eighteen. Dad helped me set up a speculative real estate company. Showed me a simple way to buy a home, lease it, buy another home, least it, all through a corporation. I have a home in Aspen, Dana Point California, a place called San Arcos along the Mexican Peninsula where the Lorem is headed right now. I think you might not like the heat in Mexico if Las Vegas was bad."

"I saw Satan looking for shade in Vegas." Jack said.

Sarah giggled and squeezed his hand.

"Dad was smart and locked my company up so I couldn't ruin it by being stupid and, so mom couldn't touch it. When he died she tried to take it and managed to impose herself as a safeguard conservator over my inheritance and corporation until I get married because of my drug habit. I was so stupid, you wouldn't believe the shit I pulled, being a spoiled little heiress. My success went to my head." Sarah sighed and frowned. "Here is the kicker Jack. I have read it a hundred times at least. In my dad's will he decreed that my inheritance will be released to me when I marry a suitable and respectable man deemed worthy of my class and wealth. This is where my mom, the conservator cunt from hell, has a grip around my neck."

Jack nodded, took a sip of champagne. He held his glass up towards hers for another toast. The crystal chimed a delicate ting!

"Here is to new love, let us deny it nothing." Jack said. He did not finish the rest of what Michael had said - determined to enjoy the give over.

The give over was Sarah's sweet valley between pleasingly rounded thighs, feelings of love and lust, elation, and joy. Good, happy, positive stuff. Best to immerse in its seductive depths. And money. After his conversation with Karin, either way, there was money. The good way, Sarah got all of it. Or the bad way - he returned the coke whore to her mother to marry her jack ass fiancé, took the five hundred thousand dollars, and seduced Karin Lohtelli before he left Port Townsend.

BOXES OF ACCOMPLISHED PEOPLE

Hamaul drove the big Cadillac with a deft precision through New York City traffic. Jack put the privacy partition down so he could see. The same logic as his distrust of pilots he could not see on a passenger jet applied to drivers. That, and the view of the city was amazing. It was dark, city lights, tall magnificent buildings soared like a cubist forest up above. Jack had been to San Francisco, Los Angeles, many big cities. The lives of the people who inhabited them fascinated him. In movies, the poor seemed stifled and repressed, the wealthy privileged with luxuries.

"Is there something you needed Master Jack?" Hamaul asked.

"No sir. Just curious, wanted to see out the windows better." Jack said.

"First time to New York?"

"Yes, for me. Sarah has been here before."

"When I was a little girl with my dad. All I remember though is the hot dogs and the big balloons during Macey's Parade."

Hamaul smiled and nodded, his teeth were stained, worn, and uneven, natural. He looked to be in his fifties, very handsome, and, as Jack had noticed when they shook hands, very fit, a body builder. As a driver and head of security the man most certainly had some mean skills with knives, guns, fighting and driving.

"You are a warrior saint?" Jack asked.

Hamaul laughed. "Yes! You know a bit about us then?"

"Just a tiny bit. My instructor was Nirvair Singh Khalsa. I admired the man and wanted to share my experiences with lucid dreaming with him, to learn of his thoughts on the subject. I read a bit, did some research. Imagined living as he did even."

"You know more than ninety-nine percent of those I ever meet." Hamaul said.

"I am interested in how lucid dreaming ties in with Sikhism. Nirvair told me many things, but from a warrior saints perspective I am almost sure it must be different."

"From my perspective, not so much a warrior saints, those days are long over for me." Hamaul said. There was a certain happiness to his words about those days being over. "We don't have time to speak of such things here." Hamaul said. He handed Jack a card. "My calling card, any time Master Jack."

Jack smiled and nodded. He studied the card. Nicely embossed, Hamaul Sing Khalsa, Director of Security, and his numbers including a fax number. A simple symbol of a triangle with a circle inside it centered at the top of the card.

"Interesting choice of symbol." Jack said.

Hamaul pulled the car over in front of a building on a tree lined street, nodded politely, his expression firm. "Mr. Neufeld is expecting you now Master Jack." He said.

Jack lifted his duffel bag and gazed up at the building they were parked in front of. It was an immaculate soaring structure, lit up the side by street lamps and further up by large windows which glowed warm testament to an individual life on the inside. Not just any life, but an accomplished life, a person of wealth and achievement.

"It seems odd to me living in a tall box, inside of smaller boxes, in a forest of tall boxes." Jack said.

"It has its charm." Sarah said.

"Yeah, but you like ninety-five-degree heat also." Jack teased.

The walk into the building was a modest granite sidewalk and steps. It was hot, muggy, and moist. Jack inhaled and smelled the scent of earth in the undertones of car exhaust, flowers, fresh cut grass and a most delicious smell of baking bread on the breeze. He understood the trees across the street and meadows through them to be Central Park, the building before him to be the San Remo's. The rest was Sarah's domain.

"Wow." She said. "I can't believe your friend lives here. This is where rich people and celebrities live." Sarah said. She too was gazing up at the building as they made way to the entrance.

"You are impressed?"

"Most certainly. You amaze me. I have noticed that you have a way of making friends with people that kind of bonds them to you, at your service."

Jack nodded, shrugged. "It's a skill. But more like in league with me, not at my service, simply an aligned purpose. It sure didn't work on your mother though.

Sarah laughed. "She is evil. That is what you are saying."

"Her purpose is selfish, to steal your money by controlling you. Most difficult to align my purpose to hers when it is of the other side of good because, yes, she is evil." He gave Sarah a sad smile as she nodded her agreement. "She would buy me off and force you to marry Corbin. Not that she likes Corbin, just that he is aligned with her. They both want to control you and that way your money. They are both evil." Jack said. He, again, did not mention that Sarah's mother had offered her body over as part of the deal, was a bit miffed with the evil that ran in his own veins for finding it tempting.

The lobby of the San Remo was marble and plants, lit up gold and warm. They followed Hamaul at a brisk pace toward the correct bank of elevators. Jack paid close attention to the layout of the building. He noted cameras, a guard desk with a middle-aged man sitting at it who gave Hamaul a quick respectful nod, his face going blank as he studied Jack and Sarah. Jack smiled and gave him a respectful nod for what it was worth. The man's expression remained the same.

The elevator took them to the twenty second floor without a stop. Cool thing about that, Jack found out, was that it was dedicated only to the twenty second and twenty third floor, and that it automatically went back down once exited because a shorter wait in the lobby was safer.

He was surprised that the elevator exited into a wide warmly lit hallway rather than the entrance to the apartment. The hallway was carpeted in thick tan colored weave with a double black stripe that crossed over itself along the edges, laid on top sleek marble tiles right down the middle of the hall. To either side of the carpet was bare marble, a light blond with lighter streaks, where there was placed, small, mahogany chairs, to either side of beautifully burnished wood tables with a lamp on them, an ornate wood mirror behind them. The effect was warm and comfortable.

Marble, it seemed, equaled wealth in the lower forty eight, in Alaska, concrete, stained with moose blood and engine grease, was a sign of a prosperous person. Jack then colored a bit at his own presumption. His home on Onney Drive had some marble counter tops, and the garage had never seen moose blood, though the beasts walked through his yard on occasion. In Anchorage, it was illegal to kill them within city limits.

Hamaul led them to the right from the elevator doors about a hundred feet, then to a door to the right. It opened as they approached and Michael Neufeld stepped out into the hallway. He wore what looked like a Moroccan's flowing pajamas only in dark blue satin and his handsome dark features were adorned with a broad smile.

"At last you visit me in my circle of power, my home base, where I don't feel so small and tiny against mother nature and the raw beasts of Alaska." Michael said. "Ziggy told me of a great many adventures he had this summer, as well as the lovely Miss Sarah. Who is now officially Mrs. Jack McKnight. Congratulations you two."

Jack found himself blown away. As Michael said, 'my circle of power' Jack felt it. Powerful charisma.

Michael hugged both Jack and Sarah, a constant, genuine smile on his face. He was a bit shorter than Jack but a head taller than Sarah. Jack watched his brand-new wife look up at Michael and instantly fall in love with the man. Yes, power.

"We had many good adventures and it would be great to hear of them as told by Ziggy because most of those adventures were had saving his ass."

"Oh? He saved yours in the ones I heard." Michael said. He smiled good naturedly and gestured with his hand that they should enter his home.

"I invite you enter my home and find it yours." Michael said. Sarah beamed a smile at him, utterly, totally enthralled, charmed.

Jack smiled. She would do anything that Michael suggested. This was already working out.

They entered Michael's home. Jack's smile broadened as a tiny bit of awe struck. It was a work of subtle art and aesthetics that intrigued his senses, brown marble inlayed with accenting shades melted upward into a faint gold, bronze that mingled into darkness lit by pools of rich light accented contours of architecture, alcoves of art and furniture. He studied the range of wood and bronze, sculptures and carved wood trim. The effect was near elfin, as if he had entered a Tolkien scene. Beyond the foyer lay the living room and beyond that was a huge bank of windows, city lights beautifully framed with an explosion of plants with huge leaves and bright flowers, some with giant yellow flowers so heavy they hung downward like big bells.

"First allow me to show you your rooms where you can stow your gear, bathe, and dress in appropriate house clothes. I took the liberty of having some laid out for you in three sizes."

Michael led them through the living room and to the right of a large kitchen to a hall. He opened one of the doors and entered.

The room had a four-post bed like one would find in a medieval castle but in a modern style, an area was pillared off and within the pillars was a large bath tub that promised a relaxing and sensuous bath.

"House pajamas are a custom here that I hope you find to your liking. It is my way." Michael met Jack's eyes with an intensity. Jack nodded with a polite smile.

"Your house, your way." Jack said.

Michael laughed. "Good Jack! I see you understand. Shall we meet on the balcony for drinks in one hour? I have a few things to see to before I can relax."

"Sounds great!" Sarah said. Jack nodded.

Michael left the room. Sarah sucked a whistle in through her puckered lips.

"Your friend is um…" Sarah unzipped the back of her dress.

"Very cool, like I said back in Vegas." Jack said. He didn't want her to gush, felt an actual pang of jealousy. She had really been digging on Michael.

"Yeah! But way cooler than what you said, he is handsome, rich and has a, a presence like, um, like my dad, I guess, you better hold me close Jack, he could have his way with me in a New York minuet." Sarah giggled. "That came out kinda wrong. "

Jack laughed. "Way to close to the dad reference." He said.

Sarah nodded, tossed her dress at Jack. He caught it and inhaled it's scent as he watched her quick hands strip off her bra. The scent was a delicate potion of feminine essence, something that perfume manufacturers would make a fortune with if they could capture and bottle the aroma of a woman after wearing the same dress for a couple of days. On the other hand, this could be why Michael insisted they bathe before meeting.

Jack smiled as he let the dress slip from his fingers, a rumble in his chest left his throat in a turned on affirmation. "MmHmm!" His eyes riveted on Sarah's panties.

"That's right Jack…" Sarah stepped back a bit, traced her panties with her fingers. "Come and take this." She whispered.

"We shall deny young love nothing…" Jack said. The give over was good. Convincing.

Jack and Sarah walked hand in hand through a large glass door open to a marble balcony overlooking Central Park which was a dark patch lit by trails of lights within lush trees surrounded by tall buildings, windows bright - the living spaces of the wealthy - lit gold and warm, thousands of them. Jack nodded slightly, eyes wide, it was his turn to feel small as had Michael when confronted by the great Alaska wild. Each of those lights represented the lives of wealthy and accomplished people who lived powerful lives that he could vaguely imagine, certainly not comprehend.

The night air was very warm and humid, the balcony lit a warm yellow in tasteful amounts that highlighted the plants, and path to walk. A rich smell of spices and cooking meat filled Jack's nostrils. He inhaled and made a hungry sound. Hamaul and a woman of stunning stature, olive complexion, long black hair, beautiful brown eyes, sat on cloth chairs placed around a table set with decanters of alchohol and heavy crystal glasses. They both smiled as the trio approached, stood.

"Don't you worry Jack, I have anticipated your hunger, and there is dinner to be had soon as Hamaul makes it magically appear. "

At this Hamaul snorted a laugh. "My cooking is not as good as my driving, but is better than my security measures." He said. He gave a quick bow and excused himself from the balcony. "Better fetch Massa Neufeld's supper." He added, which caused Jack to laugh.

He was swept up, realized it, and was enjoying it. Michael had that power, a knack for placing people at ease with him, yet under his spell. In Jack's memory, every time Michael met with him, to hunt, or to visit, there was a reason. Michael was a teacher. Jack a student. That was their role just as to others Jack was the teacher and they were the student.

"Allow me to introduce you to my wife, Mrs. Agatha Neufeld." Michael said with a flourish.

Jack nodded towards Agatha but did not extend his hand. She nodded her eyes moving from him to Sarah. Agatha wore the same flowing, comfortable material as did Jack and Sarah now, house pajama's, and as she bowed slightly, the loose front fell away from her breasts enough to cause Jack to quickly divert his eyes, but only after noticing. The intense flicker in her eyes showed that she was aware of his 'notice', her smiled broadened.

"Ah, this is Sarah, also, um, my wife." Jack said. He laughed at his lack of finesse.

"It is a pleasure to meet the two of you." Agatha said. Her voice was as beautiful as she was, rich, exotic.

They took comfortable seats at a table of dark wood. Set on the table was cigars, and three decanters, one wine, one whisky, and one scotch. A leather clad bucket of ice set at the ready next to a silver tray that contained the cigars. The balcony, half covered by the floor above, gave the little outdoor oasis a nice cave like feeling of security. The night sky was black, no stars, the myriad lights from the other high-rise apartment buildings dominated here. The setting was made cozy by well placed, ornate lanterns.

"This is amazingly beautiful." Jack said. He glanced around at the balcony.

"Thank you, Jack, I hope you can make yourself comfortable here. Because of you, my home has lost some of its allure, having seen things through your eyes. I miss the flashes of mountains and blue water during my sleep reverie. Now, it's traffic, and, more often, my beautiful desk."

"I am already comfortable here my friend." Jack said. He felt Sarah's warm hand upon his thigh. Erotic images of her flickered in his mind as he smiled at Michael.

"Tell us more of your situation." Agatha said. Her voice was warm, pleasant, that of a trained speaker or diplomat.

Jack listened to Sarah speak of her mother and the legal situation. Was surprised at how much Sarah opened up to Agatha's questions, inwardly chided himself for not asking Sarah the same questions. He watched Michael's expression's, his eyes, his nods of recognition of what Sarah was saying.

"The wording is subjective, 'a mate suitable' is in any case. The part about wealth and stature of equal basis is rather specific." Michael said. He shook his head and gave a little frown. "I will consider the documents if I can procure them, just that process alone involves several filings. But, for tonight, let us eat, drink, and speak of other things." He said. He made a dismissive gesture with this hand as he spoke - which turned into a reach for the decanter of whiskey.

"Full glass of ice, half full of whiskey if I remember correctly." Michael said. He smiled at Jack.

A young woman in a white chef's outfit rolled a tray out and served plates of glazed duck, steamed vegetables, and rice. Bread on the side. Small plate, appeared laden with food, yet the portions were small.

Jack wolfed his down before the others had taken a few bites. He wiped his mouth on a soft towel, placed it back in his lap, took a sip of whiskey.

"That was delicious..." He looked at the remaining food on others plates.

"You have the appetite of a young man." Agatha said. She smiled as she placed a small piece of glazed duck on her fork and placed it in her mouth, fork upside down, European style.

"It is late." Jack said. "That was the perfect stomach sized portion, as Michael taught me while deer hunting on Knight Island. Also, that Americans are chronic and glutinous over eaters."

Michael laughed. "Yes! You recall. I know an apt mind when I find one Jack."

"Yeah... That duck was delicious though. I might sneak into the kitchen in the morning and polish it off."

"You are welcome to more now Jack." Agatha said. "I want no one going hungry at my tables."

"No, I get the wisdom of it. As a life habit." Jack laughed. "I can resist."

"That and to avoid chronic indigestion. You take care of your stomach for the first fifty years of your life and it will take care of you for the next fifty years." Michael said. He patted his flat belly, made the fabric smooth over a washboard stomach. Agatha giggled, her eyes drinking Michael in. "You are such a show off." She said. She looked at Sarah and rolled her eyes. "Men." She said.

Sarah raised her glass, "To men!" She said.

Agatha smiled, gazed from Sarah to Jack and raised her glass. "May they always be just as they are." She said. Jack and Michael heartily raised their glass with the ladies, took a first sip of whiskey.

"And may they always believe they are in control." Agatha added. The ladies chuckled.

Jack let the whiskey linger in his mouth a bit, felt the burn, savored the flavor, then swallowed the liquid flame down, following it in his mind as it dropped into his stomach. The initial swallow was the most poignant and this was, a fine whiskey.

"So, Ziggy says you are looking to expand while business is good, get a bigger boat?" Michael pushed the box of cigars over toward Jack. He took one and leaned forward in the seat as he waited for Michael to snip the nub of his own fat cigar.

"Yes. Should there be a bit of movement on my dad's end. Our business is tied together financially." Jack said. "Alta Pearl Fisheries Incorporated."

Michael nodded. "He is hesitant to move, or just being cautious? Your business is one of owning ones means to produce. Just as is mine. I own my means of production, trade my time and knowledge for an income. You own yours in the form of gear and hardware as well as knowledge. Much lower overhead. My education costs were as much as your outfit and I could not claim them as a net worth." Michael said. He chuckled at his own words.

"Agatha here owns a software company, offices in California, New York, and Germany. The stuff her company creates is amazing Jack, science fiction stuff."

Jack looked at Agatha, whose satin robe had slipped revealing the swell of her breasts a bit more. He made a conscious effort to maintain eye contact but as she reached for her drink his eyes moved to more flesh, just a flicker, but uncontrollable. He felt himself color.

"I... I have and use a computer quite a bit." Jack said. "Love having it."

"You are only seeing the tip, the teeny tip, of what is to come Jack." Agatha said. "One day there will be personal computers in nearly every home in the world."

"I can believe that." Jack said. "I rather enjoy mine, tell me, please, what your company is working on?"

Agatha nodded, a pleasant smile on her face, ruby red lips sliding over white teeth her dark eyes sucking Jack's attention into her.

"My company specializes in writing software for the aerospace companies. Nasa, Boeing, Lockheed Martin, but our side interests are towards communications and networking. A small contingency of us can see that one-day people will carry their computers with them. The information age is going to be incredible."

Jack nodded, his imagination taking Agatha's words and flying with them.

"Yes! I think so too, like, everyone will have hand held word processing fax machines."

Agatha tittered and clapped her hands. "Have you been spying on us Jack? Yes, that is exactly were things are going. Such an exciting time, a golden technological age is coming."

"And with it, all the perils for exploitation and dehumanizing daily functions to that of robots competing with people. Future shock. Science zooming off faster than people can cope with. The soul gets taken for granted, left behind." Michael said. Agatha nodded at his words.

"Caution is needed to incorporate usefulness and meaning into technology so that does not happen." She said. Agatha sighed and took a sip of wine. "So far though, the excitement of making computers work faster and faster and the demand for software to innovate with them, is an all consuming task in the competitive field in which I work. He who can build the best machine that helps speed up mundane tasks the most, wins. There is very little room for spirit, or soul at the pace we must produce."

The conversation flowed to Alaska and Agatha asked many questions about Jack and Sarah's commercial fishing businesses as they finished a cigar and glasses of whiskey

Sarah stifled a yawn, leaned over into Jack and whispered in his ear.

"I am getting sleepy Jack." Her hand squeezed his thigh, brushed up towards his balls. He felt the warm flush of whisky meld with a warm flush of lust and embarrassment. With the promise of great conversation, whiskey, cigars, the allure of Agatha's eyes and demeanor, Jack was not ready for bed.

Michael sensed his discomfort and smiled knowingly.

"I can understand you two must be tired after your travels, and it is very late for us as well." He stood as he spoke and raised his glass.

"A toast, to newlyweds. And in my profession, that is the beginning of the fees." Michael said. He smiled. They laughed.

"Tomorrow morning, early, we shall discuss your matter in my study. Then I shall see about getting you two your money. If I can do that, Jack, and Sarah, I hope you allow me to share an investment strategy with you that will make money no longer a concern for you two. Ever. So..." And here he raised his glass to conclude the toast. "Here is to your health, vigor, and wealth."

Glass chimed, a pleasant tinkle, and they nodded and finished their drinks. Jack took a final couple of puffs of the delicious cigar as Michael snubbed his out.

"I think I would like you to show me that strategy even if we don't get the money." Jack said.

Michael laughed and clapped Jack on the back. "Yes, indeed I shall." He chuckled. "Smart boy this one." He said to Sarah. She smiled and nodded, hugged him a bit tighter to her.

They followed Michael through the living room and into the guest room.

"I have the bed set up for lucid dreaming." Michael said. "On Sarah's side is a new gadget called a dream light. You wear it over your eyes and it detects the movement of your eyes to begin a series of small stimulations that can cause a person to experience their first lucid dream. Enjoy and good dreams to the two of you."

He closed the door. Jack heard an efficient sounding ping as the door latch caught.

COKE SLUT

" **I** am detecting a trend here with the lucid dreaming thing." Sarah said. She eyed the dream machine dubiously. "I don't think I will be strapping that thing to my head before I pass out tonight though."

"It is because Michael is a Lucidian that we are able to experience life in the San Remos." He said. She smiled and nodded.

"There are layers to you Jack, like an onion."

He just smiled and pulled her to him. "And your layers are like a rose." He whispered.

Sarah molded her body to Jack's and kissed him as she removed her bra. She drew his hand between her legs, up her slippery satin pajamas to her warm, moist crotch. "I know you wanted to talk more with your friends, but I am craving you right now. Sitting there and watching Agatha's tits as she made eyes at you was making me jealous. We are on our honeymoon adventure at the friggin' fabulous San Remos!" Her voice climbed upwards with girlish excitement. "I mean, duh Jack, we are in the most romantic setting in the world, and you want to chit chat."

Jack laughed. "Yes, you are right. This is very cool and romantic." He inwardly congratulated himself for bowing to her will rather than pointing out that they could have had both 'chit chat' and romantic time, that to him, the conversation was part of the romance. But it was not worth the mention at this moment for now his eyes were being treated to a most voluptuous and ripe woman. His very own wife.

Jack stripped off his shirt, watched Sarah's eyes lock on his bare belly, his abdomen still well defined from a summer of hard work. Her hungry look sent a thrill through him, made his borrowed pajamas tighter. Sarah leaned forward and tugged at the waistband of his pjs, fingers pulled at the hem. Jack felt his belly flutter with the butterfly's as the back of her knuckles brushed his skin. His pants came open, and down.

"Very, romantic." He said. His urges had, at first, been different - conversations over whiskey and cigars with millionaires was where he had been. But now... He was focused entirely on her as she wrapped her warm hand around his dick and lifted it up out of the silky soft pajamas.

"There it is." Sarah said. She looked up at him happily as she dropped to her knees. Her lips and wet tongue flicked up and down the underside as her fingers swam over his hips, to the cheeks of his ass. Shivers flowed through his groin and up his spine like a fine champagne fills an expensive crystal.

Sarah stood and stepped back, she gave him a coy smile. Her silky bottoms slid down her hips with a subtle twist of her nicely flared hips, her belly tone from working the Lorem all summer. She took a breath and shivered with excitement.

"What are you going to do to me?" Sarah asked.

Jack saw her as her mother had described, submissive, slutty, getting shared around like a runaway strawberry trading sex for cocaine.

"You want role play? Me tough guy, you?"

Sarah nodded. "Submissive little girl slut coke whore." She said.

Jack flushed as he felt as if she was reading his mind. She grinned at him, mischievous, playful. A guilty swell bloomed in his mind but had to fight even to gain the tiniest foothold against lust and love.

Her eyes went wide with surprise as Jack quickly escorted her to the bed and threw her on it.

"Keep your panties on and spread your legs for me." Jack said.

Sarah spread her tanned, well rounded thighs, a pouty look on her face. Jack's pulse quickened at how well played her acting. Or, was she remembering?

'Fuck you Karen Lohtelli, you get none of my head space... But, maybe I am excited by it?'

"Show me how wet and pretty your pussy is." Jack said.

Sarah sighed and smiled, bit her lower lip, eyes fixed on his cock. She reached down and pulled her panties to the side, spread her legs a bit wider, did a sexy little lift with her hips.

Jack began to crawl slowly towards her, hands touching her calves, the backs of her knees, stroking lightly, just a brush here and prolonged touch there.

"You have the pinkest, prettiest little pouty pussy. Just look at that beautiful little slice of heaven." Jack said. His tone was low, sincere. He sensed Sarah's heart beating a little faster. Now she smiled and nodded her head, eyes wide, innocent, riveted to his cock. She licked her lips and slowly rolled her hips.

"Are you really going to put that whole thing inside of me now?" She asked.

Jack smiled and shook his head 'no', moved his face between her legs. "Not just yet." He said, breath right over her skin, fingers gliding over her breasts, caressing swollen areola and nipple.

Sarah sighed as she pulled her panties further to the side and held her legs spread and back.

"There is nothing sexier and more of a turn on to me than the sight of you holding your legs back, that beautiful look of anticipation in your eyes." Jack said. He pushed Sarah's legs back further, flickered his tongue over her folds, her smell and taste enveloped his senses, inflamed his lusts. He delved deeper and deeper with his tongue, listened as Sarah moaned, softly at first, then louder, much more urgent.

Jack stopped and raised up over her. "Now I am going to stick the whole thing in you. Is that what you want?"

"Yes! Hurry, quickly." Sarah said.

Sarah's breathy tone warmed his heart. She genuinely appreciated his complement. Her gasp was playful, followed by a sincere groan as he lay over her, body flush against her, watched her eyes, her face, as he slowly penetrated her, enjoyed the sensations as he spread her open, watched her quiver, listened to her breath.

Jack lost his capacity for spoken language as he tuned to her breath, her excitement, and moved his body to match it, enhance it, lift her up over the peak of orgasm as he let his own pleasure pour through him. His thoughts of her being used like a whore, fucked and manhandled for drugs, came at the end of his wet spasms. He hated Karen Lohtelli for that.

A GRAND ENTRANCE

J ack watched Sarah sleep, a trail of drool running out of her open mouth, pretty cheeks flush, eye-balls unmoving as she did not dream. She had not put on the dream mask contraption. Jack had not reminded her to do so, this was, after all, their honeymoon.

Peoples disregard for dreams used to upset him. How could anyone possibly not care about what they did in dreams? How could they just disregard a full third of their lives? But he had tempered his thoughts with the realization that it simply was a matter of wiring. Some folks just were not wired for it. That level of introspection either scared them to death, if they were religious, or was of absolutely no interest, deemed unworthy of consideration - Dreams are garbage of the brain. A good friend, and meteorologist, had told him.

He slid himself from her sensual cuddle, lay comfortable on his back, hands folded in the shape of a triangle. He breathed deeply through his nose, a few relaxing breaths, smiled as images began to form, memories of the day. The chapel, Sarah snorting coke, Hamaul holding his hands, in the shape of a triangle, to his forehead, the sweep of Agatha's cleavage as she spoke of a golden age of technology, Michaels face as he made comments about human spirituality not being able to keep up, he let the images play, relaxed deeper, and entered the void.

Wind rushed around his body and he had full sensation that he was rushing through the blackness, the void before dreams, the gap, the place where only thought existed and a perception of form. He willed wings and a dragon form, as he had in the past during this phase. It did not work. Instead he felt the wind rushing faster. A twinge of fear set in. The thought that nothing could hurt him in the void came, gave him confidence enough to banish fear, that if left unchecked, could manifest an unsettling terror. Jack breathed easier, relaxed, told himself to sleep. And did.

When he awoke, he was observing a dream, floating, not actually a body, more a ball of ego energy, a floating mote of consciousness about twelve feet off the floor of a huge ballroom full of people dressed in lavish formal wear. Jack realized, as he looked at the people's faces, that they were unaware of him, he was invisible, a spy watching them. He usually would engage the dream in some way given this scenario but this was a different dream. All of the dream chartecters that filled the huge ballroom were paying rapt attention to off key random notes coming from a shiny black grand piano in the center of the room.

Jack, curious as to what they were all focused on, floated closer until he realized, to his amusement, that a woman was giving birth to a baby from inside the shiny black grand piano, her movements and writhing was making the off key notes, the thrums of life, discordant and rather, creepy. Jack pulled back within view yet far enough away he felt safe in case things took a turn. He tuned into the people beneath him again.

The throng was watching, feasting, dripping with wealth, obese with the fruits of life and emanating the fetid tinge of decadence. A plump blond in a fashionable black dress with bright eyes smiled and giggled with glee as the woman in the piano screamed in her labor pains, the strings of the piano thrumming as she moved against them. Everyone was paying rapt attention as they listened to the child being born. Two doctors in tuxedos stood near. Jack drifted higher behind the piano. He was listening and watching the people turn ugly with greedy expressions, as if they stood something to gain from the birth of this child.

There came a wail and another chaotic thrum of the piano strings. There were several women in the crowd with their arms in the air, dancing to the piano music of birth. Jack focused back on the woman giving birth, saw her knees come back and sensed the child sliding forward, the doctor's hands cradling it's skin. He drew nearer than he wanted to. There was blood, the mother's legs jerked back and forth, her back arched, eye sockets black, no white, scary looking. He was repulsed and shocked, tried to maneuver away, but a force, like a magnet, drew him still closer. Jack fought panic, realized he was in a dream, it was irrational to fear the minds holograms, accepted, knew he must let it happen.

He experienced a great sense of relief as he let go. His awareness streamed into the baby, felt the doctor's hands holding him, a sharp flare of pain along his backside. Rage filled him at having been born. He let out a shriek of power, torrents of anger directed towards all the people in the room. The closest finely dressed people died immediately, the rest screamed as they were mind raked, panicked, Terryfied to the point of a body wrenching heart failure.

Everything went black. Jack heard murmuring. He was in the back of limousine driving fast towards the BP building in Anchorage. Only it wasn't British Petroleum's building, it was his companies building. His mother from the piano sat across from him, his real mother, Rebecca. She, and a handful of others, had been spared the birth slaughter. Jack recalled all of those he had slain. By name. They were all corrupt, evil. Four in the room were good. Mom was one of them. But she was such a pain in the ass.

"It's a head of lettuce Mom. Yes. But not just any head of lettuce. It has been bio engineered to taste like a mild chive, grow quickly and easily in the bleakest of climates, cold or hot, and provide protein, amino acids, the essential nutrients a person can live on for a very long time."

His mother shrugged as she crocheted a huge, white, snow flake, doily. "Looks just like a head of lettuce to me and all that bio stuff is only going to tip the scales of nature and screw things up Jack." She said.

Jack suffered a moment of humor and hopeless affection for his mother then turned his attention away. The limo slowed to a stop at the entrance to the building. Inside, Jack knew, were board members waiting to talk to him about the project.

Jack approached the board room with a rising sense of belonging, of looking forward to leading. He was powerful. He had come of age.

All five board members stood as Jack entered the room. One of the men went from a respectful stand and smile to a nonchalant lean against; a white pillar near the big board table. Jack knew each one well. Vic was fat, very fond of food, and tended to overdo it with cheap whores. Sam was overly ambitious, eager to earn more even at the cost of his fellow coworkers. Carl was a collector of things, expensive things, but never to sell or trade them, he was a hoarder of beauty, his family a thing to him, to be controlled, just like a fine statue. Brother Man was cool, he was the one slouched against the pillar, a wry smile on his face. He was smarter than everyone in the room.

He wore a sleek black leather jacket, was holding a glass of whisky and ice. Henry was usually agitated and loved to yell at the others. He picked on Vic mercilessly about his overeating, ridiculed Carl for loving his job and never leaving the company despite heavy bombardment from other companies with better offers for his particular brand of genius. They were all different yet all brilliant minds who had shared common goals and direction. They were all, despite their differences, driven to dominate the world food markets. As Jack greeted each in turn he knew they had to die, that he had to kill them.

They began discussing the product and how best to market it to feed the world as well as carve out a huge profit and Jack knew their minds, their words as they spoke them. He knew what they would say before the words came out for they were speaking the words he put into their minds. He willed them to speak, to argue to become increasingly angry until one by one they began to kill each other. The order of deaths was surprising.

Henry was the first to die at the hands of Carl who had been made to feel as if he might lose his job because of something Henry knew that could ruin him. Next was Vic, choked out by Sam who accused him of holding the company back with his stupid antics and laziness. Sam got his skull crushed in by Carl who knew that Vic was crucial to the final developments and success of the plan. By killing him Sam had destroyed the entire project.

Carl stared at the blood, the corpses, heaved and vomited on the board room floor. It was just him and Brother Man now. Brother Man had taken a few steps back from the scene his eyes fixed not on Carl but on Jack. He was smarter than the others.

"Why Jack?" He asked.

Carl shrieked with anguish as he realized what he had done, he took a sword from a suit of armor that sat in its own little alcove - a light shining up from the floor lit it when the lights were all off in the boardroom. There were eight of such suits of armor in the room. They belonged to Carl, loaned as decorative adornments for the lavish meeting place that had been their sanctuary while working together for the company. He turned as if he would charge Brother Man with the sword but ran the other way, used the heavy metal sword hilt to strike the window until it shattered. Cold wind howled into the room as Carl threw himself, the sword clutched tightly in his hands, out into the blackness of night from the twenty fourth floor.

Brother Man shrugged. "I see why you killed them. But why me?"

Tears streamed down Jack's cheek's, he did not want to kill Brother Man. He looked at his mother. She smiled sweetly was she crocheted the bright white snow flake doily.

"Yes, you have too sweaty. You know that." She said. Her long, agile fingers moved in a flurry of patterns, wielding her crocheted needles in a blur, to swiftly finish the snow flake.

He looked back at Brother Man and yelled inside his mind, as he had done to the people in the ballroom who had watched him being born, as he had not ever done since. Brother Man staggered and fell, legs twitching, to the thick carpet of the board room.

Jack took a deep breath, calmed his mind, looked again to his mother. She worked another snowflake doily, already had one full center circle done. The completed doily lay at her feet, a big, intricate, perfect snowflake, shining yellow like diamonds in the board room lights. She smiled at him and he felt her mind enter his. "Awaken!" Her voice was a strong, urgent, and compelling whisper that he still heard even after his eyes opened. His body thrummed with an odd vibration, energy pulsed through him.

Sarah lay on her back now, arms over her head, legs spread, sheets kicked off, snoring. Jack resisted the urge to hold her gently He knew he would benefit from it. He knew he would feel calmed by the sensation of her skin against his. The thrum! thrum! of energy swept through him still and he was concerned that it would transfer into her, awaken her, frighten her. He breathed deeply, checked his heart rate. It was elevated, coming down to normal. Her vagina lay open, relaxed between her legs. The ambient temperature of the room was very comfortable with no covers. She made a light buzz noise as she snored on the inhale.

Jack stealthily gently slid from the bed and padded into the bathroom. The clock said 4:27 a.m. He had slept for two hours and fifteen minutes. The dream memory felt like everything had happened in five minutes but those five were spent in the body of a being who held a lifetime of achievement and knowledge. From birth, to killing his board members. He flicked the lights on and stared at the beautiful bathroom. Light orange marble walls with black marble of a different kind lining the corners, where wall met ceiling floor and corners. Jack spread his arms and stretched. He felt fantastic, elated, and empowered somehow buy the psychic baby dream.

After taking a piss he sat at the desk positioned near the bed and pondered the meaning of the dream, wrote it down in every detail he could remember. It was a very significant dream, this he knew, but why he had it, where it came from, what the symbolism of the snowflake was, the mother, the psychic baby, the bio engineering, and all the deaths, was beyond his mind. He needed to speak with someone. Needed insights. Audrey would be so cool right now. Sarah, well, she had not even put on the mask out of curiosity. She was one of those disinterested and uncurious people that achieved a lot but rarely introspected. She was young, vital, and he could see his children being birthed and raised by her... A coke whore's past and an angel's present. That excited Jack, that she had been a slut, that she chose him to marry and put all that behind her was an honor. The naughty thought that perhaps she was still a little wild and may stray to other men merely presented itself as a challenge to keep her. Jack let out a happy sigh. He pushed his books away, flipped around and turned his attentions to Sarah.

Sarah's eyes flashed open the moment he nudged his cock between her legs. Her face registered a surprised disorientation then realization.

"Jack... Let me be... Don't... Fuck me now." She giggled and angled away from his probing dick. "Jeez! Let me sleep, so tired." She said. Jack backed off.

"You sure you don't want this?" He said. He sat on his ankles, leaned back to stroke his cock. Sarah peeked at him and giggled. "Later, I will want it later. Your man ego is so funny right now." She said. Sarah sighed, rolled over to her belly with a flump of her hips. "Sleepy." She said. Jack shrugged as he made a disappointed dog sound. He did feel a bit silly. Rejection sucks. But it wasn't that unreasonable seems how she had awoken to being molested. Audrey had karate chopped him in the neck when he tried that on her.

Jack lay down, determined to sleep, to dream of pleasanter things, to allow himself to go longer in the morning. It was his honeymoon, his lover lay next to him, sated, life was good.

He looked forward to showering with her again. The shower in Michael's guest bedroom had four heads. From his cursory examination, it looked like it was made to enhance sensual soaping and stroking - all showers were made for that. In fact, Jack mused, his hand fondly cupping himself, one might say that our progression of showers has been quite amusing...

A GRAND EXIT

Jack and Sarah sat in Michael's study. Michael was furious. He had just gotten off the phone with Sarah's mother. His last statement to her had instantly produced tears in Sarah's eyes. - "I am sorry we must do this in court Mrs. Lohtelli, I had hoped you would save yourself the money only to lose in two years."

Michael tried his best reassuring smile. "I was just putting her off the real timeline. Helps people procrastinate." He said.

Sarah sniffed and looked at him, there was no stopping the flow of tears, or the soft heaves. Her chin quivered as she attempted to form words.

"She... Is such... A bitch." She managed.

Michael nodded in agreement. Jack moved to put his arm around her but she leaned away. He felt awkward as he reversed the motion and intent of his arm. Words were not coming to him, not the right ones anyway.

"You mother is very much... A most unreasonable woman. Just listening to her smug new money tone made me want to see her in a nasty car accident." Michael said. He chuckled, "Oie! That felt good to say!"

Sarah accepted a tissue offered by Michael and wiped at her nose, then folded it, dabbed at her eyes and cheeks to sop up the tears.

"We can wait two years." Jack said. "Just pretend that you don't actually have millions and live our lives. I have a nice home, a great family. We can build an amazing life together."

Sarah smiled and nodded, her eyes brimming with fresh tears.

"Yes Jack, I know... But we are talking about a lot of money and I... I don't know. Things are so complicated and confusing for me right now..."

Her words sent a small chill through him then a larger twinge of cold dread flared through his stomach. Jack knew this scene was changing, toward scenario two, take the money, sneak around at the Oregon mansion and screw Mrs. Lohtelli.

"What chances do I have of getting the money, guaranteed, within two years?" Sarah asked.

Michael shook his head, a flare of anger on his face. "It will cost a lot, and yes, she could win, but I like a challenge, usually because a challenge costs a lot." He chuckled at his own humor then sobered a bit. "In this case. You are my friends. A twenty percent contingency fee with fees paid to me should I lose would be my deal for friends. Thirty-five percent is for not-friends, and the fees would be higher. In your case, young Jack, I would caution you that the fees may be close to a hundred thousand, two hundred to not-friends."

Jack nodded. Sarah began to cry.

"You wouldn't talk of fees unless you believed there is a chance you may not win." She said. Her voice was soft, sad, watery sounding.

"True. You have a fifty-fifty shot here. Your mother has made great strides in perverting the system and intentions of your fathers will to her own ends. Your own choices with drug dependency and rehab did not help at all I am afraid; gave her the conservatorship. I spoke with a Judge about it on a similar case a while back. He said statutes in Oregon allow for such a thing."

Sarah's eyes brimmed with fresh tears, her chin trembles resumed.

"It's' so... Frustrating. Unfair." She said. "But I did it to myself..."

Her hand tightened around Jack's hand a bit as she spoke. He patted his hand on top of hers.

"We can win. Fifty-fifty shot." Jack said.

"I would bet on me." Michael said. "But I wouldn't bet a hundred grand." He let that sink in, and it did. Jack felt ice gnaw at the pit of his stomach.

"I... Understand..." Sarah said.

"I will take a second mortgage out on my boat if I have to." Jack said. "I would love to see her defeated, destroyed."

Michael shook his head. "No Jack. I won't have you destroy your business, or risk it even, and, when you seek to defeat and destroy, the other side of that is you receiving those things. You can easily destroy yourself seeking vengeance through legal means. I have seen it, used it to build my own fortune, and refuse to do that to you. In fact, nowadays, I advise all my clients to take a step back and carefully consider their own ruin. Then, if they still insist, I take their money. I win most. Loose some. The ones I lose often file bankruptcy."

The sinking sensation grew as he listened to Sarah breathe wet, sad breaths.

The evening view from the balcony of Michael's home was spectacular, Central Park and its ponds below, lined by high rises with windows lit and shrouded by haze on the far side. Sarah sat on a plush leather chair, Jack's feet up in her lap, hers in his, surreptitiously brushing his cock with the soul of her foot as they sipped whiskey together as the sun set.

Jack had let Sarah be alone after the upsetting news from Michael. She told him she needed to think, to put things together in her mind.

He spent the time brooding, fuming, then exploring the San Remo and Central Park across the street. Brooding usually meant sitting with his pen, notebook, objects of power arrayed in a semi-circle on his desk. In this case, he did not want to interrupt Sarah to get his things out of the room. Instead, he asked Hamaul to take him to a stationary shop where he might purchase a pen and paper. Jack found the store to be amazing. It sold a huge variety of pens and stationary, books.

He found an ink pen, of fine flow and weight, very well crafted and when he asked the price he discovered it was a seven-thousand-dollar pen. Jack carefully put it back in its little silk lined box, sort of a mini coffin to him now, and handed it back to the lady who had showed it to him. She smiled, put the pen back under the glass counter, then directed him to pens that very much felt like and wrote like the one he had first selected. Jack purchased a pen for two hundred and fifty dollars and the coolest leather-bound note book he had ever seen for one hundred and twenty dollars. The note book was biblical in appearance with inset gilded writing that Jack assumed was Arabic, but later was told by Michael, that it was Hebraic. It translated to:

"Don't be too sweet lest you be eaten up, yet don't be bitter for you will be spat out."

Jack justified such an expense because he was sensing that he would need to be very thoughtful, mindful, in this new marriage, on how best to elevate his own wealth to compensate Sarah for losing her wealth just to be with him. That, and he also felt, as an odd intuition, that things were about to change. Fresh objects of power for his meditative semi-circle fit the gravity of his situation.

Jack poured Sarah a fresh glass of whiskey over ice - her second, and certainly contributing to her improved moods - as she repeatedly brushed her bare foot back and forth over his groin, an impish smile on her face flickered from time to time.

"And I just want you to know Jack that I love you very much, that I feel... Really torn about what I need to do." Sarah said. She sighed and looked away. "I would be happy with you. I know it. But I just can't let go of the idea of controlling my inheritance and thumbing my nose at my mother."

Jack forced himself to smile, to relax. Sarah had been beating around the bush for the last half hour with her thoughts. He had shared with her his plans, hoped she would find them reassuring. He knew that she did not. She was focused on losing money. He was focused on selling himself for twenty-six million dollars.

"I believe that Michael will win. He is not one to lose." Jack said. He waved his hand around at the opulent terrace they were enjoying waggled the crystal glass of ice and whiskey to emphasize his point.

Sarah nodded, smiled, put a bit more pressure along Jack's inner thigh with the soft pad of her foot.

"He said it himself - he would not bet a hundred grand on winning." She said.

Jack considered, his eyes focused on Sarah's breasts, her nipples erect through the satiny fabric of the house pajamas that Michael had presented them with. He called them wizard clothes. They were very comfortable and, as Jack discovered, not Satin but rather something Michael called Pleasure Silk.

Sarah's blue eyes met his. Her lids were hooded as she gazed at him, a look, Jack read, of love and sadness. But the two did not have to go together. That there was those two together told of failure, of his inability to communicate with her, to persuade her.

"You need to take me back to my mother and take the money she offered." Sarah said. Her voice was soft, but firm. "I will marry Corbin, get my money, divorce him, and marry you."

Jack felt the cold wash in his stomach that correlated with his mind hearing what he dreaded to hear yet it was what he knew she was going to say. He knew, and had been trying to keep the words inside her mouth, wash them from her mind with pictures of success with him, without the money.

He stared down, at her belly button where it sucked in a bit of the smooth dark blue 'wizard' pajamas, opened his mouth to speak but Sarah cut him off.

"I have thought about it a lot Jack, we go back, you get the five hundred thousand, build your businesses for me, the fishing and the furniture design shop you told me of, and in two years I divorce Corbin and marry you, I make a good game of it. I have gone over the scene in my head over and over, you get the money, and in two years you get me, the money, everything." Sarah smiled as she lifted her hips to accentuate the word 'everything'. "At least this way we have a win, we pull one over on her."

Jack met Sarah's eyes as he considered her words. He recalled his plans he had made just this morning, while he couldn't sleep after having the Grand Piano Dream, what he would do if he had a limitless supply of income that twenty-six million would provide. The list had been extensive and excited Jack's imagination which always brought up the energy of motivation. Sarah's eyes were conspiratorial, her little grin, sly. She nodded slightly and Jack believed she knew that he was intrigued with the idea of taking five hundred thousand. He knew that she didn't know that the other implications were that he would find himself obligated to fuck her mother. That was not something he had told her, felt it would be too hurtful.

"Ok... So, I take the money, lose you to Corbin for two years then get you back at the end of two years... Or will the fact that I took the money wiggle into your mind as a nagging doubt, until it is turned around so you begin to resent me for it and your feelings for me grow dim and then you become angry, spiteful, regretful that I sold you out for cash, that I let you get screwed by another man while I waited like a drooling dog for the money? Then, in the end of that scenario, your mother wins. She gets us to compromise our values, and that is like a seed she plants and will take delight when it comes to fruition."

Sarah studied him like a bug and shook her head 'no'.

"Stubborn Irish." She grinned. "That is what my dad always called Irish people he did business with. Said he had never met a more obstinate race and he resented losing ground to them... A lot. He had a grudging admiration for them, that is why I began to date Corbin, he is Irish, like you, last name Cole but his mums is Byrne, and he is indeed, stubborn but stupid also. It is a combination that is disgusting to me after meeting you." Sarah said. She nudged his prick and balls with her foot as she spoke, smiled, and sighed. "You have a perfect cock, it gives me great pleasure, I will be wanting it back in two years." She began to giggle and took a large swig of whisky. Jack chuckled with her, took another sip, he had no intention of going to deep in the cup.

Sarah was proposing a con. He liked that idea. Separate the bitch mother from a fraction of her money with the secret plot, the twist, being that they did it together, and planned to marry once Sarah got her inheritance signed over to her any way. There was a very big part of him that wanted to go through with the deal. So much so that Jack had a hard time dismissing the idea as possible or something to do.

"I admit. The plan intrigues me. It could be fun, like cloak and daggers type secrecy... But, I can't go through with it. I won't take the money..." Jack said. "It is like selling you and... I won't do it. It would be a stain on our souls to do it."

"Are you serious? You are so holy that you can't just beat a woman at her own game for fuck's sake?" Sarah snapped. Jack was taken back a bit, the pressure of her foot on his crotch grew with the intensity of her words. He pulled back from her a bit.

"I won't sell you and I don't need the money, I am wealthy, by most standards, have plans and vision. You are being just as stubborn as I am. You can take a fifty-fifty shot and have Michael beat her in court. That would be justice and I honestly believe in justice."

Tear spilled down Sarah's cheeks but she was beaming a red cheeked smile at him."

"You are being a stubborn Irish fool. But noble." She said. "Justice is for hire, bought and sold, she with the most money to burn wins."

Jack knew she loved him more for not taking the money. A fool. Yes. An honorable fool. The world was full of them. They wrote the constitution, founded the country. Jack, felt he was in good company. He did, however, feel like a stubborn Irishman right then, utter conviction blazed in his eyes, his chest broad, proud. He nodded his head.

"Did you father loose ground often to the stubborn Irish?" He asked.

"Yes, Jack, he did at times." Sarah beamed a smile at Jack, her eyes rimmed with tears. "Two years. I go to Corbin prison for two years, then I get you back." She said.

Jack awoke as Sarah moved silently to put her clothes on. It was seven in the morning. Haumal had agreed to give her a ride to the airport so she could catch the first flight back to Oregon.

He pretended to be asleep. It was difficult. He wanted to leap from the bed, tell her she was being stupid. Tell her she was being a whore for her own money. They had fucked much, drank too much, argued, kissed it away, fucked, argued some more. She wanted him to take the money, do the con, he wanted her to take the risk and do the legal battle. There were tears, frustrations, rabid argument, anger that rather embarrassed Jack. It had been a long night and well into the morning. They had fallen asleep, holding each other, sideways on the king-sized bed somewhere between four and five am.

She left a note and slipped away. Again.

Jack leapt from the bed as soon as he heard the door snick shut and snatched the note up.

"I am, in my heart, your wife, and always will be. I love you with an abandon that I have never felt. Two years, Jack, and we will marry. We will be wealthy. You can use the money to build and create anything you wish. You wouldn't sell me for half a million. You love me. You let me go. I promise I will come back to your arms. I am your wife, and always will be."

Jacks eyes brimmed with tears, his throat closed as if a sad pair of fleshy tongs pinched it together. He folded the note and put it in the middle pages of his newly purchased leather journal, ran his fingers over the soft surface of the beautiful book, and let himself cry. It was better to let it out, get rid of it, than hold it in. His mom had taught him that.

"Fuck Sarah and her family bullshit and her millions and her stupid mom." Jack fumed. He stood in front of Neufeld's bathroom mirror. He ached though. Inside. The painful welling in his throat took his breath away. Before he could finish uttering the words tears spilled down his cheeks again. Love. Pissed away for money. When he had more than most... A nice boat and purse seine permit for Prince William Sound. A lifestyle of freedom and beauty that few would ever know, danger and strategy, craftsmanship. A leader of industry, a scion, heir of Prince William Sound. He punched the ornately stained concrete wall by the mirror three times. Not so he would break his hand. Just so he could feel the skin on the knuckles tear and burn a bit. Then took a breath, looked at himself in the mirror and locked eyes with his image, and did the take back.

"*She wasn't right for you, not like Audrey, still likes her cocaine. This way is better. You should have taken the money.*" He smiled and nodded. Anger flowed through him, there was nowhere to direct it, he did not want to punch the wall again. He did the take back again. "*She wasn't right for you, there are better out there somewhere.*"

She left him for twenty-six million dollars. That amount of money... Maybe he would leave her too. The place they were staying was worth well over ten million. Jack stared around at the bathroom's opulence and design. The shower was an amazing curl of stone and marble work, tastefully done to resemble stepping into a tree. Once inside there was six different shower heads that jetted hard or could be tuned to sprinkle soft. The bathroom was worth more than his boat.

"I will make her mother pay for this. I will become wealthy and spend it all on private investigators to poke and prod at her every movement, surround her with spies she thinks are friends, and eventually, will have her put in jail where she will become a glove for bull dyke's amusements." Jack said between clenched teeth. He was breathing hard, amped, every muscle straining as he spoke.

He took a breath, forced himself to relax, to calm, shoved his mind into a more rational space. His body shuddered as he let muscles loosen, his breath turning deep and even. The memory of the Grand Piano dream flooded his mind. He knew what it meant. Clearly. Like a sudden revelation, unbidden, very welcome. He smiled at himself. The violence and symbol of the dream flooded him and he felt his pain morph into and odd knowing, acceptance mixed with determination. Jack knew, he had just killed Carl, the man who held onto things too much.

FRANCE. WHY NOT?

Jack circled his items of power. The expensive pen, crafted by Aurora, the cheapest pen they made, bore an important weight in his fingers, new significance. He had purchased it believing that the pen and book would represent a new, married, happy, and wealthy, phase of his life.

A sad grin formed on his face as he opened the ornate leather-bound book to a fresh, crisp, white page, admired the feel and quality of the paper he was about to ink with his Aurora. His intuition had been correct, the new pen and book signified change. He began devising plans that were within his own means, of his own creation and elation grew as he did so - this was pure, no con money, no married money, just his own, that which he had created. A bit of humor began to tick away at his foul mood and soon the foul mood, was gone. The pen flashed over pages as Jack formulated and postulated plans, ideas, and plots as inspiration poured through him.

Jack's smile was huge as he closed the book, sheathed the pen, sipped the last of his coffee. He felt as if he had been rewarded for doing the right thing with inspiration and motivation, anger channeled into productivity with the drive of revenge behind it balanced now by gratitude for his inspiration, for his reverie.

With this sense of elation Jack made his way to the kitchen, hunger rumbling his stomach. There was a young lady there, dressed as if she were a combination of a chef and a chemist. Her apothecary gown also had an apron sewn into it.

"Hello Jack." She said.

"Hi, um…" He raised his eyebrows for her to fill in her name.

"Amanda." She said.

"Amanda!" Jack said. He extended his hand but she smiled and bowed instead.

"Hands are filthy… Especially honeymooner's hands." She said and giggled.

Jack smiled sadly and shook his head. He bowed back, eyes on hers as he did so.

"We decided to get an annulment and she went back to her fiancé."

"Yes, I heard that, I would leave you for the money too if that helps you feel better." She said.

Jack laughed abruptly and loud. "It does. It makes me feel a lot better." He smiled a broad smile.

Amanda beamed right back at him.

"I can see why Michael likes you so much. So… You know what's great after getting dumped for money?"

Jack nodded vigorously. "Food." He said.

He cast his eyes about the kitchen. Amanda had rows of bottles set out and was pouring a mixture of something into each one then sealing them with a well-crafted lever worked into a glass and rubber stopper that latched the stopper down tight.

"Oh…" Amanda said. "I was going to say break up sex." She winked and slid one of the bottles closest to the large refrigerator over the stainless-steel counter top towards Jack. "Drink one of those and wait twenty minutes, then tell me if you are still hungry."

The liquid inside the bottle swirled with chia seeds, Jack could see that much, they looked like fat little frog's eggs.

"What is in it?" He asked.

"Mr. Neufeld's breakfast. Chia seeds in a mixture of green tea, ginkgo biloba, ginseng, honey and cinnamon." She said.

Jack uncapped the bottle and took an experimental swig of the concoction. He savored the texture of the seeds swollen fat with the elixir Amanda had created. The cinnamon and sweet honey mixed well with the ginseng and ginkgo biloba.

"It is delicious." Jack said. He took another longer drink, then downed half the bottle, paused to let the thick liquid settle in his stomach.

"You know what chia seeds are?" Amanda asked.

Jack nodded. "Super food, I have had a hippie girlfriend or two and am very fond of them."

"The hippie girl friend or the chia seeds?" Amanda asked. As she spoke she worked. Her hands automatically moved doing something she must have done a thousand times. There was a fluid grace and care in her actions.

"Both." Jack said. He chuckled as he watched Amanda grin and shake her head.

"Tell me about your life and boat and fishing and Alaska." She said.

Jack smiled and nodded, charmed by her candor, her enthusiasm, and, he was shocked with himself to admit, her playful sexiness. She had wavy brown hair that was mostly in a bun, a longish nose, humped ever so slightly, and warm, merry brown eyes, lashes done perfectly and large to frame them. He suppressed the urge to be the noble hurt beast, the noble victim, just dumped by his love, and instead embraced the idea of being a bit of a rogue. Mark Remua's voice popped into his head then, "Love is just a chemical trick in the mind. Lust, that is the better chemical's, less binding, less... forever and ever until death do you part." Jack giggled a bit as he recalled Mark's tone and expression. He stopped short as he saw that Amanda looked a bit put off by his odd laughter.

"Sorry, I just had a bit of an epiphany. I do that often." He said and grinned.

Amanda nodded thoughtfully. "What was the epiphany? If you care to divulge I would be interested to know."

"It was that... That I am free, no longer bound to love one person, that I can take you up on your offer of break up sex if you want and that I need to call my friend Mark in France."

Amanda burst out laughing, nearly spilled a bottle of dry powder. "I made a bad joke... I am married myself." She said.

Jack shook his head; an apologetic look on his face. "Oh, I am sorry, I respect the union of man and women in holy matrimony. Was going there myself until just recently."

"Are you still determined to do so?" Amanda asked.

Jack considered her large brown eyes thoughtfully, noted the twitch of her lips, the direction her eyes moved down his torso then back up to his eyes.

"I am not sure right now." He answered.

"I made a bad choice with my husband. He drinks a lot and is always at work." Amanda said. She shrugged and licked her lips, eyes hungry, walked towards him from behind the counter, her hand releasing the loose bun to allow her wavy long brown hair to fall around her shoulders. She looked like a hungry lioness as she prowled up to him. She placed her hand on his face and pulled him down a bit, her lips parting, tongue slipping against his. Jack felt odd as they kissed. It was sweat, a nice kiss, a hungry kiss, the kiss of lust. He slipped his hands into her pants, cupped her ass and pulled her to him with a sigh and a little laugh. His knuckles stung where her pants rubbed against the swollen split open skin, reminded him that he was only a little while ago hurt and upset and betrayed.

"Break up sex is exactly what you need right now, Jack." Amanda said.

Jack wondered, as they entered his room within Michael Neufeld's home, if the wile lawyer had set him up.

It was a vigorous and pleasurable half hour or so later that Jack strolled with a confident gate to the living room where, in the far-left corner, he had noticed an area that looked like a leather drenched desk and lounge. It was on a platform that two long steps reached from the living room, had a half wall at the top for a bit of privacy. He was pleased to see that it was indeed designed to provide a quiet space to concentrate, to focus. He took a seat at the small desk and immediately felt enveloped in the pleasing aesthetics. To his left were windows framing the garden terrace, to his right wooden book shelves placed just a bit higher than the half wall. It was an alcove adorned with clever drawers and cupboards.

Jack ran his hand over the surface of the desk, studied its thick varnish. He chuckled when he noticed the name 'Ziggy' carved into the wood had been varnish over rather than sanded out – then wondered if perhaps this had been Ziggy's desk while he lived with his father.

He placed his near empty bottle of Chia Tea on a felt lined wooden coaster. It was his second bottle – Amanda had given it to him from the refrigerator, told him it was even better with a chill on it. As she spoke she flushed a beam at him, strands of wavy brown hair pasted to her cheek with sweat, saliva and perhaps a bit of other bodily fluids. She had told him that she wanted seconds once she was done with her work in the kitchen, that he would need the extra energy from the super food.

Jack pulled up the chair, sat, and found it molded to his body just right.

"Man, I want to be rich someday." Jack said. He glanced about appreciatively at his surroundings and inhaled the subtle smells of wood polish, leather, and a hint of sandalwood incense from a small brass brazier set on one of the clever shelves worked into the alcove. He associated sandalwood with being lazy, with being stoned and lethargic, wondered if it was Ziggy's or Michael's.

The phone on the desk was a cordless. Jack picked it up, saw that it had the buttons in the handset as he studied it. This was the first time he had used a cordless phone. He had thought having phone service on the boat was damn cool, now this, even better, he could walk around the dock with one of these. He placed the phone into his circle of power, Le Pen next to his Aurora, at the ready, Chia Tea, new leather-bound book, and his spiral notebook that he kept his addresses in. The notebook looked shabby next to the leather one yet held far more value as its pages contained information where the leather bound elegant book was near empty. He briefly considered transferring, by hand, all the information into the new book and chuckled as he rejected the notion. Tedious. Let the new book have a life of its own, and evolution of its own.

Each of Jack's books, in his imagination, were magical tomes. He wrote things in them, worked to make them become real, and they did, sometimes. Magic, to Jack was real, it was prayer with action and sweat, that resulted in a new thing created, a new situation better than the old, a positive change in conformity. Magic.

Jack settled in and dialed Mark's phone number on the cordless phone.

He found his friend open and excited about the idea of him paying visit. Mark had a couple of weeks to burn. Also, turned out that he was intuitive regarding Jack's sudden decision to visit.

"Don't worry my friend. I will introduce to you many beautiful girls and you can have them all. Ha ha. A rich boat Captain from Alaska. We shall have such an easy time of it."

When Jack finished his phone call he had a new gleam in his eye. He stood and whooped. "Fuck it! I am going to France. Why not?"

The day dream was hatching more day dreams. He now had to arrange other things, like passport and cashier's checks to travel with. Jack took a long drink from the glass Amanda had given him.

"Chia Tea kicks ass!" He growled. Jack stood and stretched confident that he would be able to introduce Amanda to some fun Otter Tai Chi once she was ready for another go.

THE HIEROPHANT

"Your hand looks as if you punched a wall or something." Michael said. He chuckled knowingly.

"Young love is a bitch and her mother certainly is as well." Michael busied himself making coffee for two as he spoke. They were on the terrace, it was a little after seven in the evening. Michael stood at the bar set behind a row of tall potted trees with the huge yellow flowers, Angel's Trumpets Agatha had told him they were.

"Yes, young love is to be denied nothing…" Jack said. He gave a short laugh as he fiddled with his smokes and relished the scent of strong Turkish coffee brewing.

"I did appreciate the excellent Chia Tea that Amanda let me have from your kitchen." Jack said. He studied Michael to see if the man had a flicker of mischief in his eyes or face. He detected nothing.

Michael smiled. "Amanda is a skilled apothecary. I am glad you had a chance to meet her." Michael said. "It is unfortunate that she is married to a cave man. I am sure she told you. Tells all my house guests that." He began to laugh as Jack reddened.

"It is amazing how fast a beautiful, intelligent, and willing woman can help ease the frustrations of being dumped for money isn't it?" Michael's eyes were warm, merry, he was not in the least feeling guilty for having arranged a tryst.

"I suppose not." Jack said. He nodded, smiled, and sipped his coffee. "Can we talk a bit? I need some wisdom of the ages advice."

Michael faked a hurt look. "I might be getting a bit up there in years but I certainly don't think I qualify as aged wise one... However, I am willing to hear you out and give you my take on things. "

They retired to the seats where they had dinned the evening before and there, Jack finally lit the cigarette he had been fiddling with for over an hour. He sat back on the comfortable chair and exhaled a plum of blueish smoke away from and downwind of Michael. The air was warm, humid, the smells of plants and soil competing with the smoke.

"I need to know where to take my business. Commercial fishing in Alaska is all I know. I have seventy-seven thousand dollars in savings and my boat and gear are worth half a million. I only owe a little over half that on her. People are getting faster boats, some with three engines that power along at 15 knots. Um... I am going to France to visit for a couple weeks so let's say I have seventy thousand." Jack said.

Mike nodded, his eyes knowing. He pulled a wooden box from under the table and opened it.

"Cigar? I recommend the third one from the left."

"Cuban?"

Michael made a spit noise. "Certainly not. Virginia grows much better tobacco."

Jack laughed. Nodded. He selected a cigar and sipped his coffee as Michael produced glasses, ice, and a half full bottle of Scotch. Michael said nothing as his hands arranged the glasses and ice, poured, snipped the end of his cigar, handed Jack the tiny guillotine.

After each had gotten their cigars lit Michael raised his glass.

"The coffee was great, Scotch is better for relaxation and it is much better with a full glass of ice. Trust me. It's true." Michael said with an odd grin. He had poured each glass half full over the ice. Jack raised his glass and clinked it against Michael's.

"If you say so, it must be true." He took a sip. It burned with a slight wood smoke after flavor.

"At your young age, you have accomplished a lot. I was taught that I must own my own means of production to be wealthy. So, I became a good lawyer. I certainly own me. "Michael smiled, sipped his Scotch. "Your boat and fishing business is your means of production and you own it, at least so long as you make payment to the bank. But it is like farming. It is subject to circumstance. What if the government suddenly decided fishing is bad and shuts it down? What if your equipment breaks at all the wrong times, two years in a row?"

Jack laughed. "Now you sound like my mother, she is always painting worst case scenarios."

Michael nodded. "You should listen to your mother as well." He said with a grin. He then leaned forward, his face serious.

"If I were you I would continue with the college." Mike said. "You have a massive mind and will do well in any field of study you take on. You keep your business with fishing, learn finance, keep great credit to avoid high interest rates." Michael shrugged. "That is really the best advice I can give. You do those things and you will be better off than ninety-five percent of everyone in the United States financially. In that you get to work a beautiful boat in the waters of Prince William Sound, well, that part, young Jack, is a wealth that few will ever know."

Jack looked at Michael and nodded. His words were true. He let them sink in, the sincerity of Michael's voice was that of experience, he had been there, a silly grin of gratitude on the man's face most of the time. Jack now felt that same gratitude and his regard for Michael grew fonder. The gratitude lessened the suppressed pain of having Sarah return to her mother. His desire for revenge, while still hot, lessened, cooled a bit, with letting go. But just a bit, a moment of no wind to fan the flames.

"Better off than ninety-five percent isn't what I am after. I want to be in the top one percent. I want to be able to pay people to legally hold Mrs. Lohtelli down while other people I pay piss on her, and get away with it because there is a statute that I twisted that says I can get away with it." Jack said.

As he spoke felt his blood surge. He clenched his fists as rage and a lust for revenge surged through him.

"Her mother offered me five hundred thousand to return Sarah to her, offered me a little more than that actually." Jack said. He pictured Sarah's mother, on her knees, his cock in her, it would have been an angry revenge fuck thinly veiled as a 'good fuck' - felt ashamed, yet excited, the rage now mingling with lust.

"You did not take the money?" Michael asked. His eyes were alight with a keen flicker of interest and curiosity.

"No. Sarah wanted me to. She said she would play along, escort her home. But, I said no. I feel like such a moron right now. I mean, Sarah was fun, she even liked my Sea Otter Tai Chi." Jack said. "I was just getting to know her better…"

Michael laughed. "What is Sea Otter Tai Chi?" He asked.

Jack grinned. "It is a sexual thing. Shall I go on?"

Michael nodded eagerly.

"Male Sea Otters brutally rape female Sea Otters, or so it seems as we humans watch and anthropomorphize. I watched them. Mating. Violently. And slowed it down into Ty Chi." Jack said. He shrugged, felt a bit self-conscious. "The way Otters behave sexually was pointed out to me by a young Eyak girl, she then asked me to wrestle with her, I just took it from there."

"I see." Michael said. "So, you… Raped Sarah?"

Jack shook his head and laughed. "No! Not at all. It is a dance, a measured resistance, slow, consensual."

Michael frowned and shook his head. "I guess I don't get it, or, maybe I do, it just has to sink in. I will try it with Agatha after explaining it to her… She is a third-degree black belt."

Jack laughed at the earnest expression on Michael's face, it delighted him that he had taught his teacher something that the man found interesting.

"So, tell me, please Michael, what you see, in the way of aiding me business and life wise. Right now, I am sitting on this most amazing balcony overlooking Central Park, I just lost a love, and twenty-six million dollars, and am about to say 'fuck everything' and go to France." Jack began. His switch from laughing to his serious 'appeal to the father' voice caught Michael off guard.

"I blew off registering for this semester of college so I could chase Sarah. If I stuck to my plan, I would be in college, studying Psychology towards my Masters, business being my minor to help me learn about my own business and how to run it…"

Mikael laughed with a sort of downward tone. His derision a bit unsettling. Jack shut his mouth and stared at him.

"You must trust me on this. And remember that you asked my sage advice. Drop the Psych degree and just major in business. You will be better off.

Even better, major in Computer Science. That is where our economy is heading. Everyone wants a computer. Everyone plays games. Get a degree in creating video games and you will live a charmed life. Had you majored in business you would have taken the half million as Sarah suggested."

Jack gazed at Mike for a moment not believing that he had just told him he should have taken the money. His decision to let Sarah go without the money element was honorable, the right thing to do. Out of everything else, this part made him feel intact.

Mike saw his look and stopped talking for a moment. Shrugged.

"You asked for my 'sage' advice. Think about it. You two pull a con on mom. You get the five hundred thousand, or at least have a chance at it, and I could have advised you very aptly in how to go about locking her in on that. All the while you profess your love for each other in both scenarios. So, the honorable and noble thing you did is nullified. Her mother got her back either way except you don't have five hundred thousand. In a sense, Jack, taking the money would have been the more-right thing to do. At least her mother is compensating you for your loss in some way, for the two years until you two can reconcile your love. However, and I concede this, I have a higher level of respect and regard for you because you gave up the money. I just like the argument that the money was also the right path." Michael shrugged, smiled his charming genuine smile once again. "Indeed, that you did not take the money, that you sacrificed that, means a great deal, not financially, financially it was the um... dumber thing to do, but on a soul level, you preserved a portion of it, a spiritual purity, hands clean, conscious clean, much more valuable pay off long-term."

Michael said nothing as Jack digested.

"I weighed your argument, your position, with Sarah, she said much the same."

"When you refused, she was relieved, loved you even more." Michael said in soft tone. He puffed his cigar and studied Jack for a moment then leaned forward once again.

"Jack, do you have any knew names to add to the list?" He asked.

The question took Jack by surprise for a moment. It was usually him who brought up the Lucidian agenda with Michael.

"Yes, a couple, you?"

Neufeld nodded. "I do indeed, eight in all." He said. His voice was lowered, conspiratorial. "The people whose names I am going to give you Jack have to be very secret. They are not ones to be taken lightly, the connections and power runs deep through this country and the world. I have been think-ing about whether to give them to you." Michael's eyes held Jack's, the full weight of his words hit him and a flush of prickles swept up his spine.

"And because I turned down the money you have decided I am worthy?"

Michael laughed. Nodded. "Far more valuable long-term young Jack." Michael sat back in his chair a satisfied expression on his face.

"Twenty-six million? The names of Lucidian's I give you are of very inter-ested billionaires my friend. What you do with them, how you find the right path, is going to be interesting."

Jack shook his head, smiled. "You are kinda scarring the shit out of me right now. You and I talked about forming a thing, a Lucidian thing, but I thought it was just a collection, like if I needed a good mechanic, look at my list, find a Lucidian mechanic and hire him, a common mind support system of sorts, like the Mormons do, like a sleeper cell."

Michael laughed. "Well yes, it was fun drunken conversation we had but over the past two years since the idea has resonated with other people dur-ing fun drunken conversations and those conversations evolved into plans. You Jack, are the father of those plans. All these people want to meet you and I have arranged an introduction, no easy task I warn you." He eyed Jack, dead serious. "Do you agree, beforehand to meet with them, should I arrange an introduction?"

Jack nodded automatically before the doubts came flooding in to make him hesitate, to stop nodding his dumb head. He had no idea what he was agree-ing to.

"They have one thing in common with you Jack, vision, lucid visions and they fear death, the events that they have experienced in dream and life are much weaker than those you are feeling and dealing with. I had you moni-tored in your room. You awoke on fire, literally, from a dream, reached for Sarah and pulled back, you knew you were on fire, the Kundalini, it would have transferred into her body and you knew it would have startled her, made her think you are weird."

Jack felt his jaw tighten. He took a sip of Scotch.

"What do you mean you had me monitored? Even while I was naked? Sarah?"

Michael shook his head no. "Of course not, just the dream time, we are not interested in sex."

"We?"

"Agatha and I."

"Oh." Jack sipped the last of his Scotch. "Can I have more?" He asked.

Michael smiled and poured. "Will you wait two years for your Sarah?"

"Do you think I should wait for her to come back to me?" Jack asked.

Michael shook his head."Love advice I am not good at. I know it hurts. That I know. More when you are young. But... Life is short! Live it! Go to France. Enjoy the pleasures there. Your friend is well connected if his last name is Rembua. Luke Rembua is one of the best nuclear physicists in the world. He has aided France in dominating the nuclear energy field."

Jack nodded. "Yes, I met him, an interesting man, was difficult to talk to at first but he loosened up a bit after a while." He took a sip of the fresh Scotch let it linger in him mouth as he stared at the Central Park skyline.

"I was not suited for psychology. You are right. One time, I wanted to slap a woman as she was talking about her cold-hearted father and tell her to just get over it, she was beautiful, didn't need his approval. When I told my Professor, who I ended up in a two-year relationship with, she laughed and said that I may lack the needed empathy to be a good psychologist."

"Ah? You got to do the teacher? Good for you. "Michael smiled and nodded. "Not me, all my professors were men."

"She is a good woman. I left her for Sarah. She really wasn't one for monogamy anyway. Life is short. I wanted kids with Sarah. "Jack sighed. He felt, for a moment, sheepish about dithering over his love issues with Michael but it was a convenient shift from the weight of being spied on like a lab rat and the prospect of their fun Lucidian thing turning a bit more real.

"She left. Without daring to argue with me any further. Just. Left. Second time." Jack inhaled, got a mental grip, shifted subjects."Computers huh? I have drawn designs for a computer room with video cameras. Sort of a mad scientist fantasy. I am interested but suck at math unless I am using it to count money. Then I seem to get by ok."

Mike laughed. "If they taught kids the correlation between math and money and how to use it to make money many more would love math... I don't do the higher math well at all myself. That's why I am a lawyer." Mike smiled at his own humor for a bit and then his face took on a look of keen interest. He reached into his pocket and pulled out a small red leather-bound book and handed it to Jack.

"I want you to have this, it is a copy of my own list of Lucidian's. Your name is among them. I have been compiling them ever since you and I spoke long ago of dreaming while awake. Agatha, I am very happy to say, is also in the book."

Jack nodded, his heart thudded with excitement. He reached out to accept the book, a happy elation flooding through him, followed by staggering weight, gravity, the very reason he had purchased a two hundred and fifty-dollar pen, that, and it was amazingly well balanced.

"I will arrange for you to meet these people when you get back from France, your time there will no doubt season you a bit for things outside your comfort zone.

Jack spent the rest of the evening on the phone. He paid for an open-end round-trip ticket to France, spoke with his father to let him know where he was and what had happened, also to let him know his itinerary. Robert McKnight handled the news with a good natured grunt, told him to fuck often and varied for a while. That, to Robert McKnight, was the answer to a good deal many issues. More surprising was that Neufeld not only agreed with Robert on that accord, but had already set up a hot session with his own Apothecarist. It was no wonder that Robert and Michael had clicked so well together so many years ago.

Jack then began to work on a passport - which meant a call to his mom was in order. He smiled as he compared his relationship with his mother to Sarah and hers. He felt gratitude as the phone rang.

"Hello?" It was the sing song voice his mom answered with when she was in a good mood.

"Hi Mom it's Jack."

"Jack! What are you up to? Off gallivanting around with that girl?"

Jack smiled. He knew his dad would tell her everything. He also knew his mom would want to hear it from him first.

He told her the story. She was excited for him even as she expressed her usual doubts.

"You are young. Have a great adventure. And send me some post cards from France. Nothing bawdy, only tasteful because I want to share them with some friends I sit boards with. That way I can brag about you and maybe get you an introduction to one of their daughters."

"You know, mom, that sounds a bit like Sarah's mom, but on a much more acceptable and reasonable level." Jack said. He laughed as she giggled.

"Guilty I suppose..." Rebecca said.

"I will send you both mom. You and dad can enjoy the bawdy ones and the tasteful ones I will tailor to attract the ladies. I need you to overnight my passport to me here in New York."

Jack stopped talking as his mother made a happy little sigh.

"Oh Jack! It was so wonderful to hear you say those words. It delights me that you are going to France on a whim, that you value having different experiences."

"Focus mom, the passport is at my house, in a lock box. Key to it is in a magnet box, under it, in a little hidden drawer. The lock box is under the desk in my bedroom. Brian is renting the place so please call him before you go over."

"Oh Jeez. Yes. I can. I will bet you need it sooner than later too. I will call him. Got your guys number still from when you were living there."

"Thank you! You are my favorite Mom. "

Rebecca McKnight laughed.

"I am your only mom you turd."

"Yes mom. But I have met other people's mom's and you still rank at the top."

"What? Just at the top?"

"Well, there are some pretty hot moms out there." Jack said.

He laughed as his mom gave a gasp of mock indignation.

Rebeca then sighed. "I am sorry that girl picked money over you. I was thinking it would be nice to play with some grandkids."

"Yeah... That was something I found rather pleasing to think on too mom. But I guess it just wasn't meant to be, yet."

WINTER 88 INTO 89

AK ZEN

Jack sat at the computer in his old bedroom in his parents' house in Anchorage. He had rented out his own home to Brian and company and was too proud to ask Audrey if he could move back in with her, so it was back home for a semester, like he was eighteen all over again. His father, Robert, had chastised him for the poor planning at first, then admitted that at least he was sensible enough not to waste money on a rental. Truth was though, Jack could have moved back into his house on Upper O'Malley, there was a bedroom coming free in January when one of the tenants headed to Kodiak. Intuition kept him from moving back in, he knew on a level that it would be better to stay with his folks for a short time.

Jack took a sip of his coffee, it was still hot, fresh and had that acrid zing he liked. He inhaled the scents of date and pumpkin bread baking in his mother's kitchen, heard her talking with his father as she stirred another batch of bread in her big green Tupperware bowl that she had used since he was a child. Good things came from that big green plastic bowl. Jack took another sip of his coffee. All was right in the world. His warm peaceful feeling was replaced with determination and a grim set of the jaw as he returned his attention to the computer monitor, stared at the drawings.

Christmas music played from the house speakers. Something Jack loved. Built in speakers. He was designing a top house for his dream boat on the computer. He could see it in his mind, sketch it out with detail on paper, but translating it into a usable format on the computer was painstakingly slow. Frustrating. He worked with the cheap little Computer Aided Drafting system he had purchased all the while fighting the urge to use pen and paper.

The Top House of a commercial fishing boat was essentially a command center in Jack's mind. Being able to communicate with not just the crew on the deck or in the cabin but the rest of the world as well was important. The radios, the PA system, and the SatCom all had to be neatly arranged out of the way, yet convenient to the reach, of the navigation electronics. Incorporated into his designs were built in speakers with the ability to pipe the music all through the boat or just one area or the other, then cut out the music so the voice could over-ride and be heard by the crew. The captains seat placement and adjustments were what he was fiddling with now, adjusting the likely dimensions needed, however, required an actual physical reality. Jack worked for a good while then stood and stretched, shook off his frustrations with the slowness of the CAD system. Or was it his slowness? He didn't care.

France had been a very good time. Simultaneously relaxing and exciting. Mark had taken him under his wing and showed him around, introduced him to some of the best brothels where Jack realized that sex with the emotion of love attached to it was far better than sport fucking. His lusts were sated but not his heart. Sarah was ever present in his mind.

"You are silly American! All bound up like... Like constipated with this love for zat blond. She will only get fat and dumpy via time. Surely you know this?"

Mark's sage advice. Jack grinned as he recalled the look on his friend's face as he spoke.

In spite of his moral high ground on the love and sex mixed thing, Jack was quite pleased that he could say he that he had been to a brothel in France. Learned a couple new techniques - something he might share with Sarah. He lingered longer in France than intended, visited many villages along Route Du Vin that had him convinced that J.R.Tolkien had visited these same areas and used them to describe the Hobbit's Shire in his books. The wine was good, hearty, deep purples and reds, tasted of the earth and soil he could run his fingers through. He met families that had lived and cultivated wines for centuries, developed a great love and respect of their heritage. He steered Mark towards less of a planned debauchery across France to a more educationally significant experience. Jack sought fervently for French Lucidians, talked long nights, in broken English with respectful attempts at the language of the Gaul's. He fell in lust with and seduced several young country girls in little local dives and found this far more exciting that the polished feminine charms of the courtesans that delicately spread their legs for any gentleman with the right introduction and cash payment.

Jack's hopes of landing Sarah were still high. There had been six letters waiting for him when he got home. Each one full of promise and love. She was with Corbin, the wedding set for January. But Sarah was faithful in her heart. Jack took solace in that amid feelings of betrayal and an odd sort of conspiratorial excitement. Sarah detailed out her steps towards gaining her money and divorcing the drug ridden clod in each letter. Then filled the rest with sexy love stuff that made Jacks heart pump.

It was cold. Just a week before Christmas. Minus twenty. A rare cold snap. The big house his dad had built on Zurich Street occasionally made a snap-creak noise, it's complaint to the cold outside. Inside though, the home was warm and smelled good. The tree was trimmed, warmth and gold light flooded the big open kitchen and living room. Jack had helped his mom and dad decorate earlier in the afternoon while sipping hot buttered whiskeys and telling tales of France and his travels.

From his bedroom window Jack admired the sheen of the Cook Inlet and Kink Arm. The ocean glowed pink with the last rays of the setting sun. It was a bit past four in the afternoon. Golden hour in Anchorage in December. Jack considered both ends of the suns journey, morning, and night as a beautiful design that proved god loved his children. The very thought made him feel a pleasurable reassurance, a resonance and appreciation of the work that went into creating the world. Whenever he could, he paused in his day to catch the rising or setting sun and just watch, in awe. Today his admiration was especially appreciative because it drew his attention away from the frustration of using the cad program over a more fluid sketch on paper.

Jack rolled his chair away from the keyboard and monitor to the corner of his desk where he faced the window. His fingers pressed a section of wall paneling inward to release a catch then open outward to reveal a small ventilation fan he had installed to hide his smoke habits. He flicked a toggle switch, also hidden between rows of books, to the on position to activate the fan he had installed in the wall and pulled open a drawer containing his cigarettes, ashtray, and lighter.

He stood and stretched as he looked out the window then glared over at the computer monitor. Like it or not, the CAD program was, in Jack's mind, a magical portal that his ideas had to pass through to reality, so he was determined to master it. It looked so much more professional to describe a project using the computer generated prints, was an industry standard he had to meet and best.

Jack turned his attention back to the sunset and smiled as it dawned on him that there would be a day when he would sketch out a design and have someone push it through the CAD portal for him. Save time, be more creative. He nodded, satisfied in the assumption that he would one day have help in building things.

Bright sparkles of ice crystals filled the air, made halos and beams of the street lights. Dark clouds overhead... Jack marveled at the contrast of the bank of dark clouds, heavy with coming snows, the bright band of sunlight on the horizon and how it lit up the underbelly of the black clouds. It was an ominously beautiful effect that meant it was going to warm up a bit and snow. A white coat of fresh snow for Christmas, could be a couple inches, could be a couple feet.

The desk Jack sat at was one of his own design that he had built, and continued to modify while he was in high school. It was a simple g shape that took up the width of the room curved down the walls, an L shape at the window end and a wraparound at the other end. He had been very proud of it, prior to being at Michael Neufeld's desk. Now it seemed a bit drab. Neufeld did not even have to sketch things, he could just tell someone what he wanted to create and pay them to do it.

Jack sat down and lit a smoke, his hand on his coffee cup, eyes on the horizon and steadily shrinking sunlight. He watched the fan suck the smoke out of the room. This was a clever piece of work he had done while in high school that required clandestine planning to hide the fact he was cutting a hole in the outer wall of the house to install the fan that he wanted to suck his pot smoke out of the room, so his mother and father wouldn't smell it. His mom, however, found it - helped keep the secret because she liked to sneak a smoke in now and again even though dad had quit. In time, it became their special thing, a late-night smoke.

Rebeca began to get increasingly open as Jack grew up, became a man. She shared things with him regarding his father that he found amusing and rather adventurous where as his father rarely talked of his youthful exploits and dealings. Their life in Cordova had been rather fantastic and Jack certainly had not wanted to leave at the time his father sold the big house, built the place on Zurich.

The fan was rather ingenious he thought. It sucked air out of the room at a high rate. He could smoke near it and it not only cleared the room but pulled in the better smells of his mother's cooking from the rest of the house. Jack hated the smell of cigarette smoke lingering in a haze in the air. It limited his oxygen intake when it came time to dream. Oxygen he much needed to convert to dream energy, he also hated that he smoked, so relegated it to certain times, only smoked after preparation and ritual.

Golden hour was over. He put out the cigarette then turned back to his design on the computer, grunted in disgust, and turned to pen and paper. A crisp black line from a Le Pen, a fresh white piece of paper. He quickly finished his built-in speaker design for the Alta Pearl's new top-house and realized, as he let go and flowed, what he needed to do with the CAD program. There was a click, an aha! moment, and it was just as the song "Opportunities" by the Pet Shop Boys began to play on the radio. Jack chortled with glee, shivered with pleasure then began to work with an increased determination. He quickly began to see form come out of the effort. Elated he pushed on, to a congratulatory smoke break, poured a fresh cup of coffee from his carefully prepared thermos.

"Jack are you smoking in here?"

Rebecca's voice made him flinch as his reverie popped. A flare of anger at being disturbed was quickly squashed. He had been deep in thought, imagining the interior locations of electronic equipment, radar, radio, stereo, compass, auto pilot and then. Mom. He forced himself to smile, at first, it became real as he gazed at his mom's smiling face.

"Yes, care to join me?" Jack waved at a chair near the window.

Rebeca took a seat near the vent - her usual position when they were sneaking a smoke. His father hated smoke, was an ex-smoker of the worst sort.

"Did Dad leave?"

Rebeca smiled and nodded. "To the store. We have to hurry."

Jack handed her the pack of smokes she kept in the room. She was fond of Japanese brand, Parliaments, that had an odd carboard tube as a filter on the end of a short filter.

"What are you working on?" She asked.

"Top House design for the new Alta Pearl. Next step is to contact a fabricator for the frame. Aluminum I think will be best. Then fill it in. But need to get some expert advice."

"Sounds expensive." She always started with her assessment of cost. "Expert advice is usually expensive, especially if its legal advice." Rebecca tittered at her own joke.

Jack grinned. "I think it is worth it. "

"You got a call from that girl Sarah today. She said she would call back at six if she could." Rebeca said. There was a gleam in her eye. She liked the intrigue.

Jack felt a happy jolt and smiled at the news. Despite his romantic flings, while in France, he was still in love with Sarah, still held a flame for her, though now he was not so sure they would make it the two years without growing apart. One thing that was helping keep it together was the long conversations they had been having at around six in the evening. The time was convenient for Sarah because Corbin and her mother were rarely home by that time.

"That makes you happy? That she called? She sounded very disappointed you were not here."

Jack nodded. "Makes me happy. Hopeful I guess. If I had my way she would be here and not thinking about her millions..." An idea suddenly hit Jack. Since his conversation with Mike Neufeld he had reevaluated his education direction into finance, business, and computers.

"What Jack? You look as if you just discovered the wheel?"

"Just a thought. I will run it by Sarah. She gets an annuity or stipend every month. If she simply reinvests the money each month, in her own account, it can keep paying her and there is nothing her mom can do about that. We just invest it. Soon, she will have more than the original amount and the original amount will double. "Jack smiled.

"Sounds ok to me, pretty stable but what if her investments fail? It would take a lot of time to get the millions. Could just get it in two years."

"You are ever the optimist mother. Do you advocate that I play the game and get her back and the millions?"

Rebecca laughed heartily.

"I really am just offering balance. You and your father are so optimistic. And yes, I think it's full of plot and intrigue, you two sneaking around, marrying later for millions. Think about it, you get to spread your wild oats, as most all young men like to do, and then, in two years you get together, you get the girl back, and she has her money, but, always remember, it is her money. No matter how kind she is, there will always be the division that you must breach, then the stigma of being a 'kept' man."

Rebecca was a remarkable woman. At fifty-one she was very attractive, kept her hair long, her body toned, took great care of herself. Her garden during the summer was nothing short of spectacular and she was always humming as she forced plants to obey her will. Watching Rebecca garden was like watching a military commander put together a platoon of the best soldiers and train them into a superior fighting machine.

When Dad was just starting out in Purse Seining it was the three of them. Mom, dad, son with Uncle Conner as the skiff man. They crewed the Alta Pearl for the first two years. Rebecca did her time commercial fishing as the cook and lead line person. Stacking lead line was the worst job on the boat, right under a steady stream of jelly fish as the corks, webbing, and lead line, dropped from the big power block high overhead for two crew to stack, a cork stacker, and a lead line stacker. His mother had insisted on doing the job as lead and ring stacker and suffered burns from strands of jelly fish jelly fish and the occasional big brass ring smacking her in the head as they stacked gear aboard a rocking boat. When a grinding day was over she would then prepare dinner that was designed to be breakfast and lunch during the next day by using left overs.

She took all the weather, storms, arguments between Robert and Conner, shouting matches between father and son - and made brownies, comfortable, soothing, brownies. There were a lot of brownies during the fishing season. It got to where if Jack saw brownies he would wonder who had been fighting.

"I did have a good time in France. Even have gotten a few love letters since I have been back. "Jack said. He smiled as his mom slapped his knee.

"See? You are spreading your oats, getting it out of your system. "She ran her fingers through her hair, beaming at him, body language shifting.

Jack was surprised at his more relaxed attitude towards his mother's sexuality. Perhaps it was France, the looser inhibitions there regarding sex was very... Cool. It was obvious Rebecca had started some erotic thinking and was becoming aroused but it still surprised him when she leaned forward in a conspiratorial manner, jade green eyes bright and mischievous...

"You know your father messes around but you probably never suspect me... But I do, it's fun and exciting and he even found out. We agreed to keep our sex life good and all else was to be discreet and just fleeting sex. "

Jack swallowed a tiny nervous lump in his throat, shrugged of an odd tension that suddenly twanged at his shoulders. France was liberating, yes, but this was... Mom. His mind pictures her with another man, and he quickly rejects it while, at the same time he pushed away anger, strived for acceptance. His mom was looking at him, studying for signs of disgust and anger.

"That... Would explain why you are cool with her and Corbin and me and whoever I guess. But you know... All during my dating experiences, you recall the girls I was crazy about, they all ended up being unfaithful and screwing someone else. Even Audrey." Jack said.

Rebecca smiled. "In Alaska Jack, you don't lose your girl just your turn in line."

"That is a horrible saying because it is often true. Kind of our Alaska Zen regarding relationships huh?"

"Alaska Zen. I like the sound of that. "Rebecca said.

"Does that make it acceptable then because a few do it? "

"I am not sure just a few do, more like sixty percent of the men and, in Alaska, maybe a bit higher than forty percent of the women."

"Would make an interesting psychology paper if I hadn't changed my focus."

"It's a bad stereotype, though isn't it?" Rebecca asked.

"Yes, but like fairy tales and folk lore there is an observation made that leads to the stereotype. "

Rebecca nodded thoughtfully, sniffed the air, smiled. "Cookies are done!" She sped from the room just before the kitchen buzzer sounded.

Jack had a fresh cup of coffee, a plate of pumpkin spice cookies, smokes, ashtray, and phone, all ready to go at six o'clock. Sarah called at ten agonizing minutes after.

They talked and laughed for an hour and then Sarah worked him hard for information about France and the girls he slept with. Jack resisted gently then allowed the allusion and finally, as gently as he could, admitted. Sarah was glad. Jack was surprised. The conversation left him bewildered but feeling relieved. She had spoken something about Leo Buscaglia and a book called Love. It sounded interesting to Jack so he jotted down the name of the book and author. Sarah promised to send him her copy with notes in the margins she made just because she loved him. The notion was very romantic to Jack. When their conversation was over he had a fresh sense of optimism, a new view of the potential success of he and Sarah's plan.

Christmas time in Alaska was both cold and hearth warm. Inside his mother's abode, warm light, good smells, conversation and laughter, was a pleasure that Jack had anchored many a good memory down with. His dad, Robert McKnight, loved being host to all other family, Anchorage, Palmer, Wasilla, Kenai and Cordova McKnights all gathered for three days at the house in Anchorage one year, his Uncle Conner's home in Cordova the next. Jack was fond of his cousins and they of him. Three of them he had taught to Lucid Dream. Three out of six. The others were a bit too stubborn, atheistic, indifferent or to young.

Jack was also much closer with the three lucid dreamers for they were all Uncle Conner's kids and Jack shared bonds with his Uncle Conner that no one in the family knew, save the twins. They knew. They were silent to all others. Jack loved and trusted them for this.

Cousin John became adept at Lucid Dreaming then shunned it as he became a very devote Christian for a year, then embraced it once again with a renewed fervor when he broke up with his girlfriend, who was a Baptist. Jack and the twins fondly referred to him as John the Priest because he related his lucid experiences to Christ and biblical lore.

Cindi and Marci, the twins, were very good at keeping dream journals, and phenomenal in their dream proficiency. Each family gathering Jack would ask them of their experiences and they would put their heads together and compare notes. He would ask them if they had found any one else like them.

This year would be a bit different after Jack's conversation with Mike Neufeld and the establishment of an affiliation of Lucidians. The names on the list that Neufeld had given him were of a surprising array of wealth. Five men and three women. Michael had arranged for a meeting with these folks at a fund raiser in New York. The room was huge, filled with people who lived in boxes of accomplishment. One by one he met and spoke with the eight names on the list, was a bit shy, but able to laugh and get them to laugh, which, to him, meant things went well.

BETTER THAN RIGHT

Jack sat on the long couch near the arm and table lamp, Cindi to his left, Marci next to her, then John, Aunt Wanda, his mother's sister, and her husband, Uncle Ian. The room smelled of cookies and hot buttered whiskey, ever present whiffs of rogue vapors from the fireplace. Jack was thrumming with the pleasure of family conversation and his second tasty hot buttered as the McKnight's shared barbs and banter, laughed, made merry.

His father, Robert, stood at the fireplace hearth next to Uncle Conner the two of them motioned for attention. The room only quieted when Robert's voice, his boat voice, boomed a thunderous, yet polite, request for silence.

Jessica, Daniel, and Franky even quieted down. They were of an age to understand the repercussions of ignoring Robert McKnight each of them having felt the knuckles to the noggin a time or two. Especially Franky, who was seventeen. He had stubbornly collected the absolute most knuckles to the noggin. He was now utterly quiet as he awaited Robert's speech.

Robert McKnight's voice carried his words like a bass megaphone as he spoke to the family.

"I am expanding the business a bit." He announced. Jack stopped whispering to Cindi and tuned into his father's voice.

"Conner and I have contracted a boat builder to build this..."

Robert unfurled a poster sized picture of a huge boat. A long beautiful cabin and a beautifully designed work deck. Jack's breath caught in his throat. They had talked about doing a combination yacht-purse seiner over beers at the Anchor Bar in Cordova, one that could accommodate tourists for charters during the off season.

"You went with our drunken idea!" Jack blurted. His father beamed at him and laughed. "Yes! That is where all our best ideas come from!" He said. Rebeca rolled her eyes but smiled at Robert as he winked.

Aunt Felice sat very still, looking even paler than normal, ice cold blue eyes fixed on Uncle Conner told that this was the first she had heard of the plan. Conner gave her a comical grin shrug that was applogetic and begging of acceptance at the same time. Jack saw Aunt Felice inhale, restrain herself, and give a teeny tiny nod, her wide, thick lips, however, pursed, also a tiny bit, telling Conner that they would speak about this in private.

"It is time for you to move up a bit, your little boat only holds forty thousand pounds. It is getting embarrassing when you must deliver because she is packed and we are still fishing, most people think you pack as much as we do, damn it, making us look bad!" Robert McNight said. The group laughed, except Aunt Felice though she did flicker a smile, was warming a bit.

"You need a bigger boat son, the Emma Dawn is now costing you money. Besides, who the hell wouldn't want one of these?" Laughter filled the room as Robert ran his hand down to the cabin area of the blue print, a big smile on his face, as he exaggerated the sweep of his hand and the movement of his body, like a con man pirate giving his best pitch. He then straightened, the more serious Robert McKnight at the helm. He nodded at Jack.

"And yes, to acknowledge my son, Jack and I thought it would be a good idea to do tourism and purse seining using the same boat. We hatched a grand business model based on the ever rising tourism economy in Alaska. We love Prince William Sound, especially when we get to share it with those who have never viewed such beauty and wildness. Granted, we were a bit drunk at the time, but hell, that's when Irish Scott's get their best ideas!"

Everyone laughed. Jack beamed with excitement.

Robert then snapped back into his pirate con man act, one of his favorites at family gatherings, and the bars where Jack had watched him ham it up with this friends, all laughing and carrying on.

"Here there be nice state rooms for guests. Three to sleep six people. Captains quarters are in the top house, two full sized heads, 'cause we know owe the ladies like a nice bathroom and we McKnight men like our long shits."

Rebecca laughed the loudest, her sister, Wanda was right there with her. Thin smile from Aunty Felice.

"I set it up so the three of us get one, sister ships and its cheaper for three. We get a 'volume' discount."

"What about four? "Franky Murphy said. He was currently working aboard Roberts boat as crew during the summers. Winters, he spent in school, doing well. Franky would make it in life, but with few friends. He was a pain in the ass to Robert. But, family and all. Rebecca's sister didn't know what to do with the kid. Some are just bad seeds and Franky Murphy was a selfish arrogant asshole as a young kid, and instead of growing out of it, he grew into it. Fishing changes most people for the better. For Franky, it made him a better asshole.

Robert though, smiled even bigger. "Yes, four would be better actually. The more we do, the cheaper they get. In fact, our job for the rest of this cold winter is to find as many people as we can to buy into this boat and boat design. I am targeting about six as a reasonable number. "

Jack rocked in his chair a bit as he sipped at his hot buttered whisky. Some called it Hot Buttered Rum and some Hot Buttered Brandy, the McKnight family called it Hot Buttered Whiskey. He was finding great humor in the exchange now taking place, non-verbally between Conner and Felice. Her demanding inquisitive look at first was now a confirmed rage that she struggled to contain and Uncle Conner knew he was in for it so kept giving her an apologetic shrug and a huge smile and a batting of his eyes, that was just pissing her off even more.

Aunt Felice finally lost her composure. "Son of a bitch Conner! You did not consult on this with me!"

Conner flinched, one eye closed his other wide as took a Popeye stance and raised his fists. "I am what I am! A Fisherman!" His impersonation of Popeye, a familiar family schtick, made them roar with laughter – until Aunt Felice hurled her mug at his head, which he caught with his huge hands. Now Conner shot Felice a look that Jack had seen, right before the man's fist knocked him across the room. The playfulness, however, was not all gone.

"Easy me lady, this is the tellin' and after comes the talkin', no money has been committed as of yet. I was just having a bit of fun." He did the apologetic shrug and a smile again. "This is one of Rebeca's favorite coffee mugs."

He handed it back to her… Felice nodded and took it, a flicker of relief flaring across her face. She looked at Rebeca, gave an apologetic shrug. Rebeca laughed. "I was hoping you would hit him in his big head, that would have been funny, like, THUNK!, for teasing you like that."

"Yeah, you knew about this already though?"

Now Rebeca looked down a bit, a wry smile on her face. "Yes, but that is because I am the accountant for the family…"

Felice nodded and let it all go. "He is what he is. Knew that when I married him. Just thought he would grow out of it."

Robert liked to think big, to expand on what he finally believed was a good idea. It took a while for dear old Dad, to come to conviction and movement, but when he did, and he asked Jack if he was in, he whooped enthusiastically. Yes, he was all in. He cast a glance at Rebecca and she was nodding, a beam of a smile on her face. Jack was relieved. She usually frowned at the beginning of a bad idea.

A special Christmas, where everything is just right and magical happens more often with the right attitudes all blending together. As a child Christmas was always a happy jumble of food and family. Then the awkward years where gratitude and expectations begin to battle, then the adult years where delight is in watching the children. It occurred to Jack, as he sat listening to his father talk about his boat and the banter of uncles, aunts and cousins, that he was living a blessed life. He relaxed and absorbed the moment, the taste of his Hot Buttered Whisky, the excitement of committing to an inspirational idea, the warm lights of the Christmas tree blending with candles on the hearth. The faint smell of wood smoke from the crackling fire, moose chili and corn bread scents from dinner still lingering.

Rebecca snapped pictures with her Polaroid and passed them around. As Jack looked at them he smiled. This was a great memory, a wonderful present. He looked up to see his mom smiling at him from across the room.

"I love you." Her lips moved, silent. Jack smiled big. Rebecca snapped the picture. He was locked into the memory. The world was better than right.

SEEDS

Christmas Eve. Snow swirls into the house and around a huge array of boots as Jack and his cousins enter at the mud room. They carry bags of gifts they shopped for all day for a secret Santa gift exchange Rebecca put on each Christmas Eve, and for others besides.

"I am so glad to be safe out of that horrible car!" Marci said. She kicked off her boots next to Cindi's. Snow melted in the twin's hair, glistened in the light of the mud room. They were now fifteen and getting scary pretty. Dark auburn naturally curly hair, hazel green blue eyes like his, a McKnight trait which made Rebecca's constantly jade green eyes seem mysterious and exotic. Marci and Cindi were well rounded, curvy, not fat, but... full. They were beautiful, and good. Their older brother, John McKnight, was a thick, muscular young man at sixteen, handsome and quick, with a wry sense of humor. His mischievous mannerisms and acting outs stemmed from having twin sisters supplant his only child status at two years old. John had been at the wheel, fish tailing the old sedan whenever he got a chance, nearly loosing full control on several occasions.

The car Marci spoke of was an old Lincoln that Jack bought cheap to get around Anchorage. It was long and spacious, seated seven in a pinch and rear wheel drive. Fun in the snow until it met a hill.

The four of them entered the warmth and cheer of the kitchen. The fireplace blazed, nearly every couch and chair was occupied. Smells of turkey and ham cooking prevailed over subtle spices and sweet smells mingled with the ever-present wood smoke smell. Jack kissed his mom as she stirred the turkey gravy. Aunt Wanda gave him and the twins a hug. Aunt Felice, Conner's wife, had overheard the girls speaking of John's reckless driving and stood with her arms folded, foot tapping, a sure sign of her consternation.

"You will not drive the rest of the time here in Anchorage John McKnight." She said. She did not yell, barely raised her voice, but enough, and with the authority of a magistrate, which was her profession. John stiffened a bit and nodded. "Yes mother." He said softly.

Cindi and Marci stood by Aunt Felice, small grins on their faces as they stared down brother John, their positioning artfully placed outside of Felice's peripheral vision, so they could tap into mom's righteousness, mock her, and intimidate John with their wit all at the same time. Jack laughed and clapped John on the back.

"I was not going to let you drive again anyway."He said.

"I already figured on that." John said.

They made their way through, large bags in hand, to Jack's bedroom so they could wrap and label the Christmas gifts. As they worked at making nice gift wrapping Jack told his cousins of his conversation with Mike Neufeld. Told them of the eight names he had been given, of the coming together of an abstract thought, or one he thought was abstract, to form a more active group, with a purpose he did not yet realize.

"You are a nut you know that? "Marci said.

"One of these days you will have your own dream religion." Cindi added.

"There is only one religion." John said. He had recently met a girl, who went to church, a different one from the previous girlfriend, which had revitalized his religious side.

"Tell the Jewish people that, or Muslims, or Wiccans. They all believe they are right but between all of them is the very bright reality of lucid dreaming." Jack said. John nodded thoughtfully. He was nowhere near a fanatic.

They were wrapping gifts as they chatted, one of the ways to avoid the plague of Franky's criticism and negativity was to work. Franky avoided work when possible.

"I like the idea of a religion actually. "Jack said. He paused in his taping of the Christmas paper.

The name he had drawn was Daniel's - eight-year-old cousins from Aunt Wanda on his mother's side of the family where he was working on cultivating two other lucid dreamers, Jessica, and Daniel. Potentially. They were young and he was gently planting seeds. He had purchased a book about a boy who dreamed he could fly and a small cassette player for the boy. Daniel already liked music and was at the age where listening to it in his own room might start getting cool. The book was a seed that might bring together Daniel's thoughts and stimulate that first Lucid Dream.

"You could do it." Cindy said.

"I can see it happening." Marcy said.

"It would tie all religions together." Jack mused. The tone of his voice was known to John and the girls. John groaned. The girls giggled. "We could rule the world!" Jack said. He gave an evil chuckle.

Jack shook his head dismissively." I don't think I have time for all that, but like Napoleon Hill said, "A group of like minds with common goals can accomplish anything." Or something like that... What Michael proposed is exactly that. Anyway, how have you guys been harvesting your dreams?"

"I have been writing of this world called Taka. Hawk in Nippon. There is a sentient jungle and it manifests itself into humanoid ant warriors to represent its interests to the civilization that is encroaching on its boarders." John said. "The twist is that the ant warriors begin to rebel against the Jungle controlling their forms. The want to be separate from what created them."

The room was silent for a few seconds, just a few residual wrapping paper crackles, then warm laughter.

"Wow! You were just waiting to say that, weren't you?" Jack asked.

John's face was a big smile as he chuckled. "Yes, great timing too. Got you away from religious sacrilege."

"I want to read what your writing! "Marcy said. Cindy nodded in agreement.

"We have been dreaming of a game, so we tried to make it but it is impossible."

Cindi's lip stuck out in a comical pout.

Jack lifted a book off his dresser. "I have been reading steam punk novels lately, before that anything by Michael Moorcock, and have found that certain writers write in a way that enables me to enter the book world they are creating... I am wondering John, if this has anything in common with you. Will your writings inspire me to dream in the world you create?"

The girl's eyes were big.

"Yes! Yes! We do that too... But with romance novels. "They giggled.

John rolled his eyes. "You two are so mushy with that stuff. You meet a guy and neither of you knows what to do but you are experts when it comes to the books. "

"We know what to do!" Both replied. "How much money you got? How big is your dick?" Cindi said and snapped her fingers. Marci laughed uproariously. "We have been dream practicing. "Marci giggled.

"I wonder about you two sharing a dream connection, shared dreams have been documented." Jack said. He smiled and studied the girls as they glanced at each other.

"Yeah, we do that sometimes. Kinda spooky. "Marci said.

"Kinda invasive. I mean..." Cindi began but Marci punched her lightly to hush her up.

Cindi began giggling harder.

"I walked in on Marci doing it in her dream and thought it was my dream and..."

"Shut up!" Marci cried. But she was not loud or forceful, more exasperated with her twin.

The door opened and Franky stuck in his curly blond head. "Hey? Doesn't sound like much wrapping is getting done in here." He said.

"We still have a bit to go. You want to help? I don't think anyone got your name. "

"Nope. Wrap your own stuff. And no one got my name because I didn't put it in, didn't draw one either." Freddy said.

"Well aren't you a bucket of fuckin' sunshine." John said.

Jack was irritated by the interruption. He resolved to quiz the girls separately regarding their shared dream times. See if they were imagining it, or if he could verify. A bit of a chill passed down his spine. It was a common thought that twins shared a near psychic bond, Cindi and Maci could very well be capable of a great deal on a psychic level.

THE MCKNIGHT'S BUY THEIR BOATS

Vern Doken smiled and raised a glass of whisky. He was a short dark-haired man, strong from work, hands calloused in the peculiar areas people get while working a trade. Those traits plus a tour of his facilities where the boats would be built, made for a good bond of trust.

The four of them raised glass, clinked, and downed a whisky double. Jack followed the burn with a sip of beer, eyes tearing a bit. Uncle Conner was aglow, his face a bit ruddy from drinking the last three days. Robert was a bit more conservative with his alcohol and Jack like to think that he himself rarely drank, which was the case, also why the room was beginning to warble, not near a spin, just a bit off balance, an over burdening urge to grin. This was night four of waltzing around the subject of contracting with Vern Doken, and his start up boat building company, Commercial Cabin Craft Marine.

They had toured the facility, with Vern, twice now, examined and sea tested a beautifully designed purse seiner, a new build, destined for Kodiak, studied the blue prints for the new boats and discussed options, gear, and electronics. Each day Jack became further convinced they were on the right path with this company, that Vern's vision of building boats that had both a very well-designed cabin and work deck.

He liked the concept, 'Commercial Cabin Craft Marine' had a good ring to it, and potential. Like one of his own ventures. Potential, but not quite all there. There was a very new, start up, element to Vern's business of building boats, something that Vern admitted readily. A start up, but he was coming from Little Hoquiam where he built boats for over ten years for them and decided he just wanted to do it better. It was the start up feel, and the sale that Vern made, his passionate pitch of what he believed he could do and where he wanted to take his company, that his father and uncle sought to prey on.

They were at a restaurant just a few blocks from the marina warehouse. Vern was buying, again. Their money was no good while Vern was around.

"Your orders are very much appreciated gentlemen. The designs for the boats are already approved and now the work begins. Once your loans go through that is. "

Robert paused and gave Vern a look that Jack was glad he was not the recipient of. He knew the look well, it usually came just before a very important lesson in respect and communication skills, or a dressing down.

"We have discussed, in depth, hiring you, of all people, to build us these boats. We believe that you can produce a product that fits our vision of multiple fisheries combined with tourism and have already secured our financing. It is all now, a matter up to you to accept our offer of five hundred thousand per boat. You do that, draw up the contracts, we sign them tomorrow over whiskey and cigars." Robert grinned and nodded a happy affirmative, eyes set upon Vern's with a proud, sincere gaze.

There was silence from Vern as his face ticked. Robert said nothing but smiled, took a sip of whisky. Conner nodded, said nothing. Jack held his breath. He would not speak. If he did his father would back hand him, figuratively, with a fierce gaze that bellowed 'shut the hell up boy!'.

"You want a larger discount? You are already getting eight hundred thousand-dollar boats for seven hundred thousand."

Robert nodded and put out his hands to show they were empty.

"We mean no offence to your skills. We are utterly convinced your product will be superior, your company will be very successful. It is just that we have limits on what we can do, we are not wealthy, we must ensure that our simultaneous purchase of three boats is the best possible deal we can get, which in this case, is also all the bank has already approved us for, and for which, I hate to add, our accountant also advised us that we should not go over due to a market and financial analysis of our success to purchase ratio. Our success ratio goes through the roof at five-hundred thousand. Your success ratio improves by a forty percent margin based on the fact that your three boats will be famous because we are famous, well, notorious is more like it. People will see your finished product, what it can do, and they will want one. Once that happens, you charge them a million, they still will buy from you." Robert said.

Jack was impressed. He doubted it would work, but he was inspired by his father's words, his tone, his self-perceived skills at negotiation. He hoped to one day, have balls, as big as Robert McKnight's.

He watched carefully as Vern held his face as still as possible, took a sip of whisky and shrugged, his face sliding into a smile.

"I respect the three of you." He said. Vern raised his glass. "To Family." He said. They all drank. Vern smacked his lips, his eyes moved between the three of them.

"I tell you what I will do for you, and yes, for me. I will build your boats, but for six-hundred thousand each and that is because I would break even at your offer. I know you have done your homework, and also know that you do have the means to provide the price I ask. My spot is right in the middle, and I have moved for you, because of family, and because you are correct, these boats will be my advertisement into your market. If you ask me to build such a craft for you, and break even, just on the 'maybe' people will be inspired to purchase my product, I could do that, but I could do it even better, faster, more motivated, knowing I was going to make a profit that could fund further success of my company. I also have family, a son who works for me, three sons who commercial fish out of Kodiak, and a new wife with three daughters." Vern rolled his eyes and nodded as if he was seeing them in his mind. "They are my life." He said.

Jack held his hand still on his glass. He had noticed that his palm and fingertips left little traces of sweat on the dark red vinyl table cloth. He glanced at Vern's hands, saw that he also was leaving traces of sweat when he pulled his hand away from the table top to grasp his whiskey glass.

The pause was not as long this time. Robert nodded after a few seconds. "Fair enough." He said. He held his large hand out to Vern. "I agree." He said.

Vern studied Robert's hand as if he were double thinking his counter offer. Jack saw him wipe his hand on his shirt on the way up to shake his father's hand.

"Damn it! Ok." Vern said. He smiled and shook his head. "I feel like I just gave you three boats, and yet feel good about it by god." He waved at the waitress to come over.

"Reasonable profit is acceptable." Robert said. "Though I believe you could produce the boats for five hundred and still make a profit."

"I could, by eliminating content, cutting corners, and producing something substandard to my vision." Vern said.

Robert laughed. "I like your honesty." He said.

Vern shrugged. "We are all in now." He said. "Let me reassure you, I want these boats to shine!"

Jack had his moments of doubt. His father as well. A week earlier, after a long day with a loan officer from Alaskan's First Bank, Robert had put up his house and boat as equity. Jack committed fifty thousand of his remaining money and tied his boat up, which was almost paid for, as equity. Conner laughed as he committed a hundred and twenty thousand and the equity in his home to secure his financing. There was a lot of sweat at the signing. Everything was on the line.

The dinner was delicious. Steak done perfectly, mashed potatoes, green beans; the whiskey and conversation flowed. Jack had a great deal of respect for his dad, how he had handled the negotiation. He had been ready to lay down his commitment at seven hundred thousand, had been caught up in the potential the boat represented, in how Vern had expressed interest in his top house designs for the boat, had studied his amateur engineering designs for the rigging and told him that there was some good stuff he could incorporate.

Jack smiled. It now occurred to him that Vern may have feigned interest in the designs as part of his charm, of the sales process. His father had not been so easily sucked into the deal.

Not entirely sucked in, he had a list of concerns, questions he wanted to ask, all written out during an all-night circle of focus session. The paper was neatly folded and in his back pocket, full of questions and doodles as he dreamed of what the boat would look like, the design of the name in paint and a symbol for the front and sides of the top house. Jack wanted the boats completed before July or at least by August of 89'. He was a bit miffed by the timing, which was for September 89' at the best for all three boats, but felt he was striking while the iron was hot. His father had to co-sign for him to get a boat at the same time. Robert argued that they would save two hundred and twenty thousand on the price of the boats, the time was now. Jack had much to hesitate about. Business this interlinked with his father bugged him a bit. He liked his own thing. Conner had made a larger down payment, which made Jack give him a knowing look to which Uncle Conner just grinned big and told him it was from perfectly legal investments.

"It's only paper! If we go down - we go down big." Robert had boomed. Jack had laughed. Yes! He wanted this badly. He signed quickly, eagerly, and appreciatively at the next dinner with Vern.

THE SCHOOL OF DAD CONVERSATIONS

Tax time was approaching. The boats were being built. Jack had already had his mom do his taxes. He had to pay. A lot. He went to a specialist and found that he would pay much less if he took small risks. He took them and got the bill down from eighteen thousand, seven hundred ninety-five to seven thousand, forty-two and fifty-six cents. That left him with roughly seven thousand dollars for startup capital for the season of 89, thanks to Bart who had run the Emma Dawn during two successful Halibut openers and was currently fishing for Black Cod. But now he needed to work to make it until start up June 15th. It cost a good deal of money to get everything ready. Drop the boat in the water, de winterized, gear up, inspect and repair, safety improvements.

Jack had enrolled in computer science. Was taking to it very well. He found a much better CAD program at the University of Alaska Anchorage. With a copy of the new boats blue prints he began to design a Top House that integrated the same space utilization of the sleepers he had observed on semi-trucks. There had always been a fascination there. While in the Seattle area he had dragged his father to a convention for Semi-Truck drivers and RV owners.

Jack loved the time they spent there, the combinations he imagined building into his boat were both innovative and inspired. Robert was impressed. He suggested that get in touch with Vern and have him provide a set of blue prints so he could design the top houses a bit more thoroughly than the ones he had already put together and presented to Vern that did not fit the actual dimensions of the boats they were building. A task that Jack tore into with inspiration and drive once he returned to college.

Robert was constantly on the phone with Vern or Vern's Forman a fellow they had met during the site tour, Sam. His father wanted to be involved in every step of the process. Listening to those conversations one would think that Robert McKnight and Vern Doken were long time best friends.

Money had been transferred and daily reports and questions were an obsession with his father. Jack, decide he felt a bit sorry for Vern on that account. He wouldn't want to be micro-managed by his father, had been for his first year of owning the Emma Dawn.

The new boats would be limit seiners, fifty-eight-feet in overall length with a twenty-eight-foot beam. Huge and incredibly wide. His current boat was much smaller in comparison. The new one would tank down and haul one hundred thousand pounds of salmon, his current boat was deck loaded at about fifty-five thousand.

Jack lingered in the kitchen as the coffee brewed. Rebecca had insisted on making it but she liked it week, Bean Counter Coffee Jack like to call it because she made it more to conserve coffee than for flavor reasons. Rebecca ran a well-structured house, militant style, much like her gardens.

Prior to beginning his studies Jack had a set pattern, his learning ritual as he liked to call it. He would brew a pot of coffee, lay out his materials while it brewed, pens, paper, note books, book to study, ashtray, cigarettes, lighter. On the wall above his study desk was a picture of his family, a copy of the blue prints for his boat being built, a yacht he admired, Sarah, a design for an oval shaped desk, and an idealistically styled stone home set in an estate of agricultural and maricultural production he liked to call the Prince William Sound Farms. Things he loved and worked for. These days he would glance at the photo of Sarah, the one they took for them at the wedding chapel in Las Vegas, in her clinging peach colored dress, a happy smile on her face, sort of. Now he could read a hint of sadness and doubt in her eyes and features.

Jack would affirm to himself that she would remain true in heart to him, even if she did have to spread her pretty legs for Corbin to get her millions.

He would also affirm that he would have millions of his own in the next few years while staring at the boat and the miniature stone castle house.

There were things, mostly mental, on his agenda, as he entered the kitchen to make coffee to find Rebecca already making the coffee, her way of saying she wanted to talk. At first Jack felt a twinge of irritation at having his ritual interrupted. He shrugged off the mild patrern inturuption, gave her a hug and squeezed her shoulders, understood that she was about to express her doubts, yet again. But she surprised him.

"Your father is going insane over this boat deal Jack. You should talk with him more. He is thinking you are rather... nonchalant about the whole deal. He needs reassurance. "

Jack couldn't stifle a snort of doubt.

"Dad? Needs reassurance?"

Rebecca gave him a look that told she was serious.

"I guess that never occurred to me, that's all. The mighty and powerful Robert McKnight needs... Reassurance." Jack let the concept settle in a bit. His father was human after all.

Rebecca laughed. "You think that your dad is ten feet tall and made of stone, and that's good, 'cause I do too sometimes, but what I fell in love with was your fathers surprising sensitive side. For a man raised in his era, he is rather... Evolved. I guess that's a good word. "

Jack poured himself a cup of coffee from the quarter brewed pot - the only way to get it strong enough. Usually Rebeca would smack him for doing that. Now she just gave an exasperated sigh and Jack was not sure it was the coffee thing, or his response regarding his father.

"I will talk with dad. He might be surprised but I am obsessing over the strategy we used myself. With both positive and doubtful fear stuff, but more positive. I have finished the cad designs and sent them to Vern. He approved them with the shipwright, for all three boats, with no increase in cost. In fact, Vern said that cost went down and helped increase his profit margin because my designs were more efficient than his original plans which called for a lot of expensive wood work where I want fiberglass and carpeting."

"Robert knows that. He thinks you took the quality out of the top house design that Vern originally had." Rebecca interrupted.

Jack nodded furiously. "Yes, I know. We had that conversation." He said. He set his jaw, eyes alight with pride. "The approval of my designs means that I can sell or lease them out to others. I have the rights to the designs, like a patent, only an intellectual property."

Rebecca nodded, an apologetic smile on her face. She had her long auburn hair down, a white blouse, tight blue jeans a fuzzy black pair of house slippers, mostly for grip on the wood floors but also to protect the feet from chill. She ran cold. At that moment, Jack found her very wise and very pretty.

"I know Jack. I know your father is upset. He told me today he told Vern to not put your top house design in his Alta Pearl, said Vern called him a stubborn Irishman." Rebecca laughed. "You know your father likes to think of himself as Scottish, not Irish, even though his family has a six-hundred-year history in Ireland."

"Wow, really? He told him not to? I bet I can get him to change his mind. I just need to show him why my design is better, once he knows what he is saying no to he will change his mind."

"No, Jack. He thinks your design is great, better even, just worth less. He thinks that people will find it odd, unconventional when the time comes to sell the boat. That people will pay more for the conventional wood work you find in a top house."

Jack laughed. "The designs are mine, every boat in the harbor will have a top house like what I put together. No one will want a boat without a built-in command center. There are no others like it now, but soon, no one will want a boat without this design. There is a long-range plan at work here mom, fabrication and design. My own production, my own shop where I can create shit."

"You fancy yourself a visionary Jack McKnight, I get it. I am just saying you need to talk to your damn father. He is driving me nuts. Ok?"

"You are so beautiful mom when you are feisty. "Jack said. He smiled his most charming smile.

"Don't try and charm me you devil. This is a serious conversation."

"I know Mom and I will talk with Dad, I promise. In fact, this very night, whisky and conversation. "

Rebecca rolled her eyes but smiled at the same time.

"You two and your whiskey, I want a civil conversation not a shouting match."

Jack winked. "Sometimes that's what needs to happen. But you know I will avoid it using my highly-refined diplomacy skills that I have learned from the school of Dad conversations. ".

Rebecca laughed. "Yes, I suppose so huh?"

ANOTHER NAME FOR THE LIST AND A VIRGIN SACRIFICE

Jack awoke after a series of pleasant dreams at five in the morning. He picked up his tape recorder and spoke all he could remember then realized he forgot to push play. Did it again.

"I was on the Emma Dawn, traveling up a river. My son was on the boat, I knew it was my son, but also that I didn't yet have a son and this made the dream lucid for me. It was a pleasant day, the river waters blue and we entered a busy port where I accidentally hit another boat and scratched it. An oriental man began to yell at me. I apologized. He kept threatening. I grew angry and told him to fuck off with the lambasting, that I had apologized already and would pay for the damages, end of fucking conversation. The guy laughed. Apologized. Invited I and my son to dinner at his father's house. We accepted. As we approached the father's house I noticed a sports car sitting on the porch, only it had no wheels, no engine compartment, was just the cab. Curious as to what it was for I opened the door. As I did a young man opened the door to the other side and told me to have a seat on my side and we could game together. I slid into the seat and he pulled a screen off the windshield and set it in front of me. I was amazed that the screen was flexible, he handled it like it was a piece of heavy rubber yet it lit up with the beginning of the game in brilliant color. I studied the controls for the character on the screen, they were set into the arms of the sports car seat. I settled into the big, leathery and comfortable car seat and began to get excited as I realized I was sitting inside the desk I have been designing and doodling about with for years. I woke up at that point."

Jack snapped off the tape recorder, dropped it on his bed, and strolled, in his shorts, to the bathroom across the hall from his bedroom for a shower. It was to be a busy day. Three classes, CAD, computer engineering, and computer science. But the most exciting was an appointment with Glen Volstead at nine am at Alaska Fabrications. He showered quickly, two minets, crossed the hall in a towel back to his room to dress, moving quicker now, fully awake from a last few moments of cold water on his body from the shower.

He made a pot of coffee as quietly as possible. He did not want to awaken his parents. As much as he loved them they liked to talk in the morning. Morning time was for silence, forethought and vision.

Jack had many talks and debates with his dad after Rebeca directed him to be more communicative. He had shared with Robert his plans to open a fabrication shop, to create many more designs like his top house command center, convinced his father to tell Vern to go ahead and install Jack's design. Jack had pointed out to his dad that one-day computers would manage boats, that he had used Computer Aided Design programs to enhance the design of the pilot house on all three new boats and that he could earn a significant amount of money from these designs being used on thousands of boats.

He poured water into the coffee maker in an even stream, ears tuned to the telltale floor creaks in the house that would indicate an awake parent. He breathed in the pungent, crisp smell of the coffee as it made its noisy way into the pot. It occurred to him that the smell would awaken his mom for certain. It was too strong. He laughed at the thought, pulled a pitcher of chia seeds and green tea, Amanda the Apothecary's recipe, from the refrigerator, poured the mixture into a tall glass and watched the frog egg like seeds swirl about.

Fiberglass molds. His appointment at nine. Sweat equity in an avant-garde computer desk he had contracted to have built. He was helping a guy he had met at Chil-Koot Charlie's on a frolicking Saturday night. Glen Volstead. A nice synchronicity. Synchronicity was something that happened to Jack more and more. He noticed, long ago, that lucid dreaming guided him to do things that made happy coincidence occur more often. In this case, it was his back that ached after sitting for hours at the computer. No matter how he adjusted the chair it did not help so he stood, stacked cardboard boxes on his desk and wedged the monitor on the top, then another stack and used that for the keyboard and mouse. Gave him a bit of relief and amused him with thoughts of designing a more comfortable desk using the CAD system that was causing him long hours at a desk in the first place. - That night he dreamed he was in class in an advanced college. The desks were eggs with computers in them. That morning he sketched out a new type desk, a productivity station, where a person could work both sitting and standing. The monitor at the stand station connected to the pc via a long cable so the stand station screen was the same as the sit station screen. He also designed the office chair to be more of a automobile seat, as in his dream, with power adjustments, only without the size constraints that come with an automobile.

The following Saturday night he met Glen Volstead after both had given up competing for the attentions of the ladies against five other guys. The following Monday they had worked out a more practical, and beautiful, desk design as well as brainstorm several other ideas together. Tuesday saw the beginning of the work. The desk was rapidly taking form under Glen's skilled craftsmanship.

Jack poured a tall cup of fresh coffee, thanked god that he had not awakened his parents, and silently walked to his room. There he spent the next few hours on the computer to prepare more fully for his classes.

9:00 AM

Jack pulled his big Lincoln into the parking lot of Alaska Fabrications. He proceeded to the back doors and found Glen sanding a large round piece of fiberglass.

"Wow! That was fast!" Jack said.

Glenn smiled showing tobacco stained teeth. "I don't screw around man. Not when I am onto something cool like this. Clock in and I will line you out. Got an entire piece for you to work on today. "

The piece was the molded pockets for books, lighting, pens. As Jack worked on the mold, which had to be built in backwards mirror image of the actual fiberglass, he visualized the finished product. It would be something to behold. It was shaped like a staple with no hard corners once against the wall. A semi dome would hold the computer monitor at the end of it. Lighting inside the dome hood was to be on a dimmer switch, the switch set into the side of the dome. This would give a private sort of environment in which to relax while on the computer or studying a book. A u-shaped lip with room to slide a good sized office chair into, one that reclined - Jack wanted to integrate a power automobile seat into the desk. There was a grooved area for the coffee cup, a hole to attach his smoke sucking fan, and ample space inside the cockpit for pin boards and files. When he wanted he could slide the chair backwards out of the cockpit and use the large work surface of the L shaped desk which was multi-level, flat spaces and clever storage shelves built in like he had seen the security guard's desk at Mike Neufeld's condo, area to stand, stretch, continue working on the same computer screen as inside the cockpit but at a standing station, the signal carried via a long monitor cord from a Y split in the back of the harddrive.

Glen and Jack paused to chug water and smoke at 10:30. Class was looming, but Jack decided to skip it. He had studied. All class was for was to prove it and receive reward, and flirt with the curly haired girl. But she would be in the next class as well.

"It's coming along nice. Fast." Jack said.

"Yup. I believe we have a rather cool design here. "Glen held a camera. He had been taking pictures of the project as it progressed.

"Once it's finished and we piece it together I think others will want one."

"You thinking about a scaled down version? Or going with this piece?" Jack asked.

"Thing about fiberglass is once you make the mold you can reproduce it over and over." Glen said. "I will see how many of these I can get sold before making a smaller desk. "

Jack smiled and pulled from his briefcase a pad of yellow legal paper and tore off the first four sheets.

"I had some ideas for designs. Scaled down. Different sort of feel to it. And one for standing that will mesh nice into the one we are building."

"Standing huh?" Glen took the designs and scrutinized them.

"Yes. I realized last night that I enjoy standing. So, you see, part is podium style, and part is flat space, then sitting. "

"Hmmm... The entire point was to be comfortable. Big easy chair rolling between work areas, everything at arm's reach. "

Jack laughed. "Even the most comfortable chair in the world gets uncomfortable when you sit in it very long. I have found that when I stand and read at a podium I feel very focused, like a wizard scanning magical tomes."

Glen smiled and nodded. Jack had grown fond of the him while they worked on the design and molds for the desk. "I do most of my work standing up actually so it is nice to sit at the end of my day. "

"Once we get the molds built and the bugs worked out how much will the cost be on these?"

Glen shrugged. "About three hundred, materials and about a thousand in labor. "

Jack nodded. "Think we can sell them for around twenty-five hundred? Take a dividend down and finance the rest for those that don't have all the cash up front. We charge interest and build in a recovery process at the time of sale if we must repossess one."

"More for the big one. Around thirty-five hundred I think. I have had a couple of people stop by and look at it already. And... What do you mean we?"

Jack smiled. "We as in I want to hire you to run a business for me. I have been working out the details on purchasing my own fabrication and design shop. Something I have been thinking of and planning for a while." Jack could see the interest and curiosity in Glenn's eyes, right there alongside some doubt and scrutiny.

"Our company will be called ErgoDyn Inc. We will build things like this desk, a far superior couch to the ones we have had for centuries, boats, specifically top-houses for boats, but I think maybe entire boats would be fun and profitable. A bill was recently passed making companies spend a set percentage of their budget on ergonomics. Have you heard of ergonomics?"

"In this business? Of course, I have... No, actually, I have not heard about it. I am kept busy in the main shop stapling together furniture. "

Jack nodded and grinned at his friend's wry humor. "There is a huge opportunity to put together a more comfortable modular office desk and sell them to businesses and office building developers nationwide. Four percent of the buildings budget must be allocated to ergonomics to keep people productive and out of the hospitals for things like typing elbow and meta-carpal-tunnel syndrome, also to stave off the workman's compensation claims for these things. I have written a business plan out, done everything but apply for the loan, and have been waiting to meet someone like you to make an offer you can't refuse."

Glenn shook his head, then nodded, shrugged. Jack's read of him was that he was skeptical but curious, interested.

"I have a commercial fishing business, as you know, it keeps me busy during the summer months. During the winter months, I go to college, and recently just signed on for four more years because I changed my fields of study. I needed to find someone like you, someone passionate about what they do, with vision, and a will to get rich. Would you like to run my company for me? I need someone to run it while I am gone, manage a sales staff, production, product lines, and develop and propose more and better ideas all the time."

Glenn's eyes gleamed at the idea as he unconsciously nodded his head.

"Not so sure about the sales staff bit, but I like the idea of my own shop. I have many ideas and things I want to create, like trucks, I hate the uselessness of trucks, a cab and a bed, why not a bigger cab with more function, and a bed that is customized for the work a person uses the truck for, like a built in generator, electrical plug ins for running power tools, hydraulic pole arms for lifting a heavy load into the bed of a truck. Things like that..." Glen nodded as he spoke, an enthusiasm overtaking his reluctance. "I will do it if you reassure me that I will be able to purchase and modify trucks and resell them."

Jack nodded. He looked Glen square in the eye.

"Have you ever seen an idea for a design in a dream?"

Glen looked at him, a new flame igniting in his blue eyes.

"I have had a few ideas from dreams. Your desk came from your dream, that's what got me interested in it. "

Jack nodded. "You are a visionary. Like me. Here..." Jack pulled a small Lucidian pamphlet out of his pocket. He made them at college. They were brief. To the point. The cover was a simple symbol. Inside were the keys to the universe. On the very last page of the booklet was a PO box address, a request for donations, and an enrollment form in exchange for more pamphlets.

Glen reached out, took it, opened to the first page, smiled, put it in his pocket.

"I will read it later. "he said.

Jack nodded.

"I am a Christian though so it might not appeal to me that much. "

"There is no conflict. If you keep an open mind you will find that using dreams for inspiration will only strengthen your belief and faith." Jack said. "Worked for my cousin John, who we now call Preacher John."

Glen nodded, "I am just a Christmas and Easter Christian in any case." He said.

They went back to work, only now they were tossing out ideas, laughing at the absurd ones, and jotting down the feasible ones.

11:30 AM

Computer class was rather epic. Jack turned in his spread sheet assignment. He had done it on a real-life scenario rather than the one the Professor suggested. As he completed the project he kept repeating, "Computer... Calculate the price per pound of salmon average pound per salmon, to number of salmon that need to be caught..." While visualizing a day when that Captain Kirk Star Trek computer would exist. Only seemed natural.

Jack sat at the top row all the way in the back next to Terry, a cute freshman who shared two of his classes. She had flirted with him on day one. He had politely flirted back then settled into ignoring her, yet being friendly, while delighting in her increasing desperation. Today Terry wore a white blouse, tan pants. Her curly brown hair framed her pretty face, big brown eyes and a light smattering of freckles. Jack watched out of the corner of his eyes as she slowly undid her pants, pulled them, and her panties, away from her curly bush, dipped two fingers between her legs in a slow and deliberate manner. Jack had a great view of her pussy mooshing to either side of her digits. She zipped up and put her fingers near Jacks nose.

"Do I stink?" She whispered.

Jack inhaled and smiled. "Not at all."

"Oh ok. Just checking. I was beginning to wonder. "

"Would you come to dinner with me tonight?" Jack asked. He smiled his best smile, his glee with Terry genuine. He had been cultivating this moment with her, but in no way expected the star pupil in Professor Johnson's Computer Science course to become so brazen.

"Dinner? No. I won't. We could just go to your place and fuck though. "

"Umm... I have roommates. "Jack said.

"Put a sock on the door knob." Terry said. She winked.

The professor droned on, others were whispering as well.

"A sock on the knob means we are fucking?" Jack asked. It was one of those awkward moments when all others stopped talking in time for his voice to ring out quite audibly. The entire class went silent.

Professor Johnson glanced up at Jack and Terry.

"Yes. In the dorms. That's what it means. "He said. The class burst into laughter. Jack reddened a bit, Terry was crimson. Johnson gave a patient smile, went back to his lecture.

Jack got Terry's phone number and promised to call her. He had decided to skip his CAD Design class and get back to work on the desk he had designed using CAD. Figured that it would qualify for extra credit and if it didn't then the Prof didn't understand that Jack was not looking for a CAD job with a big company. He wanted to be the big company employing the CAD designers.

He strolled quickly through the campus to the parking lot. The day was cold, the sky dark grey. Piles of snow lined the parking area like micro glaciers at the end of the lot where the plow trucks all pushed the snow. He had parked his car sort of up on the edge of one of these so it sat at a sharp agle. This was the only spot available to park, and was not actually a parking spot, but when running late, it is ok to improvise.

The noon day sun flickered between thick grey clouds that were clearing, lit up the leading edges like giant white cauliflower contrasted against the black, snow bearing clouds. He breathed in the fresh air happily, his head upward, looking at the sky as he walked.

A truck honked behind him. Jack flinched sideways, boots slipped on thick ice. He lurched and jumped to keep from falling, turned to see who had about hit him.

Audrey smiled merrily at him from her truck window, her blond hair framed her face where it poked out from her Parka hood, her bright blue eyes beaming at him.

"Got you good Jack." She laughed. She jumped out of the truck and Jack gave her a hug, purposefully inhaling the scent of her hair, light perfume filling his senses.

"You smell even better when you are awake." Jack said.

Audrey laughed. She pulled him by the hand toward the truck.

"Get in! I have a surprise for you." She said. Jack looked at her, amused and happy to see her.

When the semester began she had informed him that she was in love with a man near her own age, two years older. Jack was glad to hear it, happy for her, and even happier that they were still friends, even though he had hoped to have an ongoing fling with her, which is how she came to tell him she was in love, and attempting to be a good woman - something she had said with a blush and a sexy sigh, then told Jack that she wanted him as a dear friend forever if that could be possible.

Jack got in her truck and she pulled into a parking spot, now available, near his car, left the truck running and shifted on the bench seat to face him, her formal professor skirt slipping up her nylon clad thighs a bit. Jack smiled as he admired them openly. Audrey didn't mind and stretched just a bit more for his pleasure.

"My surprise is that I am getting married." She said. She removed a thin glove and showed him a large diamond ring on her finger. "I already told your mom so I thought I should tell you before she did." Audrey said.

Jack nodded, his mouth suddenly dry, he averted his eyes as silly thoughts of a parking lot blow job, as in days gone by, flitted away like cockroaches in sudden light.

Audrey giggled. "You look stunned Jack, it's ok, I know your mind silly boy. And yes, those days are over. For now, at least. Never know if he is going to remain good in the sack or not." Audrey winked.

Jack nodded and sighed. "I was hoping to keep you on the list of excellent sex."

Audrey, oddly enough, did not change her receptive body language, just gazed at him and nodded.

"I was hoping you would marry me Jack. But I get the whole age thing, and you wanting kids, even though mine loved you and were free, silly man." She winked.

"Are you doing this then to get revenge? To show me that you are a desirable woman and I have missed getting you? You should know that even when I was with Sarah I felt very strong memories of you and actually missed your mind, your sex, wished you were her age." Jack said.

Audrey sighed. "You and I will always be soul mates despite time difference, I am forever yours to love. If you want me right now I will give myself to you, willingly."

Jack nodded. "I do. I want you, I want to be your hot, dirty little secret." Jack said. His eyes again explored Audrey's thighs with open lust.

"I am planning a wee vacation at the Alyeska resort during one of his business trips." Audrey said. She winked and smiled playfully.

Jack slid out of the truck, looked her in the eye. "Call me." He said. "Love you Audrey."

"I love you too Jack McKnight." Audrey said. She smiled as their eyes met. She sighed and blew a strand of hair out of her face.

"You better come when I do call or I will be crushed." She said in a quiet tone.

"No, you won't, you are way more resilient than that shit." Jack said. "And I will answer, and come running."

He watched her tail lights depart, swirls of steam and exhaust shrouding her truck as she turned and was gone.

When he fired up his car on the fourth try it was with cussing and prayer, the battery near dead in the winter cold, the steering wheel freezing his fingers, 'I Wanna Know What Love Is' by the Foreigner came on and he began to laugh. KWHL had it's sappy moments. He plugged a cassette in, Tantric Buddhists choir by Jerry Garcia and listened to the deep chants of the Tibetan Monks as he sped across the slippery Anchorage streets towards Alaska Fabrications and the magical desk they were creating. Glen would be busy with his day job until the evening but he would join in the work at five thirty or so when he got off and could spend time in the rear of the shop.

7 : 4 2   P M

Jack made some calls and arranged to bring Terry to his former roommate's place. Brian Smith had been Jack's friend from way back in third grade in Cordova and was recently his roommate, he and two others, Matt, and Brad. Cordova friends, the three of them gillnetters since they were fourteen years old and doing well with it. They rented his house from him while he was living with Audrey for the last year and a half, stored all his stuff in the bottom level bedroom of the home.

Upon his return from France he made the decision to live with his folks rather than move in with his friends and make them return his Master Bedroom to its former glory. He knew them too well and would be prone to partying with them more than he cared for because, after missing a semester and changing his major, he loaded up with eighteen credit hours and a three-year plan rather than four to his degree.

He explained to Brian that Terry might not think it cool if he lived with mom and dad. The house was a big hillside home that had been abandoned when the oil people made an exodus out of Alaska after the price per barrel of oil plunged. The realty company was desperate to sell it, the bank very reasonable, of course, after he bought it, the value continued to plunge. One would think that buying a million-dollar home for under half a million would be a safe bet. Not in Alaska's oil based economy. Oil execs were fleeing, rumor had it that they were tapeing payment booklets to the door knobs of their homes with a note that said, "Please move in and take over payments."

Jack pulled up to Terry's parents' house in his rumbling Lincoln and she ran to it and jumped in with an excited giggle. She shut her long winter coat in the door and tried to give Jack a quick kiss only to have the trapped coat not allow her to reach him. Terry groaned with frustration until Jack met her half way and kissed her. A quick peck on the lips. She then opened the door and jerked her coat out of the way, closed it again, slid over and pressed up against him.

"My parents will be home any moment, lets' get outa here." She said. Jack obliged and eased on down the road between piles of snow three and four feet high, veritable frozen barriers left by the city plow crews.

"Your parents are right to keep a tight leash on you." Jack said. "You have a very naughty side from what I can tell."

Terry sighed and nodded. "I do. They however, are simply control freaks who think that because I need them right now while I go to school they can still tell me when to be home. Even though I have a naughty streak, I am really a very good girl and love the control freaks very much."

They talked. Jack probed and prodded at Terry with questions and humor, found himself very much liking her answers, her wit. When he began to drive up O'Mally Terry fell silent for a moment.

"You live up here?" She asked.

Jack smiled and gave the big Lincoln some more gas for the momentum he would need to get the rear wheel drive car up the hill ahead.

"Yes. I have a room with lots of roommates." Jack said.

Jack sped the rest of the way up the hill, made the car go sideways around the hairpin corners to keep his momentum up to make it to the top. In his rearview mirror, he could see the lights of Anchorage far below.

"Why are you suddenly tense?" Jack asked.

Terry gave a thin smile. "A boy took me on a bad date up here once, at some weirdo's house. There were naked women in a big birdcage, it was scary to me."

Jack nodded. "I know the place. My place is an entirely different scene."

As he spoke he turned the Lincoln down the drive to his home on Oney Circle.There were six cars in the v shaped driveway in front of a big square home with square windows, a cubist representation of a home. Jack had been ecstatic when he purchased it. The architecture, a modernist combination of Art Deco and Mediterranean gave the place an exotic feel, especially in the sunshine. The home held its warmth even through winter, though the design would look better on a Caribbean beach or hill side. Fishing had been great, his need to invest a burden, and the oil people were bailing out of Alaska fast which drove the price down to what he could barely afford. When the housing market recovered from the oil executive's exoduses there was no doubt in Jack's mind that the home's value would sky rocket.

"Very cool house!" Terry said.

"It is indeed lovely, isn't it?" Jack said. He grinned at her amazed eyes.

"Are you rich?" She asked. "I mean, that has nothing to do with the fact that we are coming here to screw, for all I knew you lived with your parents, like I do, when I used un-lady like tactics to gain your full attention."

Jack laughed. "You did kinda put it out there." He said. "I was interested in you the whole time though, looked forward to sitting in class with you and observing your squirmations."

"Squirmations?" Terry giggled. "Don't think that is even a word Jack."

"Nope, but it is communicative so it's valid."

"Well, I don't believe that I was 'squirmating' at all."

"You were. You squirmated until you pulled your panties down and gave me a whiff of your pussy, which, I must add, smelled very yummy. Yup, I would say you were definitely squirmating."

Terry giggled as Jack parked the car. It was cold and dark out, a wind blowing, as it most always did on the hillside.

"So, you don't park in the garage?" Terry asked.

"I actually do live with my parents." Jack said flatly. "It's a long story, but involves women, love, breakups, ends with me at my parents' house, safe and warm while I study and build, with this house rented out to friends. Really, really good friends." Jack said.

Terry nodded. "I would like to meet them. I would also like to squirmate all over you when we get the chance."

Jack laughed and gave her hand a squeeze. Her brown eyes were warm and merry, her cheeks a slight pink over a cute smattering of freckles. He went to her side of the car and helped her out, walked her towards the big, dark green double doors, entered to faint music coming from the living room, conversation, and soft laughter. The kitchen was to the left of the foyer and smelled of a myriad of meats and spices. Jack kicked off his boots, slung off his coat, hung it on a bronze hook between other long heavy coats then helped Terry remove her long coat which she had tucked around her the entire time she had been in the car.

She was dressed in a white blouse and sensible blue jeans, smelled good, was excited and eager.

"Hi Jack, welcome home." Brian said. He held a plate in one hand, a large stein adorned with a dragon and iron bands in the other. His smile was charming as he eyed Terry and nodded to her.

Brian had curly blond hair, bright blue eyes, a pug nose and handsome face. He had been valedictorian at graduation, was currently studying Financial Economics towards a doctorate. Sharp guy. He was also a gillnetter, had been so since he was fourteen which was the age that most boys in fishing families began to desire being their own boss instead of dad. The other two friends, Mat and Brad, had also started at the age of fourteen in their own gillnetting operations.

Jack shook Brian's hand. He hadn't visited but once since he had been back.

"Terry this is my best buddy Brian Smith, he and I grew up together in Cordova."

"Cordova?" Terry asked. She nodded to Brian as she shook his hand.

"Yes, Cordova, where the odds are good but the goods are odd." Brian said.

Jack felt Terry press up against him and slid his arm around her as if they had been together a long and intimate time, felt that way. His fingers stroked her side, felt her soft warm baby fat near her hip.

She laughed at Brian's comment. "I believe I read that article. Thought it was written by a stuck-up bitch when I read it."

Brian smiled. "She was right. And she was funny, but you are also right, she is a twizzle head." He nodded towards the kitchen. "The chefs in the group cooked up some killer food, broke out some summer reserves for the occasion."

They entered the kitchen and smells of spice and garlic filled Jack's nostrils.

Mat and Brad hailed him from the living room where they sat with plates of food, a fire blazing, candles nicely placed and the lamps gave the living room a comfortable glow. They sat with their girlfriends, talking, the ladies smiled and nodded at he and Terry.

"We didn't wait to eat, it is bad luck to not eat fish immediately once it is ready, against some kind of Native law I think." Brad said. His bass voice carried very well from the living room to the kitchen.

Jack's stomach rumbled as he eyed the foods. Baked King Salmon from the look of it, sat on a metal pan next to battered halibut, a large bowl next to that held what he was hungry for – beer battered King Crab legs.

"My god there it is!" Jack said. He grinned seized a plate, placed two of the fat, crispy, battered crab legs on it, scooped a copious amount of Brian's famous spicy tartar sauce next to them.

"It has been a long time between dinner parties, I wouldn't dream of having you over and not fixing up some legs." Brian said.

"Yeah," Brad spoke. "You don't have time to play with us anymore cause your all growed up and want to focus on yer studies." His voice carried over the polite conversation and dim background music. Jack just shrugged and smiled at his friends. "Nah, I just really wanted to live with my parents."

They laughed and went back to their conversation. Jack heard Mat say, "No seriously, he does actually live with his parents." Jack shot him an 'I will kill you' look but Mat just shrugged and grinned.

Brian offered Terry a choice of beer, wine, whiskey, or scotch. The later beverage perked Jack's ears up a bit. Terry dished up a smattering of salmon, crab, halibut, and a pile of asparagus, mashed potatoes, and gravy thick with deer liver bits, onions, and mushrooms. The dining room table was still littered with plates and as they moved to sit the others rose from the living room and joined them at the table. Introductions were made, Jack had not met the winter girlfriends his friends had made. He smiled at this thought as Terry's knee pressed against his. Was she going to be the Winter Girlfriend? If so they had little time, winter was about over. Jack shrugged at the thought. Cordova boys had a bad reputation for leaving to fish and dropping the girl.

Terry was only eighteen, the youngest in the room, and the only under-age one among them. He had thought she was twenty at first impression because she carried herself very well.

"This is much nicer than the last Hillside party I went to." Terry said.

"Thanks, this type of party is more my thing." Jack said. "It's a Thursday Night Dinner Party, a tradition we have all had for a long time, Friday Night Rumbles happen tomorrow."

He laughed when Mat cocked his head at the statement, caught on, and shook his head.

"Do you go to Hillside parties often?" Mat asked.

Terry shook her head 'no'. "My parents keep pretty tight reins on me." She said.

"There are a lot of killer parties all the time up here." Cloe, Mat's lady, said. She wore her hair in large blond curls, like Fara Faucet, a thing that took some doing with a curling iron and hair spray. Her hair swept to and froe as she spoke and hugged Mat. She was standing next to him and picking off his plate bits of King Crab meat as he shucked for her. A bit tipsy she was with wine, face aglow with the comfort of friends, drink, and feast. The other two ladies, Tanya, who was with Brad, and Sandy, with Brian, were sitting and sipping wine from large glasses as the guys reloaded with seconds from the selection of meats tatters, and veggies.

Jack waited until the others got settled into the big wood high back din-ing chairs with fresh plates of food, before taking an appreciative bite of the beer battered King Crab leg. He felt the crunch of the batter, savored the flavors of the beer, the sweet, rich crab, garlic, and onion salt, as he breathed through his nostrils the scents of the delicacy.

"Mm! That's so good... Damn, Brian, thank you, I missed these so much." Jack said. His tone was a low moan that made Terry giggle.

The ate and talked then retired to the living room with a glass of scotch in hand, and cigars. Jack showed Terry how to ready her cigar tip with the little guillotine snip as she smiled and stared into his eyes. They varied the conversation to include the ladies, otherwise it would have all been fishing brags. Jack told his friends he had just invested in a new boat.

"No shit? How big is it?" Brian asked. "You are doing it at the right time buddy, fishing is going to be killer next year and we all did fantastic this year."

"Moving on up!" Brad said. "Gonna' grab you a piece of the sky."

"Thanks Jefferson." Jack said. He laughed at Brad's botched imitation of the dance George Jefferson always did at the intro of The Jeffersons.

"It's a limit seiner but get this, will be rigged for multiple fisheries and tourism for the off season. Thinking about having people pay to come out during the seine season as observers."

"Hell yeah, like the dude ranch that I visited this year, it was cool, I got to rope some calves and drive cattle, got to feel saddle sore to. We went out for four days, great experience."

As they chatted and bantered back and forth Jack began to feel a bit nostalgic as he sat with his friends. Whenever they got together they spoke of their dreams and goals, of building empire, of expanding and innovating equipment, compared notes on new stuff that was coming out. He realized at that moment that he loved his buddies.

"You remember when we were all fourteen, had skipped school and went to the Eyak River to drink beer near Happy Joe's house?" Jack asked.

"Yeah, we were all standing in dead fish and mud. The smell was that of money we missed on the grounds." Brian said.

Jack nodded. "That day, in autumn, after you guys had finished your second season and blown away our parents expectations I sort of took a look at us, from outside the picture, while we were skipping school and drinking beer on the banks of the Eyak River. We were so young, so hopeful an exuberant... I realized then that we were all princes, set to inherit Prince William Sound and the Copper River Flats and right as I was having that thought the song "Sweet Emotion" by Aerosmith, came on. The sun was just right on the water... I will never forget that day."

Jack raised his glass.

"Here is to our inheritance, may we prosper, may we grow, we are the new era."

They all raised their glasses and called out an exuberant agreement as the glass clinked together.

"Maybe someday your mom will let you come fish with us on the flats." Brian said.

Jack laughed and shook his head. "Even if she did I would be happier Seining, bigger boat, calmer waters. My hat is off to you guys but that muddy chop out there is forever ruined for me after it took my cousin."

They all nodded solemnly. "Here is to David McKnight." He said. They drank again.

"He was a good guy." Jack said and nodded. The Scotch burned on its way down. He took a puff off his cigar and leaned into Terry, whispered in her ear.

"Are you ready for me to put the sock on the knob?" Terry's cheeks turned red as she giggled. He took her hand, warm and soft, and led her downstairs through the other living area that was set up with a theater and comfortable chairs for gaming, a wet bar, and a work out area. Mat was residing in one of the bedrooms in the downstairs and Jack's stuff was boxed in the other bedroom. When he turned the lights on he found a bed that had a pile of blankets placed on it, a thoughtful gesture from one of the three, and his boxed belongings that had been in the master bedroom. A bit unromantic but neither cared.

Jack ran his hand up Terry's slender neck and tangled his fingers in her hair as he pulled her in for a kiss. Her body was warm, soft, she shivered at his touch. He sensed her lack of experience, found some blankets and a big comforter in the closet and spread that out on the bed. By the time he had it organized Terry was already naked. Inexperienced, but willing. She giggled as the look of surprise on his face when he first lay eyes on her. He glanced appreciatively at her body. Her breasts her small, very firm, capped by perfectly round areola and long hard little nipples, the sexy little fat pad of her belly descended into a smoothly shaved cleft, something that he was not used to seeing, something he found very alluring. Just a few hours ago she had some nice brown curlys.

"You are adorable." Jack said. "You shaved right after class?"

Terry nodded. "Thought you might like it, all the girls are starting to do it. She looked down at herself. "Do you like it?" She asked.

He nodded, smiled, moved towards her as he skinned his shirt off.

"I like, very much." He said.

Jack took her in his arms and felt the soft, smooth warmth of her belly against his. He studied her eyes, as he gently pulled her to him for a first kiss.

First kisses were everything, the tell of chemistry, the sage of lust, the oracle of love. Terry's tongue flickered over his, thrust into his mouth with an innocent eagerness. When the kiss was over he was erect. Her hand grasped him and pulled as she lay back and spread open her legs.

"Just do it fast." Terry said. "We can kiss and explore later."

Jack hovered pressing just his erection against her, slid it lightly over her abdomen, downward, the swollen head grazing her smoothly shaved cleft.

Terry nodded with enthusiasm, her eyes big, round, fixed on his belly and crotch.

Jack nudged gently and felt a bit of resistance. She was wet, breathing heavy. He leaned over her and kissed her neck as he slid into her a bit then met resistance again.

"Hold still!" Terry hissed. Her legs wrapped around Jack's ass and she pulled him into her as she thrust her hips. He felt the resistance grow taunt, her eyes widen in fear, mouth open, lips making a little 'oh'. There was a release and he entered her, held still while meeting her gravely concerned and determined eyes.

"Ah!! Ohhhkkkk..." Terry had a mischievous grin on her face. "Now you know I am a good girl for reals." She giggled.

Jack sighed, trembled with pleasure. He had never taken a virgin before and felt as if he had been the one who was being taken, could feel every pulse and heart beat through her vagina, the pleasure extreme as he continued a bit deeper. Knowing she was a virgin, wanting to get rid of the status, and chose him, unexpectedly, helped prolong his pleasure for some twisted moral reason that he didn't, at the moment, care about. Jack made double sure he was a gentle animal with her, felt a certain responsibility to set the stage for the rest of her sex life. She screamed and whooped when he went down on her. Then she wanted more! more! more! Terry was a delight.

BLACK FRIDAY

FETCHED ASHORE
MORONS PLOT A COURSE OVER BLIGH REEF WITH A SUPER TANKER
THE LIES OF PREPAREDNESS
GROSS NEGLIGENCE

1989, MARCH 24ᵀᴴ, FRIDAY, 7:00 AM

When Jack awoke the next morning, he was a bit hung over, crusty with Terry glaze. She was still asleep next to him. He suppressed his urge to pee, for just a moment longer, - had awoke from a dream where he was pissing all over the papers on his desk - and gazed at the girl. Her eyes were closed, cheeks a light pink, lips moist, comforter pulled up to her neck. Beautiful, innocent, and sweet. The phone was ringing upstairs. Faint.

Jack pissed and wobbled a bit. The phone started ringing again. Annoying. What time was it? He glanced at his wrist watch. Seven in the morning. He dressed, washed his face, combed his hair a bit, made his way upstairs knowing full well the phone would stop ringing by the time he got there. It did.

Brian had made his way to the living room. He looked sodden, but smiled through bleary eyes.

"Who the fuck is calling at this hour?" Brian said.

"I was going to check." Jack glanced at the AT@T recording machine. "Two messages." He hit play.

"Jack, it's mom, you better turn on the news, then get home, or get home and turn on the news, your father is flipping out. It's... A huge disaster... Just watch the news... I love you honey."

Jack stared at the answering machine. Stunned. His mother's voice was panicked. Everything bad went through his mind.

Brian turned on the tv. A Sandlers's furniture commercial was on. After brief consideration Jack decided he would wait for the tv rather than call his mother back. He found a half pot of coffee, poured two half cups and ran hot water from the tap into them. He handed Brian a cup and sat on the couch. The commercial ended, the news came on. Special Report.

Jack watched and listened, there had been an oil spill. In Prince William Sound. Yeah. The environmentalists would be pissed about that. He figured they would have it cleaned up in short time. Bligh Reef... Hmm... Monumentally stupid. Even he charted well around Bligh Reef and he only drew six and a half feet of water.

He then saw a chart depicting the oil spreading outward. The size of it sank in. Happened just after midnight. About the same time, he had been taken by Terry again, for the fourth time.

The tanker had been gushing oil for... Seven hours.

"Fuuuuuckk!" Jack finally exclaimed. He leapt to his feet. "Fuuuuuck! Fuuuuuckk! That's going to wipe us out! Why aren't they doing anything?" Jack felt anger flood through him, amp his breathing, tighten his muscles. He stood and bounced about while watching. "They need to plug that fucking hole! What the fuck? There aren't even any boats there with that company... What the fuck is the companies name? Why aren't they there?

Brian stared at him, eyes wide, mouth open a little then said. "Alyeska Corp.?"

"Yes! That's it. Where the hell is Alyeska? They are supposed to be there, if this ever happened, and... It's fucking happening now for seven hours!"

"Fuck!" Jack picked up a recliner and heaved it across the room.

"I gotta go!" Jack said. He started towards his coat, then remembered Terry.

"Yeah. Before you destroy my stuff! Put that fucking chair back and calm the fuck down. They will clean it up. "

"They? Who the fuck is 'They'? It's been seven hours and 'They' haven't done shit!"

Jack felt rage surge through him. It was raw, powerful, but not entirely unchecked. He used it to heave the recliner back upright, drag it back to the square indent it left on the carpet. As he crossed the room with it he knew his dad was freaking out. They could lose the boats. They could lose the fishing. Jack slammed the chair into place.

"Jesus dude. That's my favorite chair. "

"Don't you get it? We are fucked!" Jack waved his hand at the television.

"I said relax!" Brian snapped. It was a sharp bark. Jack stared at his buddy. The guy looked furious. But he didn't know. Didn't know the hoops and weaves Jack and his father had gone through. Everything was tied up in the new boats. He had done a second mortgage on the house they were now standing in even though the first one had no equity, he had done it on, expected equity. The house could be gone as well. Poof. Boat gone, fishing gone, house gone... Because some moron Exxon employee was actually stupid enough to plot a course, with a god forsaken Super Tanker, full of crude oil, over Bligh Reef, a plainly marked fucking reef, it might as well have run into Bligh Island. He sucked oxygen in through his nose, deeply, told himself to get rational.

Jack began to run several scenarios through his mind.

Cancel everything!! Call Vern and tell him no deal... It's too late! We shook hands, exchanged money, signed contracts. The financing is done. Fuck! They were a bit creative on the financing. House, boat, permit, everything tied up.'

Jack groaned. There were huge payments to be made.

He blinked. Brian was staring at him.

"You ok? You just went away..."

Jack realized his face had been frozen, eyed staring off, mouth and jaw clenched so hard it hurt.

"I just bought a new boat. I have sixty thousand dollars I must pay by the end of September for the next thirty fucking years! I mortaged this place to the hilt... After this shit the value is going to plunge even more, first the oil people flee, then they destroy my fishery on the way out! Cocksuckers!" Jack felt his head swelling painfully, a lance of ache stretched from his forehead, down his spine, into his left foot. He realized he was holding his breath, forced himself to release this mess, gain some damn self-control, wondered if he was having a stroke. He let out a miserable sigh.

"I gotta talk with my dad. He is worse than me when it comes to this shit. Has probably destroyed the entire living room by now…" Jack chuckled at the imagined carnage. McKnights were famous for their rage.

"In fact… I must talk to lots of people in a short time. I need to go to Cordova. We are going to get hit the most by this. We only have fishing to sustain us."

"Yeah. I am thinking I should go too. We should. "Brian said. "I will call and make reservations. Ferry. Are you taking your truck?"

Jack nodded.

"Good I am driving down too. My girlfriend of a month ago introduced me to her dad, a Russian family. He travels around the world running oil skimmers. Told me some tall tales. But the bottom line was that he was very wealthy from doing this - working on oil spills. I bet there is going to be money to be earned. "

Jack nodded as the info sunk in. Work would be good. Money. But then next year? What then? So far in debt. He smiled and nodded at Brian. Of all his friends the guy was the most sensible, a rock he was grateful for.

He helped himself to Brian's coffee and brewer and in five minutes, he and Brian were at the kitchen table, chain smoking, a fresh mug of coffee in hand, note pads, pens scratching, the two of them sounding out ideas back and forth, making notes of shit to do. The action felt good, was the best defense against dismay.

"Get reservations for Ferry." Brian wrote. He wanted to go right away.

Jack did not want to go right away. He had college classes to consider, fourty-two-hundred wrapped up in that. Semester would be over by May, better than half the value was already had from the investment.

"*Talk to profs and see if I can finish classes by corresponding.*" Jack wrote.

"*Get Truck Packed for ferry. List of calls to make: Dan Gartney, Fish and Game guy. Dad.*"

"Dad first." Jack said aloud. He picked up the phone and dialed his dad. He let the phone ring six times and Robert answered.

"Hi Dad, Jack."

"Goddamn call waiting. I am on the line with Uncle Conner. I will talk when we are done." Robert said.

"Ok, I am at Brian's. Bye." Jack hung up.

"That went well. "Brian said.

"We are brief and to the point. He is conferring with Uncle Conner. He got a boat along with us. They will probably come up with the same conclusion as us. That we need to be there."

Jack shook his head. "We don't need to if they get some boats out there and clean that shit up."

"We might be the boats Jack, Gyles Knowles is there now, let me call him."

"I would call my Uncle Conner but Dad is talking with him right now." Jack said.

Terry entered the room looking a bit embarrassed until she noticed they were agitated.

"What's going on?" She asked.

"There has been a huge oil spill in Prince William Sound. I own a business there, commercial fishing." Jack said.

Terry's eyes registered and widened. "That's right, you are a fisherman. Ohhh... That would explain those big muscles you got there." She giggled and squeezed his arm, eyes alight with merriment. Jack smiled, thankful for an easing of the heavy situation. He pulled Terry over his lap, jean clad butt up in the air as she giggle- gasped. He smacked his hand on her ass.

"This is serious you wench!" Jack said.

Brian, who had been talking with Gyles, grinned at the sight of Jack smacking butt. He hung up the phone.

"Gyles says he has never seen so many helicopters buzzing about town. There are lots of suits and media people already showing up.

Jack let Terry up. She pulled her T-shirt down to cover her belly, leaned into his ear and whispered. "I am not a wench... But that made me wet." And walked off, a glance over her shoulder and a cute wiggle of her ass.

"Excuse me for a minute, or twenty. "Jack said.

"You run off and fuck. I will worry for the both of us. "Brian said. He made a dismissive gesture.

When Jack and Terry returned, Brian sat with Brad and Mat. All were frantically scribbling notes and making calls. Sandy was bustling about the kitchen making some eggs and sausages.

Jack sat and lit a smoke. Mat hung up the phone. The phone rang. He snatched it back up. "Mat here... Oh, hello Robert, yes, he is here." He handed the phone over to Jack.

"Sorry kid. I just hate the interruptions of call waiting. It insinuates that the other call may be more important."

"I understand. What does uncle Conner's take on all this?"

"He is calmer than me that's for sure.

"Usually the case.

"What the fuck does that mean?"

"That he stays calmer than you."

"Yeah, I know that, he is my brother, I know him better than you do. He thinks that Alyeska Pipeline Company has a plan for this kind of event. They have oil boom - they will get around the oil."

"Then why aren't they out there yet?" Jack asked.

"Nobody knows that. There are not even any signs of mobilization in Valdez."

"No? What the fuck?"

"Conner plans to run his boat out with several other Cordova fishermen tomorrow. He is getting ready today."

"And do what? Glare at a tanker?" Jack snapped.

"No smart ass, they are going to start dipping the oil aboard using brailers full of oil absorbent rags while the media copters fly overhead. That ought to make the news and shame the bastards into action."

Jack nodded. "Yes! I can see it. Great idea. Fuck. I want to be there. "

"You have school to worry about kid. Let the pros handle this. Things should be ok. Besides, if things don't work out you are going to need an education in the future."

"The pros? Captain Cook avoided the reef before it was named after his first mate, there are no pros involved in this. It has to have been done on purpose."

"Don't start in with the conspiracy theories, not now, that shit gets old. What is happening right now is nothing, they are doing nothing, probably stunned that it has happened. They promised there would be a plan, a rapid response, but so far, they have shown that they lied about that."

"Dad, it's a conspiracy. They did it on purpose." Jack said. "Bligh Reef has not been run into since it was marked on the map."

"Not a conspiracy kid, gross negligence and incompetence. Jesus Christ kid, I gotta go, make arrangements, you stay in school and I will let you know when you should come, if it means to quit the semester."

"Alright, yes sir. See you soon."

THE BAD NEWS AND THE GOOD NEWS

1989, MARCH 25ᵀᴴ, SATURDAY, 5:00 AM

Jack awoke, made a pot of coffee. Thought of his yoga and went into the dark living room and began to stretch and breath. He did not want to watch the news. Today was to be spent working with Glen on his desk project. He imagined the birth of ErgoDyn as he breathed into a yoga pose. His recent dreams flooding back to him.

> A large house decaying at the edge of the sea. Boats floating on crystal clear ocean, gold fish flitting about under water. A voice clear and soft. "There is the path, there is the way." As Jack watched the clear waters the rocks grew until they constricted the flow and pressed the gold fish together. The little fish darted about confused, then lined up and began to swim in what was now a narrow creek. Jack reached down and found his hands on the controls of his boat. He pushed the black knobbed lever forward and then idled up to speed with the red knobbed lever. His boat followed the gold fish down the narrow stream to a steep hill. With a rush his boat plunged over the edge. Jack was elated, and held on as he steered and saw he was on a mountain side steering down towards Cordova harbor. Only the mountain was above Anchorage. The dream had not been Lucid. But Jack saw its symbols clearly. Clearly as mud.

'What path? Where? When?'

He sighed and stood. Coffee yoga this morning; he poured a cup. Now was time to manifest a long-time day dream, the desk, and the fab shop. ErgoDyn Inc. shimmered with potential in his mind.

7:00 AM

By seven o'clock he was at Glen's shop working on his desk. Fucking things up. Glen cursing and showing him the right way.

"I know you are distracted by this bullshit oil spill but common man. You don't gotta' sand all the way through the form there."

"Shit! Sorry." Jack looked at his work. Not as bad as Glen made it sound, but only because he had stopped him before he did any damage.

Jack's arms were sore. He had been in a bit of a trance as he sanded smooth the cockpit cowl so they could gel coat it a final color then add layers of clear coat. In a trance of worry and fret.

"I have so much debt. Payments on the Emma Dawn, the new boat, this house... nearly two fucking million dollars... Why didn't I listen to my mom? Now she is going to say 'I told you so!' Jesus, what a mess... Uncle Conner is out there now... that should shame Exxon and Alyeska into action, if the media isn't already bought and paid for... No way, the media delights in destroying large companies, just look at what they tried to do the General Motors...

His back ached, with the exertion of sanding, and an additional amount from the effects of his mind in reaction to the news of the oil spill. It was like every muscle was tense, like there was a constant, blunt, dagger wedged between and under both shoulder blades.

Jack dusted off the spot he was sanding and stood back to admire their work. They were both very proud of the piece. It was sleek, unique, and flowed in function and form. It would be a rich maroon color with lighter shades of gold and darker brown swirled into it. Much like marble in appearance. Glen had made four boards with different color choices. They were each so good that they decided they would be retained and offered as model choices to potential clients.

Glen lit a smoke, offered Jack one.

"I got my ass chewed out yesterday for clocking out early to work on this thing."

"Shit, really? I don't want you to get in trouble over this."

"Trouble? I run this place. If Paul fires me he will have to do all the shit I do. We have an agreement, I can side project all I want, if he is taken care of. Profits are up. Cause of me. But he acts like the business is failing because of me, last couple months here have been bullshit."

Jack nodded. The last time he had talked with Glen he had grandly offered him a job, a new company, and done so with confidence. Now he was looking at losing his fishing operation. His entire perspective on his future was now a haze of fear and worst-case scenarios.

"It seems that my grand plan, ErgoDyn, may have to wait." Jack muttered.

"No, it isn't!" Glen said. His voice was raised, made Jack jump a bit when Glen waved a paper in front of Jack.

"That is an order form for three desks like this one from Gillian Robinson. You familiar with the Robinson family here in Anchorage?"

Jack nodded even though he was still trying to recall why and what they had done.

"Bankers? Alaskan's First Bank? Big money and politics? Anyway, I am dating Gillian, their daughter, and ahem, President of the bank. You know the pamphlet you gave me? It rang a bell with her." Glen laughed and shook his head. "Actually, it sent off klaxons. She kinda flipped out when she read it. She does it too, dreams like you do. Then I told her about the desk design and how we met... Well, not everything about how we met." Glen laughed. "Fact is, bud, when she saw the desk she said you are the real thing. A Lucidian. She told me that she lucid dreams which got me more interested in it. Said it totally changed her life. That you are a visionary because you put into words what she felt, but couldn't express. And... She wants to meet you..." Glen frowned. Jack saw in his friend's facial expression and heard in his purposeful tone that he had his doubts about having the two of them meet.

Jack laughed. "I would love to meet her and you think she will be interested in financing ErgoDyn? It is good to date the President of a bank.

"Ha, not at all... Actually... yes, it is good. I am already jealous. She is going to meet you and forget all about me."

"Then I can bring my girlfriend. "Jack said.

"I thought your girlfriend was marrying another man for a while." Glen said.

"She is, we talked, it's cool for me to date. So, I asked out a young freshman, well, she picked up on me in truth, a virgin as it turned out. I believe she is Winter Girl material. Met her in computer science class. Very smart and super cute and I don't mean, kinda cute, I mean adorable cute, and smart, a keeper by all other standards."

Glen nodded, shrugged. "I am not that insecure, just reasonably logical. You don't know Gillian like I do. She is very… forward thinking, I guess. But this means that this has great potential for a loan scenario. Honestly, I question whether I would sacrifice her to get the loan, that is how bad I want to run my own shop." Glen said. He let out a sigh, gave a wry smile and shook his head as if accepting the scenario and it's adverse potential.

"Gillian is going to give us an interview for the financing for ErgoDyn. She even loved the name. "He said. His eyes blazed now with the enthusiasm and intelligence that had attracted Jack to him in the first place.

"That's… Very good news. I need some of that right now." Jack then burst out laughing. "Sarah's mom controlled the money, clung tightly to millions, and this guy signed over the task of running a multi-million-dollar bank to his daughter? Roughly the same age I assume? How nice, exactly, is Mr. Robinson.?"

Glen shrugged. "Never met him. I have only been dating Gillian for a month. I don't exactly want to meet the parents just yet. Her Dad is a lawyer, chairman of the board, oil wealthy, the list goes on. Intimidating is how Gillian describes him. He knows judges and calls Senators friends. Kinda makes for an awkward meeting given my past… Enterprises. "Glen said.

"And what might they be?" Jack asked.

"Grower. I had a huge operation. The officer that popped me obtained a questionable search warrant. I got off. Mr. Robinson is no doubt friends with the prosecutor. "

"Holy shit! You're a grower, or were?" Jack asked. He had known a few. Odd sort, but very knowledgeable about cannabis and horticulture. His tone, therefore, was one of admiration rather than scorn. Which he suspected that Glen feared. He saw Glen's face light up a bit.

"The best in Alaska! A strain of Matanuska Thunder Fuck, Quadriplegic, a nice breed of Indica and stronger Indica…" Glen smiled. "I don't smoke it any more… Or any less actually… Ok a lot less."

Jack laughed. "I smoke it per my code. Tiny amounts, know your grower and the source of the seeds and hybrids. But... Let's get back to the money my friend. "

"Right... The interview. That's gonna be as soon as possible. We need to talk to her about it."

Jack frowned. He didn't know where he would be in a week if things didn't go well in Prince William Sound.

"I have no way to commit to a meeting right now with this fucking oil spill threatening to wipe me out. I mean, I could lose everything." Jack said.

Glen nodded, a stern light in his eyes, then said something that stuck with Jack for the rest of his life.

"When you know what you want, you will make a fucking commitment. I want this. I even read, and dug, your little pamphlet, puts things together for me. I suggest you use what you wrote and cause this meeting to happen, because it is exactly what your Lucidian thing is all about. It's one of those 'clicks' where shit comes together, where the doors open and things advance in your desired direction unexpected and in uncommon hour."

Jack stared at him for a moment then broke out laughing. "You are mingling Thoreau in with your persuasive speech." He said.

"Yes, I am, you handed me the keys to the universe, but Thoreau did as well, you aren't the only brilliant one in the room."

"The keys to the universe... Yes. I want it too. Ok! I am committed. We will do it!"

He extended his hand. Glen shook it. "Gillian is going to like you, way too much, I know it."

Jack shook his head. "I will bring Terry, she is fresh, cute, pretty and bouncy in all the right places. Best student in the classes I have with her. You will love her."

"Ha... Wait, are you suggesting a swap?"

"Yeah, if I must sleep with your girlfriend to get the loan, so be it." Jack said.

"Fuck you Jack." Glen said. He was grinning though, as he made a fake punch to Jack's chin.

They worked with a fever and vision to finish the first product of ErgoDyn inc. until eight in the evening, then placed the pieces that would be joined together close to each other so they could see what they had accomplished. Jack whistled his enthusiasm.

"It is a thing of beauty. I can't wait to get it together and get the layers of clear coat on it." He said.

Glen nodded, a huge grin on his face. There was a fine white powder that coated his sandy blond hair and clothes. He fished for his pack of smokes, offered one to Jack.

"I only smoke on special occasions." Jack said. He took a cigarette when Glen gave him a stern look and shook one out.

"And yes, this is a special occasion." Jack said. He chuckled as he lit the smoke.

"We have about eight solid hours of work to do and this thing will be real." Glen said.

"Yah, I have a hard on just looking at it after thinking about it for a year or so." Jack said.

Glen barked a terse laugh. "If you get hard looking at a fancy desk you are going to love meeting Gillian. She wants to meet with us tonight at Asia Gardens, you know where that is?"

Jack nodded. "I frequent the place, about every other week or so. Great bar and even better Chinese food, a winning combination."

Glen tilted his head inquisitively. "Really? I am surprised I never have seen you there."

"Yeah, odd. We were not supposed to meet until Chilkoot Charlies I suppose. Just how the universe clicks."

Glen nodded thoughtfully.

8:45 P.M.

Asia Gardens was on the south side of town on Old Seward Highway, just across the street from Jack's failed Float Center business. His sign, white, with blue waves, and the words Float Center in black in the middle, was still there. He often stared at it as he drove by and thought about what might have been if all went well. Lost it just two years ago, when the price for a barrel of oil fell dramatically and all the oil people began to make a mass exodus out of Alaska. He and his partners had overextended, expanded when they were in the black, and then, boom, the oil economy dropped. The big 'Float Center' sign was a part of the over extension, cost twenty thousand dollars.

The bar was a bit of an older crowd than Chilkoot Charlie's. He knew the owner and it had great Chinese food. The waitresses were Thai girls, the owner, Shay, Thai as well. They were experts at flirting and stroking the egos of the patrons, so much so that if Shay hired an outsider the Thai girls would quickly have the new girl broke and in tears as they maneuvered the crowds to their tables and advantage. Fun to watch them hustle. The regulars were mostly business people from the neighborhood. A good crowd of people who worked hard and smart for a living.

Glen had arranged for Gillian to meet them there at nine. Jack pulled into the parking lot fifteen minutes early, eager to down a drink, a bit of liquid courage. Glen had built the meeting up to such an extent that he was feeling excited and nervous, little shivers of anticipatory energy flooding through him.

Once in the lobby he used the pay phone and invited Terry to meet with him. The girl was thrilled, talked fast, promised to dress conservatively so she wouldn't get carded.

Jack took a seat at the bronze plated bar on a comfortable bar stool. A rock would be comfortable after all the work he had done on the desk, bending, squatting, lifting, sanding, cutting, shaving. He felt the ache in his muscles, reminded himself that he had a rather soft winter in France bounding about the country side. He looked down the long bar, smiled and nodded at a few people that he recognized and then caught the eye of Lisa, the bartender right as Glen joined him. He slung his coat over the bar stool next to Jack and slapped down his pack of smokes and a green bic lighter.

"Gillian doesn't smoke, so I gotta have a couple before she gets here." He said as he took a seat.

Lisa was smiling at Jack and sauntering towards him, hips swaying, delight in her eyes.

"Shit! I didn't know that two of my favorite guys knew each other!" She exclaimed. She was short and stacked, stood on her tiptoes and leaned over the bar, lips pursed for a customary kiss.

Jack leaned forward and gave her a lingering kiss and she broke it off to move over to Glen who looked over his shoulder first, comically, then gave her a quick peck on the lips.

Lisa smirked. "You meeting a girl tonight? Haven't seen the two of you for a while so I figured you both got married or something."

She was a striking blond in her mid-thirties, bright blue eyes, voluptuous, sexy, and a very experienced bartender. She had worked the Elbow Room in Dutch Harbor for three years. Lisa had a thin scar that showed through her eyebrow from a hurled shot glass to prove it - that and pictures of the bar fights aftermaths.

"I bet you are needing a shot and a Heineken right now." She glanced at the tv behind her. The news was on CNN, currently talking about drivel. "It's been about every ten minutes with an update."

"Yes, two shots of tequila, and two beers. "Glen said. "My tab."

Lisa bent low to grab the beer, enjoying the homage paid to her breasts by both men.

"I have been avoiding the news all day but yeah, it's been heavy on my mind." Jack said.

"He has been bitching about it under his breath all day." Glen said. He and Lisa exchanged a smile and an understanding nod.

"So fucking stupid." Lisa said. "The Captain ought to be shot for hitting that huge clearly marked reef just off the big obvious fucking island with the same name."

Jack raised his tequila. "I will drink to that Lisa."

"Ah, Gillian just pulled into the parking lot there." Glen said. He was looking in the mirror, through the smoked glass windows behind them as they faced the bar. Jack looked but could just see the headlights. Gen stubbed out his smoke in a hurry and downed the shot of tequilla raw, no salt or lime, chased it with a beer.

"It's not like her to be early damn it. It's you Jack, she has a hard on for you already." Glen said. Jack looked at his friend, sought to put him at ease but could see he was of good enough humor, was faking his simpering.

Glen was being a bit over dramatic Jack thought, then froze, like a dear caught in headlights, as Gillian strode into the entry, took her coat off and shook it to remove melted snow flakes. All that she had under a very nice red blouse bounced and wobbled above a black skirt, shapely legs, high heels. The way she angled her hips as she hung up her coat accentuated the big round curve of her bottom. She strolled confidently towards them and Glen met her half way for a hug. Her hands slid down his back and cupped his ass as they gave each other a greeting kiss and then hugged. As she hugged Glen she looked over his shoulder and locked eyes with Jack, smiled a steamy smile. Jack felt his attraction to her, recognized hers to him. His heart rate elevated, his crotch lust meter swelled. It was an obvious approval and attraction. Glen was right, this could get a bit awkward, not being overly dramatic at all.

Jack sighed with relief as he noticed Terry's car, a little Ford Escort, pull into the parking lot as Glen and Gillian finished their hug.

"Jack, this is Gillian, Gillian, Jack." Glen said.

"I have a present for you Jack." Gillian said. Her voice was rich, calm, soothing, it helped ease his sudden sexual tension which was adding to his nervous waves of pricking excitement.

She held her hand out, palm up, and on her palm, was a metal broach. He recognized it immediately. It was the Lucidian symbol he had sketched onto the cover of all the pamphlets he handed out.

"Holy crap! Wow!" Jack blurted. His excitement peaked once again, chills swept through him. He knew he was not exactly being eloquent but did not care, his amazement was to great.

"Holy shit! That's my symbol!" Jack exclaimed. He could see a merry brightness in her eyes and knew immediately that this was what it felt like to mesh with another Lucidian. Felt it with Michael, Glen, and his cousins when they spoke of Lucid Dreaming. This, however was a bit different. The attraction and power that Gillian yielded were palpable. The significance of their meeting flashed across Jack's mind. This was a piece of the puzzle, of destiny… He glanced at Glen who gave him an odd look of happy remorse. "I told you she is incredible." He said. Gillian tittered and kissed Glen's cheek then shone the warmth of her gaze back upon Jack.

"I am very pleased to meet you Jack McKnight." She said. She lifted the broach a bit higher for him to take. He did. Held it in his hand, studied it, turned it this way and that.

"I had them made just out of pewter for now. Beautiful isn't it?" She said.

Jack burst out laughing. "Yes! It is!" He held the symbol up and studied it again. "How the heck did you get this done so quickly?" He asked.

Gillian laughed. "I have a sweat shop I run out of my house." She said.

Glen nodded. "You should see her shops, awesome, she had designers who work for free for her just so they can use the tools and environment."

Jack nodded, he caught sight of Terry approaching behind Gillian and Glen and greeted her. She had chosen wisely, a white button up blouse, black slacks. She smiled merrily at Jack as he took her by the hand and whisked her in front of him an introduced her to Glenn and Gillian.

They took seats together at the bar as the news came on. There was a moment of decision about the seating. Jack felt it appropriate that he sit on the other side of Terry, with Gillian next to her and then Glen. He took a seat and guided Terry to her position.

Lisa, being ever the fantastic bartender, pretended she didn't know them as she asked for the ladies' orders. Jack smiled thanks at her as he saw her note Terry's age and shrug it off, turn to prepare the drinks.

Then all Jack's attention went to the television screen as the Exxon Valdez Oil Spill update came on. They were covering the purse seiners hovering around the edge of the spreading oil, dipping the oil into barrels and lowering them into the fish hold! He whooped and raised his shot of Jose Cuervo.

"Yes, that's my Uncle's boat out there, and several other Cordovan fishermen. Right at the edge of the friggin' oil spill! And a day early! That will shame those bastards into action! Start cleaning it up without them!" Jack cheered loudly. Several patrons clapped. Lisa whooped. Glen raised his glass and the four of them drank.

Terry hugged him as he settled down, warm hand stroked his back. Gillian had a question on her face, then recognition. She let out a little gasp, "Glen didn't tell me you were a fisherman. "She said. "I think it's a horrible mess what they have done. "

Jack nodded, a grim smile on his face. "Now that the news crews have shown the fishermen, hell, even made them look a bit heroic, out there mobilized while Alyeska and Exxon do nothing, I hope one of those giant organizations mobilize whatever equipment they have and get to it. They better do something fast, it's spreading, it's huge, but once the tide takes it, or worse, a wind storm..." Jack clenched his jaw.

"Ok! Ok! No more news tonight! I buy you guys a round huh?" Shay came in. She was the owner of Asia Garden's, had been listening quietly from the corner. Jack smiled. She never, ever, bought a round. She was a good bar owner, was liking the dynamic of the bar and didn't want the news to piss everyone off, cut down the drinking, and hence, cash flow. Smart lady.

"Anyway, yes I am a Commercial Fisherman and am a bit concerned that this might affect my income. My... Everything." He said and stopped. Glen was glaring at him to shut up. He then realized that he and Glen needed to appear stable and dedicated to attract a loan. "Um... However, I will bet there is a way to make money from this spill." Jack said. He caught Glen give a tiny nod.

Gillian shot Glen a glare. He shrugged.

"VECO has a huge operation here in Anchorage. I am sure they will be involved." Gillian said.

"VECO?" Jack asked. He had never heard of them. Shut up before he admitted it.

"You might want to talk to someone there. See if you can get some insight?" Gillian said. "There are three oil field service outfits based in Anchorage, VECO is the largest, and I know Bill Allen, the owner, personally. "

Jack shifted his thinking from that of being a little guy, squashed by an oil spill, by Ayeska and Exxon, to a little guy who might be able to profit from the disaster.

"You know the President of VECO?" Jack asked. He didn't know where else to go, wanted to avoid Glen's panicked expressions.

Gillian smiled and nodded, eyes merry. "Yes, we have worked some financing for them. You meet all sorts of cool and diverse people when you loan money for a living." Gillian said.

Glen made bigger eyes at Jack in such a comical way that Jack almost laughed into his beer.

"Oh... I thought that was your dad." Jack said.

Glen just stared at his beer, head sagging a bit.

"Father doesn't do much. Owns the bank. Worries and stuff with the board members of which he is the chair. I am his CEO., I run the bank which is a bit of a side thing for him really. He um... is wealthy and is looking at politics, or other avenues of doing something good to pay his penance for being wealthy."

"Oh. Well... That's good then... Right?"

Gillian laughed at Jack's charming clumsy mannerisms.

"It was until I found out you are wondering how to make money on an oil spill Jack McKnight." Gillian said. She laughed and shook her head as Jack's face fell. "I am kidding, teasing, sorry, no, no! Don't look sad! Give me back that happy, angry, serious face."

Jack smiled then winced as Glen mad a fleshy gun with his thumb and fore-finger and simulated blowing his brains out – outside of Gillian's line of sight as much as possible.

"Glen…" Gillian said sweetly. "I see you… In the mirror." She turned and giggled as he pretended to be innocent.

"Four more shots please Lisa!" Glen said. "Just for me." He chuckled as Gillian again gave him a look. She turned her attention, all warm and rosy back on Jack.

Jack felt Terry's hand squeeze his inner thigh. Her agitation was growing as the two talked past her position. Jack gave her side a reassuring stroke. It didn't seem to help.

"You are fortunate to be a fisherman. We loan money to fishermen all the time. Good investment; my dad always says, 'people will pay to eat, and those who work the business of feeding them are a worthy investment.'"

Jack nodded. "Salmon is great food. High in protein and readily available. God designed a steak for us that is born, leaves for few years to grow, then returns ripened and ready to be eaten, to the exact same spot it was born in."

The shots were poured. Glen raised his.

"Here is to God and his awesome team of genetic engineers for creating the salmon." Glen said.

Jack laughed.

"Exactly!" Jack agreed.

They downed their shots, chased with lime, then a swig of beer. Warm smiles and hooyaaas with body shudders - huge ones from Terry, made them all laugh a bit. Jack admired the wobble of her breasts as she shivered. Her breasts were small and perky, required no bra, and the blouse had come unbuttoned yet another notch.

Gillian snapped her fingers in front of Terry's tits. Jack looked up at her and smiled. Her eyes were bright blue, merry with intelligence. Even the white of her eyes showed a faint blue that enhanced her eyes blueness. Jack wanted her. He knew that. Glen was right to be concerned. The man was sharp.

"I am sorry Terry, that was rude of me, just trying to get your man's atten-tion." Gillian slipped her hand over Terry's shoulders, long fingers stroked the back of her neck as she pressed against her. "And I admit, they are very pretty." She said. Her lusty tone and manner put Terry at ease perhaps, or she didn't want to seem prudish. She leaned into Gillian's sudden closeness and gave the woman a kiss on the cheek.

"I am glad you like them." She said. The two of them gave Jack a smile.

"Four more shots!" Glen said. They shared a laugh.

"If you have the time tomorrow I would like for you and Glen to meet me for breakfast at Jackie's and you two can discuss your business plan. Don't worry about a written proposal. I can aid with that when we need one."

"Ok. Sounds good." Jack tore his eyes away from Gillian's. He guessed that she didn't want to discuss in the bar because of the sexual tension building. He guessed right. After the round was had Glenn and Gillian excused themselves to leave.

Jack stood as they did and Glen stepped close to him. "I see the way you and she are making moon eyes. I don't care. Just want the loan so we can make cool shit. Her dad scares the shit out of me anyway."

Jack nodded. He felt guilty. Glen was right. The parting was a good thing even though it felt like the fun was leaving the room.

Jack stepped towards Gillian. Checked his woozy as he extended his hand towards her. Gillian took it, shook his hand then pulled him forward for a hug. "Stop pretending you don't want me Jack." She whispered, voice feather light. Jack did so, immediately. Gave Gillian a lingering hug goodbye. Glen rolled his eyes, walked towards Terry and took her in a hug, hands free down her back - if he was hurt he hid it well.

"It was very nice to meet you Gillian." Jack said. "Thank you very much for making the Lucidian symbol, it is even cooler than I imagined."

She beamed a smile at him, winked. "It was my pleasure as well Jack McKnight." She said.

Glen took Gillian's arm and the two made a little bow and strolled towards the door.

On their way out Gillian stopped at the juke box, programed a couple of songs.

She and Glen made their exit as the song 'Opportunities' came on. Jack laughed. "*You got the looks, I got the brains, let's make lots of money.*"

He hugged Terry close to him. He leaned in close to her ear. "I was wanting to tell you that you look very sexy and carry yourself very well. And..." He stopped, inhaled the scent of her warm neck.

Terry inhaled also, he saw her arms goose pimple. "Let you know that I want you so maybe we shouldn't get too drunk."

Her hand went to his inner thigh, a warm and gentle pressure.

"You and that woman just met? She sure seemed to know you well. Made you a pin and all." Her big brown eyes held Jack's gaze as he formulated an answer that would not turn her warm and gentle hand, now in his crotch, into a raking talon.

"We did just meet, she read this..." He pulled a Lucidian pamphlet from his coat pocket, his hand brushing past something soft as he did so.

"I had given one to Glen because he is a Lucid Dreamer... Like me... Um and many others."

He put the booklet on the bar next to the ornate pewter symbol. The symbol on the cover jacket matched perfectly by Gillian's pewter rendition.

"That is just... Weird." Terry said. She picked up the booklet and thumbed through it. She paused and set it down, looked at the symbol and the matching pin side by side again.

"Ok Jack. You are the weirdest interesting person I have ever met. My first, a cult leader, commercial fisherman, and what exactly was the loan meeting about?"

Jack laughed. He found her amazement very flattering, was enjoying her look of bewilderment for the moment.

"It's for a loan to create a fabrication shop for, a company we are creating called ErgoDyn; design and engineering via contract and personal lines as well."

The crazy perplexed look on Terry's face made Jack giggle maniacally.

She joined him and giggled a happy giggle. "Ok so you are a cult leader, who commercial fishes, and who designs...furniture." Terry leaned in, hand slipping back between his legs. Jack kissed her gently, slid his hand from her hip up her side to her smooth armpit. She melted into him.

"I am not a cult leader, it's not like that. You are very intelligent. I think you will like the booklet. It contains the keys to the universe, or at least that is what Glen described it as. You can read it tonight. I suggest we catch a cab though. To my place, you, and I. "

Terry nodded enthusiastically. "My first man is a gentleman, as well as a very busy character. Her cheeks were pink and her nipples poked through her sheer bra to tent her blouse.

"I want to please you, to hear you moan, make you quiver." He said.

"I want that too. "Terry said. "Are we going to be going out? I am a bit old fashioned and..."

Jack kissed her, hand stroked up her back to grasp the hair at the back of her head. He did not want to have that conversation just yet. Soon, yes, but not tonight. She might not think her 'first' was much of a gentleman when he told her about Sarah.

"You are my girlfriend and I am your boyfriend. We have great chemistry, and we are young and free. Let's think later, fuck now. "Jack said.

"Ha! My mom warned me about you." Terry said. She pushed Jack away from her and mocked a pouty face.

"I will read your booklet. I know who Gillian Robinson is by the way, sharp woman, if she liked it I probably should."

Jack nodded, two more rounds were set before them.

"From the man down there. Says he liked watching you two lovers and wanted to thank you for the entertainment." Lisa said. She gave the two of them a patronizing look then rolled her eyes. "Personally, all the mushy mating ritual turns my stomach. Seen it a lot, rarely ends well."

Jack glanced down the bar and nodded thanks at an older man who had dark hair, neatly groomed, black wool long coat just being pulled on. The man looked vaguely familiar. He smiled at Jack and walked over.

"Just wanted to thank you two for the entertainment. It is refreshing to see young love." He said. His face was handsome, in his forties, he reached in his pocket and pulled out a card that read,

'Drake Smith

Sales Manager

Worthington Ford

"Look me up if you need a car or truck in the future. I take excellent care of my clients. "He said.

Drake extended his hand to first Jack, then Terry, whose hand he lifted and kissed very gallantly. He smiled a charming smile, turned heel, and strode towards the exit. Jack noticed a little pink flare up on Terry's cheeks. The man had taken her, for the moment.

"Hmmm... A car salesman. Kinda a sleazy bunch huh?" Terry said. She wiped the back of her hand on her slacks.

She had no way of knowing that Jack had applied for a job selling cars to supplement his income this semester. They had asked him if he was going to return to fishing in the summer, to which he said yes, and that had ended the interview. They were looking for year-round employees.

"They are not so bad actually. You sure seemed a little smitten with him."

Terry giggled.

"I did huh? Let me guess, you are reading my cheeks? Nice. Everyone does that." She hugged up close to him. "Well, not everyone, my dad and mom, and brothers. I guess I was 'smitten' with him a little. He was handsome in his long overcoat. But then I found out he was a car saleseman."

Jack shrugged. "I applied at Alaska Sales and Service, hoped to get the job, but they didn't hire me because they knew I would quit to fish during the summer, did the math, they make over ten grand a month, something college students hope for when they graduate." Jack said.

"Really? That pretty damn good. I think I could sell cars to pay my way through college." Terry said.

Jack nodded. He was beginning to genuinely like her. Not the hot flame of love like he had felt for Sarah, but a slower progression, an interest, a potential, with hot chemistry and a good level of wit.

He put Drake's card in his pocket. He had not yet applied at Worthington Ford. This time he would lie and say he was looking for year-round employment. As he did so he pulled out the something soft he had felt earlier, glanced at it without Terry seeing, which was easy because she was glued to one side of him. "I want your baby, call me sometime!" Was written on it. Jack's heart pounded a bit harder. The song, 'I want your sex' by George Michael came on the jukebox. The second song she had programmed.

"She is such a bitch..." Terry said. "Could she be more obvious?"

Jack laughed.

STORM BREW

Jack's eyes opened. He recalled his dreams. Just barely. Hung over from the tequila. Terry was next to him. He cupped her breast as she slept, felt her nipple harden, breathed in her scent. She had been sheer joy even though they had to be whisper quiet because he had brought her to his parents' home. Jack wanted to be near his clothes, and familiar ritual, to shine his best for the meeting at eight with Gillian and Glen.

Terry stirred but did not waken as Jack stroked his fingers down her belly. He stood and gazed at her in the dim light from the electronics at his desk. There was a twinge of guilt that pulled at his mind. He was her first and had made extra certain that she enjoyed herself. But what if he was too good? What if she would never be satisfied with a man? He snickered at his own conceit.

There was a certain gravity though. He knew she was falling for him, sort of swept up in that charming, dynamic, interesting man magic. Jack had it, he knew he did. And since meeting Gillian, he was sure he had never met a woman with it. But Gillian changed his mind about that with one glance of her bright blue eyes. Eyes so blue that even the whites were a faint blue. He knew her level of purity immediately. Had seen those kinds of eyes only twice before in yoga class.

Jack focused on Gillian's face as he stretched into his morning yoga. Her blue within blue eyes. He smiled as a scene from the movie Dune popped into his mind, then melded with the saying, '*The sleeper must awaken!*' Gillian's face smiled at him and said, *'tell me of your business idea Jack'* as George Michael sang, 'I want your sex' in the background. His yoga instructor smiled at him. *"Her eyes are like that because she processes high levels of oxygen and very few impure foods or toxins."* Nirvare Sing Khalsa said. *"In other words, she doesn't smoke, drink or eat shit abomination foods."*

Jack snickered to himself as he imagined his holy man yoga instructor cussing.

Gillian Robinson... Guilt pang for Terry... Then for Sarah...

Terry was breathing soft snores behind him. He raised his arms upwards, inhaling, held the pose, clenched his anus, sucked his testicles upward into a protective pocket all men have but only a few in martial arts know how to willfully use. Exhaled big on the way down.

He picked up a heavy padded bamboo Kendo practice sword and began to strike and parry, dance, stretch his arms, until a fine sweat broke out and his heart rate was elevated. For fifteen more minuets he pushed himself until he could smell the alcohol and tobacco in his sweat, then showered to wash it all away.

Coffee Yoga. Jack silently poured the water into the coffee maker - ears tuned to his parent's room. He could hear the wind outside, the icy scrape of wind driven snow, the ticking of the fire place, but, no creaking of the floors as his mother crept up on him. She often tried to sneak up on him. It was about twice a week that he caught her. She would laugh and shake her head - then set into lecturing about making the coffee to strong. This morning Jack could just hear the wind. A strong gust hit the big living room windows. Ice particles hissing across the double pane storm windows.

Jack nearly dropped the pot. Wind! He had been worrying about wind and oil! He picked up the phone and called the weather. As he listened the blood drained from his face. There was a storm brewing in Prince William Sound. It had started building last night while he was busy with Terry. It would spread the oil. While they debated who should do what and how.

"Fucking Alyeska and Exxon are not doing shit!"

He stared at the window as he crossed the dimly lit living room and clicked on the television. In his peripheral vision, he noted his mother in the hallway as the light from the TV came on. Sneaking under cover of the wind noises. She might have had him.

"There is a storm brewing..." Jack said. He smiled as he watched his mom stop sneaking and silently snap her fingers, her mouth formed the word, 'Damn!'.

"The wind woke me. Your father is still sleeping, thank god, he would be cussing and ranting right now if he knew." Rebeca whispered.

Jack nodded. There was a commercial on TV. The surge of rage came back only this time Jack checked it. His heritage was about to be covered in oil, his playground, his livelihood. Wind had been his greatest worry even though his mental focus was on the positive, there was no denying the probable. March was stormy seventy-five percent of the time. His jaw was clenched tight as the surge of rage and sorrow flowed through him. He breathed, focused on the potential income he could pull out of the oil. Gillian had spoken with absolute certainty that there was money to be made to the point that he felt foolish for not realizing it on his own. He resolved to shove aside the emotion and see the situation for what it was, clearly.

He turned his eyes from the screen, to the window as another strong gust hit, sprayed it with tiny silver ice crystals. They were going to state the obvious anyway. But were there any efforts made by Exxon and Alyeska to contain the spill yet? That's what Jack wanted to see even though he knew, in the pit of his stomach, that was not the case.

Rebecca stood with folded arms frowning at the television, alongside Jack, as the latest update came on fifteen minutes later. It was local news, from Anchorages KBBY. John Jones reporting. Nothing being done... Storm expected to peak around noon Monday, the 27th... Fishermen still circling the edge of the oil spill... Being warned off by an Alyeska pilot boat. Now that was ironic.

"The wind will spread the oil..." Jack whispered.

"Oh Jack... It is horrible..."

"I have to go Cordova now, get the boat ready. I met a gal last night who knows VECO people. Maybe I can get something lined up to help. Maybe I just go do what we decided to do without help like Uncle Conner and those others."

Rebecca shook her head. Jack pushed the knob that turned off the television console. The living room darkened.

"I know you snuck a girl in last night. And on Easter Eve no less. Do I get to meet her?" Rebecca asked.

"Sure, if she wakes, a wonderful girl. Terry is her name. "

Jack sighed. Reached for the pot of coffee. "Black Friday this year instead of Good Friday huh?"

"Yes... I suppose so. And speaking of black you made the coffee way too strong."

"I will just add some hot water to weaken it down for you mom." Jack took Rebecca's mug and poured his mom a half cup, then turned the water to let it get hot while he poured his own. It was a ritual he and his mother performed often. He had diluted her coffee for her a hundred times.

"Your dad has ferry tickets already, managed to finagle something with the people who told him they were all booked up. He wants you to finish your semester. I am swamped with work, bought a ham, we can do something small and simple for Easter or, just wait until we can all get together and be thankful Jesus is risen."

Jack nodded, sipped his coffee. "I have a lot going on today as well Mom. In fact, to me, this has been a time of my life where it seems God is working with me, helping me to get my ideas into reality. It is... Most bizarre and um... Delightful... and then this oil spill... It's like he also hates me and has plotted against me."

"No one hates you, god doesn't hate you silly, you see it through your anger. I see it as if he gave you some gifts because he knew this was going to happen."

Rebecca dipped her head towards his bedroom door. "God gave you the strumpet you brought home."

Jack laughed. "That 'strumpet' is a straight A student in my computer classes, pretty sharp."

"Well good, maybe she will keep you in college like your dad wants, not skipping off to go..." Rebecca shrugged. "I know you are going. It's the right thing to do. But I promised your Dad I would talk to you..."

"I know it is important to dad, college education. But the point of it is to earn good money doing something I like. I already got that. Fishing. I think it would be stupid to continue my studies while this is going on. I could lose my business." The thought sent a wave of cold panic that Jack felt through his body.

Rebecca looked at Jack, he saw the sadness and compassion in his mother's eyes.

"I know you will go Jack. You will go son, and try to save your ocean lover." She hugged him. "I will try and get you some reservations right away."

Jack sighed and relaxed, his mom's embrace making, for a moment, everything better.

"Oh! I just remembered!" Rebecca said. She snapped her fingers and moved silently out of the room. Jack could tell from her body language that she had good news, or what she thought was good news anyway. She quickly returned holding a large cardboard tube.

"Vern Doken sent these..."

She spread out large photographs of what would be Jack's Alta Pearl.

Jack also saw an equipment list and specs. He pulled that into his view. The frame of the boat was in place. It looked enormous. The men working on it tiny in comparison.

"Wow, that's impressive." Jack said. "You mind if I take these and go over them a bit?"

"Of course not, honey, you paid good money for them."

Rebecca reached out for another hug. Jack squeezed his mom affectionately and inhaled her scent, faint lavender soap and mom-ness, something Jack imagined was a mixture of chocolate chip cookie, sweat, and Gorgio all mingled together. His muscle tension slackened a bit. He closed his mind to the oil spill and flooded it with warm memories of his mother, then with thoughts of his morning appointment with the lovely Miss Gillian.

THE ERGODYN PITCH

Gillian had ordered for them. Omelets, hashbrowns, toast. Jackie's diner was already full but she held a booth. Glen and Jack took seats, Glenn next to Gillian, Jack facing her beautiful blue in blue eyes.

"Thanks for ordering." Jack said.

"I figured you might be hung over a bit."

"I was indeed." Jack said. That had been three hours ago.

"Tell me of your business plans gentlemen. I don't care if we eat and talk I am starved." Gillian was eating with speed and finesse as she spoke. Amazing. Except she was eating fruit and having a tea that she brought herself.

"ErgoDyn shall be a small-scale fabrication shop where we design and build custom furniture for people as well as provide a specialized line of services for hire, fabrication contracts, things like that. "Glen said. "I wanted a better desk. So, we built one. You liked it yes? Ordered three?"

Gillian nodded. "I thought I would try one at home first, then see if a few others at work would like them."

"I would think a more productive workspace would be a private work space." Glen said.

Jack nodded. "I think we can tone down the whole cockpit thing if it is a bit much for a bank setting. I think that one-day people will want music, computer, chair, photos, all to be integrated into a home productivity center. It will be the norm. And I would like to be the Xerox of that norm. Imagine with me for a moment... You get off work, it's been a long day, your feet are sore. You are looking forward to your man rubbing your feet as you sit in the plush Intimacy One. Two swept line padded seats that face each other at angles. You can talk and massage each other's feet at the same time. Got a super short wife or husband? No problem, just install via Velcro the padded addition to either side. Feeling a bit horny? Each chair is designed not only for foot rubs and conversation, but for... "Jack stopped and smiled at Gillian as her cheeks tinged pink. "...a sensual variety of consensual adult activities and looks great in the master bedroom or the living room where guests who don't own one will not suspect a thing!"

Glenn glared at Jack, jaw clenched. Gillian burst out laughing. Glenn exhaled and lightened up.

"Ok... You surprised me with that, not your normal slant on furniture. But yes, I can see it and I like the foot rubbing, so would any woman I suppose. But I want to know where the money is going to come from, you know, the part where you pay back the loan? I am not investing in a chair, am I?"

Jack nodded, then shook his head. Glenn gave him a look that said it was his turn to talk. He inhaled and began to speak with a purpose and intent that impressed Jack.

"We want to design and market smart furniture that challenges the norm of ninety degrees while capitalizing on the ergonomics laws that have recently passed and providing innovative products that make people more comfortable and healthy while at work, or at play. The money will come as business invest in complying with the ergonomics law. We will install our well-designed work stations and cubicles, as well as carry lines built by others. On one end we design our own advanced style, on the other, we contract to install whatever the businesses would like to set up. If we can sell them ours, great, if not, we can still contract for the installation and sale of many lines already in production." Glen began. He continued with numbers and cash flow expectations for quite a while.

Gillian nodded as he spoke, kissed him on the cheek, when he concluded.

"Well-spoken, lover. I believe you two can make it and am willing to help." Gillian said.

Jack felt her foot slide up his calf under the table. He wanted to move, politely, but didn't dare break contact with her.

"But I want to be involved. I want to run the sales team and take care of your books every Friday."

Jack was taken back. Gillian was crossing a line but he wasn't sure if he minded.

"We could use your help... But are you talking a buy in, or a loan?"

Gillian gave a little frown, either from Jack removing his leg or at his question. Perhaps both.

"I hadn't thought that far into it, but eventually it could be a buy in, once there is something more than testosterone and inspiration to buy into." She smiled sweetly. "The loan I can get you with or without me helping if that's what you mean."

"I would love for you to help." Glen said. He nodded and smiled at Jack.

"I am aware of the attraction you two have for each other. It's ok. This is bigger than getting all petty and jealous. I have my charming qualities as do the two of you... I feel like we are, well, family."

Jack remained as unreadable as possible. Waited for Gillian to respond. He finally met her eyes and was riveted once again. She smiled a faint smile, eyes imploring.

"There is a very strong attraction..." Jack said. He saw relief flicker across Gillian's face.

She nodded. Then glanced at Glen.

"There is an attraction between I and Glen as well, chemistry, we are good together." Gillian said. She hugged Glen. Then moved over to Jack's side of the table. She hugged him to her and kissed him, tongue hot, hand hot on his inner thigh.

Jack's eyes went to Glen and he saw his friend color up, anger, rage? No, embarrassment perhaps. But Glen smiled and nodded, his lips ticking a bit.

Gillian released Jack from her lips and then embrace.

"Whew! Glad we cleared the air on this!" Jack said. The three of them began to laugh.

"The look on your face was priceless." Glen said. He giggled insanely for a few seconds. They laughed again then sobered a bit and sighed.

"What about Terry?" Gillian asked.

"What about her? I like her, a lot, she quizzed me last night after you left, has a good mind."

"I mean do you think she will take to being a Lucidian?"

Jack shrugged. "We planted the seeds... She wanted to read the booklet... "

"If she does we only need two more." Gillian said.

"Two more what?" Jack asked.

"Two more believers, followers, members of the group. It takes five believers to register as a religion." Gillian said.

Jack laughed but stopped short, caught by the blaze in Gillian's eyes.

"Oh... Your... Serious."

"Yes, Jack and you should be as well." Gillian said. "Now is the right time for something like this. People are looking, searching for meaning and not finding it through conventional religion, all the while technology is rising faster than people can keep up with. There is a huge rift being created between science and religion and there does not need to be. We can step in and tie it all together, science, religion based on experience and practice that lends itself to innovation and inspiration. Just look at that beautiful desk idea you came up with, from a dream, and it integrates human comfort and physicality with technology. That is what The Lucidian Church can do as well. I mean... I am Catholic, right? When I go to Mass on Sundays they use fear and then god loves you, all on faith. There is no meat and potatoes of 'How To'. The 'How To' is Lucidity. I told my priest, Father Jacob, that I dreamed I walked with Jesus and spoke to him and that Jesus showed me a snake in a figure eight biting its own tail painted on a pyramid shaped wall of a temple. Father Jacob then said that the bible often references dreams and their portents and patted me on the head. The next time I saw him, we talked about it again but when I told them that the dreams awaken a sense of closeness with God, that they aid in manifestation of things, he drew back, said that it sounded like I was saying we are, somehow, gods..." Gillian stopped talking when she noticed how intently Jack was listening. "What?" She asked.

"Oh, sorry, I was just absorbing what you were saying. I have given little thought to how a Catholic Priest would regard the idea of having a Lucidian Church next door in the neighborhood."

Gillian was a bit out of breath. She took a sip of coffee. "I will be seeing him for twelve mas today in fact." She shrugged. "Mas isn't as great as what I have in mind but it's all I have right now." She said and tittered a bit. "I am hungry for spiritual knowledge. Have been since I was a little girl."

The expression on Gillian's face then grew intent, conspiratorial. "We need two more believers. The papers are in my office for you to sign and submit to become a religion. After that, you have a tax free real estate license."

"And then we do what?" Jack asked. Chills were sweeping up and down his spine as Gillian spoke, the goose pimples rose on his forearms and were noticed.

Gillian smiled and nodded. "I got them too Jack, the chills, like when things are clicking that are good and meant to be and in line with god."

Jack nodded. He held back in telling Gillian, just yet, about Michael Neufeld entrusting him with eight names of people from Neufeld's 'special' list.

"I have my cousins, certainly they will be onboard, this was their idea actually." Jack said.

He had been amused by the idea of a new religion when John and the twins had suggested it during Christmas, had added a few more layers to the idea in his notebooks, but was primarily focused on his other, more concrete and urgent, projects.

"I also have a list of people, names, addresses, phone and fax numbers, who I and others have compiled. I have cultivated my own list, or a line, and those on my list have been adding names to their lines as well. For example, I gave Glen a booklet, he gave it to you, Glen is in my line, you are now in Glen's line."

Gillian nodded and beamed a smile. "That is more than we need. Then Jack, we make and take donations. I will be first in line. Two foundations that I work with will donate money, I personally will tithe, Glen will tithe, you shall tithe. We will print more of your booklets. I have already sent out info to people I believe are potential Lucidians, took the liberty of having a couple friends reproduce them, also faxed over a thousand copies out to people I know, people from a list I had compiled of likely candidates for donations in other ventures. You know, people who had bought books along those lines. I made them a bit more formal than small sheets of paper stapled together. They have a request for donations and to order more, in the back two pages. A request to join and learn and prosper. I haven't slept more than thirty minutes since I read your little booklet." She placed a booklet on the table, same size as his rather crude paper ones, nicer card board, glossy black with a bright blue Lucidian symbol on the front.

Jack took it all in. Gillian was near breathless when she stopped talking. She smiled. Raised her eyebrows. "Then we purchase land, begin to build the first church."

"Wow, a church... Sounds pretty... Big." Jack said. "I like the idea and where we are thinking. This feels very good, the three of us talking and making plans. We need to schedule some more time tonight to brainstorm."

"Sounds wonderful! How about my place?" Gillian said. Her face was bright and cheery. Impossible to say 'no' to.

They agreed and made ready to leave.

"I will need you and Glen to sign the loan papers Tuesday. Create a business plan Glen, that says in writing and more specific numbers, what you just told us."

Glen nodded.

"Good... I will set the two of you up with a line of credit. Go find a suitable property for your shop, I already checked your credit, excellent, should be justifiable and easy to push through the underwriter."

Gillian took Glen and Jack's arm and sandwiched herself between the two handsome men. Jack felt ten feet tall. Giddy.

"I hope you two don't mind my sexual freedom, but I might have to fuck a couple of board members to smooth over approving your loan." Gillian said as they breezed out of the Restaurant. She giggled when they took her serious.

RITUAL LOADING AND ASS CHEWING

Jack returned to his parents' home on Zurich street, slid to a stop on two inches of fresh snow in the driveway. He stepped out of the warmth of his big Lincoln, saw his dad in the garage, was torn about going in and helping or bypassing and seeing if Terry had the good sense to stay in bed so he could give her a good morning.

The old man hailed him though and threw the weight of his internal argument on the side of dad. Jack made a bee line to the garage. Dick would have to wait.

"Give me a hand while I chew your ass about a few things." Robert McKnight said. He had a small smile on his face as if apologizing for being dad.

Behind him his Ford F350 was mostly loaded with Cordova gear. Robert was very efficient with his garage and work shop space. Pull the truck in on the left side, load with hunting and fishing gear for the interior of Alaska, the right side, Cordova gear, rain coats and pants, wools, red rubber Extra Tuffs that most fishermen wore on the boats because they did not slip as much as other boots and were water proof.

Jack jumped into the bed of the truck and began to consolidate space there.

"You need to stay in school while I sort out what needs to be done son. If there is something you can do then I will call for you. No sense in both of us being there." Robert said. He heaved a box of mending twine and needles up to Jack. He caught it, fit it neatly into a slot.

"That sounds reasonable I guess. "Jack said.

Robert cocked his head, confused for a moment.

"Your mother led me to believe you would be resistant to the idea. Don't you let that little piece of tail in your bedroom distract you from the big picture. Your dick already cost you a semester mooning over Sarah and now look at you - Sarah who? You see? Easy to forget when another one loves you."

Jack began laughing at his father's antics.

"You know, old man, I love the shit out of you."

"Yeah, me too kid. I know you got a few irons in the fire here..."

Jack hadn't told his dad about ErgoDyn coming together, or the religion thing.

"But you gotta focus on what the future may look like. Fucking oil spill is a game changer. We may be out of business. Then you can do something with your education. You got to always have a fall back plan. And as far as your education goes, you just changed course right when you were about to get a degree, and now you are cramming to make up for your sudden shift in mind." Robert tossed Jack two sleeping bags, neatly ensconced in water proof oil skins, as he spoke. "Now... I know my buddy Neufeld had something to do with that, god damn guy is always up to some grand plan, but now you might be caught without the cash to continue school if the fishing fails and you have another three years to your degree instead of this last one."

Robert reverently handed Jack a hard-plastic case containing his prized 300 Win Mag hunting rifle.

"Not only that but every time you start a new business you drop out of school. You are twenty-five and have been going to college and working your angles since you were seventeen. You should have your degree by now son. Society doesn't give a shit if you have the equivalent of a Ph.D. invested in your education – if you don't have the actual degree, you don't get the job."

Jack nodded, acknowledging the weight of his father's words. "You are right dad. I have been working on my fall back plan, and Neufeld did put me off Psychology and onto Computer Science, but the man is correct, I am seeing an entire new playing field of opportunity with the computers. I just regret I did not jump on it first." Jack smiled at his dad's survival gear and rations to the front of the garage, to load that up you had to back the truck in. Pre-packed backpacks were all in a row. Six of them, though there were only three people in the house. Just in case any neighbors needed a hand.

"You have been adding to our bug out packs." Jack said.

"Yes, that's my hobby, a backup plan, and a damn good one. "Robert said. He chuckled. "You want to see the new stuff? And don't think you have successfully ended your ass chewing." Robert smiled knowingly. Jack had to laugh.

He had received his first two weapons, a 22 caliber, bolt action Remington, and a Luger 22 semi-automatic pistol with a 25-round clip, for his ninth birthday from his father. Robert then proceeded to teach him not just how to shoot, but how to shoot very well, and not just how to be safe, but to be very safe. Any time even an unloaded gun's barrel past the plane of a human being, Jack received a cuff upside the head. Not liking the stout cuffing, Jack quickly learned extreme gun safety. At the same time, Robert introduced him to survival skills and preparedness. He and his father had spent countless hours packing and repacking the 'ultimate' survival pack, shopped for improved tools and weapons. Then taking them hunting for deer and moose in Cordova. The packs had evolved into quite the interesting trick bag over the years. Trip wire traps, snares, Kasul 454, 200 rounds, 270, 200 rounds, fire starting kits they practiced with in winter and rainy August in Cordova - well rainy any month in Cordova. Arctic tents, tiny stoves that left no smoke trace. Chemical packs that cooked food, water filters for drinking on the run...

The kind of stuff that almost made a person wish they had a reason to use it. Jack had certainly spent a lot of time visualizing scenarios where he would use the gear, earthquakes, nuclear war, an attack on U.S. soil. He also had vivid dreams where he was being hunted and used the packs to survive and fight back. Fun stuff. Often, he would present his father with an idea or improvement to an existing piece of equipment based on one of his inspirational dreams.

"I don't have time to go over all of it right now son. Ferry leaves at four this afternoon. I need to catch the train at three into Whittier. Leave here at two..." He tossed a large blue tarp. Jack caught it and slung it into a tight-fitting slot.

"Conner said that he was made to run his boat into Valdez because it is so oiled from his efforts that it would oil up clean water. They have a cleaning station there. He is waiting for them to clean his boat."

Jack caught another tarp, everything was stashed. This tarp would cover the trucks contents and keep it free of snow or rain.

"I got this kid. Go ahead and sneak that girl out of your room. She is still sleeping. Your mother tells all. Telephone, telegraph tele-Rebeca."

"Her name is Terry. Nice girl I met at college."

"Don't knock her up Jack. That's rule number one. These young ladies are very fertile at this stage of their lives. How old is she?"

Jack laughed. "She is eighteen Dad. Turns nineteen in May."

"Shit! That reminds me. Sarah called. I spoke to her a bit. She will be in Cordova once her boat gets there. Said it was heading up from Baja California, or was just passing Baja, said it would be about eight more days."

Jack stopped at the doorway. "Did she say anything else?"

"Just some mushy nonsense." Robert said. He laughed as Jack shot him an anxious look.

 "She said she loves you and that she knows you are in agony over this."

Jack felt a pang of guilt. Not about Sarah, but about not actually feeling agony over the spill. Anger yes, and frustration. But they were shelved. Put in the background while he dealt with college and the pleasurable swirl of synchronicity that was forming ErgoDyn Inc. while it lasted.

"Thanks for telling me she called. Did she say what time she would call back?"

"Six tonight." Robert said.

Jack walked slowly into the house. He was in no rush to see Terry while his mind was on Sarah. A pang of loss struck him as he realized that his feelings for Sarah were fading, still strong, but changing. He had set himself free with Terry, forged a powerful alliance with Gillian, who he was dangerously attracted to, yet still clung to the belief that he would re-unite with Sarah after she freed herself up via divorce in two years.

"I *wonder if I would so stubbornly be holding onto her if she did not have millions...?*"

Terry was still asleep when Jack entered the room. He gazed at her and recalled thinking of relieving his sexual tension on her lithe little body. She was only five foot one or two Jack guessed, breasts small, about half a handful. Jack looked at his hands, they were big. He laughed.

Terry stirred but did not waken. He studied her eyelids. They were fluttering as she dreamed, eyes darting back and forth beneath the thin skin of her lids. Jack inhaled through his nose as he concentrated on her mind, an image formed of him stroking her back as he piloted a magic carpet over a blue water harbor with bright while pillars and alien crafted boats. He attempted to insinuate the image into her current dream as he meditated on them. Nothing happened as far as he could tell. Her face was a bit puffy as she slept, lips open, breathing through her mouth. Jack pushed her lips together and she quickly switched to breathing through her nose. That was a good sign. Mouth breathers tended not to be lucid dreamers and he wanted Terry to learn.

Sarah had expressed no interest in learning to lucid dream even after learning that Mike Neufeld was a lucid dreamer. Jack felt a twinge of objective doubt regarding Sarah. What was it about her he loved? She turned him on. Simple chemistry. The days in Prince William Sound had been powerfully romantic. Her laughter at his antics rang loud in his mind. Her touch, her kiss, her moans.... She was very enterprising, invested her stipend from the trust in an Alaskan work boat, her own form of rehab, to clean up from drugs and get away from her mother and Corbin. She had not, however, told him of Corbin, or even that she, in fact, owned the boat...

"Why are you staring at me?" Terry asked.

Jack jolted a tiny bit. Smiled.

"Because you are cute and sexy." Jack said. "Lay still and see what you were just dreaming."

Terry relaxed, closed her eyes, opened them.

"I was dreaming about you fucking me." She said and giggled.

"No, you weren't." Jack said softly. "Honestly try and see if the images come back to you."

Terry shrugged. Remained still for a few breaths.

"Close your eyes and relax. Move your eyes back and forth slowly to see if that stimulates the memory."

Terry lifted her head after a few seconds. "Umm, I do remember, now! I was driving my car through a parking lot and hit this kid. The cops came and I was so worried that I would go to jail... Hm, interesting. Do you recall your dreams every morning?"

Jack nodded. "Several times during the night and early morning I awaken and recall. Write down or record the interesting ones." He gestured to the desk near his bed, it was situated so he could sit up, rotate to the left and be at the desk, his butt still resting on the bed. This allowed for a minimum of physical movement. Jack found that moving the body a lot made it harder to recall the dreams, that part of the waking process was to transfer energy to the muscles so the brain switched into a mild flight or fight mode which somehow short-circuited memory.

Terry sighed and rolled onto her back as Jack caressed her. He turned some music on so any moaning would, hopefully, blend.

TESTOSTERONE AND MANIFESTATION

MARCH 26ᵀᴴ, EASTER SUNDAY, 12:00 PM

J ack gave Terry a ride back to the cold, white, snow drifted parking lot of Asia Gardens so she could retrieve her car. He had taken a cab there and gotten his Lincoln earlier for his meeting with Gillian.

She needed to shower and change her clothes then go to her Grand Parents' house for Easter dinner. He helped her scrape snow and ice off her car and then stroked her to orgasm in the warmth of his Continental as they waited for her car to warm up. She had doubted he could do it but he told her to pretend his finger was his tongue and talked dirty to her.

Jack watched her little butt wiggle as he helped her negotiate the slippery parking lot back to her car. Cute. Adorable really. She had asked him if he was leaving for Cordova, and if he would meet her folks the next Sunday if he was in town. Jack had agreed he would if he was in town but gave her a spread of probability in Cordova's favor.

The sky was grey, cold but no snow, not yet. It had snowed during the evening, made his morning drive a bit challenging but now everything was crunchy with a glaze of ice. Not the greatest traction. Jack put his car in reverse, caught a bit of traction and began to pick up speed. He checked his mirrors, more gas pedal, more speed. He was half way across the empty parking lot, going fast, towards the exit, in reverse. He cranked the wheel hard left and slammed on the brakes. As the big Lincoln snapped around Jack whooped and shifted into drive. Now facing the exit, he quickly checked the street and gunned the car out of the parking lot sideways down old Seward highway in an easily controlled fish tail. He whooped and laughed manically as he brought the car under control and slowed way down to a safe speed. Taking off in a fish tail was good fun but the car was hard to stop and had little steering maneuverability in a slide. Jack understood, from experience, that there might be other drivers, like him, screwing around ahead.

He found Glen in the back cleaning up the work area, no sign of the desk.

"Boss man bitched me out again, says I am using up valuable space with this project. Accused me of stealing materials to build your desk and claimed that I have been slacking." Glen slammed the broom he had been using into its slot on the wall.

"Almost quit the fucker but realized he is right, not about stealing, but about slacking off. I let a few things go in favor of working to get our desk done. Which it is by the way, look." Glen waved the way towards the door to the main shop.

Jack entered and saw, assembled and beautiful, the desk. Its sleek cowl looked very much like the cockpit of an F-16 only roomier. Jack had peeked into a real F-16 cockpit and felt sorry for the pilots that had to fly in such cramped quarters. Compared to an actual fighter jet cockpit, this was comfort, luxury. The black and red marbling in the clear coat looked as if a deep crimson fire burned through the blackness. To Jack the paint job symbolized bringing forth ideas from thought, burning through the black infinite potentiality of the mind to manifest in reality as a solid thing of great use. Formlessness becoming form, the immaterial becoming material, the magical act of manifestation.

"Wow... It's... Beautiful..." Jack said. He reached his hand toward the shiny smooth surface.

"Don't touch! Clear coat is still setting!" Glenn barked. He nodded though.

"It is a fine product. It took us seven days to make, given my relentless drive to complete it."

Jack laughed. "It is fucking amazing! You, are fucking amazing!"

Glen grinned, nodded, then sobered.

"We need to talk about Gillian." He said.

Jack nodded though he did not want to talk about Gillian.

"I agree. I..."

"In the nights you are with her I want Terry, just to make it fair."

Jack was taken back by his friend's words. Glen was constantly surprising him.

"Did she tell you about the note I slipped in her pocket?" Glen asked.

Jack shook his head, 'no' stunned. "Gillian slipped me a note too..." He pulled the napkin from his pocket.

Glen shrugged, smiled."Gillian told me she gave you that note. You didn't call by the way." He pulled a crisp hundred from his pocket, a clever grin on his face. "I won the bet on that. Lunch is on me."

Jack's confused face must have appeared funny because Glen burst out laughing.

"I have been having a serious moral dilemma with this whole scene all the while you two are plotting out everything? I suppose Gillian knew you put the note in Terry's pocket?"

Glen nodded. Terry did too. She caught me, then let me, played it off with a hand up your leg and a giggle as I put the note in her pocket."

Jack felt a pang of betrayal tug at his anger strings as a bunch of thoughts regarding Terry and women in general, played through his mind. At the end of the thought strings he could tie them all together with a few rationalizations, a justification, and perhaps a touch of denial, and came to acceptance, even humor.

"That little slut..." He shook his head then grinned. "And I thought she would be a baby bird, imprint on me at first orgasm. I was her first you know."

Glenn nodded enthusiastically, a lecherous grin on his face.

"That's really good to know. So, you are cool? I can pursue? Because, just to be up front..." Glen grinned sheepishly as Jack shot him a raised eyebrow. "...from here on out? Terry did call me and Gillian blew me while I talked dirty to her on the phone."

Jack just stared at his buddy for a split second then began to laugh. "Jesus Glen. You have a way with words, blunt, but clear, with vivid imagery. And that is a scene I don't want in my head."

"Well, we are being up front from now on right?" Glen shrugged. "In the interests of being 'up front' and all, I don't see any reason to mince words."

Jack nodded. "Just let me know when it happens, I would like to give her time to... Freshen up... Should I even still be in town. We can be each other's Jody."

"I have a feeling the spill is going to demand your attention... I mean, Gillian did, and I agreed with her." Glen said. "She wants you to call her and I believe you had better stop repressing your desire to be with her for my sake."

"Shit... I am a bit intimidated. She is that sexy."

Glen sighed. "Allow me to put you at ease on that. Gillian is a submissive, likes being controlled, just take her, she wants you to, don't pussy around, and don't make it so fucking obvious that she knows I told you either. You are right about her in that she is powerful and sexy, that is her role all day, leader, boss lady..."

Jack nodded. "I will play it cool."

He focused his attention back on the desk, it's crimson writhing, burning through the black marbling, then inspected the cockpit, everything in it at arm's reach, cup holders, fan controls, lighting, floating keyboard and mouse pad designed to slide out over the chair rather than be used at the desk, though it could also be used at the desk if wanted. The cockpit was chair-centric. Glen rolled him a beat-up office chair to sit down at so he could slide inside.

As he took the seat Jack had a twinge of déjà vu that morphed into a memory of a dream. He chuckled, pleased with himself, with everything. While not quite as sophisticated as the egg-shaped desks in the college dream, the real thing was tangible, and inspired from the minds imagination within a dream. He took the sides of the desk in his hand and pulled himself into the cockpit. He turned on the interior lighting with a plastic rocker button.

"We need a cooler chair." Jack said. "Black leather, red trim, cool pattern, to match the desk."

"Yes, we spoke of that." Glen said. "I did some research. There are some very pricey executive chairs that use polymer gel that molds to your body better than a cushion. Other than that, not much. "

"I just recalled a dream of this chair... Thought it was déjà-vu but then recalled the dream..." Jack paused. "I wonder if all déjà-vu is repressed dream memory?"

Glen looked at him as if he were suddenly trying to give an answer for the sudden shift in thought.

"It is." Glen said. "I thought of that a while back..."

Jack cocked his head inquisitively.

"Ok, no, I didn't think of it. Back to the desk, you odd duck."

Jack laughed at his friend's humorous expression as he spoke. Glen had a certain charming charisma about him that made him easy to like. He didn't blame Terry for keeping her secret.

"I dreamed I was sitting in a Nissan Skyline, inspiration for this desk, using a flexible magnetic monitor that could be moved around, where ever you wanted it." Jack looked dead serious into Glen's eyes. Glen nodded for him to continue.

"The seat had game controls built into the arm rests, was very comfortable, and massaged my back and ass while I gamed. We need to model our chair after an automobile seat."

He smiled at Glen as if that explained everything.

"Ok, I am buying, so any suggestions on a budget cool way to do that?" Glen's eyes bugged out a little as he said, 'budget cool' to emphasize that Jack was still paying him to work.

"My car seat is very comfortable, and powered. It might work for our desks, lengthen the existing wiring, put the controls at the side of the armrest."

"I can see that..." Glenn's eyes darted back and forth over the cockpit area, measuring. He moved to a wall shelf, returned with a measuring tape.

They quickly measured and noted dimensions.

"I bet there is a Lincoln Continental at the junk yard with nice seats just waiting for us." Glen said.

"That has black leather seats like mine." Jack said.

"Now that's getting specific with the wishing."

"Hell, if it doesn't work, we can swap mine for it." Jack said.

"Yes! Either way, wish fulfilled."

They continued to laugh and joke as they prepared to move the desk to Jack's parents place, both feeling a creative bit of genius working in their lives.

THE GETTING OF THE TRUCK

MARCH 26TH, EASTER SUNDAY, 2:30 PM

Anchorage still had up its Christmas lights only they were referred to by the city as Winter Lights. These were to make less dark, the long dark hours of Alaskan winter. Midafternoon and the low sun was straining to penetrate thick dark, snow laden clouds. Small intermittent snowflakes landed on Jack's windshield as he drove, beaded up into droplets of water and began to travel up the windshield.

Jack turned on the wipers. He and Glen were on their way back from picking up his truck at his Jesse's place in Peter's Creek. This had involved a quick shovel job and a jump start. Glen drove behind him in the 86 Ford f350.

Just as they reached the Glen Highway snow burst loose from the heavy dark clouds, began to blatt the windshield with large white flakes. Frosted flakes Jack had called them as a child. He smiled at the sight as he slowed to a safer speed in the diminished visibility. He popped in a cassette and jammed out to Ozzy Osborne's Crazy Train beating the steering wheel with his hands to the tune.

Getting out the four-wheel drive symbolized mobilization towards Cordova. Time to go, get out of Anchorage, back to real Alaska, back to Cordova. He felt it in his guts. Time to return to the Raven's, the Eagles, and Crows, the cousins and Uncles, the boats, warehouses and bars. He had not been there during winter for ten years. March was usually quite snowy but giving way to

April, which, in his foggy memory was wet and sloppy with a few snow storms left before winter sputtered out.

Jack popped the cassette out and switched on the news as he made a careful exit off the Glen Highway at Muldoon. The news was on, they estimated four hundred miles of oil would spread in the storm that was building in the Gulf. Jack stopped breathing as he pictured swirling Black Death coating every inch of surface area in the Sound. In one mile there was often twenty miles of coves, bays, jagged points, and rippling coastal shores. Snug Harbor, where he had first met Sarah, Yellow Bluffs, Bay of Isles, Marsha Bay... Green Island... wouldn't be Green anymore. Knight Island, the host of a hundred scenic bays, was right in the path of the wind driven oil.

He had practically grown up in Snug Harbor. His uncles, dad, and their friends used to raft up and barbecue fresh fish, visit, share needed gear and, most memorable, have the occasional banya or cold shower at the water fall on the beach. He had lost his virginity in the Snug Harbor banya to a nineteen-year-old British girl who was crewing aboard his Uncle Conner's boat. Snug Harbor would be ruined. He had started calling it McKnight Island because he felt it was only fitting and it had caught on in some circles, his family circle most prominently. Jack pictured the oil seeping into miles and miles of unspoiled beaches. He had found beaches in Prince William Sound where every rock was four-inch disks worn smooth and arranged like fish scales all down the tideline of the beach, looked like giant serpent scales, as if a snake lay along the contours of the beach. When looked at from still water 'as' the scale like stones reflection gave it a rounded illusion. The Serpent Beaches would be coated in black tar.

Jack's hands were clenched around his steering wheel, his driving aggressive through the snow, passing people fishtailing around turns as his anger transferred through to his driving. He realized this as he nearly rear-ended a dump truck full of snow at a red light. That awoke him a bit and he lessened his pace noted that Glen was still, right behind him. Crazy guy. The truck sucked in the snow, took longer to stop, had a higher center of gravity.

Jack mashed his foot on the accelerator as he entered the wide, Sunday empty parking lot of Alaska Fabrications. He cranked the wheel hard then slammed the brakes to send the Lincoln in a sideways skid until it stopped, near the back door of the Alaska Fabrications.

He exited the car as Glen jumped out of the truck and tossed him the keys.

"If you can't find a black leather seat use mine, just replace it with what you do find." Jack said.

Glen opened the driver side door, squatted, and looked at the Lincoln's power seat.

"The controls are in the arm rest of the door. Wire might be long enough already. Very cool idea. I wonder how to convert the power to wall socket though, right now it is powered on twelve-volt battery... "

Jack nodded."We can get an electrician involved if we need too. I have proven, on my boat, that I am not the best electrician. I have a great reverence for Nicola Tesla, I see electrical routing as magical and mysterious and deadly and... "

Glen grinned and shook his head. "I am with you on that but not so afraid of twelve volts. I will tinker with it a bit, see what sparks and melted things happen."

Jack clapped Glen on the back, gave him a smile. "This shit is going to happen. We got to find a place to work out of."

Glen nodded. "We have a line of credit. Lets buy some stuff. I got a list!"

"We need put some things on paper and go from there." Jack said.

"Yeah, like my salary, for sure. Need that worked out right away." Glen grinned.

Jack used the good feelings he had about the creation of the desk to summon the courage to use the shop phone to call Gillian. It wasn't so much the courage, he had that, but it was the needed confident tone, the happy enthusiasm he was feeling, that had to carry through the phone conversation. Anyone can call and speak, but the right timing, the right voice inflections, that was a different matter altogether. Turned out, he could have been drunk and slurring his words and Gillian would still have been agreeable. She was delighted to hear from him. They confirmed the get together for dinner and what time in the evening. He also called Terry to see if he could pick her up at eight, after her Sunday Dinner. She talked in low, excited tones, her parents monitoring, said she felt like a bad daughter sneaking out for an Easter Sunday date.

He did not tell her of his plans just that they would be having dinner and drinks. This was rather new Terrytory for Jack and he was enjoying it, immensely, even though he was uncertain of the outcome. He was, however, certain of the desired outcome, that of a swap of partners that didn't ruin things between them all as friends. Jack intended to keep things out front and honest with her. They had both hidden little notes from each other from interested members of the opposite sex. Best to come clean.

HORMONAL LEMONADE

Jack sat at his desk in his room, coffee, note pad, fine tipped black ink Le Pen, at the ready. The phone rang. Sarah!

"Hello?"

"Hi Jack! It's Sarah! Remember me? Your soon to be wife?"

"How can I ever forget my super sexy little vixen?" Jack said. He felt guilt and hoped it didn't come through his voice.

"*Is she being accusatory in her tone? Or was that all in my head?*"

"I will never forget my horny Captain Jack. I miss you though, a lot! "Sarah said.

"My dad said you are coming to Cordova as soon as your boat arrives?" Jack asked.

"Yes, I think he will get it there about the eighth of April. I, happily, will be coming alone. Corbin will be staying here because of a little trouble with the law. Our friend, Officer Addington, has proved to be a most helpful ally in dealing with Corbin."

"He is a good man, Sarah. I am looking forward to sneaking around with a married woman in Cordova." Jack said.

"You know it. Corbin sucks in bed! His dick is too coked up all the time and... Oh shit. Sorry Jack. You don't need to know the details."

Jack's cheeks were blazing a bit with hot anger but he suppressed it well enough with thoughts of Terry and Gillian until he began to feel guilty instead. The result was an oddly mixed bag of compassion, understanding and lust.

"It's ok. I know you must be with him, um, in fact, I am open to you sharing more. You know, if it turns you on, I am open to weaving it into a hot little phone fantasy for you." Jack said.

Sarah gave out a little moan of delight. "We could do that, I love your voice and how you make me cum with your stories Jack, it's, magical. Right now, though, we must keep it short, I have an appointment to get to across town." She said.

They had talked with each other every other day or so and she always called him from her real estate office. Her day job, buying and selling properties, gave her lots of Corbin free time.

"It's not magic so much as it is Neuro-Linguistic-Programming, that and knowing the little hot button fantasies your filthy whore mind comes up with." Jack said. He lowered his tone just a bit to that regular, sexy tone, he used. It didn't work.

"No, I mean, not a quick fantasy, I don't want a quick one right now. I am all dressed up to show a place and am not... Jack, going to screw up this dress or the tiny little white cotton panties I am wearing." Sarah said. Her voice was pleading though, more than stating.

"Come on Sarah, you are getting wet because you don't want to, and a man can tell, when a girl like you is in heat, like that big black janitor you told me about? What was his name?"

Sarah giggled into the phone. "Jack, not going to happen, sorry."

"Ok! Ok! I give up. You can put away the semi-reluctant-cheerleader voice." Jack said. "I am just glad I get to see you, even under the shitty circumstances."

"When life gives you lemons you make lemonade Jack." Sarah said. "In our case, it will be hormonal lemonade, and knowing you, adventurous and highly experiential lemonade. God, I miss you!" Sarah said.

"I miss you too. It is hard being so far from the girl I love."

"Corbin is such a dick..." a soft sigh. "Anyway, we will get to see each other soon. What have you been up to?"

"When we last spoke we discussed me loosening up, so I have been out socializing..."

"Good Jack, I am glad, lets' keep our secrets though, I mean I know you will share every detail if I ask, or..." She laughs. "If I don't stop you from rambling."

Jack felt relief sweep through him as the nag of guilt was erased by Sarah's words.

"Are you going to be in Cordova when I get there?" Sarah asked.

"Yes, sooner probably. Got the truck out today. Need to get the boat in the water, maybe when you get there we can stay on the Lorem or my boat? I doubt there will be any hotels available."

"Who wants to stay in a hotel? We will stay on the Lorem! I have a surprise for you! I can't wait!"

Jack grinned and pictured Sarah's smile. The flame of his love for her burned a bit brighter - his lust, pictured her smiling from between wide spread trembling thighs and pink capped breasts as she lay on her back.

"Sounds exciting, and yes, we will make some lemon aid! Hopefully we will be together all summer." Jack said.

"Would be wonderful, but Corbin has started talking of joining me on the Lorem. He can't for a while though because of a contract he is seeing through. He has a mess on his hands, bad management on his part, and must fix it. Might even land him in jail. I am working on a few more sabotages to keep him here longer, one of which is a highly lucrative bid that is most certainly going our way..."

Jack laughed. "Ain't love grand?"

LIVING THE DREAM

MARCH 26ᵀᴴ, EASTER SUNDAY, 8:30 PM

Gillian's home was... Amazing. Six thousand square feet of coolness on Upper O'Malley jazzed up with Christmas lights. It was nowhere near as architecturally sophisticated as Luke Remua's but very nice for rugged weather in Alaska. The outside was three modernist boxes meshed together, four if you counted her garage, which is where he had been instructed to park. The garage was large, could fit four trucks, two deep, in the front. Jack parked his truck in one of the rear spaces closest to the garage door, next to Glen's car, a hot rod VW Bug with skinny rubber all studded up for winter. Jack had the pleasure of driving the thing and found it better than a four by four in the snow – rear wheel drive with the engine over the wheels made for great traction on snow and ice. Glen had welded additional skid plates under the bug and a black diamond plate cow pusher to enable him to plow through thick snow berms and skid along on top of deeper snow far better than a regular car. Jack told him that those three things, skinny studded rubber with an aggressive tread, skid plates, and a diamond plate cow pusher, or Russian leg breaker, could be called the Alaskan Drift Package - could come with an optional recovery winch welded into the cow pusher, and that they could offer such things with their own fab shop in keeping with Glen's demand to modify trucks to his heart's content.

The VW bug now sat dripping upon Gillian's garage floor, it's modified Porcha engine ticking as it cooled. Jack admired the car as he passed and laughed with amazement. Glen had already installed a winch just behind the cow pusher.

Jack pulled Terry to his side happily. "Wow, look at this place, it is amazing." He said.

Behind the parking area was a large central machine shop and to either side of that were two work bays, four total, one obviously set up to smith jewelry. He figured this was probably how she got his Lucidian broach, worn proudly on his cashmere winter long coat, designed and finished so quickly. After seeing how fantastic the paint job on the desk and the finish of the desk itself turned out, Jack had been imagining all sorts of useful items to be made from fiberglass, or something finer. The mold process for fiberglass is what held his imagination. Once made, they could be used over and over. Pour the liquid, tack the fiber glass and you have another item like the broach Gillian gave him made of pewter. Set up a process to do this and production could be sped up considerably.

Terry tugged on Jack's arm.

"You can inspect Gillian's toys later. They are waiting for us."

"Relax sweet meat I was just taking a moment." Jack said. She gave him another tug.

He allowed her to pull him away from the garage. The workspaces were half walled cubes with convenient shelving and comfortable standing and sitting positions. One for smelting, jewelry making, one water colors, one a personal computer and chair. He knew now, why Gillian loved his desk design. She was predisposed to do so by her own level of inventiveness. Jack's dick got hard, his Gillian respect meter rising, sexual performance anxiety increasing.

They entered the mud room, which was a wide tunnel connecting the garage to the main house. It was lined with closets, washer and drier, a bathroom and shoe racks. They removed their winter wear and found their way to the kitchen via the smell of garlic.

Gillian was tossing a salad, her long silky blond-red hair all the way to the sweep of her buttocks. She wore a sheer ankle length wrap with patterns to hide nakedness beneath. The fabric clung in an alluring manner that accented her body, reminded him of Agatha Neufeld dressed in Michael's pleasure silk. Glen sat at the counter, his back to the living room, which the kitchen was two steps higher than, to frame the city lights in the large living room windows.

When she saw them, Gillian gleamed with delight, let out a little cry of joy and clapped her hands together. Glen smiled and raised a tall drink. The smell of garlic bread broiling dominated the kitchen.

"Here is to us being naughty and drinking on Easter Sunday." He said. Took a swig, and winked at them or was it just Terry. Her blush indicated that she thought it was just her.

"Hope you two like lasagna because its what's for dinner. And don't think I made it either, this is way better than I could do. I get pans of it made from Romano's when I want to impress people." Gillian said. She strode over, a joyous smile on her face and gave Terry a pleasant kiss on her cheek then hugged her, her eyes meeting Jack's over the girl's shoulder.

"Yum. Romano's is my favorite Italian place." Terry said. Jack nodded, his eyes on Gillian she moved to bend over and remove the lasagna from the oven. Was that her nipples he could see through the fabric of her dress or was it the pattern and his imagination? There certainly was a lot of natural, wonderful, wobble. He glanced at Terry to see her eyes also on Gillian, her cheeks tinged faint pink.

"You like scotch Jack?" Glen asked. "I recommend that you do. Gillian's dad liked it until he quit drinking and he has bequeathed his collection to her." Glen made emphasis on the word 'bequeathed' as that of an ivy league snob which made both Terry and Gillian giggle.

"I do like it. Not really an expert at the stuff."

There were glasses with ice at the bar already, a tasteful setting, wine glasses, four of them on a silver tray with a bottle of wine mellowing, table cloths, plates, lasagna, salad, and… just about done in the oven, garlic bread that smelled good.

"You should save your palate for food and wine, much better than a pre-dinner Scotch." Gillian said.

Jack nodded. "Sounds good to me." He said. Their eyes met and he enjoyed the flush of her approval.

"And so, it begins. The little control wars." Glen said. He smiled mischievously as Gillian shot him a look. Jack poured a glass of wine.

"Actually… she has a point, wine is better with food." Jack poured a glass of wine, set it in front of Terry. His hand touched Terry tenderly as he guided her to sit next to Glen at the kitchen bar. He kissed her ear lightly, whispered, "Its ok, Glen is yours tonight. No man owns you." Jack saw her give a slight nod, her cheeks flare pink, as she settled into the bar chair.

They ate at the slender marble bar, the four of them cozy, sitting on padded stools with high seat backs and foot rests angled just right. Jack next Gillian, facing Terry, who sat next to Glen who faced Gillian. At either end of the bar was lit candles in uniquely twisted candelabra. The lights were dim, the ambiance very intimate. Jack could smell and feel the sexual tension even over the fresh garlic bread cooling in a cloth lined wicker basket. There was great food set before him. He was hungry. But not for the meal.

"Have you got two more people for our goal of five yet?" Gillian asked. She smiled prettily at Jack, eyes fond, engaging. She radiated out at him. Her foot stroked his calf. Jack flushed. It was not missed by Glen.

For a moment, he thought of her as an enchantress, casting a spell of lust over him, then decided that was exactly what she was doing. As in a dream. Jack met her eyes and beamed a push at her, showed her his own light, was amazed as her cheeks pinked up. His intimidation of her waned a bit, confidence rose.

"I have not thought on it. Terry, did you read the Lucidian Booklet?"

"Uh uh." Terry said. "Been busy with studies n' you. I will tonight. Unless I am busy with you. But I want to join your religion, I will sign up, so you only need one more." Terry looked at him hopefully, a cute, I want you look on her face. Then she looked at Glen, same look, smile growing as he gave her a wolfish gaze.

"I actually have three people, my cousins John, Marci, and Cindi. Avid Lucid Dreamers. Pretty much sure things." Jack said. "I have not called them about it yet, but I am certain they would sign up. I have many other names, and each of those people keep a list as well. Have thought about a way to co-ordinate getting in touch with them, having them get in touch with the people on their lists, and so on."

Gillian smiled. "Good. As soon as we get them with us... The sooner we can register as a religion. I have the proper paper work all lined up to send. Just need to add the names of the believers, figure out a doctrine, list the administrators." Her eyes flashed merry at the thought. Jack felt his pulse quicken.

"I want to learn how to do it. Lucid Dream. Sounds pretty fantastic." Terry said.

Glen nodded. "It's a life changer. That is for certain. And you are a very smart young lady. You will be able to do it easily enough. The good news is, you don't have to be a Lucid Dreamer to be a Lucidian, just believe what Lucidians believe and you are one of us." Glen's tone was enthusiastic and genuine, his smile at Terry encouraging, not wolfish. Under the act, there was a good guy, or Gillian certainly would not have chosen him for a mate. Jack felt sure that Terry was in very good hands. He nodded in agreement with Glen, but had not, yet, accepted his words as true in his own mind until he had heard his friend speak them.

"A Toast." Said Gillian.

All raised their glass.

"To the first four Lucidians. May the religion Jack has founded prosper and aid the world."

"Amen!" Glen said.

They clinked glass, took a deep sip of wine. Jack sputtered a bit after swallowing his drink.

"I don't claim to have founded anything... Just yet." He said. He laughed a bit of a crazy chortle, made a steeple of his fingers before him. "It is crazy, Gillian, that we are talking so matter of fact about this. Founding a religion is... Huge."

Gillian nodded. "Yet it is all coming together whether you like it or not. The synchronicities are just too huge to ignore. You meet Glen, you both have been dreaming of a fabrication shop, he knows me, we meet, Terry and you meet, she is a genius with computers, the list goes on."

Jack nodded. Terry glowed from the compliment. It was not, however, a compliment, it was an observation, Terry was a genius with computers, far better than he was in the classes.

Jack nodded thoughtfully, stared at his half-eaten meal, really wasn't hungry, had eaten with his mother prior to picking Terry up from her parents' house. He sampled a rich bit of cheese crusted on top of the pasta and sipped at the wine, savoring the swirl of flavors.

"Excellent recommendation." He said. Nodded. "This is really good wine."

Gillian laughed and clapped her hands. "I am please you like it." She said. The ball of her soft little foot travelled up his calf. Distracting and exciting. Jack shifted away from the Terryble weight of the thoughts of founding a religion. '*Like changing mental gears, relax into the moment.*' He thought. He also, in the far back of the mind, acknowledged Gillian's logic regarding synchronicity, with memories, chance encounters, Michael Neufeld at the center of them. He had not yet told the others everything about Michael. Had not yet shared with them the depth of the Book of Lucidian Names he kept, other than the mention of forming the practice at the end of his booklet, nor that he knew others who also kept their own book of names. There was already a network. In his mind, he saw a web spreading across the world, France, Japan, Russia, New York, all starting in Alaska. A shiver passed through his spine, radiated in cool joyous prickles across his skin like a wave of rain drops across the surface of still water.

"Founding a religion is scary." Glen said. "So is founding a business like our shop, scary, new, but a religion, my friends, pays no taxes, and can have lots of perks." Glen nodded in agreement with himself.

Jack nodded as well, laughed. "I can dig the no taxes thing the most I think." He said. He finished the wine and reached for the Scotch, an asking eye on Gillian's. She shook her head 'no' and he flinched his hand back as if scorched, gave Glen a look. "Power struggle lost." He said. Glen shrugged. "Told you man."

Gillian made a harrumph noise, eyes playful and fond towards Glen and Jack both.

"I just want to go to the smoking room first." she said. "I have cognac, scotch, and cigars laid out. Then it's tub time. Suits are optional." She laughed. "Relax Terry! Sheesh, your cheeks are like little flames." Gillian gave her a warm gaze as she stood.

"Leave the dishes for later." She said. Gillian led the way down two wide steps into the soft light of the living room then up again along the windows and to the right where she opened a heavy wood door and stepped inside.

They followed to find a large plant laden room, polished wood floors, warm to the feet, a huge rock fireplace and mantle with couches around it, a wood table with cognac and cigars between the couches. A large glass enclosed room off the smoking room held a jungle of plants. The kind of plants that required special knowledge to grow and grew huge. Behind the plants and within them was a large hot tub bubbling, the light from it was a dim red color so they could enjoy the view of the angel wings spread of city lights silhouetting the shore line of Turnagain and Knik Arm.

Gillian moved in front of the fire, stoked it, the brightness of the flames made her dress disappear, her ass and legs appear. She bounced it a bit, knowing that she was see through as she poked at the fire. She then turned on music at a stereo mounted along the mantle, turned and smiled.

"I noticed you boys smoke like chimneys while you drink and clang ideas about so I hoped to recreate that atmosphere here." Gillian said.

Jack's eyes were on Gillian's ass and legs as she stood before the fire. She was magnificent, totally aware of the power of her form, her sexuality. A Godess... Terry pinched him to break his stare. He slid into a comfy seat and began to pull his smokes out of his pocket.

"Oh... Lets' do cigars first!" Gillian said. Again, Jack flinched his hand away from the smokes. Gillian giggled. "You are much easier to train than Glen every was." She said.

"But train him you did. I am just saving us both some time." Jack said. Glen rolled his eyes.

She took a seat, her wrap sliding far up her thigh. Glen situated himself at Terry's side and looked at Jack, moving his eye balls to indicate that he should get closer to Gillian.

"Well, it is a good idea. Here, let me get them for us." Jack stood and picked up four cigars from the table, handed them out as the others reclined then sat next to Gillian on the couch. He smiled at Terry as he noticed, even in the low lighting, her cheeks flush as Glen placed his hand on her leg, whispered something in her ear.

Gillian pulled Jack's hand to her thigh and sighed, a happy contented little sound. They were silent, for a few ticks of the clock, reading each other's faces.

"Let me get the scotch." Gillian said. She scooted forward and Jack moved his hand to stroke her side, near her hip as she poured. His fingers grazed her panty line beneath the silky fabric of her dress. Gillian lifted her butt a little and he found more curvature to explore. His fingers traced the accessible sweep and valley of her butt. She shivered with pleasure, tiny goose pimples lifting along her arms.

Glen whispered in Terry's ear something that made her gasp, then giggle and cover her face as his lips kissed the nape of her neck, hand moving up her thigh, subtle, sexy. He was playing her music and she was listening. Her eyes fixed on Jack's and he read lust and excitement in them, hoped she read approval in his smile and nod.

Jack lit his cigar, held the lighter for Gillian to puff on the end of her own. He gazed at her as she hollowed her cheeks and sucked on the end of the cigar, not her first time. She smiled at him and blew smoke to the side while making a satisfied little affirmative sound. Jack was reminded of Michael's balcony at the San Remo.

"The last time I had a cigar was on Michael Neufeld's terrace in Central Park. We talked of the Lucidian church then. Fitting we shall do so now, with cigar's."

"Odd coincidence?" Gillian asked. She gave a wink and a nod, tinkled the ice in her glass of scotch. Jack raised his glass, "Here is to synchronicity, our confirmation that life is but a dream, and that God's hand is in play." They all raised glass and drank. Jack sank back in the couch happy in the moment, his thigh pressed against Gillian's. He sighed contentedly.

"Ok, I will take the bait, who is Mike Neufeld?" Glen asked.

Jack studied his friend's face as he considered the answer to his question.

"I believe he is behind every move I have made. My mentor of sorts, but more powerfully, he mentors by example of great success." Jack said. The others looked at him with curiosity. He explained the relationships, that led him to be taken under the wing of such a man. Told them then, of The Book of Lucidian Names that Michael had suggested they each keep and how that sparked the thought of a religion at his cousins playful prompting when Jack suggested that the three of them also keep their on Book of Names. Jack spoke fondly of both Michael and of his cousins. Of how John and his cousins made the suggestion that he start a religion then just gazed at him, with utter confidence, like it was only natural that he do such a thing.

When he finished telling his story he took another pull of the scotch, felt it's warmth swell through him. The fire popped and crackled. The scotch went down like molten fun and immediately flushed through Jack's system a heady sense of wellbeing and healthy lusts. His leg pressed a bit more against Gillian's soft thigh as he lit and puffed his own cigar to life.

"You know; I was thinking..." Jack said.

"About world domination? I go there too sometimes." Glen said.

They laughed.

"No... I was thinking about us being the first four Lucidians... What if this all goes huge? Multi-millions of followers. Who would run it?"

"We all could." Terry said.

"We could, yes, but who is the pope? The grand wizard you know? It's not that kind of thing. Lucidians give everyone the knowledge they need to be their own spiritual leaders, there is no need for priests, or authority figures." Jack sipped his Scotch as the others considered his words.

"We could make everything light and fun. Not take ourselves too seriously, yet, at the same time, provide people with the knowledge and access to the dreamtime, to experience other dimensions and potentialities, show them how to unlock their own potential, live better, wealthier, healthier."

Glen chuckled. "A religion based on experience and results rather than faith, and in addition to faith. We would be letting people know they don't need to die to go to heaven, they can get there from a nap."

Silence... Gillian started and they fell in with her, laughing, from the gut, full on mirth.

"Glen, you have a way of saying profound shit. I love it." Jack said.

"Profoundly common sense is what my mom called it as I grew up. "

"Exactly." Gillian said. "You got it from her then."

Glen nodded. "We may have a hit religion. We may have a hobby. Who cares? We are Lucidian!" The last he spoke as if he were saying Spartan instead of Lucidian.

"What happens at the church? We just tell people to go home and dream? Or what?" Gillian asked.

"That's where my thinking was headed. I spent some time at this beautiful home in France. Luke Remua's, a nuclear physicist, another very wealthy guy, who showed me a higher society than I was comfortable with, taught me how to speak in higher society, tried to anyway... Jack laughed as a memory came to him.

"He found my straightforward mannerisms refreshing but told me that honest people get eaten, that I had to learn how to pick up on attacks and counter them, learn to give someone a compliment that really meant they should go fuck themselves." Jack said.

Gillian nodded. "Oh my god Jack, it sounds like you have been to my board meetings."

Jack nodded, smiled. "Luke's home was amazing. He had these peaceful pools of water staggered in tiers that spiraled around his place in four levels. Each pool was accessible from each level and off each pool was a grotto, each unique, with a hot mineral bath like our spas only all in stonework, smooth and glazed."

"Sounds dreamy..." Gillian said. She sighed, rubbed her hand along the inside of Jack's thigh.

"It was amazing, and between each pool was a slide you could take to get to the next pool below, and not with a whoosh of adrenalin but at a relaxing pace that curled around his entire house and into the next pool."

"Wow." Terry said. "He must have been mega-rich."

Jack nodded. "He is an incredible human being. But, you know, rather busy. Hard to pin down. I did manage to bond with him a little regarding inspiration coming from somewhere, got him to share with me his aha! moments, but mostly, I was just a guy who had provided him and his son with a service. His son, however, is on the list of Lucidian's and stands to inherit his dads fortune one day, or, even, create his own in partnership with his dad." Jack said. He puffed, blew smoke, took a sip, guided Gillian's leg to drape over his. She let him, smiled and raised an eyebrow.

"You know where I am going with this." Jack said. "You have a spa room that would rival one of his. Those trees in there with the huge yellow flowers, Angel's Trumpets? Neufeld had some, they add to the steamy sensual feel to your home like they did his."

"You like my Angel's Trumpets?" Gillian asked suddenly. She nodded towards the big plant with huge yellow flowers pointing downward.

"They are spectacular." Jack said.

"It's from Columbia, grows there like a weed. They call it Devils Tears there though. Don't get to close. The CIA and Columbian criminals use it for mind control."

Gillian smiled mischievously and placed her hand on Jack's thigh press lightly upwards. Jack inhaled deeply as pleasure rippled through him.

"Do you use it to control people?" Jack asked. Curious thoughts of Neufeld's use of the plant crossed his mind. A high-powered lawyer could put such a thing to rather diabolical effect... And he did have a sexy apothecary in his employ...

"Certainly not. The idea is abhorrent to me, that our own government finds it useful sickens me." Gillian said. Her tone was serious.

"So, before the mind-control-plant conspiracy, where were you going with what you were saying?" Glen said. He leaned forward, let Terry's hand slip from his. "Are you saying we design spaces like Gillian's spa? You are thinking of an indoor pool type setting for the Lucidian Church?" Glen asked.

"Exactly. An indoor sanctuary, a grotto, several grottos. A place we can go and be at peace and network together. But for kids and adults that way we are family oriented, we bring up young Lucidians." Jack said.

Glen clapped his hands. "Yes, I was hoping you would say that, and who would design the interior spaces of all the Lucidian Churches? ErgoDyn! That's who."

Jack nodded his agreement at Glen. "Good thinking, I like it, built in contracts from the church. Could keep us busy for a long time, if anyone besides us joins."

"Mm, I can see it, parents enjoy a soul rejuvenation and the kids get to thrill on water slides." Gillian said. "We could design the Water Parks around a sort of Disney theme, a magical show case for things people have 'dreamed' up. I love it... I also love that we can employ ErgoDyn to build, but ErgoDyn will need a general contractors license to do that. Glen, you should get one."

Glen nodded. "Ok. I get one. No problems. Maybe you share with me how tomorrow?"

The group laughed at Glen's expressive facial expressions and tone. "So, how many people do we need to have join, how do they benefit, what is our thrust? Our 'holy vision'?" Glen asked. He sat back, pulled Terry to him, stroked her head with his fingers while he thought things over, Terry's eyes rolling as he did so.

Jack puffed his cigar, leaned back on the couch in a comfortable reverie. Mind working over several options to define what would be the main mission of the church. Gillian's hand warm on his thigh, nuzzling ever higher, was a distraction. He met Glen's eyes, saw that his friend was alight with an idea.

Glen parted from Terry, sat on the edge of the couch and leaned forward to speak. "Our purpose is to blend the science of direct experience of higher intelligence with technology through productive inventions and innovations, like the desk we built. We join science and spirit. We create, use the lucid experience to tune up with god, higher intelligence, shiva, whatever you want to call it." Glen said.

Jack smiled at his friend and nodded. "Sounds good, and is a great description of exactly what we are doing now, creating." He shivered. "I can feel it, it feels good."

"That is brilliant Glen." Gillian said. She nodded. "We can build around that as our 'thrust'. We create, we 'dream' things up. We bring together science and spirit." Her hand moved warmly up Jack's thigh at the word 'thrust' and a tad higher with the word 'up'.

"We put this water park up on the south side, on O'Malley, we will have a neighborhood of around three thousand people..." Glen said. "Land is cheap there now, if there is a willing seller."

"Or we put it in Muldoon for much less, with a larger population base." Gillian added.

"The Church and neighborhood thing is the old way. We are new way." Jack said. "We put our Water Parks anywhere and people will not only attend Church, but also pay to use the facilities like a public source of entertainment, right? So, we optimize our facility with making it easy to get to for as many people as possible but limit the public access hours while church is in service."

"Yes!" Gillian said. Her hand jumped a bit higher, was now directly on his crotch in her enthusiasm. "That way even nonmembers can donate to the church and have a tax write off."

"Yup, and while they are visiting the Water Park we cultivate their friendship and membership. We put our churches according to the greatest flow of traffic out that way, they are using the best roads to arrive in the fastest, easiest way." Jack said.

Glen smiled. "That's pretty big thinking Jack."

"I see something is getting big." Terry giggled, eyes staring at Jack's crotch.

"Mm, mm... Is it big Terry? You can tell." Gillian purred. She now worked her fingers along Jack's jean clad bulge. Jack coughed and shifted, to allow a bit more room for growth.

Terry giggled again and nodded enthusiastically. "The biggest I have ever had."

Gillian's hand slid gracefully over Jack's swelling crotch.

"Here is to thinking-big." Glen said. Terry snuggled into him a bit more intimately.

They raised their glasses.

"And to the first Lucidian Water Park." Jack said. They drank. The moment was locked in Jack's mind. It felt good. Gillian's closeness felt good. The church was born... On Easter... His mind went to the day he had realized that he and his friends were heirs to Prince William Sound, Princes of the

Sound, prayed that this too, was not something that would be destroyed, just as Exxon had most likely just destroyed his fishing business.

"And here is to Jesus rising, historically, on this day, or close enough to Astarte to be ok." Jack said. The others looked at him. He shrugged. They drank. He had just wanted to get away from worrisome thoughts regarding the spill, the boats, everything.

"Now, how we going to pay for this?" Glenn asked. "Investors? Memberships? Loans?"

They sat in silence, each looking at the other for an answer.

"We become a religion, we network with those already on the lists, ask them to send their lists."

Jack nodded. "Michael has a list, I have a list and Michael is on it, as well as you guys."

"I have already begun the process of getting donations." Gillian said. "I am very good at that sort of thing." She beamed and gave an innocent smile. "We will begin soliciting donations via a marketing blitz to interested parties. That is also something I am very good at.

"You have?" Jack asked.

"Yup, now that we fleshed out a few details I can make it all come together. This is going to be so much fun! I need your book of names first thing tomorrow morning Jack. I will get an invitation off to them as well.

Gillian leaned forward, raised her glass towards Glen and Terry, Jack joined suit, a bit stunned at the prospects of this being more than a brainstorming session.

"Here is to being Lucidian, to being creative and with god." Gillian said.

The heavy crystal drink cognac snifters 'tinged' together a musical note. Jack downed his remaining Scotch, felt a warm rush in his belly, his mind pinging, his spine tingling.

"And now would be a good time to end our first committee meeting and relax in the spa." Gillian said. She stood, grabbed a bottle of cognac, and led them into the spa. The plants were placed well away from the actual hot humid water coming from the bubbling spa. Blue lights at the bottom of the tub lit the room with a rippling water effect.

Jack glanced around the room, picked up on the energy of Gillian's use of this 'grotto' to recharge and relax. He breathed deeply through his nose, told himself to calm down. His excitement was intense, his arousal with Gillian, with the situation, placed his mind in a euphoric cloud. The struggle to remain composed and confident was aided by the peaceful vibe of the spa grotto.

"There are suits in the shower room. Suit up if you wish, shower, then use the spa." She said.

Jack felt her squeeze his hand and give it a little tug to indicate he should stay at her side.

"I am going to give Jack a tour of the house. You two can jump in there if you want. We will catch up to you a bit later." She said.

The tour was more of a beeline to her bedroom. Her room was warm, rich bronze and subtle reds, a mahogany canopy bed to the right, fire place on the opposite wall. The art on the walls was of people embracing, loving, screwing Kama-Sutra style. Her warm hand in his squeezed a little then let go. She moved to the fireplace and pushed a button, fire leapt up to lick at ceramic logs, dance along and between them as if eager to obey her command.

Gillian turned to face Jack, her back to the fire, legs spread so her dress became see through. Jack just stood there, gazing at her, eyes purposely lingering on the silhouette between her legs then up to her eyes. Her cheeks were a little pink, lips parted, nostrils flaring as she breathed.

He met her eyes, blue within blue, hooded with lust and desire. There was a pulse, a wave of energy and hormonal chemistry that took Jack's breath away with a surge of sexual excitement. He inhaled sharply to compensate, noted Gillian's pupils dilate, as she smiled and nodded, a knowing between them. Jack stepped forward and took her hands in his, heart beating faster, his prick swelling harder as she came to him, pressed her body against his. He stroked the small of her back, his other hand slipping upward, under her silky hair to grasp her neck. Her lips parted as he kissed her, tongue lightly flicking against his, her lips soft, her saliva warm in his mouth. Jack felt his breath quicken with excitement. Gillian let out a little moan of pleasure, a tickle of vibration, in his mouth. When they parted from their first lingering kiss all pretenses were off, gone, stripped away. Both were breathing hard, bodies pressed together, hands quickly removing each other's clothing. Gillian pushed his pants down as he undid the clasp holding her wrap on and let it fall to the floor. Jack drank in her the upward curve of her breasts, the crinkle of tight, light brown skin surrounding erect pink nipples, the sweep of her hips framed light downy hair above her smoothly shaved vulva cleft. His cock was rampant, throbbing, the skin tight. Gillian looked down at his erection, sighed another happy sigh, and pulled him by the cock to the bed. She lay down, spread her legs and guided him into her. Usually Jack spent a bit more time at the foreplay stage but it was obvious that neither of them needed it. The kiss was enough.

The bedroom was filled with wet slapping noises, moans, gasps, and a sweet funky, intoxicating sex scent that was ambrosia to the mind.

Jack fell next to her and pulled her to him. Gillian wrapped her legs around him as they kissed.

"Oh my God Jack that was…"

"Mythical? Intense?"

"Yes! Oh my god… I am such a lucky girl!" Her hand stroked his slippery prick. "I want more!"

"Of course. From now on you will always be after me lucky charms." Jack said.

Gillian laughed as he nudged her to her back again and spread her legs, hovered over her, his prick brushing her soft belly as he kissed and nipped at the side of her neck. He then moved down to her feet, and began to kiss and stroke his way up between her thighs, his hands lightly touching feeling her jerk with pleasure, listening to her moan. He loved her unique Oh!-Gasps, each one sent a pulse of desire through him, like a reward for doing good. He moved higher then latched his mouth over her clitoris, his tongue lightly flickering up and down as he listened to her O-Gasps get nearer together as he found the right cadence. He watched her belly ripple and tense, felt her thighs tremble against his hands as he held them back and open. She let out a wavering moan that turned into a strained shriek.

"Oh, my god! Glen! Oh god! Oh fuck, oh stop, no more! No more! Please." Gillian cried out. Her stomach tightened more, legs strained and quivered, the expression of intense, surprised, ecstasy and just a touch of frantic panic in her blue eyes made his cock strain just a little harder. Her entire body rippled with pleasure. Gillian held her head up, hands pushed Jack's head away from her overly sensitive clitoris, mouth locked in an 'O' shape, eyes frantic. All poise, dignity, and self-consciousness was gone. Gillian was stripped down to the bare primal essential human being. She arched her back and let out a final loud wet moan sound.

"Oh, my god, that was…"

"Mythical." Jack said.

"Yes! Fuck! You licked me sooooo goood and your cock... Oh my god!" Gillian giggled.

Jack felt his head swell a bit, his ego so nicely stoked.

"You are gorgeous... and sensual... Incredible." He said. His hands stroked the swell of her breasts, caught her nipples between the fatty pads of his fingers.

"You are the most incredible man I have ever been with." She said. She gazed down at him and Jack felt like the world had just flipped over. He smiled and nodded. "You inspire greatness. Your twat is incredible!" He said.

Gillian laughed. "Crude boy!" She said. "I will bet there is a lot more to you than just some good missionary Jack." She winked and ground her crotch against his cock, then pouted.

"Oh... You didn't cum and I am rubbing on you so nice..." She rolled off him. "Save some for later I guess."

"I don't think I have much more left in me."

Gillian handed him a robe after they took a quick shower together. She had on a warm fluffy pink one with a swan embroidered across the back. As the two of them made their way out of the bathroom, Jack noticed the way she had arranged things; easy desk from bed much like his, red walls, gold and bronze candelabras, four post ornate canopy bed. Large arched windows with tastefully patterned curtains and a private bath were to the west, over-looking the city. Mirrors were placed in strategic places, to accent a curve of wood or piece of art, rather than just for vanity purposes. Music played, volume low, a female artist Jack had never heard. Voice powerful, slightly Irish, lilting, rising, then soft, then rising to a torrent of passion, vocal rage, yet still clear, beautiful. An image came to him of Ireland.

"Who is the singer? She is ringing my bells..." Jack asked.

"Sinead O'Conner. You like her? So, another epic female already caught your attention?"

Gillian lifted her hand to clasp Jack's as he shrugged and nodded. She smiled, a sudden mischievous flash in her eyes.

"We should sneak down and surprise Glen and Terry!" She said.

The house was dark, Gillian's hand warm in his as she led the way. They were silent, stealthy, could hear the house creak and tick. Jack was reminded of a game he used to play with his cousins when the house was pitch black.

Sneak tag they had named it. One of them was 'it' and would turn out the last light, then, in pitch blacktry to catch the sneakers as they tried to transfer as many balloons from one corner of the house to another. It was great fun and developed a great sense of stealth. It was also a lesson in listening.

Hand in hand he and Gillian crept down the hall toward the spa room until they could peek through one of the steamed-up windows. There was no sound, no sign of Glen or Terry.

"Knowing Glen they are in the kitchen." Gillian whispered.

"That was ten minutes ago!" Came a booming voice from behind them.

Gillian shrieked. Jack jumped in surprise, turned with his elbows out, grazed the top of Terry's head.

"Ow!! Fuck Jack!" Terry yelled. She held the top of her head, but began to giggle.

"Oh shit... Sorry!"

He took her in his arms and hugged her to him. She was hurt but laughing.

Gillian smacked Glen's shoulder.

"See what you did? Poor Terry about got her head knocked off!"

Gillian kept smacking Glen as he laughed and fended off her blows.

"Serves you right for peeking you pervert." Glen said.

"We just..." Swing and a miss... "Wanted to make sure..." Another swing and a miss... "You two were not fucking in there." Swing, and a good solid hit to the gut. Glen made an 'Ooof!' noise and laughed.

Terry used the moment to cling to Jack, hands stroking him through the robe as if she were apologizing for being with Glen, or letting him know she was ok with the scenario. Jack felt an awkward conflict as he considered that Gillian might get jealous. Then he turned and saw she was in a tight embrace with Glen, kissing him and it was, in fact, Jack that felt the pang of jealousy. He suppressed it with the thought that they all, most likely, were feeling a bit odd.

Gillian picked up the half full bottle of Remy Martin. "I vote we finish this off in the spa." Her robe dropped to the floor. Terry giggled and dropped her robe as well. She took Gillian's arm and they ladies led the way.

Glen and Jack watched their butts jiggle as they walked arm in arm into the spa room.

Glen gave Jack an apologetic shrug and smiled.

"Living the dream huh Jack?" He said.

"That and more." Jack said. He smiled and nodded.

"Hey, I thought I heard my name called out earlier. You notice anything like that?" Glen asked.

He skillfully dodged Jack's playful punch.

The water bubbled and steamed, the mind controlling Angel's Trumpet shimmered with dew in the corner, it's heavy bright yellow flowers hung downward, strong stamen's jutting proud and confident, out of the open yellow bloom. Its presence was intoxicating to Jack's imagination. He could see the potential dripping out of the plant. The water in the spa was warm, not hot, but very comfortable.

"The plant intrigues me." Jack said. He was chest deep in the big spa, Gillian next to him, fingers sliding over his thigh, breasts warbled by the waters surface as she relaxed, head on a padded rest. He took a luxurious sip of Remy Martin and a judicious puff of the pungent cigar. "It arouses me and intrigues me that its powder can be used for mind control. We should make some. Just to experiment with. See if it really works."

"I am sure that if it worked, it would be illegal for me to keep in my house, and it is not." Gillian said. "To me, it is a symbol, of mind control, of focus. You don't need it though, you are walking, talking, Devil's Powder."

Jack smiled, both flattered and doubtful of her words. He sighed happily and relaxed, felt a wave of love for Gillian. He gazed at her blue eyes, her hair, wet, was flat to her head. Reminded him of a beautiful seal, a silky, but he knew he could not have her, to try to keep this one would be to push her far away. She was a wild horse, a creative spirit, a very good strategist, a woman at play, dancing, yet very focused. He was devils powder, a commercial fisherman, out door adventurer, who just had his livelihood and way of life covered with thick, viscous, crude oil. A knot of pain and fear swelled in his guts.

ABOUT THE AUTHOR

BRIAN BUTLER

Brian Butler operated a rescue boat during the Exxon Valdez Oil Spill, worked with experimental oil absorbent fabrics using tidal forces to naturally scrub bluffs and rocks, then bailed on his contracts to return to fishing. Because, by god, that's what a fisherman does.

He lost his fishing business in 1991, got married, moved to Japan, became something entirely different from what he believed he would be.

Today, Butler enjoys the shorelines of Orca Inlet, the Delta Dunes of the Copper River, the banks and rainforests of the Eyak Lake and River, and the Cathedrals of God in Prince William Sound. He takes pictures and writes of the vast beauty he finds in those places in hopes that others might be inspired to visit the area and enjoy the peace and beauty for themselves.

The trauma of dealing with the Exxon Valdez Oil Spill, combined with the need to share the magic of life with others was his motivation behind writing the books. Here you will find memory woven into fictional character as the historic tragedy of the Exxon Valdez Oil Spill unfolds.